PART ONE

Those were the Days
A Two Part Triangle
Love Story

A.Miguel Trujillo

To quote writer extraordinaire Harlan Coben

"Cherish and take care of what you value"

"Happiness is fragile"

*"Appreciate every moment and do everything
You can to protect it"*

Those Were The Days: The Early Years

Copyright © 2024 by **A. Miguel Trujillo**. All rights reserved.

No part of this publication may be reproduced, stored in a retrieval system, or transmitted in any way by any means, electronic, mechanical, photocopy, recording, or otherwise without the prior permission of the author except as provided by USA copyright law.

The opinions expressed by the author are not necessarily those of Moon Shard Media

5202 Corbridge Glen Ct., Katy Texas 77449 (254) 254-4712 |
info@moonshardmedia.com

Moon Shard Media is committed to excellence in the publishing industry.

Book Design copyright 2024 by Moon Shard Media. All rights reserved. Cover Design inspired from painting by the author.

Published in the United States of America

ISBN: 979-8-3302-3133-1

eISBN: 979-8-3303-5921-9

PROLOGUE

The Early Years

This story is being told and expressed as in the mind and eyes of Michael as he portrays his own feelings as well as those of Mira Rose.

This was in the summer time, I was working hard in construction that summer, so that I could save my money to fund my tuition, books, clothes and other misc expenses this coming fall. I had recently inquired about a part-time position as a draftsman with a local architectural firm down town so to not be far from the university.

I had been taking trips to Taos every 2nd or 3rd week-end to visit mom and dad. I would on occasions also visit with some guy friends and some girl friends that we would take dancing at some of the local dance halls.

Trust me, there is not much to do for entertainment in that town. Aside from the one theater there are several dance halls where mostly young people take their girl friends for the local music. I did have several date nights with 2-3 girls slightly younger than myself who attend the Taos High School. It has been interesting to say the least.

I had two very interesting past encounters with a very charming girl named Rose Ledoux . She was someone special, at least 3 years younger than myself meaning she will be a junior in H.S. We had 2-short and rushed dates on 2 weekends when I had come into town to visit. I am now curious how soon I may see her again when a date is not so rushed. Since then I have lost contact with her and I need to start looking for her very soon.

The surest thing in life, is that
"The past is never where you left it"

Chapter One

I know she is out there some where in our home town I come from, she is too young to have gone off on her own or to another high school.

My first attempt to contact her will be to through the high school in their records of photographs taken last year for their year book of; sophomores and juniors, just maybe I could recognize her and identify her in a photograph.

My second attempt which is rather weird, but it might help me find a source within the high school students and so I set out one Friday afternoon in early May to talk to various students as they are leaving classes.

I specifically found out which group of students was the sophomore group, so I was there and I was asking many of them if they knew Rose. The problem was I did not have much to go on, so I was just looking at all the girls and their classmates. About 2-3 dozen were leaving the grounds and then a group of 4 girls were together of which two were not her, but the other two were alone and the one with the shorter hair style happened to be Rose.

I walked over to meet the both of them, I said hello in a quiet pleasant manner so as not to scare them. As our eyes met and she looked at me and turned her head to one side with a very inquisitive look, with a sense of recognition, that gave me the opportunity to say, "Rose is that you, have I really found you?" I am so relieved now."

"I hope I did not scare the both of you?" She smiled and I knew immediately that she recognized me and said, "well hello Michael, what a surprise." Why are you so relieved?"

Rose turned to her friend and said, "excuse me Joyce I need to talk with him, so I will see you on Monday for classes?" As she moved away from her friend, she looked at me again and smiled and we both walked towards each other; I was so relieved that I had finally found her and that she did recognize me, maybe she was pleased to see me.

Her smile was even broader than her initial response and more acceptant now that we were close enough to touch; I could not hold back, I gently touched her face looked her in the eye and said, "Rose, I have been trying to find you and contact you. I had not stayed away from seeing you on purpose, but have been extremely busy with work and with my classes at the university this past first part of the year." "although I have thought of you many many times in the last few months." *I am so glad I finally found you, because I knew I would find you!*

"I recently realized last week that I really was crazy not staying in touch with you through the school year and I only have myself to blame. Now that I have found you, I want to apologize and ask for your forgiveness that I did not stay in touch with you." "Will you forgive me?"

She raised her left hand up to my hand that was on her cheek and squeezed it lightly, saying, "I really have missed you too and have wondered were you were and why had I not heard from you. I also had no way of reaching out to find out where you were.

As she finished her statement, she started to tear up a little and she seemed sort of sad, but maybe they were tears of joy or comfort, maybe the same thing I was feeling towards her. I reached further took her in my arms, squeezed her and said, "I am so glad to finally see you again."

She says, "I know you have your mother here in town but I had no address or telephone number to call about you."

We stayed close as I held her and I moved back, we looked at each other, she sniffled and said "I too am so glad you reached out to look for me, you just do not know how pleased I am and happy to see you again and do not ever ever leave me again."

I was stunned to hear what she had just said and it just impressed me so much.

I quickly said, "are you ready to head home and can I take you home? so that I can know exactly where you live and the address as well?" "Yes please, I really want to ride with you so we can spend more time together, It is Friday and I have nothing else to do." "I want you to tell me what you have been doing all this time that I had not seen you or heard from you, I just thought to myself, well, he is gone."

I drove away from the high school as she gave me directions to the next connecting street where she said I should turn left towards the El Prado area. She said her street was about 6 blocks from where we turned and she guided me as we maneuvered the side streets towards her home.

As we were driving she managed to move to the center of the seat towards me; I was somewhat surprised that she was wanting to be much closer to me. She says to me, "Do you mind if I come closer to you while you drive?" "I blurted out, "no of course not, I like that if that is what you want."

We finally arrived at her home and she showed me where I could park. She looks to the right and says, "Oh my mom is home early. Do you mind if we go in for a few minutes, I would like you to meet her?"

I quickly said, "I would be glad to meet your mom, even though she may not be expecting that someone Is bringing you home today." She took hold of my hand and we walked into the house; she calls out, "mom where are you, I am home and I have someone I want you to meet?"

Her mom walks into the living room, smiles and says, "Oh you are home already, usually it takes you longer to walk from the high school." Rose quickly says, "mom I want you to meet Michael, he is here from Albuquerque to visit and he did pick me up at the H.S. He and I have been friends since last year, but he had not visited here in town recently."

Her mom walks over to us and extends her hand out to me and says, "I am very pleased to meet you. Rose had not mentioned you recently, but I was aware of you by name and that at another time you had brought her home one night."

Rose was still holding my left hand. Her mom asked us to sit down so we could visit. She asks, "you have family here in town?" "I answered that I did and they were my mom and dad, so when I can, I come to visit them over a weekend, but always have to go back to my work and my studies at the university."

I looked over at Rose and said, "I guess I should get going as I still have not gone home to my mom's; she is expecting me this late afternoon as it takes me 2 1/2 hours to travel here. She lives over on Montoya Street off the road to El Canyon." Rose says, "I will walk you to your car." I said goodbye to her mom and thanked her for taking time to visit.

Rose held my hand tightly on the way out to the car, she says quietly, "I am so glad you decided to meet my mom as she is very fair with me but does expect me to be honest with her on my personal behavior; I think she likes you as she was very pleasant." I have never brought anyone home to meet and visit her or my dad; they are somewhat strict with me; just so you know what to expect from them."

I stopped short, turned to face her and said, "I am pleased that you asked me to meet her maybe now there will not be any concerns as we see more of each other, right?"

She had a nice smile and opened those beautiful green eyes and said, "Can I see you tonight, I really want to see you so we can visit and catch up for the lost time that we did not see each other?"

I could not refuse such a request from her and said, "What time would you like me here?", at least by 7:15 pm ?"

I told her that I want to visit with my mom, have dinner with her and then break the news that I need to come see you for at least a couple of hours. "What if we just stay at your home, visit there; We can take a walk, sit outside and just visit and look and be visible and normal?"

"Your parents will see that we are not going to run off. I think they will have a better opinion of us, because I want them to have a good opinion of me as they do not know me at all. I want to make sure your dad feels comfortable with me with you, does that sound okay to you?, Dads always look out for their daughters, I know I would if I were a dad."

Her eyes sparkled as she smiled and said, "I would like for you to kiss me, but we can wait till later tonight?" and do not forget." She squeezed my hand and I understood her message, how little I knew about her, but now I feel she will be very affectionate and how my little friend may well be a passionate and loving person to whom I will return the same feelings.

I am fully prepared to treat her with respect, kindness and show her that she can lean on me and trust me from now on.

We said goodbye and I promised to be here at 7:15+ p.m. She waved goodbye, seemed a little sad, so I will not let her down, I will be here I will keep my promise as I think she does finally deserve it, especially from me.

I arrived at my mom's house a short time later, I parked around to the side of the house, grabbed my bag and clothes and went to door, knocked and she came to the door, smiled as she was glad to see me again.

Mom and I visited, had dinner and later talked about her position with the seamstress shop and she was still able to carry on with that type of close and delicate work. She said she was still able to do the work for at least 6 hours a day. I helped her do dinner dishes and put foods away so that I could be helpful.

About 6:45 I said to her that I wish to visit my friend for at least 2 hours or so and that I would be back early so we can talk about taking her to the grocery store tomorrow..

I was at Rose's home by 7:10, I found her sitting on the bench under the porch where it was cool and out of the direct sun. As soon as I pulled up, she jumped off the bench and sort of rushed to the car to meet me, I opened the car door stepped out and walked forward to meet her,

She extended her hand to meet mine, squeezed it and said, I have been waiting for you and am nervous because I want you to meet my Dad. They are both relaxing in the living room; I hope you are not too nervous, or are you?"

I thought about what she said for a moment and then I answered her, "I think I can manage and will try not to be too nervous, so let us see how it goes, okay?"

We walked forward from the car towards the front door and then she opened the door and allowed me to walk in ahead of her and steered me towards the other end of the Living Room where her parents were sitting and relaxing.

She says to her Dad, Dad I want you to meet this friend of mine from Albuquerque, but is originally from here in Taos.

Chapter 2

Her Dad stood up from the chair he was in and walked to us both as we entered into the living room; I extended my hand and he did the same, I said to him, "Hello Mr. Toledo I am Rose's friend from Albuquerque I am very pleased to meet you and make your acquaintance."

He was very nice and invited me and Rose to sit. He started by asking me what I was doing in the big city, so I told him about work and my class studies at the university, he seemed impressed and congratulated me for my efforts.

Rose spoke up and said, "we are going to go sit on the porch bench and then go for a walk while it is still sunny; so I quickly said to both her parents. "it is a pleasure to meet you both; hope it is okay to visit with Rose for a while, because I also want to go spend some time with my mother tonight."

We sat on the bench, she next to me only as close to, but not too obvious or too intimate to draw attention from her parents. Soon she put her left hand on my shoulder and said, "I think we need to go for a walk, now!" I looked at her with raised eyebrows as if to say, okay I am ready too.

She went to the doorway and informed her parents that we were going for a short walk, would be back soon. I was up and ready to go as she approached me and we walked out towards my car,

Just behind the car she stops, turns to me and stands against me and places a soft tender kiss on my lips, pulls back and then puts her hands on my face and gives me a full mouth kiss, the kind I have never had the likes of. I placed my hands around her waist and gave back with the same tenderness.

We pulled away and began to walk towards the roadway, she with her arm around my waist and I with my arm around her shoulder in a tight embrace. I looked at her and said, "that was quite a kiss, your kiss took me by surprise." She says, "I know but I needed that kiss and that was my way of welcoming you back to me and I hope it is only a start for both of us."

"You just do not know how much I needed that; the night you took me home from that dance and we were very close and short of time, I remember how your touching and moving your fingers in and out was so pleasing, but that was all we did."

"What happened that night I never forgot and it left me yearning for you for more and it has lasted this long." you never called, you never came back, why?" I said, "I want you to know that *the image of your smile* has plagued me ever since we last met."

As we walk on I stopped for a moment, looked at her, how she was holding back the tears with a bit of sadness but also maybe tears of joy? I gently touched her face, lifted her chin and said, sweetie that was why I came to ask for your forgiveness and to apologize for not have come back or been in touch, I also want to experience your smile again."

"I know it could have been very puzzling to you and very cruel of me, why did I not at least come looking for you much sooner? "As I explained to you yesterday; now I really feel bad and you had every right to be puzzled and even upset at me, but I did not know how you might be feeling after that day, that night."

As I cleaned her slight tears from her cheeks, I said, again "please forgive me, I am now here and I will never leave you again and from now on I am here for you and I do hope you are here for me."

She finally smiled and said, "I am sorry to be so emotional, but I wanted you to know what I had felt all this time that we were separated and I can now understand what you may have been experiencing on your own as you mentioned, after all you have a life of your own to keep up." "Can we now be more honest and sharing with our own thoughts, needs and tell each other what we are doing or experiencing?" I said back, "I agree with what you are saying."

We stopped and decided we needed to turn around and go back to her home, as I needed to get going myself.

The sun was starting to set as we arrived at her front doorway, she opens the door and announces to her folks that we are back. She says, "Mom and Dad, Michael has a request. I quickly said to them, "I ask your permission if I can take Rose to the movies tomorrow night?" I believe there are two shows, but we may only stay for one show."

Her mom and dad look at each other and shrug their shoulders and said back, "I guess that is okay.

I said goodbye and good night to both, Rose said she'll walk out to the car with me. We stood together, I pulled her close and kissed her tenderly and said, "see you about 6:45 pm tomorrow; I really look forward for us to be alone together without any concern about time, okay?" I waved goodbye to her as I left, she threw me a kiss.

On the way to my mother's home I thought about how well the evening had gone and how receptive her parents were and they seemed comfortable with me coming to see Rose there at their home.

Mom was still up when I arrived back, she doing some ironing; she says, "I have been waiting for you so we can have some dessert. I baked a pie earlier and it is waiting for us. Come sit down so I can serve us at the table." "How was your visit with your friend, did you get to meet her parents?"

Earlier in our sharing personal thoughts, I asked her, "I hope you do not mind if I ask you what your full names are, do you have a middle name and what is the family name?"

She says, "I do not mind sharing my names with you, after all we are sharing personal information and that is okay. My first name is Miranda, my middle name is Rose which is what I go by. The family name is Ledoux. The reason I use Rose is because I think Miranda is better when I would be older as an adult if I wished to be called that.

I paused for a few seconds and said to her, "Rose I believe both your names are beautiful names and it is your choice how you wish to be known. I have a similar issue; for my first name I was named after my grandfather and middle name after my own father, so we are in a similar situation."

Chapter 3

I told her yes, "they were nice and very friendly and they gave me permission to take Rose to a movie tomorrow evening."

Saturday morning I took mom to the grocery store so that she could buy a few items of food for her next week. As she always needs someone to drive her to the store. We have had time to talk about what I am doing with work and with the university classes.

It is always important that I know how she is doing, even though I am away as a rule. My older brother works at the Los Alamos Laboratories and can respond to any of her needs within an hour or so.

My mother will be here in Taos until approximately the first of November then she will either go to one of my older sister's home for the cold month or go to Calif. to visit and stay with her older sister and family. She gets the chance to work in that family's restaurant and be helpful.

It can be imagined what it does to my period of time from early November throughout the winter until maybe May of the following spring. During the holidays I come to visit with my Dad on a long weekend, as he works at the Los Alamos Labs during weekdays, goes home for the weekend and travels back to work early Monday morning.

Most of those holidays when I am not working and not attending university classes, I find myself staying at the boarding school and making the best of it. The school is closed down for the Christmas holiday; 10-12 days. Those 10-12 days can be very lonely, cold with very little companionship from my fellow university students.

Mom and I had an early dinner Saturday, I helped her with cleanup of dishes and other items. Once we were done I excused myself to take a shower and shave, as I had not done since yesterday. That took all of 35 minutes and then I could get ready to leave for Rose's home.

I told my mom that I would not be too late, not to wait up for me and since I had a key I would let myself in the kitchen door and promised to be quiet.

I arrived at Rose's home at 6:45, knocked on the door and her mom came to the door. She gave me a big smile and said to come in, that Rose was still getting ready. She asks me, "Did you have your dinner, because if you did not, we had plenty left?" Rose's father has gone to town to pick up some items we need for tomorrow Sunday."

I said, "No thank you, my Mom had a very good dinner and dessert; she likes to cook she always cooks for me when I am here. She does not cook much when she is alone, so some times she over does it."

Within 5 minutes or so, Rose came in from the bedroom and greeted me and said, "I hope I did not keep you waiting." I responded, "No I just got here a few minutes ago and was just visiting with your mom."

"I am ready when you are." Then her mom says, "you two go ahead so you will not miss the first show and be careful out there." Rose says to her, "we will mom, see you when we get back." I could not believe how beautiful and radiant she looked.

I could hardly wait till we were outside and in the car so I could compliment her. I made sure she was in and comfortable; and I went around the other side, slid in, wasted no time in saying to her, "Rose, sweetie, you look so great, beautiful, and so grownup I can hardly believe my eyes, so I reached over and gave her a tender kiss on her cheek, I did not want to mess with her lip stick.

She reached over and gave me a big hug and a great smile and a look with her head slightly tipped; that smile was a charming sexy message that I would have to think about for the rest of the evening; it could get me into some sort of trouble She was dressed in a dark blue blouse. A light grey skirt and mid-high heels; like I observed, she did look like a young woman who was proud of herself, happy and meaning to please. I hope I have not brought that on her.

As we are driving away she says to me in a way to get my attention, very quickly it did happen, "I want to please you, that you'll be proud of me and I did want to look more grownup then normal." I am so pleased to be with you and to be by your side, you do mean so much to me."

I drove us to the plaza theater, she held on tight to my waist and I just smiled within and marveled at how with a very small amount of effort she was literally transformed into the young woman that I can cherish, admire and learn to care for and love as never before.

As we arrived I went to her side of the car and helped her step out smoothly, we stepped up on the sidewalk and walked the short distance to the ticket booth to secure the tickets for the first showing.

I can hardly express the pleasure and joy I felt inside of me as I had Mira Rose sitting next to me, actually tight against me; really I would not be able to move unless she shifted over to the right seat space.

We managed to get through the first 1½ hour showing and then, dim lights came on, a couple of cartoons started playing and we both were back to the reality of where we were. She looked up to me and said, "I can not believe we are here together, a totally new experience for me one I had only dreamed of, but did not expect to happen."

I raised her chin up, looked in her beautiful green eyes, kissed her tenderly, with her eyes closed she smiled and said, I have been waiting all this time for that kiss, a kiss that tells me a lot without so many words." "I can only say I feel the same as you have just expressed with your kisses."

I asked her, "what story can I read from looking deeply into your eyes, what can you share with me or is it too early to express those thoughts that are bouncing around in your mind, waiting, struggling to be released as a response that has been building up in the last few days and hours?"

"Talk to me sweetheart! Oh may I call you sweetheart from now on? as I will always say it with full meaning of how I do feel and will feel about you from this very moment?"

I took her by surprise, as she just looked at me with a bit of caution as to how to respond to a question that was far from her immediate gathering of her own interpretation and what meaning that form of affection would now have from now on.

As she sat there in a daze, I guess thinking as to how to respond to a question that did take her by surprise, so she must be wondering how she can react and respond, but meanwhile the theater lights are turned off and the title of the second show comes on with all the music and fanfare that is part of starting a movie. This was probably a nice way to delay what her response would be.

She quietly, in a shy way after the movie started, said to me, "If you want we do not have to stay for this showing. I am okay if we leave now; I think we need some time to be together before we go home." I looked at her , nodded and then said, okay let us go and spend some time alone."

We quietly walked out of the theater and went on to my car. It was a quiet and pleasant evening time, shortly after 9:00 p.m. I drove off wondering where we would go to just be alone and be able to share our time together.

There was a drive-Inn on the main highway, so I drove there; at least there we would be safe, could enjoy an ice cream sundae or a soft drink.

We parked, a young girl came and took our order and would be back soon I looked at her as she moved close to me with the same look in her eyes and her lips slightly parted; like she had shown me before in the theater.

The first thing that she voiced to me was, "I love the fact that you want me to be your sweetheart and it pleases me that you asked, what more could I ask for than to be your sweetheart, but now I have a same feeling and wish to be able to affectionately call you what I think of you too."

"I wish to call you in a manner that is you and you alone. I can only think that I want you to be my "Honey" nothing else or nothing crazy like others call themselves." "May I call you my honey, because it means you only?" I responded, "I am pleased with your response, what can I say, other than what pleases you is fine with me."

Chapter 4

I reached over to her, brought close to me and took her face with both hands, kissed the tip of her nose, then her eyes and then those precious lips I was longing for, how much more could I ask for than this precious person. She gave me the tightest hug with both arms around my neck and would not let go and said, "I really care so much for you that it is hard to express myself now, but time will tell."

Again she looked at me as if she was experiencing a joy that I could not fully understand, but she was expressing it with that great smile of hers', those eyes I really do love so much and her tender touch on my right cheek.

Just as we stood struck by each others expression on our faces, the girl with our sundaes knocked on my window, so I had to take care of our order and then be alone again. We were having, hopefully, one of those, sharing moments that we would have from now on.

We ate our sundaes in silence, I offered her a spoonful of cherry ice cream, she took it in the blink of an eye and said, "I liked your kisses better, but that cherry taste is good." After we finished we left for her home to be there at a reasonable time.

I wanted her parents to feel good that we did not stay out beyond a reasonable hour, I very much wanted them to trust me and feel that they could trust me with their daughter and that we both would behave in an acceptable manner still enjoy being together within the time in which I was here to take her places that they found to be acceptable for their young daughter

about her and her family and how the parents were very nice to me. I informed her that Rose was someone I had met last fall and had not been to see her since.

Mom wanted to know how old Rose was and was she still in school. I told her Rose's age and yes she is still in high school here in town. She seemed to be acceptable to all of the answers I gave her, She did ask, "Are you interested in her to continue seeing her?" I answered that I was and would only be able to see every two weeks when I can come to visit her and Rose; like this weekend.

At approximately 2:15 p.m. I told mom that I needed to get going, that I would make a stop to see Rose for a few minutes and stop and see Dad and apologize for not spending time with him, next time.

I arrived at Rose's home, knocked at the door and she came running to the door, saw me let out a little cry and was all smiles, she rushed to me put her arms around my neck, kissed me passionately and said to come in. I expected to see her parents, so she says, "Mom and Dad went to church and then to visit an aunt in El Prado whom they had not seen for several weeks. My brother also went."

She could not contain herself now that we were alone, so I kissed her and she was so affectionate and would not let go of me, so we could get a breath or two in between each kiss. I know she just wanted to make up for time we lost last night due my bringing her home too early.

I was feeling the same, because here I am ready to leave town, she knows and dreads to see me leave for at least 2-weeks; I feel the same way, because it will be 2 weekend until I may come back.

Mira Rose looks at me with those teary brown eyes and it is beginning to make me sad too. All I can say or do is: Sweetheart, "I know it is tough for us to part for the time being since we have been so close this weekend and we have much more to share, experience and look forward to."

"Please do not be sad for now just think that in two weekends I will return; I wish I could come every weekend, but it is just not possible, at least right now." She says, "I am going to miss you very much, so I need to find things to do to use up time, but I will be thinking about you all the hours that I am awake."

"Listen, let me offer a suggestion, you may be able to find a part-time job. Go visit the two drugstores, and even the La Fonda restaurant/ hotel and see if you can talk one of them to hire you part-time to occupy your time and make some money, how does that sound for a start?"

I have to go now, I really hate to leave, but I should and I am not happy that I have to leave you for now. I kissed her one more time, she released her arms around my neck and said, "Okay I know you need to leave, I will miss you."

I said to her, "I will call you at 7:00 this evening, so wait for my call; this is not goodbye, we will talk later, okay?"

My drive home was uneventful and all went wall, traffic was a bit busy being that it is Sunday, mid afternoon when some people are on their way home after a weekend away from their homes, someone like me.

I stopped on north 2nd street at a place to eat my early dinner and then go on to the school campus where I have my place of residence at the boy's dormitory.

All was quiet on campus not much going on; I suspect the few students and staff were probably done with dinner and had gone to their own quarters for the evening.

I arrived at the dormitory, unloaded all my gear and put all my clothes and other items away. I was a bit tired and worn out, so I lied down for a while it was only 5:45 pm and too soon to plan on calling Mira Rose, I will wait till 7:00 p.m.

I suspect that I dozed off for at least 30-45 minutes, when I awoke I saw that it was 6:50. I needed to hustle over to the telephone booth for my 7:00 call to Mira Rose. Lucky for me the telephone was free and I was able to dial out to her home phone. It rang about 3-4 times then a response.

"Hello, this is Rose, she did not ask who was calling, but without saying so, she knew it was me, so I quickly said, "Hi sweetheart it is me can you talk?" "yes, yes she says I have been sitting here next to the phone waiting for your call. I told my Mom you would be calling at 7:00 just so she knew that." How are you honey! How was the trip back home?"

I responded, "I had a good drive home, all is well and it sort of felt good to be back, but I surely miss you already and it is going to be a quiet boring evening without seeing you, I guess I have no choice right now, my main concern is how are you doing since I left, have you had dinner?"

She started to answer, but she seemed to have become a little emotional and as if she was tearing up before she could get her words out. Finally she cleared her throat and said, " I was sad when you left and did not know what to do with myself.

It was a sudden change for me as I had not ever experienced this form of emotions." "I can now imagine how it must be when two persons are separated."

"I know it is going to be a tough 2- weeks for me; I need your help in how to deal with this separation from you. I know you or I can not do anything about it." It is sort of unreal for me, because I have never been attached or cared for someone at all. The thing is that it has just happened in such a short time since you came to see me and we are now thinking only about each other."

"Sweetheart, I will also have anxious moments or times of being alone with my thoughts about you and I, and will not be able to do anything for the time being.

For you all I can say is; try to be happy, think good thoughts think of me as probably being there near you and hope how there will be many happy days and times for us in the near future and as time goes on." I will call you again on Wednesday evening and the next weekend."

"Think of me as only being gone a few days at a time and always within a telephone call away, okay? and if we stay in touch as I said, our days can be shorter and we can share our thoughts, ideas and our own secret exchange of emotions."

"Give more thought to my suggestion about going to the drug stores and restaurant for an opportunity for work, that would keep you busy, you can be happy working with others and time will go by faster. You can look forward to be hearing from me and soon it is time for me to come see you again."

"Honey I want to tell you that my Mom came into my room earlier before dinner and asked how I was doing; had you left for the city today? She saw that I was quiet and I guess I looked sad, so she sat down and asked, "how much do you care for Michael, do you think it can be serious enough that you two will be seeing and dating from now on?"

"You both seem to have a very good relationship right away. He does seem like a very nice, thoughtful and honest young man, he seems to treat you well."

"I was surprised that my Mom would ask me those question so soon. I guess she saw right away how we were together." She said to me, "I know you are young, but not too young to be attached to someone you could care for, but you have not had any experience with boys, as we have so far been strict about you're going and staying out late."

"Oh before I forget can you give me your address where you live on campus of that school, can I write to you there?" "Let me continue to tell you about the questions my mom was asking and what she thinks about the two of us."

"My mom also said, "Your dad and I were impressed that Michael wanted to bring you home early after the movies. He seemed to want to please us, so we can trust him and we feel he will be good for you, so we can talk more later in the week, you are expecting his call, right?"

Rose did not share anything else with Michael on the phone and chose to leave it as a discussion she and her mom had after he had left. She and her mom's conversation included other comments, and ideas that her mom had about the two of them, they could wait until later.

"Mom finally asks, "do you think you can handle being attached to him, but only able to see him every two weekends?" "You need to think about that, because it could be hard on you and not be a satisfying relationship and even hard on him too."

"Also you do not know what he is doing in the city during those two weeks, he could have a girlfriend there too, have you even thought about that?" "I know it is really early, the fact that you just got together with him and know very little about his current living conditions."

"I do not wish to put negative thoughts in your mind, but only bring it up as your mother: I am or will be concerned about your feelings and ideas about the two of you."

"I do know that eventually your plans, dreams and ideas about your own future will be the most important thoughts you will be dealing with, and we understand, for your sake.

Those thoughts and discussions were in Rose's mind when she talked to Michael on the phone, but she chose to keep them to herself as issues to be aware of and to think about as she and Michael continued to be together in forming a more sincere, tight and personal bond with each other.

When Michael heard the operator come on and say to him that the call was over or he could put in more money, so he and Rose felt they were done for tonight; they quickly said goodbye for now and would talk more on Wednesday.

Michael had much to think about from now until the call to Rose on Wednesday. He was surprised the talk between her and her mother about was directed to their budding relationship, but mostly about how Rose would handle the relationship at a distance and not be hurt in one manner or another by that separation.

He began a mental search into his own mind as what was the best way to assure Rose that he was fully prepared to be honest and treat her truthfully about his own part in the beginning of their relationship and make every effort to keep her happy and informed.

He began to write down ideas about certain points that her mother had presented to Rose and the manner in which she was probing and advising Rose.

It is understandable she can be concerned about Rose's new relationship with him. He did think that most of those questions or comments were good and made much sense, so that Rose could think carefully about what she should expect from her involvement in a distance relation.

Michael also feels that the relationship could go either way and he and Rose may have a difficult time accepting a breakup later when they are both deeper into their feelings.

so it is very important for each to understand their feelings and be certain about what they want out of the relationship. Michael does need to tell Rose that he himself wishes to be loyal to her and that he wishes for her to trust in him, be happy and be there for him as well.

Michael needs to share with her the fact that their finest days together are unknown but yet ahead and that it will take the both of them to work, share and plan the days ahead.

Chapter 5

Monday started out as a busy day on the job site, Tom our boss was throwing orders and instructions at all of us and said we were running a few days late and we all needed to pick up the pace, so as to catch up.

We all had our individual assignment for the next few days, so we broke up and went about performing our own duties or related duties when it came to a specific work load that was related to other tasks. those 40 plus hours of this week were very intense and I would be glad to see the end by Friday evening at 5:00 p.m.

Meanwhile it was 5:30 Wednesday, we were done for the day and I was able to go shower quickly and get ready for dinner at 6:00 pm. I did have some free time after dinner till I would be calling Mira Rose [*I really like referring to her in that manner because she is special and the two names go together well*].

At 5 minutes to 7:00 I walked over to the phone booth by the girl's dorm porch, Good no one was using the phone at that time, so I walked quickly, got in and closed the door. I picked up the phone and pulled out 3- quarters that I did need to talk at least for 18-20 minutes.

I received a dial tone and started to dial Rose's number after it connected it took 3 rings before she quickly answered and said, "Hello", I said back "Hello sweetheart."

"Hi honey I was sitting here waiting for your call and you were right on time, it is good to hear from you it just seems like it has been a long week since Sunday, but it is only 3 days since. I was just anxious to hear your voice. My mom said I was just nervous and anxious; she was actually watching how I was acting."

"She has actually gone to another part of the house, she wished for me to have my privacy to talk to you and I appreciate that from her." "I was very lonely these last few days; first thinking about all the comments that my mom put in my mind and then me going over and over what real meaning they might really have. I did not want to be confused about those things she brought up."

"Honey, you need to help me think through all those ideas and comments she put in my head and I need to know and understand you better, as I trust you even this early in our being together, okay?"

"I do not mean to be nosey or curious about what you do with your spare time in the evenings when you are not working or doing other things. I know you are alone and have to do things for yourself." "Please forgive me for asking, I am not being distrusting of you, I care for you."

"Rose, to answer your questions as to what I do in the evenings after work and dinner, I take walks around the campus, I may visit with some of the guys or guys and girls who work here for the summer and I do a lot of reading of the mystery books I got introduced to this last fall."

"Sweetheart, I have been reading novels of a "Mike Hammer Private Eye" written by author Mickey Spillane, very interesting, full of mind boggling episodes and mysteries. It occupies some evenings and then the day is gone, time to go to bed to rest for another day at my duties on the dining room building we have under const.

"There are time when I do go see a movie with one of my buddies or even alone. I do not mind going alone, as I have been used to being alone. I have these 3- buddies, we go out riding around and I am always the driver of my car and they sit back there, drink some beer; I do not like or drink beer."

"I also purchased a drafting tabletop with drafting tools and have started training myself in their use for drawing building forms and details. I am also spending much time developing new lettering styles to apply to drawings I am preparing as I practice."

"In the next month or so I am going to contact some of the architectural firms down town to see if I can find a part-time job as a draftsman."

"I could also assist one of the architects, so I can begin to establish myself as a potential draftsman as I accomplish my course studies in the field.

"I am hoping to set up my classes this fall so they fall in the morning till 12:00 or so, that will allow me to work part- time from about 2;00 t0 5:00 pm every day during the first and second semester"

"All of the things I did to pass the time away before my effort to find you and as of the last weekend, I did without having anything or anyone on my mind, especially since school was not in session and I had the rest of the summer to work and make the best of it."

"Sweetheart now that has all taken a turn for the best, and the best is having you to think about to plan with and to just think about sharing every bit of what I think, what I need to do to keep you happy and for me to also be as happy as possible now on."

"I have not or do not date or see any of the girl students here and I have not met any girl students at the university, I live away from there during sessions at the University.

I barely have time to accomplish my studies and perform the duties I am required to do just to be able to live here on this campus. My duties give me board and room and bus transportation to and from the university, it is a great deal.

"I do have weekends off from duties, but there is always something for me to do except when I go to see my folks, and from now on to see you; what a change that is and I will look forward to those weekends now that you are there for me and I will be there for you."

"Sweetheart, you have nothing to worry about and no concerns about what I do with my spare time, from now on I will only be thinking and planning about us and visiting you every two weeks.

I hope even sooner as time allows, besides you are now part of my past, but you are now my future and I want to be part of your future."

The operator came on line and said, "Your time is up: I pulled out 2 more quarters for more time to talk.

"Have I satisfied your curiosity and any concerns that have come up after having those discussions with your mom? You may not have even thought about issues your mom said if she had not said them, right?"

"Talk to me, sweetheart, tell me what you think and what your ideas are about us and the times we will be able to be together and enjoy those times from now on?" On a daily basis now that I am here and did spend part of the weekend with you,

"I constantly have, 'that great image of your smile from Saturday night.' "I was so impressed with your beautiful smile," how different you looked, and as I said before "so grown up with that natural beauty, it really blew my mind."

"Honey now I really understand all about you and what you must have to go through just to go to school, work and keep up your duties. I am really impressed and it really makes me feel closer and more a part of you and I have no doubt that you are very sincere and honest with me, so said please forgive me again for asking those silly questions." I really miss you and I will be very happy to know what we can now be for each other."

Oh! honey "just want to tell you that I talked to the drug stores with the La Fonda owners, they will get back to me by Friday about me possibly having a job for the summer." I hope at least one will offer me something, I will wait."

She quickly says, "Goodbye honey I will wait for your call on Saturday, will miss you until then."

The operator came on saying time was up, so I said, "need to go for now but will call you Saturday evening about 7:00, so goodbye sweetheart till then okay?"

It was somewhat depressing to just hang up and have no real contact like when you stand close, very close, put your arms around her, she does likewise and there is that wonderful full kiss that tells it all; that is the way to say goodbye for now, we will be together again soon.

At this moment that is only wishful thinking, but I am sure she is probably thinking and feeling the same. This is all very new to me and I feel it is also very new to her.

I am convinced that we will now be able to express ourselves with much clearer minds considering that Mira Rose had just brought up the various questions as related to her by her mom. I now have expressed in full and answered and cleared up any doubts that could have just lingered in her mind, which would have raised mistrust of me when I am away from her during my weeks here at work and later on during classes at the university.

I also am thankful that she did bring out and present to me those possible doubts that her mother had shared with her so that she can consider and keep in mind about the beginning of a relationship with me.

I took a walk around the park and then went back to my room at the dormitory to read my novel for the evening. I did my reading until 9:30 p.m. and then I started falling asleep; I had worked hard today under the hot sun, no clouds or even a slight breeze which can also bring some relief from the heat.

Chapter 6

The work week slipped by rather fast and here it was Friday nearly quitting time from this hard work, but it was pay day and we expected the boss to come around with our weekly pay. He usually paid us in cash but we had to sign a special form to acknowledge the receipt of funds.

The usual for me is to leave the job site and go shower and then lie down and rest until dinner is served in the dinning room. I only see other students or workers at this time of the day and maybe through the early evening before we all return to our dormitory rooms.

I am not under the umbrella of rules that the summer student workers have to be, they are not allowed to leave the campus on their own during weekdays. They are allowed to go to movies in town or other activities on weekends. It seems to work well for them as they are already conditioned to the campus rules and they seem content.

I being a university student who has stayed here on campus for these last two summers will be attending classes starting in September. I can come and go as I wish in the evenings or on weekends with no restrictions: like an adult and to set an example for younger boys and girls student workers, so I conduct myself well, I try to help with tasks around my dorm building and I keep my room and bathrooms clean. I also associate with others so as to be sociable, I do volunteer for duties as needed..

This Friday night after having read my detective novel that I have been reading for the last week or so, I laid down the novel and listened to some soft music and my first thought was—Mira Rose .Recently I devote quiet time be- fore bed time to think about her smile and her responses.

Maybe she too is thinking about us in her own quiet time and wishing for us to connect almost daily just to be able to share personal private thoughts and wishes. I hope she is now more at ease since we discussed my situation here and comments shared with her by her mom.

Tomorrow Saturday at 7:00 pm I shall be calling her at home; I am so looking forward to what we have to share, at least for the moment. I thought just the other day, maybe I should try to hookup a telephone line in my bedroom just for my use and then she and I can talk almost every day early in the evening. There is a phone line in the house mother's quarters upstairs; I shall call the phone company.

Saturday was a slow day and uneventful for the most part, but I decided I wanted to go to an afternoon showing of a new movie that has been out for less than a week. I talked to some of the boys in the dorm to see if they would go and then I went over to the girl's dorm room to see if at least two of the girls would be allowed to go with us. I would actually be the chaperon for them all. They are well behaved and it should not be a problem

I kept my fingers crossed that the girl's house mother would allow two girls to go along to the movies. I had to do a lot of convincing that it would be good for them to get out for a change and I would oversee their behavior just for at least 2 hours or so. Lo and behold it was allowed.

The outing went well, all five of us fit in my car and it was a short trip down to Central Avenue where all four theaters are located. We all agreed on the 2- movies to see and we all enjoyed it. We had soft drinks and pop corn in the theater We were back at the campus by 4:30 and I personally thanked the house mothers for letting the boys and girls go to the movies.

The school has a small 8-10 passenger yellow bus that we university students use to travel to and from the university during school year. I am wondering if they would allow me to take students to the movies on some weekends?

At dinner time, I was informed by those girl students that did not have an opportunity to go to the movies that they would have liked to have gone too! They were a little upset. I quickly said, "You know? I will take you all tomorrow if you get permission from your house mother, but we need to see if there are at least two more boys who wish to come along with us. Find out after dinner, we can decide tonight and after church tomorrow we can head to the movies, okay?" I was told that both house mothers had agreed to the outing and we planned it for 1:30 in the afternoon.

I rushed over to the telephone booth to place my call to Mira Rose, Oh how great that name sounds, to me I sure need to talk to her tonight and share my day activities while she shares hers since we talked on Wednesday. The phone rang twice and it was quickly answered; it was Rose.

"Hello, This is Rose, "Then Michael, responded, "yes it is me, hello sweetheart." She says back, "I was waiting for your call, but sometimes others call and I would not want to be taken by surprise if I called someone else your name, so I am sorry I did not assume it would be you okay?"

She does not wait one single second as she admits, "I have made sure that no one else tries to call out so that I can wait for your call."

I told mom that you would be calling me at around 7:00, so she understood." "I have been anxious to hear from you as it seems that the last three days were very long, too long but I am happy now to hear your voice." She hesitated momentarily, as I gathered she was being a little emotional, but she caught her breath and said, "I have missed you although we talked on Wednesday."

"I missed you too and I could only wish I was there with you at this moment, but I am here on the phone so talk to me tell me what you've done all this past week." At the moment, I said, "sweetheart I have put in enough quarters so we can talk for about 30 minutes or so, we do not need to rush,

I waited while she gathers her thoughts and she decides then she starts out by saying, "The last few days of the week were nothing, it seems that all I did was think about you calling me on Wednesday, then Thursday to Friday I was waiting to hear from those drug stores and restaurant, so guess what?

"yesterday about 4:30 I got one call, it was the Saavedra's Drugs Store that called and they asked me to come in this morning at 10:00 am to talk about what my duties would be and so they trained me all day until 5:30 this afternoon. My mom picked me up and we got home in time for dinner."

"I was so excited to be hired and could hardly wait to tell you, so now you know! I have a job for the summer, is that not neat now I can be more independent, make some money and occupy my summer vacation." "My parents were happy for me, so now I need to figure out how I to get to work and back every day, I will let you know soon."

"Honey I am so please you interested me to look for something to occupy my time for the rest of the summer." "It will really be good to meet people, to talk to tourists and to learn how pharmacy stores do their sales; also I can see the kinds of stuff they have for sale and to learn what is out there for us to buy."

I said to her, "sweetie I am very pleased to hear you are very happy that you will be busy and the experience that you will be achieving for the rest of the summer." "Let us talk about you and I. "I have been thinking about us being able to talk more often by telephone, so I have come up with this idea."

Chapter 7

On Monday I am going to call the telephone company down town and ask what a simple telephone connection here at my dorm room would cost me, and I would need to have long distance service for us to be able to talk more often, such as every other day or so. "What do you think about that?" "There is already service here to the house mother's quarters in the dormitory."

I said, "I know it is a long time between my visits to see you and also my mother and only 2 calls a week is not much time for us to talk." I feel that I can afford the cost."

"Honey do you think it will be expensive? Will you be able to afford it? I do not mean to ask what money you have to spend, so forgive me for bringing it up." I do not want you to do something just for me; I can manage how we take time to visit when you come over and I really appreciate you wanting to call me at least twice a week."

"Honey I think a lot about us and how we managed to get together again." As you said before; you found me and I am overjoyed that you did and I am very grateful that you care for me and I care for you very much as well."

Some days I just walk around smiling and thinking. My mom has asked me at times, "what is going on, you seem to always be smiling and you walk around humming a song or two?" Usually I will just say,   "Everything is fine mom, as I smile and walk away, I know she is thinking she knows why."

Just as Rose finished telling me about her mom, the operator came on and time was up, but if I put another quarter in, I could talk for another 10 minutes; I agreed and did so, so now we can finish our conversation.

 A. Miguel Trujillo

"Honey, I will write you a letter and mail it Monday morning, I hope you get it by Wednesday, so let me know when, as I will take time to express my special feelings and thoughts that I seem to have when I have gone to bed. It is a very special time of the day for me, I am all alone and nothing can interfere with my thinking about you."

"That is very sweet of you to take time out to write to me, I will take time out to write back if it is of interest to you that I do so." She says," I would hope so and I will be interested to see what and how you answer back."

Time was up for the call, so I say to Rose, "Sweetie it is time to go and it is so long for now I will call you at 7:00 on Wednesday so we can plan for the coming weekend." Her voice sounded somewhat less than clear and saddened, but she managed to say, "goodbye honey I'll miss you, look forward to your call on Wednesday and I promise not to cry and maybe I will see you in my dreams."

It was a sad way to end our talk, knowing full well that we can not see each other until I do travel to Taos next weekend. I was surprised how she ended with a sad goodbye; I did not expect her to express those feelings or emotions tonight and it hurt I could not be there to comfort her and get her to feel better, I must tell her next time.

In a similar feeling of sadness, I too felt separated from her and the fact that all we can express at this time is our feelings for each other without being able to touch, be physically intimate and me to hold her in her hour of need for such closeness. I too need some form of being able to hold her, to touch her and caress her with tenderness, it will be the weekend.

All I can do now to make the best of the rest of the evening is bury my feelings and thoughts in the novel I am currently reading. I will still have the feelings I felt during our talk and I know she will probably be a little sad, we will talk on Wednesday.

I need to share with her that I am here and she is there, but we should think of us as one in thought and mind, so that we can be tuned into each other, be happy and be thankful for having each other to lean on and talk to each other, I am here for her and will keep her happy.

Monday, Tuesday and Wednesday, just work, days and quiet sort of lonely nights. I made and effort to walk over to the girl's dorm and found a small group of boys and girls hanging out, talking, laughing and telling jokes. They had a radio in the porch blasting some songs and music, but they managed to hear themselves carrying on.

I walked up, said hello to them all; they quickly quieted down some and they looked at me as if I was lost and had strayed away from my own dorm. They invited me to join them and I said thanks. I sat down next to Delia, whom I have know for a while, she is quite a lovely person, young and sexy looking.

One of the boys reaches out to me, asks, "How does it feel to have all the freedom of having graduated and now going to the university?" I understand you are working for the contractor on finishing the new dining room building?"

The question was two parts, so I answered the first by saying, "I enjoy having my freedom and able to go as I please, but with that freedom comes the responsibility to behave, work hard, save money to go back to school as I have no one to help me with my living expenses and funds to go to the university and to be able to get a degree."

"Yes I am working for Horton Construction and believe me it is hard work out there in the sun, sweating, being thirsty all the time and making sure that I do my tasks well so as to not get blasted for a job badly done."

"At the end of the day I am tired, worn out and ready to relax, all of that is part of my survival and accomplishing my daily tasks; but in construction one sees what we all have been putting together to last 50 years or so and one can feel proud of what we have done. You should try it some day."

"One thing that has really been helpful to me is having the good fortune and privilege of having a car to get around in because some days I am sent elsewhere to work for a day or more; I really appreciate that."

"I already had my car when I came here as a senior, but it was at home with my parent and was allowed to bring it back after graduation." "without a car you can not have a job.

They all looked at me in wonderment, one girl says to me, "I feel sorry for you having to work out there in the sun, it shows because you are somewhat sun tanned, so I guess we are lucky here because we work indoors all day."

One other boy pops up and say, "I wish we could get off the campus more often to go to town or movies." I said to him, "I would be interested in taking some of you to the movies in town; some could go on Saturday and the rest of you I could take on Sunday to the matinee shows, okay?"

Most of them were excited about that, they asked, "You would really do that for us?" I said, "Yes I would, so I can look into it with the house mothers or the front office." "Now, keep in mind that every other weekend I travel to Taos to visit my folks and a girl friend I have been seeing for awhile and I am scheduled to go next weekend."

"So the following weekend we could plan on something for all of you those two days. We do not want to leave anyone out, so lets make sure we know who will go."

We spent the rest of the next hour plus telling jokes, laughing and listening to their music. About 9:15 I wished them all a good night and I would see them again, maybe tomorrow night?" One girl says, "good night do not let the bed bugs bite", Ha Ha! and they all went crazy laughing.

I was pleased to have spent time with them, as they need a fresh body to visit with and even to pick on and it did help me feel better and not so lonely by myself.

I am so into Rose and she is on my mind all the hours in a day that I am awake. I certainly can understand if she is also somewhat lonely at times and I wish that we were together more, even in this early stage of our relationship.

It is possible that at this stage of separation, that either one of us could have a change of heart and admit that it can not work; that closeness; personal contact and holding hands and also being able to get away together is truly very important to me; I hope Rose feels that as well.

I am trying to be an adult about our new relationship and my only hope is that being so young at this stage that there may be some misgivings about how serious we should be about each other. I do adore her, have great feelings for her and I know that those feeling will only grow stronger.

Monday came and went, on Tuesday when I trekked to my room in the dorm, I was met at the hallway next to the stairs by our house mother. She says to me, "Michael earlier I slipped a letter under your door. I certainly was impressed with the fragrance it had, must be very important from someone in your hometown of Taos" I think I may have blushed after what she said and all I could say was thank you I appreciate it and headed to my room.

I quickly gathered up the letter, looked at it and I knew that it would be from Mira Rose. She said she was going to write to me, but I did not know it was to be this soon. I sat down on the bed, opened it up in a hurry and sure enough; four pages full writing. Wow! how impressive!

Lucky me, I immediately became engrossed in the first page and it is as I could not wait, my shower can surely wait for now. It starts off with:

Chapter 8

Hi Honey

I could not wait to write this letter to let you know what I have been through and doing the last few days since we talked Sunday evening. First I want to tell you how important your calls are to me, for now they are all I wait and live for without them I am climbing the walls.

My mother looks at me kind of strange on those times when I am either tearing around the house, humming a song, so she says I always have a smile on my face. Just to pick on me at times she will ask me if I am okay. She thinks that is clever, I just smile more and stick my nose in the air and walk away. She knows!

Many nights I am glad when it is time to go to bed, because that Is when I am all alone with my thoughts about you and about us. I pray that you are okay working hard at the building you are building with the contractor.

I know that we are young, me I am 17+ and younger than you, but my heart tells me that I am old enough to understand companionship, love and being true friends as well.

I am very happy that it is you and I do think we fit well together and not you with someone else or me with any of those strange guys here in town

I figure my mom and dad probably think I am too young to be serious with someone but they can not fully understand what my feelings are for you, specially since you came back and looked for me. They can not possibly know what that meant to me when you found me

You came back into my life at the best time ever, how little did I know that this could happen and you have turned my life around in just a few weeks. I am super glad

My days and nights were boring, had nothing to look forward to and staying home all the time is no fun at all. I would like to be busy

I know that we are new to our relationship, but it only means that we have plenty of time to grow both mentally, physically and emotionally. I am going to be very happy caring for you. Again I am so delighted that we are together at this point in our lives,

because you are at least 3 years older, I have much to learn about being with someone and I can hardly wait to be able to learn about what it takes to be more independent,

caring and how to share and I feel that I can learn much, much more with you and I will always have an open mind for you

I took time with this letter to say more, to express my feeling towards you because there is never enough time during your calls, but I am always delighted to talk with you; I miss your touch and smile

page 3

At times there is much more that I could say to you, but both of us are trying to talk at the same time only because there is so little time to say much more

I think that is a great idea that you wish to set up a telephone in your dorm room, how great is that. When you do call we can talk as much as you wish. I offer to pay for half of the cost since I am now working. Would that be okay?

Also, think about it this way, I can even call you just before bed time and wish you pleasant dreams, I can talk to you more intimately since our telephone is next to the dining room and away from the bedrooms. Think about that

I could certainly enjoy longer talks with you at different times during the weekdays, but only if you wish

page 4

I have really enjoyed writing this letter to you, it is so much more personal. I apologize about my writing since I do not have any experience at doing so, but some how I have really been able to express myself; I have surprised myself, I hope I have not shocked you how I expressed the feelings I have begun to gather in my mind and in my heart for you

You will be calling me on Wednesday evening? I will be waiting next to the telephone. The days always seem to be longer when I know you will be calling I can hardly wait till that evening at 7:00 that day

Please be careful at work and do not be too lonely like you say, be happy, think good thoughts. I will do the same here, for you

I could write more, but I need to say good night because it is now getting late. I am happy have good thoughts and I look forward to all that we can be to each other and for each other

I do get somewhat lonely especially when the sun has gone down and it starts to get dark. It is as if the house walls are closing in around me. My parents are in their little world, talking and visiting about their day at work

page 5

It seems that there is no one around for me to talk with about my day and what I did learn at the drugstore. My feelings are very important to me now more so then ever before. I just wish I could tell you more, express more and know that you would be there to hear me out

I am not very religious but can honestly say God bless you and I say it with all my heart again good night Honey

I am having a hard time as how I should end this special letter to you and to express myself like I feel and I hope it is acceptable to you and it is my wish that you never leave me again

I care very much for you, keep me in your heart and thoughts all day long

With all my affection, 10 times over!!!

Rose with many kisses and more to come

Chapter 9

I sat there on my bed after having read all 4-1/2 pages with such admiration for Mira Rose and a letter that has to be read at least 2-3 times just to be fully absorbed and I admire how well she was able to convey, on paper, her feelings and able to write it "from the heart" as she has really shown her ability in a very short time after our own conversation just earlier this evening.

Our conversation had ended in a manner in which I wish we could have had more time. It appears that she was able to begin her letter where we left off and carry on with her feelings in a surprisingly fresh manner.

I am so intrigued and proud of her for how she has responded and shown emotions, passion and total interest in the beginning of our relationship and it seems she is not afraid of commitment so early. I am so prepared for what could be a refreshing friendship as well as a loving relationship. We can grow in more ways than one.

I showered quickly, as it was almost time for dinner, so I will shave later after dinner and just see what the evening brings; not much I can plan for, but maybe I can visit with the younger boys and girls.

I finally realized that it is very important for me to call about getting my own telephone here in my room, what a blessing it would be, I could talk to Mira every night before bed time.

I do have one thought, I will talk to Miss Gladys, the person in charge of the kitchen and dinning area and see if I can be of some help after tonight's dinner; it will give me a chance to be helpful and productive.

My offer to help in the kitchen and clearing of the dining room was accepted, I was given an apron and some thin rubber gloves so I would not soil my clean shirt and be able to handle plates and bowels with food. Some of the student who are assigned to the cooking, serving and cleanup were looking at me as if they wondered what I was doing working alongside of them.

One of the girls was brave enough, she came up to me and asked, "what are you doing here cleaning up? after all you are not a student or a summer worker" "Were you a bad boy and are being punished for what you did?" Forgot to mention that she, Delia, the girl knows me well enough to approach me with her questions and make fun of me.

I said to her, "Delia I just decided I wanted to be helpful, since I have nothing else to do for the rest of the evening. I am feeling rather lonely and detached from my normal routine, please feel free to feel sorry for me, okay?"

Her eyes widened, she turns her head and her facial expression is weird and says, "I guess I should feel sorry for you since you must feel different tonight; poor you."

"Come visit with us at the girl's dorm since you have nothing else to do, later, but I will not say anything about how you are feeling, so that they will not pick on you."

I smiled at her and said, "Thank you, you are quite a charmer and I trust you will keep my secret tonight, so I will see later?" She walks off to the kitchen and waves and says, "See you later at the porch or on the lawn and do not be late."

I said to myself, that went well, but I continued to finish up what I had started in the dining room and proceeded to the kitchen to see if I was needed further on cleanup. I talked to the dietitian/ head cook and she thanks me for my help. She says to me, "Usually it will take an extra half hour plus to finish up, so I am sure the girls here will appreciate your help tonight, and I thank you very much."

I quickly responded, Thank you for dinner and all the other meals, you and your helpers work hard. I remember when I was assigned to kitchen duty as a senior a while back, we both know what it takes to serve meals here. "I will offer my help at other times when I have nothing else to do and help you all with an extra hand."

I made my way to my dorm to clean my hands and check my clothes for any leftovers. Once I checked myself out, it was 7:30, so I went on to visit with the young group I hung out with two days ago. I met them at the steps to the porch, they were huddled together telling each other jokes, I guess? or maybe they were gossiping about someone else.

I managed to survive the evening visiting with the group, they were nice to me tonight, since now they know I will be taking them to the movies every other weekend. It was time for me to relax for an hour or so, read my detective Mike Hammer novel tonight.

It is tomorrow that I am looking forward to; it will be Wednesday at 7:00 pm that I am looking forward to and talking to Mira Rose. Having received her letter, I will certainly have much to share with her as she shared with me in her very interesting letter.

I needed to prepare myself as how to approach Rose when she is on the phone with me, I need to be understanding of the many issues she expressed and her thoughts about our being together. It is important to share with her, after all she opened up her heart.

Wednesday a.m. it is breakfast time and those that are interested in having breakfast are there. I was just walking into the dining room when I almost bumped into Delia, she looks at me, smiles and says, "well are you feeling better today, better than last night?" Will you sit at the table with me and others because I want to make sure you are going to be okay?" I nodded that I would.

She says it with a teasing tone and in a very inviting manner. I am trying to read her expressions, I hope it is not what I am thinking. Is she trying to connect with me in more than just a friendly manner? I hope not, because I am not available for what could turn out to be just a summer romance, at least for her, as I consider myself to be unavailable.

The day dragged on and it was a blessing when 5:00 o'clock came around, I was ready, I was tired; it was a hot and clear day and I sure felt it in my bones. I readied myself for dinner, I approached the dinning room with caution hoping that it would not get complicated. I went directly to the table where the few university summer students sit. It is customary for them [and me] to sit there during classes.

The time was nearly 10 minutes to 7:00 p.m. I needed to go to the telephone booth and make sure that it is free, so that I may call Rose. Luckily it is free and I waited a few minutes so as to call at exactly 7:00. I deposited 3-quarters, got a dial tone and made the call. It rang twice and it was quickly answered by Rose.

She quickly answers, "Hi honey again I have been waiting for your call, so glad to hear from you. Did you receive my letter, I mailed it Monday morning and hoped you would receive it before you called?" I paused; please say something, talk to me, is something wrong she says in a lower voice?"

I was quick to answer, as her voice was starting to waiver and sound different, "sweetheart, I was just trying to find my voice so I could express all of the happiness and joy which your letter brought me after I had read it at least 3 times.

"There is nothing wrong, it is just me, you have no idea what feelings you aroused in me and how beautiful your letter is. I was so impressed in how you expressed your feeling, passion and honesty."

"Now I can imagine how deep your feelings go and how well you shared them with me. I want you to know that I too have deep feelings for you and I can further say that I adore you, care for you and will be able to love you with all my passion for you."

"I am not afraid to say without hesitation what I just shared with you. I herein wish to express further commitment to you to us and our future."

"No you do not need to help pay for the telephone service I will call for starting tomorrow. I really like the idea that we can talk longer, more often and your suggestion that you would call me to wish me good night; It can go both ways, providing your parents are okay with it. Too bad you could not also tuck me in for the night each time, how does that sound?" "Interesting right?"

"You are very quiet, what is going on in that very beautiful brain of yours, care to share?" She waits.

"My Mira Rose, if I was there for just a few moments, I would hold you, caress you and kiss you like you have never been kissed before; I are very much interested in you ."

As she was trying to hold back the tears, she says, "I am overjoyed and so happy; I am sorry for the tears, but they are tears of joy, hearing the passion you have just now shared with me." "I will barely be able to wait until you are here on Friday."

All of a sudden the operator comes on and says that time is up or place another quarter for more time.

"Rose, your letter really set me on fire, I too could hardly contain myself, you could not have been more open, sincere and with passion that I could not have imagined.

"I have a great idea for Friday evening, I will call my mom tomorrow evening and ask her if we can have dinner together, the three of us." "Would you like to meet her, I really wish for her to see and meet you as I think it is time, okay?" "Are you aware that there is a full moon this week?"

"Yes I would like to meet her, do you think it will be okay, since I am new into our relationship. How much have you shared with her about us, specially when you come visit me those nights that you are here?" "Yes I will be ready to meet her, I will let my parents know that you are planning it for Friday."

"I thought about the moon last night, so here is my idea; it will be full for the next few days, I am suggesting that we both do this; as soon as we finish our visit on the phone, that I and you step outside and face the moon, fold our arms as if we were hugging each other, look straight at the moon and close our eyes and think only of each other."

"We'll think good thoughts, almost as if we were there together, my first gesture would be to kiss those wonderful lips of yours and hold and squeeze you tight and say, "Mira Rose this is our Luna Blue and that we would do the same every full moon whether bluish or not." "Is that a crazy idea or what?" "It would be our personal way of connecting with each other, It can actually be an intimate gesture very personal to us."

She responds quickly, "Oh! honey what a great idea and so original, it can be our very own private way to be together when there is a full moon, I can hardly believe it; it is a very clever way to be close, happy and together and so personal.

We can have and share something that no one else feels or shares. you are so thoughtful! We tell no one okay?" Now I begin to know more about you which tells me we need to share more of who we are, what we think and what personal feelings we have that we can share.

"I understand that because I am younger and maybe I have been more sheltered here at home and in my life. I have very little experience other than the time I spend at school and I have very few friends that I can really call friends and even trust them with any of my personal feelings. I have much to learn."

"Sweetie I have had more experiences [some good and some not so good] I will share many more personal things that have been part of my growing up since I left home to go to boarding schools, okay?"

The operator came on to say time was up, either place more coins or quit in one minute. "Sweetie I need to go, time is up, but I look forward to seeing you on Friday. I will call back tomorrow night after I have talked to my mother about dinner, be happy and plan what we can do on Saturday night, okay?"

"She always seems a little sad when we are about to finish our conversation and I too wish we could talk and share more for a longer period of time.

"Honey she says, I really enjoyed our visit tonight and I know our Friday and Saturday visits will be very interesting as we can make up for lost time this last 2 weeks, till Friday, I care for you very much, good night."

On Thursday nights' call she asks me, "honey you have been referring to me as Mira Rose, I am a little puzzled about that, can you tell me why?"

I thought about it for a moment then said, "please do not be offended, I was just thinking about the fact that you have a first name which is your legal name, I was toying with the idea that you could be known by the names as such "Mira Rose" to me it really is very catchy, original in use and stands out for you as a person—a bit more classy." "All three of your names are very classy and different, so why not?"

"There are both girls or boys who have names that are together and no one seems to care and they are acceptable; it is a matter of how anyone wishes to be called. I just took the first 4-letters of your first name and shortened it to Mira "What do you think sweetie?" I think it would suit you well, you are beautiful that it would compliment you nicely and the name could give you a sort of mysterious persona."

She is quiet, is thinking, I can just see her brain working hard and finally says, "honey the more I think about it the more I like it. It would take a while for me to get used to tell anyone that I go by Mira Rose."

I will at some time discuss it with my mom and dad to see how they feel about it, because they are used to calling me Rose; "I responded back to her, " just think about it for awhile, do not say anything. I wish to, privately, call you as I have been for a period of time. I think it suits you very well, Mira Rose."

She laughs lightly and I can imagine she has a big smile on her face, thinking, thinking to herself. She finally says to me, "honey you are full of surprises what else have you been thinking that you are not telling me?"

"Well I am not sure what else I want to admit to, but my mind is always exploring ideas, thoughts and stuff that can get me into trouble, for the time being let us leave the subject as we have discussed."

"I only hope you can see how that can change your personal attitude, give you an opportunity to see yourself in a different manner.

A person's name and how that person presents itself to others can be seen as being more than just someone without any significant personality."

"I personally think you have the looks, personality and smartness to be much more than you might expect from yourself. That is one of the reasons I care for you and cherish you and want to be with you."

"Look sweetheart it seems I have talked too much and said a lot that you will have to think about until we see each other tomorrow night, so I say good night, pleasant dreams." She says back, "Honey I am so happy, delighted and somewhat excited about all the thoughts that you have talked about, I will just go to bed and think about what you have said."

"I just do not know what to say now, but just wait until this weekend, you may not be sure of what you have just started; so what time are we having dinner at your mom's."

"I will be at your home about 4:30 to 5:00 pm and then we will go from there, because I assume dinner will be about 6:00 or so. You will be ready?" "Bye."

I hung up the phone, looked around to see what was going on in the area of the girl's dorm porch, but it was quiet and it is a good thing no one was around to hear my call.

It is good that my telephone service will be installed on Monday afternoon after 4:00 pm, that way I do not lose much time at work, just a half hour. I will call Mira Rose around 7:00 pm and surprise her, because I will not mention the phone connection this coming weekend just in case.

Normally I call her on Sunday night after I return, but I will tell her I will call either that night, but then surprise her on Monday night. She might be concerned if I do not call after I return, so I better not do that as it might cause her to think otherwise.

Chapter 10

On Friday noon, I got my clothes and articles I need for the weekend and then I ended the day at 2:00, quickly showered and managed to leave town at 2:30 in order to be in Taos by at least 4:45 pm or so.

It was good to travel earlier in the afternoon, not much traffic from the city to Santa Fe and from there to points north, so I made good time getting to Taos and arrived at Rose's home shortly after 4:35 pm.

As soon as I arrived in their yard, I honked the horn 2- sharp times and then Rose comes rushing out the front door, rushes to meet me as I left the car. She threw her arms around my neck kissed me on the cheek to start and then a full kiss on the lips, I could hardly contain myself and then she just held on very tight and it seemed like a long time, how great!

She finally managed to say, "Honey I have been just so nervous waiting for you and hoping the trip here was good and safe and I am so glad to see you it just seems like so long since you were here last." "My mother was watching me very carefully and I could tell she might be just as nervous.

She kissed me again with such passion and she is so affectionate, I can not refuse such attention.

She let go, took my hand and led me toward the front door; she was all bubbly saying, "I am so happy you are here again and I am ready to go to your mom's home for dinner, but first lets go talk to my mom first."

We walked into the living area, her mom was just standing there with a smile on her face looking at both of us and said, "I sure am glad you are here, she was just going back and forth but staying close to the phone, I guess she expected you to call?"

I said, as I reached out and gave her a hug, "hello nice to see you again, may I call you mom?" I do hope you and Rose were not too nervous, because I did have a good drive here not much traffic on the road in the early afternoon."

The mom was slightly surprised that I wished to call her mom and she says to me, why that is so nice of you to want to call me mom, I am delighted, thanks." "Let me bring you both something fresh to drink, after being on the road for what, over at least 2 hours you must be thirsty?"

When she walked away I turned and looked at Rose, she had a beaming smile and looked so pleased with both my request and her mom's response that she reached over a gave me a very wet kiss, wow! how lucky am I.

We visited for a little while. I asked if I could use their phone to call my mom and tell her I was already in town and would be there soon. I was told to go ahead and make the call so my mom would not be worried.

I asked Rose's mom, "did Rose ask if she could go be our guest for dinner at my mom's?" She answered quickly, "of course she can go, it is very nice of you and your mom to have her there for dinner tonight."

"She has been talking about it since she got home and excited and as you can see she got all dressed up. She had said she wants to make a good impression on your mom."

Rose just sits there, with a smile and fidgeting like she is ready to go; those beautiful green eyes just sparkle and show off her natural beauty.

Secretly I am saying to myself, how I really care for her and loving every moment with her. From now on I could never stand to be away from her. I want to love her and take care of her, I do truly adore her.

Rose poked me lightly in the ribs and said, "I am ready! how about you?, and your mom is expecting us." She looks at her mom and says, "I am really looking forward to the dinner and a long visit."

As we were leaving Rose's home, I said to her, "I meant to ask you, how is your job at the drug store, and how do you feel about it?" She quickly answers, "I really like it, there are so many interesting things happening, people coming and going, never a dull moment and I am assigned so many different tasks that it keeps me moving around."

I asked Rose's mom, "did Rose ask if she could go be our guest for dinner at my mom's?" She answered quickly, "of course she can go, it is very nice of you and your mom to have invited her for dinner tonight."

"She has been talking about it since she got home and excited and as you can see she got all dressed up. She had said she wants to make a good impression on your mom."Rose just sits there, with a smile and fidgeting like she is ready to go; those beautiful green eyes just sparkle and show off her natural beauty.

"Honey, again, I am so super happy that you had suggested I look for a job there. I know that I am learning every day how the business works and that it gives me a sense of what products there are out there and what they really cost." "You really are looking out for me and care for me to look forward to learning and improving myself, I have you to thank."

As the sales clerks are serving customers and they happen to need a product from the shelves, they will tell me what shelf it is on and I will respond." I am getting more and more familiar how products are stored and what their code numbers are, and I am beginning to memorize many."

I noticed that she was wearing a slightly short dress with a tie around the waist, low heel dress shoes and her hair was curly and so shinny. She is so naturally beautiful that she needs no makeup at all and her lips are so naturally rose colored in such a way it compliments her green eyes.

I am so impressed that at times I just want to look and talk to those eyes that I have quickly become to love as part of her beauty.

I could not help but stand there and just admire her and how that I finally realized I was just standing there, mesmerized and not saying anything. She calls to me and says, "I am ready, are you okay?" wake up."

As we walked out to the car, she clung to me and said Honey, "I am tickled you are taking me to meet your mom over dinner; her green eyes just sparkled, and here I am not able to speak clearly. I said. "Sweetheart you are so beautiful, I am speechless."

I rushed us to the car, but I just had to kiss her and she kissed me back; deeply and wet as she held on tight and said, "Honey I have missed you so much." I just got lost in her eyes for the next few moments.

When we arrived at my mom's home, I walked Rose to the kitchen door, it is more convenient than the front porch entrance, so I knocked on the door and we walked and saw mom working over the stove and seems she had set the table and had dishes with food and ready to serve.

I called out to mom and said, "we are here and I want to introduce you to Rose. They both said hello to each other and then Rose surprised mom by leaning over and putting her arms around her neck, and again saying I am so glad to meet you, Michael talks about you all the time. I have really wanted to meet you for awhile, but waiting for Michael to bring you so I could meet and see you.

Mom was just beaming with a big bright smile and I could tell she was happy to meet Rose and she says. "come sit down so I can serve the food I still have on the stove." We all sat down and began a very delicious dinner; I believe we were all hungry. We had to insist that Rose and I clear the table and wash and dry the dishes and pots and pans. I told mom, "You take care of what is left and we shall do the rest and then we can sit and visit with you."

We were in the living room with mom and she was very talkative and interested in Rose and her family and where they lived in town. Rose was very pleased to see that mom was so interested in her family, especially Rose. Mom wanted to know how long we knew each other; Rose looks to me so that I could explain when and how.

I told mom that we had become acquainted about a year and half ago, but that we had lost touch with each other until last month. She seemed satisfied with my response and moved her head. We visited there until about 8:45, so I looked at her and said that Rose and I should get her home and that I want to come back to visit with her before bedtime.

I borrowed a key from mom so that I could come in the kitchen door. Rose reached for my hand for balance as we stepped down from the entrance landing. I helped her on the front seat. She gave me a look that I know spells trouble; I went around to my side and slid into my seat, but she quickly reaches out to me with her arm around my waist and soon her arms were around my neck and her lips were wet and sending a signal, *I want more from you, now not later.*

I turn my body around to face her, move my arm around to her shoulder, but it slips down; my open hand lands on her breast, I could not help but caress her full breast with just the material of her dress and her bra between my hand separating me from a heavenly touch that I had not yet experienced with this heavenly body so close to me that we at this time were one and only one.

She sighs a sigh I had not yet heard from her, she moves closer and her body is totally against me and I move my hand down to her leg over her dress, but soon her dress is no longer there and my hand moves further up her soft leg, reaching, moving where is it moving to?!

I could not believe what was happening, my hand did move further up her leg, but I stopped right there! we are still in my mom's driveway and this can not go any further, so I left those lips of her and said, "sweetheart, we need to go I know how we both feel at this unusual time, but we can not continue as we will be in trouble." we need to get you home, okay?"

She was kind of in a half daze and was waiting for me to assure her that it was okay and that we could not go further in the most intimate manner we have yet to experience in our relationship. She moves over slightly, looks at me with those green eyes half shut and says, "honey I was, still am, lost in the way in which you kissed me, touched me and it felt so good I was all there for you and now I really needed more from you, but I am willing to wait, just hold me, love me and be here for me."

Chapter 11

"Honey, all of a sudden I could not hold back I was over whelmed with you tonight I was resisting but could not hold back, I just wanted to express my love for you in the manner which is beyond what we have been since we began our relationship."

I drove off from the driveway onto the main street and as we were on the way she still stayed close to me and talked to me in a low tone and expressed how she was feeling. I said, "check your dress and maybe you should apply a little lip stick just so that you look okay in the eyes of your parents when we get you home, okay?"

She touches my face; "honey I sure got excited and I needed you, you were so loving, but I know we have to be careful, at least tonight. I would be upset if my parents would suspect otherwise and I do understand how you are trying to protect our relationship, we have so much to gain for us and I really care so much for you."

I quickly say to her, "tomorrow evening and night we will have the time to really talk seriously and I want to hear you express your feelings and I will do the same, as we have much that is unsaid, okay?" "Sure, honey I really want to share it all with you."

We arrived at her home, I helped her out of the car and we walked hand in hand to the front door; she knocked just to let her parents know that we back. The parents were still up as we looked, and then her mom came to the door and greeted us and said, "Oh you are home early." Rose then said, "Michael wants to go back soon so that he can visit with his mom before it gets late for her."

I quickly added and said, "My mom goes to bed with the chickens, so I want to have some time to talk with her about tomorrow, if there are errands to run and maybe I can go visit with my father too."

I looked over at her father and greeted him, shook his hand and said, "we did not get to see you before we went to dinner, I came and stole your daughter earlier; before 5:00 pm." They all laughed when I said I stole their daughter.

Rose's father smiled and looked at Rose and said, "you look so grown up in a dress I hardly ever see you in a dress, you look very nice." Rose counters back, "dad I am more grown up than you might think; there have been few places to go to in a dress, but I wanted to look nice for Michael's mom."

Rose looks over at me and says, "are you ready to go?" I look at her parents and say, "excuse me but I really should go, but first I wish your permission to take Rose to the movies tomorrow evening?"

They both look at each other and then at us and said, "Of course she can go if that is what you two want." Rose takes my hand, and says she will walk me to the car, I say goodnight and we go out. She is holding on tight as we approach the car and I turn around to face her, she is quickly against me with her arms around my neck and says,

"honey I need your kisses to keep me thru the night, hold me tight. I will treasure our evening together for a long time and I look forward to our evening tomorrow."

"Can you call me before you go to bed tonight, I want to share something. You have our number and I will tell mom I will expect your call later, okay?"

Mom was okay when I arrived, she was busy doing some tasks in the kitchen, and she was surprised that I was back so soon. I told her I wanted to visit with her and relax before bedtime, she was good with that and we visited till 10:00 o'clock and she mentioned she would go ahead and get ready for bed and that I could stay up if I wished.

I said, "can I use the phone to call Rose for a few minutes? she says, "Of course, take the phone in the bedroom if you want." I picked up the phone, it has a long chord so it will easily extend into the front bedroom.

I placed the call to Rose's home, she quickly answered and said, "hi honey I have been staying close to the phone to get your call, but in fact I was getting ready for bed, you would like what I am wearing to sleep in."

"Oh, honey you just do not know how I have been feeling lately and I am super happy with what you have shared. I I said, "I too want to just admit, but share the fact that I have been wanting to tell you that I care for you, but was sort of holding back for a little while longer." I care for you too and adore you and wish you with me from now on."

I was very anxious, I hope you did not mind to call me." "Of course not I responded, I just did not want your mom or dad to object to my call."She counters, "mom said it would be okay."

I asked her, "are you okay, I know our evening together was very short because we were in two places and not enough time to share our time?"

"Oh honey I know but it was great for me to meet your mom and enjoy that good dinner she prepared, I am so grateful and I really cared for the time with her." "What I enjoyed the most was our time in the car, I have never been so excited, so full of giving into you and I felt that I could go all night, I really wanted more, you had me so worked up."

"Michael, I need to share something special with you; as of tonight I need to tell you I love you very much, so much I can hardly stand myself with this great feeling I have for you, because it has become so special in my mind."

"I hope my saying so is not too sudden to deal with, but I can not help it and I needed to tell you so that you know how I feel, now and from now on in our relationship." "Are you okay with me?"

"honey I am so happy to hear that from you and I can not help but feel that we are now and will be so much closer and I will devote myself to you and that we will now go to greater commitments with each other.

"I really feel like we need to have a conversation about where we are going with our relationship and maybe we can even plan ahead, so let us leave it open for tomorrow evening, okay?" She was okay. "Before I go, I wanted to ask, are you working at the drugstore tomorrow day?" 'We need to plan our evening, I have two ideas, okay?'

"I am to work from 10:00 a.m. to 4:00 p.m. I asked for those hours, because I told my boss that you are in town to see me and your mom and that we wanted to go out for the evening, so she said that would be okay." "Let me ask you, how do you want me to dress for tomorrow night, I really want to please you?"

"Sweetie that is very nice of you to ask how you should dress, now that you mention it, I really liked and admired how beautiful you looked in that great dress you wore tonight. Do you mind wearing it again tomorrow night?" "I just was so impressed how it brought out your beauty, the fullness of your body and your womanhood and you are so feminine ."

"Oh honey I am really thrilled that you liked how I looked in that dress. I will do my best and even better for you so you'll be proud of me." I think you need to get your sleep and be refreshed for tomorrow, okay?"

She blows me a kiss over the phone and says, "honey I will be thinking of you while I too try to get my beauty sleep, good night."

"I will probably take my mom to the store and other places for her to take care of her needs and also any errands. I will call you about 4:30, after you get home, to see how you are doing; I will see what is showing at the theater and what time we should be there for the first showing."

I finally hung up the phone and tip toed to return it to the table in the living and then tip toed back to the bedroom and just crashed for the night.

Chapter 12

I arranged to pick up Rose at 7:00 p.m. so we could make the 7:30 show. I arrived a few minutes early and she was almost ready according to her mom. I greet her mom by calling her "mom good to see you again." She was very responsive and nice.

Within in minutes Rose came out her room with a big smile on her face and looking a little shy; I guess it was because she even looked better than last night, again I was so taken back by her beauty. I immediately reached out to her with open arms; it just seemed so natural to do so. I had not done this in front of her mom before.

She came into my arms so naturally, I looked over my shoulder and said to her mom, "you have such a beautiful daughter and you should be so proud of her and I am so pleased to be able to be with her at this very moment."

Her mom just had a broad smile and said quickly, "we are proud of her and are so pleased as to how in such a short period of time she has changed so much we are just very pleased." "I personally know why, it is because of you with her and how much she cares for you since you are back in her life."

"We are very pleased with you both and how you seem to be helping her grow up and she is so happy all the time." Did you say that there is a dance tonight?" We answered, "yes, that is what we heard."

We said goodbye to her mom and walked out to the car; we were half way there, when her mom called out, "Rose come here quick." She went and talked to her briefly and returned back to me. Rose comes up to me throws her arms around my neck and say, "she is watching us so just hold me, no kissing yet."

"Mom says she will talk to my dad and maybe they will be at the dance if we should show up. I think that is a great idea, because they need to get out and do more things like movies, dancing and even dinners." "Maybe we are starting something, I sure hope so." "They are still young enough to enjoy all the opportunities there are to go enjoy themselves."

We let go of each other and got into the car and waved back at her mom and pulled away to drive to the town plaza and the theater.

"Sweetie, again I say, you look so beautiful now, you added different jewelry, a belt and those earrings dress up your face and appearance. You will attract much attention tonight, so be prepared I am so proud of you."

"Oh honey you say such nice things about me and to me, mom is right it is because of you that I have changed so much, I feel great and am so happy, happier than I have ever been." "How can I not love you for what you are and back in my life, hopefully to stay and never to leave."

We arrived at the theater, we were walking up to the window to buy tickets when someone calls out to Rose, she turns around and sees three girls also coming towards the ticket window.

Rose hesitates for a moment and Says back, "Hi Cindy surprised to see you, have not seen you since we were off for the summer. Are you also coming to the movie?" The girl Cindy responds, "Yes how have you been and what are you doing this summer, as she introduces the other two classmates?"

It had been an interesting night and I felt that Rose and I had just experienced a night out and that it truly seemed more like a family night out.

On the way to her home, she was just so close to me and affectionate and reached up and whispered in my ear, "honey I love you and tonight we just seemed so much closer and I am so happy for us and my parents seemed to accept us more as a couple now after being with them and very natural closeness they had not seen before."

"I did notice that they seemed at ease with us and the manner in which we were just enjoying ourselves and dancing in a comfortable way." We drove up to her home and the parents seem to be there, the front door was closed, so I assume they may not have heard us drive up.

"Honey, I need your kisses, now we have not kissed at all tonight and you know it is our last night for two weeks?" I really need you, but we will need to go inside soon." She hung on to me, she is so affectionate and we just do not have the time or the place.

I kissed her gently but passionately and held her so tight, because I too knew this was our last night for 2 weeks and I wanted it to last, but we had no choice for now. I said, "sweetheart we need to go in, your parents may start to wonder were we are, okay?"

She did a short knock on the front door and she let us in; the parents were not in the living room, but her mom called out, "Rose, we are getting ready for bed so tell Michael goodnight for us and we will see him the next time. You may stay up a while if you choose."

Mira Rose looks at me with that devilish look where she slants her head left, those eyes were a twinkle of green, seemed like more green then ever.

I said, "Please do not tease me now I will not have any control over my actions, but I love how you do that along with I love you so much." "I should go, but I will think about you all night long and I promise to call you before I leave tomorrow afternoon, okay?"

She did walk me out to the car, put her arms around my neck and gave me a wet passionate kiss, she says, "That should last you at least all week?" "Then you will have to wait another 6 days till the next ones; Oh god! what am I saying, "I will have the same wait as you, honey love me, care for me and keep me in your thoughts all the days and nights."

We were very reluctant to part, so she went into the house while I watched her, she waves as I leave and I blink my lights, I guess that is it till the next time. I drove to mom's home and went to bed.

Sunday afternoon, I called Mira Rose, she was the first to answer the phone, she was surprised to hear from me; I do not know why, maybe she felt that I was going to drop by on the way out, she was right.

"Hello sweetie did I catch you at a bad time?" she quickly answers, "honey it is never a bad time when you call, I will drop everything I am doing to talk with you." In fact I was sitting here wondering, hoping that you would call,"

"Are you lonely now?" I will come by and see you as I will leave after a short visit with you." I too feel bad about having to leave and leave you behind, but I do not know what else to say." Most of the time I hate the fact that I have to leave you and go back to the city."

"Honey I know how it feels; it was a short weekend due to the fact that we did visit with our families, but it was a great time and I felt very fulfilled that we did so." My parents had good comments about you and I as a couple and that pleased me very much, I will share with you later."

"Remember I will be calling you tonight after I have arrived at the campus and my dorm room. I usually stop and eat dinner somewhere, because they do the brown bag thing for us on Sunday evening, so I prefer a full dinner." "I will be there to hear in 30 minutes or so, need to say goodbye to my mom."

As I left my mom's home she was tearful, we both miss each other, but she understands and is very grateful that I am accomplishing my work and college studies, so as to have a future. I will see her in 17 days.

When I arrived at Rose's home, she was at the door, waiting, looking for me and as soon as she saw the car she bolts out the door and ran to meet me as I opened the car door. She threw her arms around me and kissed me passionately, like always, I held her tight and I said, "I have already missed you since last night."

She did not waste any time in saying, "I too was regretting the fact that you needed to leave for home and I am sad that you are leaving. Missing you will only give me more strength to be what I need to be for you and for me." "Can you stay a few more minutes so we can visit, my folks went to visit my aunt, so we can sit here in the porch and visit.

I left town with a heavy heart, but I knew that it had been a great weekend for the both of us and the two sides of the families had enjoyed themselves in a different manner than the kind of weekends they would normally experience. Hopefully Rose and I can influence them into diversified experiences.

When I arrived in the city, I stopped, as usual, to have dinner before I proceeded to the campus and unload my belongings. It was still only 6:30 p.m. so I decided to waiting until 7:00 to call Mira Rose. I went to the phone booth to make my call, I deposited enough quarters to last for a 30 minute conversation.

After the 3rd ring Rose answers, "Hi honey I have been sitting here waiting, keeping my fingers crossed that your drive home was okay." I responded to her, "sweetie are you lonesome tonight, do you miss me already tonight?"

Before she could answer me I said, I am already missing you and I just got here 45 minutes ago." She did not waste any time, "honey I have missed you since you left this afternoon, I always have an empty feeling after you leave and it takes me till after you call to sort of get back to normal, so now at least I do feel better and can handle it."

"Did you have your dinner before you called?" I told her I had and at least felt some comfort for now.

"Mom and dad came home, I was sitting in the living room just staring at the walls. Mom noticed right away, says, "I assume Michael has already left for his home in the city?" "She encouraged me to go help her with dinner so I could perk up, she knows I will not get over it but can get back to normal."

For once my dad got involved in the conversation mom and I were having about how I feel while you are here for the weekend and how we get along so well and then I have to feel different while you are gone for nearly two weeks.

Dad says to me, "Rose you have a very good relationship with Michael, we really like him and how you feel when he is in town. I hope it is not too stressful in between times when he is not here." "We really like and appreciate how he treats you and takes care of you and you are very fortunate to have such a companion."

"I really was surprised that dad said what was on his mind about us, because he has been rather quiet, but I am sure that mom tells him what is going on." He did say that he and mom would listen to what I had to say and they support me and will listen to me."

Chapter 13

I listened very carefully while she shared what her parents had discussed and shared their opinions about our relationship.

She further says, "I know we have to be strong, have faith in ourselves and trust that we are doing the right thing." I feel very good about you and me and I trust you completely and I hope that you have the same feelings." "I feel so much more grownup now and no longer think like I did before; I had no real purpose in my life on a day to day."

"I am so pleased to have crossed the point from just being in high school to having a job and being with you, it has given me much more meaning and purpose and having the opportunity to look forward to the future; some days I can barely stand myself."

"Oh! honey I am so sorry I seem to be doing all the talking and have not let you say much, talk to me tell me things that will give me ideas, okay?"

I chuckled and she says, "I hope what I said was not funny, just sharing with you." I responded, "I am very impressed what you shared and how you shared and it is interesting that your parents decided to share their opinions about us and I am pleased that they trust me."

"Sweetie I am here for you all the way and I will be able to do more for you and share some ideas that I am tossing around in my head, but for now I too feel more grownup and aware of what a great future you and I can have in the near future, after we complete our education. We will plan it one step at a time."

We will do our best and I know your parents will be extremely pleased with the path you and I pursue for us and that you will always be protected and cared for."

"Oh! my 30 minutes are up and I guess I should go and let you do what you need to do to prepare for going to work tomorrow, I have the same purpose as well, but I will call you on Wednesday at 7:00 p.m. I too will be sort of restless and feel down for the rest of the evening, so you be happy, think good thoughts and smile; do not feel sad and especially lonesome."

"I too want to tell you, I adore you, love you and are on my mind day and night, I wish you a happy night and pleasant dreams, talk to you later, this is not goodbye but loving you till later."

"Honey good night to you too I love you, you know I find it real easy to say that and with so much meaning in my heart." The call ended and we were done for now.

I walked back from the phone booth, back to my room at the dorm; I was a little saddened but felt okay for now. Tomorrow will be different, I shall get the telephone service at noon and I shall see how that will make a world of difference in our talking from now on. It will be a blessing and what a surprise that will be when I call and tell her that I finally came thru with the service I had mentioned to her. Tomorrow night will be a brand new manner for us to stay in touch when ever we choose, I look forward to that.

Monday morning, I worked hard all morning, my boss had okayed an extra half hour off for lunch so that I could receive the telephone technician and let him in my room so he could extend service from an existing box at first floor. I sort of waited around as the service line was extended and he left a brand new telephone unit, I had it set on the night stand near my bed; more convenient for my use at night.

I worked until 5:30 to make up for the half hour at noon; could hardly wait to get off, go admire my new telephone and wait till 7:00 p.m. to make the call. I was distracted at dinner time, in fact fellow UNM classmates asked if there was something wrong, I quickly said, "No on the contrary, I was fine, just was distracted with a personal issue, not to worry.

I was just walking out of the dining room when I nearly bumped into Delia, she gives me a broad smile and I smile back at her. She says, "are you joining us tonight at the porch of the girl's dorm?" *What a surprising question.*

I did not know quite what to say, so I improvised by telling her; "listen I have something personal to take care of and then I will probably walk over, okay?" She smiled back and said, "I will look forward for us to see you and if you are lucky we might just pick on you tonight, seems to me we have not picked on you lately, so come prepared."

She walks off kind of cocky, turns and smiles. I do not know what to think of her and her smiles, her flirty actions and how she is always very friendly. I need to be careful and not to encourage her. she is a very pretty sexy girl and she has a very good approach, catches me by surprise a lot .

Finally 7:00 o'clock comes around, I settle myself in a sitting position on my bed, reach my telephone book with numbers, find Rose's home number and dial it. It rings 3-4 times, someone answers it and turns out to be Mira Rose.

She is not aware that it is me, because she just says hello. When I say, are you lonesome tonight do you miss me tonight? she just goes wild. "Honey what is going on that you would call on Monday night?" "Is something wrong?" So I say, "I do not know what could be wrong, I am just calling on my own new telephone, so what do you think of that?"

"Oh my God you got your telephone already, you had not said anything about it over the weekend?" In fact you had said nothing; Oh! I am so excited for me and for you. I had no idea it would be you

I had to interrupt her to say, "I purposely did not say anything because I had made arrangements last Monday, was scheduled for today, but one never know whether they will show up, they did and here I am calling." "Now we can talk as much as we want, I do have an amount of minutes per month, but I am not concerned, if I exceed, it only costs five cents per minute extra."

"Oh! my gosh let me go tell my mom it is you on the phone, she will be surprised"! She is back in 2-3 minutes, again excited and says" Mom was glad to hear about it, I'll wait to hear what more she says later."

"what it means sweetie is now we can talk for more minutes every night or every other night and be in touch and we can keep you happy so you will not be lonesome and the days will pass much quicker and we can hear each other's voice and you can tell me how your day went, "How is that for nice?"

"Honey I can get permission from mom to also call you too, especially right before bedtime so I can tell you naughty things even if we had already talked earlier in the evening. How great that will be and I promise I will not be lonesome anymore."

"So how was your day today at the drugstore? What time did you start work and when did your day end?" "I started at 10:00 and left at 5:00, the day went by fast, seems that when I was busy time does fly, as they say."

"Okay I will call you every night this week and let us see how that goes. I will be interest to hear what your mom thinks about you being on the phone every night, but tell her they will not be long calls, just to stay in touch. Here is my telephone number, it does start with a 505-255-0491, talk to you tomorrow?"

"Honey I love you and I will tell you what mom and my dad think now that you have a telephone. I will offer to pay for the calls that I make, so good night to you too."

I was glad that she was pleased so that now we are able to call each other and talk as we see fit. So future days will be interesting for the both of us.

Tomorrow I want to go visit a jewelry store to talk to someone about a split coin pendant for Mira Rose, she will be very surprised at what I will come up with that she may wear it. It will have a special meaning.

I went to visit the jewelry shop and completed my order for the pendant and the metal case for half of the coin. We agreed on a price and how the pendant and the case would look. He assured me they would be ready next week.

Here it is Tuesday evening after dinner, but it is too early to call Mira Rose, so I waited until 7:00 and by then I would be in the privacy of my own dorm room. I placed the call and in two short rings it is answered by Rose. "Hi honey I have been sitting here waiting to make sure I did not miss your call."

We talked about our days' tasks, but I did not say one word about my visit with the jeweler, because it will be a secret and surprise I will save for the next trip to see her. We kept on talking, she interrupted me and said to me.

"I want to share something strange and unusual that I have experience in the last few days. There is a guy who has come into the drugstore from last week and over the weekend. Yesterday I decided to walk home after work, I happened to turn and look around behind me and there he is! a little ways behind, he stops when I looked, so I continued to walk away I looked later, but he was not there."

"Today I walked home again, just for the heck of it, when I stopped to look in the windows of a woman's shop I turned to look and there he was again! I did not know what to think about that; is he following me, he somehow stopped again when I was aware that he was there, I do not think its just a coincidences that he is always where I am."

He was hiding behind some bushes that were taller than he. I really got concerned, is this guy following me and should I tell some one or report him?" When I got home I mentioned it to my dad and he too was concern and puzzled about that guy's actions. He told me to take one more day, walk home and see what happens.

She says, "Tomorrow I will walk home again and see what happens, will he be following me again?" I will tell you tomorrow evening what happens, okay?" That was a very alarming bit of news that Rose shared with me, but she did say she was to wait for one more day and walk home and see what happens.

. Wednesday I called at 7:00 p.m. and she quickly answered, "Hi honey was waiting and was anxious to hear from you so I can share what occurred on my walk home after work."

"I did walk home and I kept looking back to see if that guy was by chance following me; well he was on the opposite side of the street, but he was getting closer and closer. I think he was going to confront me, so I rushed into the lobby of the Taos Inn Hotel, I approached the lady desk clerk and said to her,

"I came in because there is a guy who has been following me and got very close to me just before I came in; can I stay here for a little while?" She answered that I could, but did I know who he is and I said "no, but he has done that for the last three days."

She offered to call the local Sheriff's Office to come and see if he is still around, but we agreed to wait for a short while. I waited about 10-15 minutes and then said to her, "I will go out and try to keep on going home, but I will come back if I need someone to come help me and take me home."

I walked out the front and around the corner around some bushes that were there, when he appeared from the bushes and extended his arm towards me and said he just wanted to talk to me, but at the same time I screamed very loud, twice, and here comes the desk clerk wanting to see what had happened, but at the same time the guy took off running back toward the plaza area. She comes out to comfort me and said, "I will call the sheriff's office right now, so come back in and sit until they arrive, okay?"

A sheriff's deputy arrived in about 10 minutes or so and came in to the lobby looking for whom had called. The desk clerk quickly addressed him and said, "this young girl was being followed and then confronted outside and she screamed, so I rushed out there to see of she was alright."

I was nervous and I stood an told the deputy what had been happening for the last few days, I gave him a description of the guy. He said he would go towards the plaza and see if he could find him and confront him. He asked if I wanted to press some form of charges and did I want a ride home.

I told him I can call my mom or dad from here and they will come pick me up. He asked me to share my name and address so that he could report back to me and my family.

My mom answered the phone I told her where I was and what had happened; she said she would come quickly and pick me up and to look for the car.

When she arrived and honked for me, I thanked the desk clerk for her help and that I appreciated what she did to make sure I was okay. I went home and just sat there; I was still shaking and upset.

"My mom was all excited and wanted to know if I had been hurt. "Did he touch you or push you around and how long has he been following you around?"

I told her, "mom I am okay he just scared the heck out of me and I did feel that he might hurt me when he reached out to just stop me, but I guess he just wanted to talk to me, but I would not let him, since he had scared me and I wanted nothing to do with him, so lets not worry about it right now."

"It took me a few hours to get over his wanting to stop me and when dad came home from work, mom had to tell him right away so that he would know what had happened on my way home." "We all talked about it before supper and we were about to start our supper when we heard a car drive up into the yard."

"Michael! It was a sheriff deputy's car, the same that had responded to the hotel." My dad got up from the table and went to the door as the deputy was about to knock on the door."

The deputy introduced himself and said, "I wish to inform your daughter and the family about the guy that had been following her." "We in law enforcement call it "Stalking", when someone is followed, especially more than once."

My dad invited him in, but he says "It is okay" he asked for me to come to the door and he could inform us both. He went on to tell us that he and another deputy found the guy down at the plaza, they stopped him and told him he had been breaking the law by stalking you and that it better quit right now, and if not he would be arrested and booked in jail.

He specifically expressed to me, that I should continue to be aware if he should again try to follow or reach you to talk, what ever it is he wished to talk about. He knows now that he could end up in jail, so if he is smart, he will just go away, but I should alert the sheriff's office in case he does; he passed on his deputy's card and wished us good evening for now.

"Michael, that sure was a scary happening, because I had never experienced such a personal attempt on me that would cause me to be very scared of someone."

I finally had the chance to speak up so I said, "sweetie I am shocked and very concerned for your safety, especially from someone who is a stranger and who may have intentions of hurting you." "I hope you will put it behind you and try to feel safe but careful as you walk to and from work. "Is it possible that at least your mom or dad can pick you up at the drugstore after work?" "I think that is most likely the worse time to be walking home, do you agree?"

"Honey that is a good idea, and much more convenient for either one of my parents, I will talk to them tonight and see what we can arrange." "Too bad I have no way of driving to work, after all I do have my learner's permit and can drive on my own."

"sweetheart, there is something I wanted to share with you and ask how you will feel about what I will present to you, but it is tied in with other issues and ideas that you may have in mind and have not as of yet been able to pursue. Now I do not want you to be concerned because I do not present my thoughts of various ideas I have recently dreamed up, okay?"

First, it is getting late for the both of us, 9:15, and you need your beauty sleep, but before we quit for the night, here is a question and something to think about till tomorrow night, are you ready?? "Yes yes she says, ask me quick."

"Think back over the past year and even a year or two and think about what sort of dreams for your future or intentions for after you graduate from Taos High School. What have you thought would be a career or job that you would wish for and would you wish for that to happen else where other than there in Taos? Surely You have given that some thought."

"Sweetheart, please do not think I am now, tonight, going to present my thoughts and ideas, okay? It will wait until tomorrow." She blurts out, "you are going to keep me guessing what you are up to until later tomorrow and expect me to be able to remember all of my ideas for my future in one day?", I hope I can."

I say quickly, "sweetheart, I should go and you need to start thinking, everything you can dream up." I wish you good night and my love and thoughts will be for you tonight and be careful tomorrow.."

Michael is now thinking for himself, can any and all of his dreams and aspirations be accomplished, can they possibly fit in with Mira Rose's dreams and what she is hoping is her destiny.

Chapter 14

Another chapter in our relationship is about to come forward and take on another meaning much different than we have been experiencing and even considered to this place in time. We both will now look deeper into our minds and then beyond our current personal involvement in this fairly new relationship.

Tonight, Thursday shall bring about Rose's ideas and dreams that I had suggested yesterday for her think about seriously, so that she can share them with me, but at the same time I too will need to be prepared with my own ideas, dreams and future plans that I had been tossing around in my mind base on just myself because there was no one in the picture.

In my current involvement in our relationship, I now will need to revise many of the ideas and perceptions of what my own future would be on my own after completion of my studies and the ROTC Program and active duty in the Air Force with serious expectations to go on to pilot training.

The time has come for me to call Rose and begin sharing our dreams that we both have held onto and have not shared with anyone. Our two minds can now come together to share our inner most thoughts.

I was in my dorm room, I dialed her home number and very quickly she answered, "Hi honey I have been waiting for just a few minutes and am so happy to be able to talk with you again and in private. It just happens that my parents and brother are out visiting my aunt and family.

I responded by saying, "sweetheart I am just as happy to call and talk for as long as we need to. Private talks sounds very good. Are you okay; happy, smiling and ready to share your thoughts tonight?" First I would like to ask how the problem with the guy stalking you turned out?

"I walked to work this morning at 9:30 to check in before 10:00 am and there was no one following me, but mom or dad will picked me up at 5:30, because my boss agreed I could work until that time. As we drove home, the guy was not on the street, so I guess he took the deputy's advise or else."

"For the next few days my parents will pick me up and we will see what happens later. Okay I gave much thought to what you suggested yesterday and I can now share my dreams, ideas and thoughts that I have kept very deep in my mind; I had no need to share with anyone, even my parents. I have always been sort of personal with what I think or say."

"Two of my classmates and I talked sometimes of what it will be like after graduation; would we go to college or get a job here in town. I never wanted to be to specific and always held back my deep ideas for the future; getting a job here is not to my liking and it sort of scares me as to what is more real for me, because I do not want to get stuck here in town.

"With you honey I will share all my inner most ideas and thoughts, especially my past dreams for me, but now I have different dreams and it is because of you, but my only hope is that they are very similar to your ideas and dreams."

"Many a times I did think about what I could do or even accomplish after graduation, I have thought about the type of courses I have taken so far until now and I am faced with being a junior. I need to take the required courses and go on to the 12th grade."

"There are hardly any special courses available that could prepare me for some special field or even a profession. It is rather confusing for me to think what I would be capable of or prepared for, I guess If I attempt to go to college I guess that is were everyone decides what to study."

"Sweetheart, were you involved in any clubs or have you taken music, art or extra curricular courses that could help you sort of plan on one or the other for the future?"

"I was in the Glee Club for one semester ; we are required to take one art course, but music or voice studies are extra curricular and I have not had any interest in musical instruments or in singing. It is really scary, so I have two years to continue to be confused and scared as what I will do."

"My mom and I have had conversations about what I would do with my life and what did I really think I would like to be. She knows I would some day leave home for college, a job or get married. I have in the past dreaded even thinking about being married; to who, most of the guys I know in school are, to me, not marriage material and who knows if they will ever amount to anything."

"When I stop to think about the whole issue of me dating, and having a relationship here, I always shutter and put it out of my mind, and I am happy and content that my parents are rather strict with me dating. Up to now!! I have not felt interested in doing so. During the last 2 years I did go to the homecoming dinner and dances; I was invited by a classmate of mine. After that he wanted to see me and go on dates, but my parents said no and I felt relieved, I was not ready or really cared for him."

"Honey do you think I am strange or anti-social by the   way that I act, talk and behave?

I jump in quickly, "sweetheart I am very impressed with your opinions, attitudes, decisions to not date so I say I am willing to say that a lot of your classmates are out there dating and running around without thinking about their reputation."

"What I do is invite two of my best girl friends and we go to the movies, eat lunch and just enjoy ourselves; we make faces at the guys when they get on our case, but we tease them and make fun of them, we like doing that, at the end of the day we laugh about it and go home."

"Honey as far as dreams are concerned, I guess I have dreamed of finishing school with good grades and by then having thought out carefully what I will set out to do to make something of myself. I talk to my mom a lot and I listen to her and my dad's advise, because I know they have my future at heart and want the best for me."

I said quickly, "There are jobs in hair solons, drugstores, department stores, grocery stores, clothes dry cleaners and in the various motels and hotels, I guess those are local choices for jobs if you were to be interested in one of those."

"Honey those are jobs that some graduates get into because they do not wish to leave town and have no other interests like getting an education."

"Sweetheart it appears you might be interested in possibly leaving town and going elsewhere, not only to get a job but maybe further your education?"

"Sit back and relax, because I have something to offer you; in two parts, first I am offering you the opportunity to take a week off from your job and do the following: "Would you like to go the city with me and be on the campus with me and be part of the day to day routine with other students your age, so think about that for a minute or two?' In a few minutes after being silent, she comes out and says, "what are you offering me and is that going to work out?" "Where will I sleep, eat and will I be expected to work with others?"

"Sweetheart, you will stay in the girl's dormitory, you will be assigned daily tasks and eat in the dining room with all the rest of us there on campus. You will have evenings free to visit with the girls there or best of all." You will be able to visit with me every single evening until it is scheduled for you and other girls to go inside and relax, or do personal things."

"You are saying we will be together every single evening?" What will it cost me or my folks for my stay there?" "It will not cost you anything, because you will be helping with chores and tasks that need to be done in preparation for the fall school semester and that will pay for your stay for the week."

"I guess my stay will be neat, I get to experience how it feels to live on a school campus in the big city, and have responsibilities; I can not really imagine how that would work out." "Rose here is the second part; are you ready for it?"

I can not see what the expression on her face is or will be as a response to what the major suggestion will be, so here goes.

"You may not be able to give an answer to this one, but you will have time to think. "how would you feel about attending school there for the next 2 school years?" "A definite answer will not be needed today but after you have been there for one week and know and have experienced if such a program might agree with you in the long run."

"You just need to think about the possibility for now, so lets talk about it for now. I want to see what your reaction is for now, so take your time to think about it and ask anything you wish."

"Honey the first things that comes to my mind are, how will my parents pay for my schooling at this school, will I still be required to work and have tasks, will it be like the one week spent there and will you and I still be able to visit and be in touch each day?"

"Your parents will have to pay a certain amount, and of course you will have chores and tasks which will help pay for your enrollment and books and what ever is needed for your day to day classes and it also takes care of your meals and there is always a nurse on duty incase you get sick."

"You will have to realize that I too will be on campus attending university classes, but will be back on campus every late afternoon. I will see you at dinner every day, walk you to the dorm after dinner and then go visit with you and we can just sit around and talk or take walks around the campus area until they announce that all girls need to go to their dorm rooms. This allows you to study, iron clothes or visit with your room mate or mates."

"Honey so you are saying that we will be together every day and also on weekends?" "Wow I can hardly believe we will be so close and able to see and visit each other." Are the boys or you allowed in the girl's dorm?"

"Yes you and I will be able to visit practically every evening and also on Saturdays and Sundays. We may also be able to go to church together on Sundays and yes the boys or me are allowed in the large living room in their dorm for watching TV, but only during visiting hours."

She says, "I can hardly believe that we will be there together as it is allowed. I was thinking out loud to my mom and said to her, "When I go back to school at the high school and are not working anymore and Michael is back in school, we may not be able to see each other, who knows maybe, for weeks at a time. If he is so busy he can not come visit.

"I said to her, "mom I will be very sad and lonely in between times, I started to cry and be upset and she tried to make me feel better." She says to me, "Rose I know that can be sad and lonely when separated by such a distance, I felt that was going to be an issue for the two of you when the time came. "You two will have to work with each other, maybe it will not be so bad after all, wait and see how school year begins."

"Honey I am concerned about us after you go back to the university and I go back to the old high school. Do you think we can work out our schedule so that we can see each other within reason every two to three weekends?"

"I do not know how I am going to manage that longer separation from you. I just can not imagine how it will affect our relationship, you being far away and me stuck here at the high school with no purpose and very little contact with you."

"I really like the idea of us being together as you have mentioned during the school year and I really like the idea of a better school and much more."

"I am very interested and even excited about what you propose, so how do we make it happen for me?" First I do want to go with you and spend a week there, it would give me a sense of being independent and at the same time a chance to experience being away from family and most of all just being there for you and I to improve our relationship, What a great idea."

"I Just feel like a whole new world would be there for me, with you." "I added, speaking of family, the real issue to think about would be, would you be sure you could be away from family this early in your life and only be able to visit them on special occasions?"

"One interesting fact is that there is a fall break, thanksgiving days off, a two week Christmas vacation when you can go home and be with the folks and brother." "Keep in mind that I too have at least 2 of those vacation which would allow me to be in town with you and still see each other.

"So you see, we will hardly ever be separated during the school year. Then come summer time when school is not in session you can be in Taos for the summer and work if you wish; be with family and I will again come up every 2nd weekend like I do now;

"I hope to be working, coming to see you and still be caring for you. I can not see how it could be any better." We just need to make sure we do not get bored with each other, we want to be able to have some space to yearn for each other, miss each other and be excited every time I come to see you."

She finally has the chance to respond to all of what I had mentioned, "Honey you have explained it all so well I do have a full understanding and again, I am excited and thrilled for us. I can hardly wait to share it with my parents, but I will wait until I have gone for the week and come back so I can share the experience I had and see how they have managed with me being gone, then I can share what you have shared with me."

"Honey I will be able to convince them, I hope, but honestly they can be open-minded and….. if I am the one pushing for the change, then it will happen. "I am so thrilled for us and I just love you so much I will feel like I will be in 7th heaven, and with you."

"Again sweetheart I will make it happen for the one week, I will talk to the person involved in student issues for enrollment, but first for the single week and also inform her that we wish to save a space for you for the school year; I'll get an application we can hold onto for the time being and when ready share it with your parents, does that sound okay?"

"Oh, I also forgot to mention the fact that there is now a full moon and it looks bigger and closer; do you remember about our 'Luna Blue' if so you need to go outside and view it. Stand facing it, raise your head to see it and close your eyes and think good thoughts and even wishes, okay? Call me back if you wish."

"I need to hang up now and wait and see what you think, okay?" We have been on line nearly an hour.

"I needed to brush my teeth, clear all reading and detail work I had been working so I could be ready for bed, it is currently 9:35 pm. Being summer time I have my window fully open for fresh air; it is cool tonight. I was just relaxing when the phone rang.

I answer the call, it is Mira Rose she is all excited and says, "Honey did see the moon and it looks great, but I want you to feel it with me can you go out side and see it like I am seeing it so we can experience it together?" I can not refuse such a passionate request, so I said okay, but leave the line open I will do the same and give us a few minutes and then we can come back and talk, okay?"

I pulled on my levis, put on some shoes, and rushed out to the front of the dorm. I could now see the moon and its glorious moon beams; it is a wonder how it can draw one; mesmerize and hypnotize one to its fullness; I stand there facing it and wishing my own thoughts to be with her at the same instant. After a few minutes I go inside.

I pick up the phone, she is waiting on line and says quickly, "Honey you saw how bright it was, I felt   separated from you but I felt your presence here, it was unreal to imagine it even though you are on the phone and waiting to talk to me. How unusual is that, If only I could have had the phone out here with me then it would have been even more real.

"Honey tonight has been one of our best nights for connecting with each other; on the phone and by looking at our own 'Luna Blue'. How much I love you, your passion for me and how you share your worldly ideas I feel very blessed and super happy we are together here or when apart, it is all the same, I hope we can further connect later like tonight."

"Honey I guess we need to close for tonight, but I will be in bed soon with such a sense of fulfillment, more then I have felt until tonight, so I wish you pleasant dreams, keep me in your heart and love me like I love you, talk to you tomorrow night?"

Friday came and went, it was payday for me and I went to the bank to deposit my check, I did keep a few dollars to hold me through the week and next weekend when I travel to Taos again to see Rose and my mom, meanwhile I need to call her to see how she is doing and if she will need anything special for herself. Need to buy her a gift..

Friday towards 7:00 pm I could hardly wait to call Mira Rose, especially and concerning the song that was dedicated to me last night; who else would know about the song except her. I was very surprise to hear the dedication; I wish I could have called her, again, but we had already talked nearly an hour last night, I shall talk to her when we are on the phone.

It is time to call Mira Rose I am quite sure she is by the telephone, do not want to disappoint her. As the phone rang three times, she picked up, all excited and said, "Honey I have several good news for you, but I do have a question for you, did you hear any thing unusual last night after we talked?" she lets out a short laugh and then says again, did you?"

"Sweetheart I know exactly what you are saying about last night. I usually have the radio on just so I can relax after a days work and that wonderful long talk we had last night. I was so surprised when they announced the song and then that it was for me and they were rather mysterious who had dedicated it to me." They said, this romantic song has been requested by a very special young lady who wishes to send a message to her one and only connection here in Albuquerque.

"Sweetheart that was a great message and I do accept it as a token of your love and devotion to me. It has been at least 2- weeks since they played it at the dance we went to. I did not realize that it had such an impression on you, but I had the feeling that you liked it. You mentioned you had heard it a long time ago and that it was a good song, at best."

"Honey I honestly mean, for you, what the song says and all of the comments I have shared with you in my letter, in our telephone conversations and as we speak tonight. I am fully devoted to you and to our relationship and I am so thrilled to be able to be honest and express all those feelings."

Chapter 15

When we finished watching our "Luna Blue" last night, I went back into the living and hung up the phone after we finished talking, so my mom walks in, looks at me with an interesting grin and says to me, "where were you, the phone was here and you were gone, where did you disappear to?" "I was not able to say anything for a few moments."

I finally got the courage to say, "mom, I had gone out to look at the moon at the same time Michael was also doing the same. We have this private time when we view the fullest moon available and we share what we have seen and take those few moments to have the feeling that we are together even though we are miles apart."

"I do not know why I am telling you this, so please we wish for it to be our secret way of connecting once a month, we feel it is very special; Michael has come up with a name for that occasion, but I will not share that with anyone, at least not now, so I hope you understand for our sake, okay?"

"Sweetheart you handled that very very well, I am so proud of you and I am sure your mom is okay with your request and will honor your secret for us. I do want to thank you for requesting the song for me and if you wish that can be our song with our secret."

"I will go to the nearest music store and find that original recording by "Patsy Cline" and bring it to you this next week." Do you have a record player that will play 45 rpm or even the 78 rpm, because it will be in one of those type of recording."

"Honey that would be great to have the recording and we do have a player for either type of record."

What I really like about that special song is she sings about far away places, some of those places I have never heard of, but it is the message it shares that no matter where the person is, that the person is always in her mind and wishes that she is not forgotten and rushes to return to her. I certainly will enjoy playing it and listening to the words and be thinking of you as I listen." "I hope mom does not get tired of hearing it, but we will see."

"Rose, I have various other songs by other singers who I wish to introduce you to and maybe you will also like them for their songs and to experience other forms of music than what you might have been listening to lately, will that be okay?"

"Honey if you have a special place in your heart for those special songs, and if you do, then I know I will also like them, care and cherish that same music you like." I need to have an open mind, experience other forms of listening and entertaining myself specially now that I am with you. You seem to have a wider knowledge and experience than I do and I just love that about you."

"Honey thanks for being so sharing, because I also will be sharing much more of many subjects and you know what we learn something new every day and I am very thankful for that. We are both still being educated, so we have a long ways to go."

"I still have more news to share with you about what we shared last night. The good news is that I do want to come to the city with you.

"I want to be there the whole week and experience what it is like to be at a private boarding school; it should be a good experience for me and so special to spend a whole week with you."

"Also the guy that had been stalking me has gone away, he has not been in the drugstore and has not been seen on the streets or the plaza. The deputy has sort of stayed in touch with me at work or in the evening at home, he talked to my dad and assured him they would still keep an eye out for him, but they feel he is not a threat any longer."

"I now wonder how we discuss the trip with my folks and how soon should we plan on me going with you?" Should I make the suggestion first and then when you come this next weekend we can both visit with them Friday evening?"

"Sweetheart, do this, sit down with them as early as Monday or Tuesday evening at the dinner table,

"Sweetheart I too am thrilled that you wish to come here and spend that week, I will be looking forward to the week myself. It will be a totally new way of us being together in a semi-private way but in the environment of the school itself." "The good news is that I already made the arrangements just in case, it is all set up with the house mother, she knows."

"Now we just need to convince your parents that it is a good thing, it will be as if you went off to camp for a week. There are plenty of adults, mostly women, who basically act as housemothers and oversee what the students are doing, so I will inform your parents as to how the system works on a day to day."

"Do you think it is too soon to plan on you coming next Sunday, the same day I will need to get back to the city. I will come Friday and of course leave back on Sunday afternoon, and with a bit of luck, you will be with me, Wow what a thought; that kind of blows my mind, so keep your fingers crossed.

"I can talk about our suggestions to your parents and I will be more informative when we sit down and decide the plan." "You can call me the following night after you talk, I will want to hear their opinion and any concerns they may have."

"Again she says "I know I can talk them into our plan; I feel by now that they have much trust in you and how our relationship is going, of course in the right direction, It will not hurt for me to be more adult about decisions and ideas with their approval."

"and honey I am just so thrilled and anxious to take the first step into some form of independence as I am now getting older and can learn to think for myself, as I can not live at home forever."

"I can see that our love and devotion for each other is very true; you have proved to me that I matter very much to you and I likewise love and care tremendously for you. I just want to be able to show you my passion and my affection for you more often then just every other weekend, am I right and is it okay to feel that way?"

"Sweetheart, as the song goes, I belong to you and you belong to me and there should be no doubt in either of our minds, right?" "We need to slowly but surely make your parents aware that we truly are together from now on, and we wish for them to have the peace of mind that goes with the that thought in their minds."

Chapter 16

Rose called me Saturday afternoon after her lunch and informed me that her parents had accepted her suggestion and would consider the plan for a couple of days. She chose to bring up the plan earlier so there would be time for them to consider, so I will not know for sure till early next week.

Rose says, honey I am anxious to see you, for you to hold me, talk to me and love me and also I wish to show you my affection and be very close to you, I really miss that closeness that we are getting so accustomed to; can not hardly blame me right?"

I could hardly wait to also say, "I miss you very and need to hold, touch and caress your beautiful face. I am spending a quiet Saturday and I am sure Sunday will not be any better. To keep busy I washed and waxed my car, cleaned the inside and then went to the drugstore to buy some essentials."

"I might see if I can take 3 or 4 students to a movie this afternoon, I prefer a mixed group 2 boys and 2 girls, those that are kind of seeing each other. We can breakup the boring times we all experience."

"Honey I may surprise you later on tonight or tomorrow and call and see how your evening went. It is a bit of responsibility taking them to down town, but I know you, you will lecture them to behave, right?"

"How right you are sweetheart, talk to you later I will be waiting to see, I'll be in my dorm room later."

I managed to receive permission to take 2 boys and 2- girls to the first showing at the Kimo Theater of a new thriller, mystery movie, it turned out be very good, they all enjoyed it. As we were driving to down town, I leaned back and said to them, "is this date night for you or just a friendly date?" The response I got was as they said it out loud, "yes for us this is a date, but we did not tell the house mother that."

After the movie I drove us back to the campus, I made sure that the girls went in to their dorm and then I took the boys to our dorm and said good night to all.

I had not been in my room more than 15 minutes when the phone rang, 2-3 times before I picked up. I was surprised to hear it was Mira Rose, it was 9:35. I said, "sweetheart what a surprise to hear from you." She quickly says, "I am bored, lonely and I wanted to see how the "movie night went" also I wanted to talk with you as my last thought tonight, because I miss you and I want to share my love with you."

Mira Rose followed her loving expression; I had a talk after dinner and after serious discussion and considerations, Mira Rose's says her parents did agree that the plan for a week that we had suggested seemed a good plan and they understood fully that Rose would be at a school campus that was secure and well controlled.

I told Rose that I would assured them that I personally would also look out for her safety and that I would make no effort to take you off campus, in fact, they probably will not permit it, as they feel it is their responsibility to see to Rose's safety, and I totally agree.

"The students working there for the summer do not go off campus unless it is with an adult to either church or to a movie on a weekend, but she will not be there over a full weekend so that would not be a concern, because we will be coming back to town at the end of that week, Saturday morning."

"Sweetheart that is just part of the conversation that will take place with your parents, but you will be there and may even ask questions of your own, so how does that sound?"

"Honey I am and will be impressed as to what you will share with mom and dad and I am sure they will appreciate all of your information." "Tomorrow is Sunday, I have nothing planned here at home so it will be another quiet day, but there is a movie playing that I could take my brother to see; poor kid he hardly has chances to go to a movie, so I will borrow my mom's car so that we do not have to walk, so there that takes care of the afternoon."

"Time to go, but I wish you a night to remember that I called, I love you, miss you and I have all that passion and affection that is building up for next weekend, so beware and I am so happy that I can call even this late and almost tuck you for the night, but that is only wishful thinking, but the day will come."

I also wished her a good night, "please have some dreams, think about us and I shall call tomorrow at 7:00 to see how your day went, I herein give you my love and wishes to keep till later."

It is Sunday after lunch, which is usually at 1:00, because there is no dinner later only a brown paper bag with goodies, so we have to make the best of lunch for a good full meal. As I was walking out, someone approached me from the left, it was Delia; I had not seen much of her lately, but there she was.

She comes up behind me, pokes me lightly in the back and says, "Hi there stranger where have you been?" I turned and greeted her in a surprised but warm way and said to her, "Hi Delia I have not seen much of you either, how are you?"

"I have been okay, they have been keeping us busy and I had been helping out in the kitchen and the dinning room after the dinner meals for the last week or so I have and I missed seeing you, have you been hiding or just being private?" *I did not know how to answer that, especially in the manner in which she worded her question.*

"Why would you be missing me as you would only see me at lunch or dinner and rarely over by your dormitory. I work all day in that crazy sun and by early evening I am tired and sometimes not interested in being sociable, I just hang around Bennett Hall and do some reading."

She comes back to me and says, When will you be going to take someone to the movies?, because I would like to go, can you take me with the others?" I look at her, she has a shy sexy look on her face, so I say to her, "I would very much invite you and others that wish to go to a movie, how about in the next few days?" She comes close, touches my arm and says, I will love to go, who will pick the movie or movies?"

She then asks, "where are you going now? will you walk with me to the dorm? so we can talk some?" *I did not know how to respond to that and not hurt her feelings, so I said.* "Actually I was headed that way to go make a call at the phone booth, I need to call my mother and see how she is doing."

She says, "Okay", so we started walking away, we were making small talk while on the way and we were at least 3 feet apart, just a normal distance for the two of us, like being friends or acquaintances and not involved in any manner.

She stops momentarily, turns to me and asks, "are you seeing anyone who will be in school here this next fall?" "I apologize for asking, because it seems you are always alone." *Wow she is really full of questions today!* I say, "no I am not and do not know someone who is a student, aside from you and I have no idea about any someone attending classes here this fall. I do know someone that is interested in coming to school here, but I'm not sure as of yet."

She says, "I know you are attending the university, are you still going there this fall?" I was wondering if you and I could be friends or even more than friends. I do like you I admire you and I hear a lot of good things about you." I do not mean to be pushy or forward, it is just being interested in you and who you are." *She really is to the point, very direct and requires answers, answers I am not capable of sharing with her.*

I pause in place, I look at her, she is a very beautiful girl, a lovely person and appears to be very smart, how fortunate if one could be with her as a friend or even as a girlfriend. I need to be careful what I say.

We keep on walking and momentarily arrive at the front door to the porch, I stop and I say to her, "Delia I am not sure how to answer your questions right now, but if you wish we could talk some more after 7:30 this evening?" I could meet you on the steps to the auditorium around that time." She gets on a big smile and says, "okay I will see you around 7:30pm +, bye."

At 7:15 pm, I went and sat down on the concrete steps that lead to the auditorium, About 12 minutes had passed when Delia showed up. Wow dressed very nicely and she just looked radiant and with a touch of perfume. I said to her, "look at you; a totally different person, you girls sure know how to be so beautiful and different from us guys." "guess we have something to learn." She was wearing bluish shorts and a dark blue button down blouse, very beautiful.

She sat down about 2 feet away, smiled and crossed her legs; her shorts were not too short , but the blouse fit here quite snug; she is a very well formed young woman. She did start the conversation by, "Well how do I look?" I responded with, "I am very impressed with how you look and you are very pleasing to the eyes, especially my eyes."

She counters, "thank you, you don't look so bad yourself, then bursts out laughing and giggling, I'm sorry I meant that in a good way, you are very handsome yourself." We both had a good laugh over the comments and then turned serious; she had a very nice smile, licked her lips in a very teasing manner.

"Michael I did not mean to be so forward with my questions and comments earlier, I just could not hold back and by being inquisitive, I was able to get you to at least say something and respond to me, I can only imagine why you are somewhat distant from me or us here on the campus."

"Delia, I do not have any concern about how you approached me and asked questions, there was nothing unusual about your questions, like you said you were being inquisitive; not too many persons are like that, I think that is an asset for you and that you will always be interested and inquisitive about people or issues around you and that is a very positive attitude you have and are not afraid to show it."

Once I finished my response, all of sudden she quickly moves over and is next to me touching me. I was a bit shocked, not having expected that motion. I would have thought that I would be the forward one and move in on her, which I chose not to do, at least not now.

"Michael will you hold my hand for now?" I chose to stall for the moment, as I did not wish to start any contact that I can not afford, so I said to her, "Delia wait for now, lets talk about my issues and possibly yours, because there is something I will need to share with you. First of all I may be quite a few years older than you ,how old are you now?,"

She answers quickly, "I am sixteen will be seventeen in September, so I countered, I will be 23 in September myself, that is a bit of a difference is it not?" "Wouldn't you rather date someone your age and have more in common than someone a bit older?" I think that relationships here in high school are short lived and only last through the time till graduation of one or the other student in the relationship."

"I know that for a fact, as I dated someone here for two school years and when she graduated, she left and I have never heard from her to this day. I had 1½ years at the university. She was 18." So I got dumped."

"Do you know any of the boys from your classes that you would consider to be in a relationship with or have even liked to be your boyfriend for how ever time it is possible?" *I could tell she was thinking seriously about what I just suggested.*

"Michael I have no one for now or for the school year coming up; there is no one I am interested in. Like I said earlier I like you very much and admire you, I guess I prefer someone older more stable."

"How do you know if I am not some crazy who looks normal but, watch out! At that point she could not help but burst out laughing and said, "You are not some crazy, I know more about you than you might think." I said back, "Oh Oh, I am in real trouble now. What do I need to correct and admit to?"

"You are being silly and I do not know stuff about you that makes you look bad, like I said you are well thought of and liked for who you are." Look I am not looking for you to be my boyfriend forever just be with me and lets see where it goes."

She looks at me straight in the eye and before I can react, she places her hand on my cheek and gives me a very smooth wet kiss on the lips, I was caught by surprise and maybe I was shocked to see that she took the first step, I did not expect that at all.

She says to me, "kiss me, show me how you kiss, I showed you." I guess I looked at her rather strange and did not respond, so she puts on a soft smile, tilts her head to the right, She draws nearer, so I took her face in my hands and first kissed her lightly then I eased in and gave her a very solid wet kiss, would that satisfy her curiosity and desire to be kissed?

I pulled away, she still had her eyes closed as if to imply the kiss was not enough for now, so I leaned towards her and placed a very tender wet kiss on her lips, by the way, she has some great lips, I kept the kiss on for a few more seconds then pulled away.

She opened her eyes slowly and she wet her lips and finally attempted to say something. She says, "I have never been kissed like that ever and Oh how great that was." "I am so glad I kissed you first, but your kisses were even better.""you do not know that?"

I asked, "When was the last time you got kissed, was it a boy friend type, just some guy and he caught you by surprise and it did not mean much?"

"Like you just said, it was just some guy who did sneak up and caught me by surprise, no big deal."

"Delia we need to stop while we can, now ! as I need to explain my personal situation, so that you'll understand okay?" " I have been in a relationship with someone for over a year, it had been low key for quite awhile until the last few months and now we are very committed to each other, so that means that I am not free to be with someone else, like you."

"You are a terrific lovely person and I hope I have not given you any encouragement for us to be seeing each other now or later this school year. I would like to be your friend if ever I can help or you need some one to talk to, if there is no one else. I did not mean to mislead you or give you the wrong impression."

"also, Delia, a part of you will be with me after today and I only promise that what you shared and were to me yesterday and   today does mean a lot, you are a precious and sweet person I will remember this initial, very personal touching, and kissing and I will see you very vividly in my mind".

It will be a very personal feeling I will have for you, I believe that there can be feelings or emotions for someone else even if one is with someone at that time."

"There is no way I can forget you as we both will be living here and around others in the same crowd. I have enjoyed seeing you, talking to you and for now I can mingle with you and the others as we have, if we can go to movies at least once a week."

"Remember I told you I would arrange for you and others to go to the movies this next week, are you still interested to do so?" I will talk to the house mothers tomorrow and get permission."

She says to me, "I will not be upset if we can not see each other, I am sort of disappointed but if it cannot be possible I understand you have an understanding with someone else, but it does not change how I now feel about you, and I am serious."

"I will keep to myself about tonight's meeting, please do not forget me and what I have said about you. We still have the rest of this summer to talk and visit and exchange ideas." Is that okay with you?" I said, "of course that will be possible."

I touched her face and saw a little bid of sadness in her eyes, she reach up and held my hand. I said, "do not be sad I will be around, we will see each other everyday and we can talk, but we can not make out or hold and touch each other unless just in passing, okay? "Maybe a little hug on occasions.

What I just said to her brought a wide smile and her eyes sparkled sending me a message; "I like that and look forward to those times, they will be very special, to me."

"I like you too and have been attracted to you; I see you have passion and are affectionate which are two very positive traits, so be proud of yourself." You have a very nice personality; just as I look back to the times when you talked to me and teased me."

"You will never know, we might be there for each other later, life is strange, there will always be changes."

I walked Delia back to her dorm, it was quiet there at the porch, actually we were the only ones there and we stopped momentarily next to the phone booth, she turns around puts her arms around my neck and place a very passionate kiss on my lips; it took me by surprise again, but I did not pull away.

She pulls back a little and says, "that was so you will remember me tonight and other times, sleep tight and pleasant dreams I'll see you around later and don't forget about movie night next week."

"Delia, I wish you to know that I will remember how you expressed yourself in a manner which was not expected at all. What you said and did is not easy to forget. I do not wish for you to think I am insensitive to your gestures, attention and affection you have shared with me and I think it was unbelievable that you would, without knowing how I would react."

"For now I will have the memory of what you expressed and I do not wish for you to feel rejected at all. Think of it as an expression that was too soon. I will keep it all to myself, so think of it as our own personal secret, as no one needs to know what our secret is, okay?"

"When we see each other from now on we will know that it was special for the both of us, okay?" "I am okay with that she responds" and I say, "thanks for that great good night kiss, I will not wash my face, especially my lips, tonight."

I had the strangest sensation after she stepped up into the porch, she waved and entered into the dorm hall. I was in a bit of confusion about what I was doing there and now what am I going to do. Am I going to call Mira Rose and then pretend that nothing happened earlier, how will that work out?

I called Mira Rose, the phone rang 3- times and then she answers, and says, "hello this is Rose" I quickly say back, "Hi sweetie it is me" ,"she says OH I did not know if you would call tonight since we talked a lot last night, I was just watching some TV programs, had nothing else to do and of course thinking about you." "Today is Sunday, did you have a busy day, I hope you rested enough to catch up?"

"I got a late start, even after the early breakfast at the dining room, I was still rather sleepy and felt from working all week long, so I laid around in my room. I also knew I had laundry to do, iron some shirts and pants and also see what else needed to be done in my room. Generally I wait till Monday evening to pick up clean linen, but I got it this afternoon so as to get a jump on cleaning and straightening my room."

"Did you work at the drugstore?" She says, "I did, from 10:00 Saturday morning to 5:00 pm, because on Saturdays it can be very busy, especially with visitors in town and of course people who do shopping on the weekends." I guess I did forget to mention last night that I had worked yesterday."

The following Friday I left for Taos for the weekend and the fact that Mira Rose would be coming back to the school campus on Sunday, so I assume it is going to happen since I have not heard otherwise.

I did bring Rose back with me and introduced her to the girl's housemother and she asked one of the other girls to take her to one of the spare rooms and get settled.

It was a bit strange to wait for her to come back down to see me for the day, but we would be seeing each other for breakfast.   She was at breakfast; one of the girls she met was helping her get acquainted with the dining room. I was able to talk to her briefly and to see how she was feeling, so far.

I said to her softly, "Hi sweetie are you doing okay for now, and have they clued you in on the task and assignments for the day?" She answers back, "yes Sylvia has been asked to introduce me to the tasks that I will be involved with her, so I expect it will be okay, I will share it with you at lunch."

I saw her at noon, lunch time is from 12:00 to 1:00 pm, so we visited briefly and then I had to rush off to my work, but we will see each other at dinner and will visit for the early part of the evening.

Chapter 17

"Well sweetie it is after 9:00 pm and I need my rest and sleep for another day at work and the whole week as well." Oh! I said, we did not go to the movies on Saturday afternoon we postponed it till at least Monday or Tuesday evening, I inquired about movies and new movies were to be showing tonight and for the next two weeks, so we will go next week.

Three weeks later
Its Registration Day !!

The new school year for all new students started one week early in order to register, confirm their grade status and financial contribution to their first year, regardless of the grade of attendance.

Mira Rose was on time, brought to the campus by her parents, participated in all of the three student preregistration requirements. Once that were completed she, with parents, proceeded to the girl's dorm to be introduced to the housemother and be assigned a dorm room, with or without a roommate, most likely she will have a roommate later.

That process went well, she was assigned a room and would have a roommate names Josie, a carry over from the 10th grade. It would be helpful for Rose to have a seasoned roommate who could be helpful in any and all daily issues in the dorm. When her parents had finished the process they were free to go and Mira Rose would now be part of the new school year in her 11th grade standing.

When it came to either lunch or evening dinner, her roommate would show her the way to and from meals, so that she could learn how it all operated, so lunch was not served on that day so that the kitchen staff could prepare for the evening meal, which would be quite larger than it was during the summer period.

I was finally able to see Mira Rose at dinner, but not able to see her until after dinner. I waited outside the dinning building and pointed out where I was so she could walk over to me.

I did catch her attention and she left her roommate and came over, I extended my hand to her and she took it and squeezed it hard, she had a little bit of tears when she saw me and she said, "Hi honey, finally I get to see you."

I quickly said, "sweetie are you alright? It must seem quite different than you expected, but it is only the first day; as days go by, you will think nothing of the day to day occurrences." She says to me, "I wish I could hug you tight and kiss you. When will I be able to do so?"

"Sweetheart we need to start out slow so as to draw very little attention to us by others."
"I am quite sure there will be questions about the two of us, most students know who I am but will wonder how I fit in; are you a sister, a friend, a relative or even a girl friend. I will not care once they know and understand we are a couple.

"Be careful what you tell your roommate and or others as the days go by when you are asked, point blank, how you are related to me since you do seem to have known me well; just a precaution for now."

"I will walk you to the dorm, you can take some time for anything you wish; put on lipstick, comb your hair and I will come back in about 10-15 minutes; will meet you just outside the porch and then we can take a walk so that we do not need to have contact with anyone for tonight.

I was there when Mira Rose came out of the porch, I waved at her, she came to me and held out her hand, I held it for a few seconds and then let go.

■■■

"I said to her, "let's walk over to that bench beneath the tree by that building which is the Library, we can sit there to start then take a walk elsewhere."

"I to am anxious to hold you and kiss you as soon as possible. Let me ask, how did your parents react to the process for registering and getting you settled today?"

She says, "Mom was more inquisitive than Dad was, but I think they were satisfied with what they saw and what to expect of my going to school here; they understood it is a safe place to be."

As the sun set and it got to be a bit dark, we managed to walk over to a larger tree, get behind it and steal a nice wet kiss and very tight hug; it was great, since we had not been together for 1½ weeks until today.

In the next 15- 30 minutes it will be necessary for all the girls, attached or unattached, to be called in for the evening and stay indoors for the evening.

As the days went on and I even had to go to UNM and register and start classes the following week, and as Mira Rose began her classes and I got involved in my own, it got to be more and more the routine of the day or the week.

■■■

We were both beginning to adjust to the routines, she was beginning to get introduced to her classes and to her teachers as well as her classmates, many of them were in most of her classes.   She would tell me of various issues that were discussed and how each student was asked to comment on the text of the assignments from the previous day.

We would meet up after dinner every day and I would walk her to the dorm, sometimes we would just meander around the campus if there was no need for her or myself to go there first if we were to spend the rest of the allowable time together.

One evening after school had been session for several weeks she says to me, "honey it is really much more interesting and different than the class experiences I had at Taos High School last year. I do realize that schools can be different, so I am getting adjusted with the manner and methods of teaching here; not bad at all, so I am okay for now and doing my best to fit in."

I say to her, "sweetheart, I am going through some of the growing pains of being enrolled in new classes and have different classmates, so it is a whole new experience with the professors and the type of assignments we are involved in, so not so different for me ."

Mira Rose responds with, "one thing I am happy about is that I get to see you and talk with you every day, much better than every 2nd weekend at home. For now it is coming together and hopefully it will all be easier going from day to day."

"The weeks and 2-months have gone by and she understands that there will be a fall break from classes and she can call her parents to pick her up and actually go home for a few days or can stay until classes resume; so that decision comes later.

The Thanksgiving break came sooner than expected and all students were to leave the campus if there was somewhere to be with families. Mira Rose was thankful that she could go home and visit with her parents and take a break from school, I as well had a few days off so I drove us home to visit and we had more time to ourselves.

Our relationship was going well and neither one of us could say we did not have enough time to be together, it was a totally new experience for both and we were trying to make it work; how will the future be for us?, only time will tell.

We were both working at keeping up our classes, after several months of this first semester, we were looking forward to her first Christmas vacation. It happens that the day of dismissal was on a Friday, so I chose to offer her that I could take her home, because I wanted to spend a weekend with my dad and then I would be back to work at the office for several days before the New Year.

My mom had left her home because it was too cold for her and she went to California to see her own sister, for at least 2-3 months, so I really did not have someone to visit there except my dad on weekends, so I was able to visit with Mira Rose some evenings of the days I was there.

■■■

The Christmas vacation all of a sudden is here, I had my last class 2 days ago and we are off for at least 5-7 days; problem is that I do not know what I am going to do for Christmas Eve and also the day of Christmas. I can not go to Taos because no one will be there. I know I can work at the office for a few days and benefit from the income for my next semester, so I will work until Christmas Eve.

I received a call from my brother at the labs inviting me for the two days of the holiday and he would check back with me a day earlier. I was made aware that we were expecting stormy snowy weather in the next few days. I did not give it much thought;

I had just arrived at my dorm room the day before Xmas Eve, when my phone rang, I pick up and my brother is calling to advise me that they were receiving much snow and was concerned about my drive up to his home up north because those roads are very treacherous in bad weather, and was advising me to not drive up; too big a risk.

He did inform me that our dad was invited to the Xmas dinner at his home and he would feel bad if I was not there, but being safe in the city was most important, so I said I would not go and wished him and his family and my dad the best of Christmas day.

On the eve of Christmas I just laid around and wondered what I could do to keep busy; I know there would be dinner at 6:00 p.m. and then a Christmas dinner for all of us, including staff, still on campus.

I thought that I would dress up after dinner and go to my church for their scheduled Christmas Eve music program, so I did go and at least I was part of the normal holiday celebration and could be around people and not feel lonely or left out by myself. I returned to my dorm on campus at approximately 8:45 p.m. sat down to gather my thoughts about the following day's activities, what could I do?

I was just sitting on my bed and listening to music when my phone rang; I wondered who could that be, since no one knew I would be here. Mira Rose was under the impression I was not in town and that I would be at my brother's home.

I answered hello and paused for a moment, next thing I know it is Delia, which surprised the heck out of me; not expecting her, certainly not tonight.

I said, "Delia is that you?" She says back, "Yes it is me, is it okay to be calling you tonight? I did not know if you would even be there" "Are you okay and hope you are well? I know it has been only a few days since we said goodbye for the holidays"

"I just wanted to hear your voice and know how you are. Please do not be upset at me, I just miss the fact that we are not near each other like on a daily basis." *I actually was pleased that she called now, as I am alone and a bit lonely.*

I said to her, "Oh sweetie I am delighted that you called and I am not expecting anyone else to call, if you know what I mean. Do not be upset as I am just sitting here listening to music and killing time until my bedtime."

"You did not know, but I was scheduled to go up north to visit with my brother, his family and my dad for Xmas Eve and dinner tomorrow day, but I cancelled due to bad snow weather."

"Tell me, how were you doing today and tonight are you and family celebrating with others on this special night?" "I went to Christmas Eve services at my church just to have something to do and see real people."

She says back, "My thoughts have been with you and just things and it seems so different now, I have never had the sort of feelings and emotions like I am having now, please forgive me I do not mean to burden you with my feelings."

"Delia you are not doing any such thing, remember we are close friends and some how or another we sort of need each other, you more so then I, but we know what the situation is for now."

I paused for a few moments and then I sensed she is a bit emotional and quietly crying, so I say quickly, "are you crying? she pauses and speaks with emotion in her response." "I did need to talk to you, you know how I feel."

I asked her, "are you lonesome tonight, what do you miss the most by being up there at home and not at school?" "I know that it is very quiet here and I am lonely and it is great that you called:" she is still crying and then she has to pay attention to; Oh! her mom is asking her what is wrong, they talk as Delia is having to explain to her why she is emotional.

Delia says, "that was my mom concerned that I was crying and wanted to know if there was a problem, also asked who I was talking to, so I had to tell her I was talking to you, she seemed puzzled but did not comment for now."

"Michael how long can we talk?" Am I causing you any expense on this call?" I told her, "no you are not causing me any cost for the long distance call, I think the cost is on your side of the call. and if there is some cost to me, it will only be for some minutes, so do not worry about it, I am not concerned, okay?"

She says, "I am concerned that you are all alone tonight and tomorrow, how about the rest of the days left till we go back?" I say, "well I have no family at home as of now and weather is bad so I will not try to travel there now, also I am working days so that takes care my hours during the day."

"Do you not think someone there would like to see you, talk to you, you know who I mean, right?" "There is not much I can do about that right now." I would like to continue talking to you now, do you agree with me Delia?"

"Oh! of course, but I would rather be there with you and I know that is not possible, so what can I say or do?"

"Well I suggest we keep it less emotional and personal for now and just talk as close friends in need of sharing issues in general; I do understand how you feel. I know we experienced a very close and intimate closeness between us and you and I have not forgotten that, but we need to put it aside for now."

"Michael it is now 10:15 so I guess I should let you go so that we can get some sleep." I say to her, "you are the one who needs your beauty sleep, me I do not know what that would mean for me."

"Michael dear, I feel so much better now that we have talked, can we do it again soon?" I said, "you tell me." We wished each other a good night and pleasant dreams.

Chapter 18

I sat down on the bed to just think about the outcome of my telephone visit with Delia, I was surprised about the emotions she expressed. I think she is very sincere and honest about how she feels. I know that I have been fair and honest with her, that I am not available to be in a relationship with her and she has indicated that she can live with it.

I need to be careful to not encourage her emotionally, because it would hurt her, also it could then cause personal harm. I need to keep our friendship at a level where she feels good about herself and just sees me as someone to turn to for support. It is somewhat unfortunate that our lives are at different stages of personal existence.

Here it is Christmas morning, no snow just a cold cloudy day, so I will go to breakfast and take the rest of the day slow since I have nothing to do or places to go. At noon they prepared a very nice meal for all of us who were there; some had visitors with them, so it was a happy enjoyable meal and visiting period for many of those there. Me I just visited a little and then went back to the dorm.

I decided to go down town and see what kind of movies were showing just so I could have some form of entertainment for time to pass, especially today. I managed to find one matinee movie that I had not seen and then there was a second showing too.

I arrived back at my dorm room at 7:45 p.m. was just getting settled when the phone rang; I wondered who would be calling at this hour. It was Mira Rose, she says, "Hi you are back in town! I did not know if you would be back from your brother's home since you were to have left early Christmas Eve morning for the two days."Did you have a good visit with brother's family and your dad?"

I finally was able to answer, "no sweetie I did not go, my brother called me the even before and told me they were have much snow and it would be falling the next day too. He suggested I not take the risk, but they would miss me, so I stayed, have made the best of it and it is now over for this year."

"Oh! I am so sorry to hear that, why did you not call me and tell me so?" I said, "well I did not want to interfere in your Christmas celebration with family and others; I hope you had a good one and I was okay, I survived and did eat well today, I also went to a movie this afternoon and saw two shows."

"I had a good time, having slept late and ate well. It was good to see my parents again since I saw them last at Thanksgiving for two days. "We too had lots of snow; we had a white Christmas !   Have you missed me?"

"Of course I missed you, it is very quiet here on the campus this time of year, no one to really talk to and visit with, but I have experienced this in years past, so I manage." When will you be back? Is it next Monday? She says, "no, we have to be back on Sunday, classes start on Monday"

I said to her, "My classes do not start until Thursday of the week and I have been working days to add to my income for the coming semester." "I will be looking forward to your return, so we can be together again for the rest of the school year."

"Honey I long for your kisses and for you to hold me tight like before, it is tough to be separated." I will Let you go so you can relax before bedtime and be ready for work tomorrow, right?" I love and miss you for now, call me soon okay?"
I sat there for a few moments and then attempted to get my clothes ready for tomorrow, so I turned on some music,

In the next few seconds the phone rang and sort of shocked me, I wonder who? I looked at my clock and it was 8:45+, so I answered quickly, said hello.

"Hi it is me Delia, are you busy and can you talk?"

"Delia I will talk to you anytime as long as I am not with someone else; you know what I mean right?" just to avoid conflict and arguments, Okay?" She says, "I am sorry to call this late, but It is the end of Christmas Day I want to know if you at least had a fair day and were not lonely."

"I did sleep late, had breakfast and laid around and stayed out of the cold, after all it is December. I was okay, after a very nice Xmas dinner in the dining room I decide to go into town and look for a movie or two to see to kill time. In fact, I saw two movies, got back to the dorm after 7:30 and am here ever since."

"How was your Christmas day and dinner?" I do hope you had a very good day with family and that you ate well and are now stretched out on the sofa?" Moaning and rubbing your tummy." She says, "you are silly, but I was a little uncomfortable later after we ate and just sat around. I must have given the impression that I was a little distant and maybe sad." My mom called me into the kitchen and asked, are you okay it seems like in your mind, you are somewhere else?"

"Mom noticed I started to tear and she hugged me and said, "I kind of think I know why, you miss someone back in the city, right?" "I shook my head, to say yes, but I said I was okay." I quickly asked, "Mom can I call him and see how he is; he has been alone all these last two days, so she said, "yes, call him."

"Delia are you okay now?" I do not want you to be sad or even lonely, with family and friends there? are there some girl friends to talk to for companionship or just to catch up on local gossip?" She did not directly answer me, but said, I do not really have close friends here in town, so no one to talk with or call to get together."

"I talked to mom and said that I was sad for you and that I know that you were alone there and that I did miss seeing you. She wanted to know how was it that I seemed to be serious for you, but you do not seem to be there for me?"

"I told mom for now we are just real close friends and I have shared my feelings for you and that you have been very kind and honest with me and supportive. I know that sounds weird but I understand and am dealing with it."

"I want you to know I have hardly no friends here; "Did I ever tell you that I went to Allison James School before coming to the school in Albuquerque, so I really know very few of the high school crowd here."

"Michael, may I ask you how serious are you about Rose and how serious is she about you?" I know that it is very bold of me since it is none of my business, please forgive me for asking and being so forward, okay?"

I had to think about that question, it really stunned me for now; good thing she can not see the expression on my face, so I hesitated a little more and then I said, "Delia it is like this, I think, okay?"

"I will be as honest as possible. This relationship seems to be only about the present, no talk or discussions about the future and with no serious commitment to that extent. She is young has been rather sheltered at home and not satisfied with the local high school."

"I had suggested she consider this high school and the opportunity to get more exposure to the world and expand her horizons. She had concerns that once we were both in school that she would not see much of me, earlier I only saw her every two weekends. I will not lie, I have cared for her and she for me, so we were wishing to be closer to each other while she attends school here for her last two years."

"I do understand the fact that you are interested in my relationship and it is difficult to discuss such an involvement with others, but I can see where you are coming from with that request." Please do not feel offended with any of my responses."

"You know we are both in an awkward friendship position as of today, you have expressed your feelings and I have been careful not to mislead you and we have discussed it."

"Can you tell me why you wish to know due to the fact that it can be hurtful to you to know personal information that you really may not want to know anyway?" "I do not wish for you to be hurt emotionally as I want you to be happy, think more about what the future may hold for yourself and even me for that matter??

She is quiet for a few moments then finally makes an effort to talk and is thinking how she will present her reason or reasons for wanting to know what she has just asked. She has been inquisitive, but honest with me and I understand; because she has to a great extent bared her heart to me without hesitation.

"Michael, I am inquisitive and just wish to know how involved and committed to her you may be at this time. I know I have been very clear how I feel about you, probably more than I should have just so as not to be hurt incase you would start being involved with me and still being with her."

"I know you have been very honest with me about not being able to be as I asked, my boyfriend, I know that was very bold of me to tell and ask of you." I do not feel hurt or offended by how honest you have been; I would have wanted for you to agree about us." "I still want to be your close friend and let the future be what it will be." Is that okay with you?" Michael for me ***it's now or never,*** me, I do not wish to be forced to walk away with a broken heart,

At this time she is quite emotional, but clears her throat and goes on, "I am sorry to be acting this way, forgive me."

"I said I only visit and see her on my trips to Taos to see my mom every two weekends. I will not lie, I have cared for her and she for me, so we were wishing to be closer to each other while she attends school here for her last two years."

"Delia you are such a sweetheart that I honestly feel like I wish we had met and known each other sooner, much sooner, then, our personal lives would not be so complicated as now." I have begun to have much more special feelings for you and I try to just keep them close to me so as not to be encouraging you any further."

"Do you understand what I am trying to say?" I just want you to be happy, smile and do not let anything get to you. Hope for the best for yourself and be planning what your future could be, it could surprise you and it may even surprise the both of us."

"Michael I am so happy we talked about what we both have been feeling all this time, I will try to be happy and content with how everything is working out and look for the future to be the best that I or we can expect as best friends."

"I do not expect you to be dishonest or unfaithful to your current relationship, but remember how I feel about you, because I remember those great kisses we shared that gave me the greatest pleasure of my life." "Delia also remember I am here for you, as much as I can be and you can always contact me; you now know."

I turned out the lights, got into bed, but it was not easy to go to sleep since I had so much on my mind. I was trying to sort out the emotions, that plays on the aspect of an existing relationship, yes the fact that there is a second love interest pulling on my heart strings for attention and my trying to stay true to my current relationship with Mira Rose.

I believe I have expressed, in honest terms, my position in my current involvement with Rose to my friend Delia. She is such a special person and so willing to express and send out the vibes, emotions and sincere affections that have sent me into turmoil that questions my own sincerity to the other person. I hope I do not have nightmares and fight any emotional battles that I am not prepared for, and that I can drift off to sleep and awake in my normal way of life tomorrow morning, God help me, I do need to be stable as I will be at work involved in difficult project tasks.

I simply can not run away from myself since there is no place for me to hide !! I will stand tight as to the rules of our friendship with minor exceptions.

Starting the day and the week with classes and then finishing the days having worked at the office at least 3½ hours each day really keeps me on the go, to say the least. Occasionally I think about my conversations with Delia, but mostly I think seriously about my relationship with Mira Rose. Is it what it was nearly 9-10 months ago when we could hardly wait to see and touch each other during my visits to our home town.

I am seriously curious about what is going through her mind; the few conversations we have had about 1½ years until we both graduate and then what would be our future.

She does not seem as excited or anxious for us to reach that point in time. She has questioned me about when I will receive my Air Force commission and mostly about where will I be assigned for active duty. She seems concerned about leaving town and also, if she is ready to leave her family.

I have tried to be honest about the requirements that I serve in active duty for a minimum of 4 years after receiving my commission. It is my understanding one does not have choices of an assigned base.

I will be sent where there are needs for one's educational back ground and to just fill open positions for lower officer positions. I am puzzled why those type of questions are so important at this time; I am within 13+ months before I reach that point; graduation and commissioned status.

The following day after dinner I met up with Delia and gave her a sealed note; to her surprise, I never looked back.

I had written a short letter to inform her of the news; Delia, I have been looking for and trying to catch up with you to share a very interesting occurrence that I learned since last night. If you can go down to the telephone booth and call me here at my dorm room, you have my number.

If you can call me after all you girls are back in your rooms, just tell the house mother that you need to call your parents, okay? I'll be waiting.

This is the next day after my note to her, my phone rings I answer and, and it is Delia, she says, "Michael Hi, I read your note but could not call last night. I have the note in my blouse so no one can see it, as I leave nothing around in the room to be visible for anyone to see."

"What is going on? I am anxious to know" "Sweetie I had a serious discussion yesterday after dinner as she and I visited for a while. In talking with Rose about school, she said she was looking forward for the school year to end next month because she has decided that she will not return here next school year. She has talked it over with her parents.

"It appears that she would rather be at a more traditional school were she can live at home, have more freedom and be able to go to movies, shopping and even out to eat with her girl friends. I was totally surprised as I was under the impression she was happy here, only because we could be together more often on a daily basis and not wait to visit every two weeks as before."

We did not have time to go into detail about how that would affect our relationship as it would put us at a distance and separated for periods of two weeks at a time. I did not ask too many questions nor wanted us to argue about personal issues.

I believe there is more to the fact that she will not be planning to return for her senior year. I will wait and see what else she comes up with.

"I want you to know those facts if of interest to you what kind of position I will be in for the summer and the next school year; your last school year and my last year at the university."

"Michael, I am totally surprised but at the same time super delighted for me, how about you?" "You know what I feel and what I want for me and for the both of us. Would you continue to be a couple or do you think that it will be a thing of the past?"

"I think I will wait and see how it plays out from now until May when school ends here, I will still be at the university till June. Most likely she will go home for the summer; I have no idea what happens after that, I will have to wait and see."

"I feel that separation will not be in my favor, because I prefer having an on-going relationship, being separated does no good for either one." "Delia what do you think?" "What are your immediate feelings?"

"Michael dear, personally I want to be with you, I need you, and hope you can also need me. We would have one more school year here, together, I cherish the thought that we could grow together and I would wish nothing but the best for us both."

"The operator is telling me my time is up, honey I want to write a letter to you for tomorrow or so and add more of what my total reaction is to your good news for tonight, can I just go and we will continue this later?" I quickly say, yes go and we'll talk more."

Chapter 19

It is now the first week in May, at least 2 ½ weeks till graduation here at the school, but about 3½ weeks till my 3rd year classes are done for the year, I plan on looking into the number of classes/hours I will need to be ready to graduate including the completion of the ROTC program. I surely need to have those fully completed.

If not at that point, I would have to take 1-2 classes this coming summer session so as to be ready for the last required hours of the 4th year.

It is Friday evening, dinner time; I had just arrived on campus about 45 minutes earlier. I need to change my clothes of the day. I proceeded on to the shower and changed. At the dining room I caught a glimpse of Delia up ahead, I did not see Mira Rose anywhere just yet.

So I pickup my pace and slipped in just behind Delia; I reached over and poked her lightly, she turns and smiles and throws me a kiss, but she also says hello, "how was your day?" I say back, "It was okay busy as always, and yours?"

I walked ahead and opened the door for them, she quickly reaches up and touches my arm, "thank you" she says and see, you later." Was there a question in that response? I did not know how she meant it and I may not really know soon enough.

She quickly asks up close, "what are you doing tomorrow Saturday, going to sleep late, be lazy or just goof off?" She walks away with a deep smile for me as I saw her get to her table for dinner. It is always interesting running into her, she is always such a tease.

As I sat down at my table and greeted my fellow university students, I turned my attention inward and in my mind I assured myself that there is always a story in her eyes and her teasing speaks louder than words, she is conveying that very secret message that only she and I know, especially in her heart.

I look across the room, she turns my way and I can feel her passion as she radiates it my way, she always lifts her chin slightly and licks her lips like saying, come kiss me.

I caught up with Mira Rose after dinner, she was smiling today different from the previous day. I walked her to the dorm and I asked, "do you need some time? I can wait for you if we are going to visit and share some time with each other."

She says, "Yes I could use a 10-15 minutes, is that okay?" I said, "sure that is fine, you will find me over there under the trees on the one bench."

When she came down, I stood up and walked to meet her, "shall we just walk around, we can always find a slightly more private place to sit and be together?" She says, "I like that idea we need some quiet time."

We were able to visit several evenings In a row, but she tells me she has to finish some reports in two of her classes and needs the time after dinner, for at least two of the next evenings. I assured her that was fine and just maybe I can use the time on 1-2 of my classes, because I will have to face final testing.

School would be over here on campus, there will be a graduation and then functions, classes and all other day to day schedules will come to an end. It will be interesting as to whom from the students stay for the summer and work as before.

Two evenings later after dinner I was walking away towards my dorm, I did not see Delia any where close by so I figured she had gone on to the girl's dorm for now, would I see her later?

I was walking away I heard my name called out, it was Delia, she motioned to me to wait, so I did.

She caught up with me, saying, "Hi Michael are you okay?" I have something for you, she comes closer, very carefully hands me an envelope, smiles with one of her beautiful smiles and says, "I love you and hope for the best." It completely shocked me that this time she would express such an intimate feeling to me.

I did take the letter to my dorm room, so I would not have it on my person, that would be a terrible mistake in case I am with Mira Rose later on this evening.

After I returned to my dorm room, I gathered up the letter I was given by Delia and I was surprised there were 2+ pages. I sat on my bed and prepared myself to read what that lovely sweetheart of a girl had to say.

Friday night　　　　　　　　　　　　　　　　*page 1*

Hi. Michael Dear

I want to share my feelings and thoughts about the conversation we had day before yesterday, the news that you shared with me. I apologize how I reacted and that I am not being selfish and thinking only of myself when I reacted as I did. I should only feel sad or concerned for you and not myself

The only real feeling I have had all along since that beautiful night we shared, was that I, my affection and caring for you has been sort of in suspension as if frozen in time, but at no fault to no one, especially you, it is almost like I feel a forbidden love for you

It has been of my own doings and I accept the responsibility (not blame) All this time I have considered it a beautiful occurrence; in the last 1 1/2 years; the feelings and experiences that I have never felt before. I have hoped and dreamed that some day you and I could be more than just friends. I admire, adore you and really care for you in a way that goes, say beyond just being friends

I have never ever cared for anyone, especially in these years since I was 14 to now that I am 17 years+ old. I feel so much more grown up being in my frame of mind at my age, I can not help myself how I feel about you. My only hope is that you may also be able to have good feelings for me, later on in the future?? I can only hope so, but who knows

page 2

I will trust in you that what ever happens in your relationship, will it turnout as you might expect or even accept because you have no choice in the final decision that she will make and expect of you?

I will certainly accept whatever the final decision that you yourself decide or not, but I will be here for you with all my heart, my affection, my passion and just someone to talk to, I will not interfere in what takes place between the two of you, as I have no right

I definitely will not say anything or express any knowledge about you, and I will keep my distance from you except when you might contact me, if you write something to me, I will cherish it, but will keep any such contact well hidden from view. A friendly hello, gesture or touch or even a tickle would sure be great !
My heart kind of always skips a beat (as is said when one sees that one special person),   every time I see

you at a distance or up close, no one could ever love you, with all my heart, more than I do, please believe me

When I do see you up close my first reaction is to reach over and put my arms around you and follow it with a kiss, I can dream can't I!, I do dream a lot

For now I am here for you in what ever way or manner you may need me at any moment. If I can get to the phone booth can I call you at your dorm room? I really would love that

I'll be remembering you, will you be remembering me as the days go by? I am really glad that I can at least see you here and there and be brave enough to throw you one or two kisses

Do you think we can work at making each other's dreams come true? It would be a great delight to me

Think of me as you go to sleep, sleep well, I care for you and think of you daily without fail

I care very much
Delia

That was the only verbal and written contact between us for several days and even weekends because there just were no opportunities to be close or even have con-versations between us.

I imagine that she was always looking out to see if I were near by or when all students and staff were in the dining room. I too would casually look around thru the crowds to see if I could catch a glimpse of her and try to reach her.

On Saturday nights, once a month, they would show a movie in the auditorium and all students were encourage to attend, no excuses were allowed; it was a matter of control so no one student could wonder off or get in trouble.

My relationship with Mira Rose was very much the same as in previous times, she is busy with her school work and I am fully occupied day in and day out including some nights as well with preparations for my next day classes.

Every other Wednesday evening at 7:00 pm until 9:00 pm, I am in charge of study hall rooms on 2nd floor. It consists of one or two grade levels. I am supposed to control visiting, talking or any other disruption among students. One particular night it was my turn with the junior classmates.

Everything was reasonably quiet and I was at my desk outside of the classroom, when out of the blue here comes Delia; she was asking for permission to visit the girl's bathroom and get a drink of water. We had a chance to say hello and she quickly reached over and kissed me on the cheek, walks off swinging her hips just to tease me; that's no help at all considering how delicate our situation is now.

We are in the last week of April, just so happens that I and my ROTC candidates are to compete with the Navy ROTC team in a swimming meet at the in-door pool on Friday evening at 7:30 p.m. I mentioned the occasion to Mira Rose and told her I could not visit with her after dinner that day. She did accept the occasion without concern, but did say, I wish that I or others could attend, but it is not a school sport so I guess not a chance.

The following evening after dinner I waited outside for her and she takes my hand and quickly asks, "how was the swimming meet, did you and your team win?" I said, "yes we did, by a slim score, we beat them by one point, not much to brag about, but very good."

I am usually anxious and ready to see and meet with her after our dinners, since it is the only time we have together. This particular time her response to me was sort of off from her usual bubbly and smiling expressive self. I did ask her if something was bothering her; she says back

, "not really I just feel sort of awkward about this one course that I am not quite prepared to turn in a presentation tomorrow. I just do not have it all together.

I said, "would you prefer to not visit tonight and use your time to better prepare yourself?; I am okay if we do not visit tonight?" She looks at me and says, "are you sure?" "of course, "presenting a good report is very important for a good grade, so you take this time to do it right and we will visit tomorrow."

She agreed, I kissed her good night, she waves good-bye and she goes on to do her homework.

I decided to go on to my dorm room and find something productive or interesting to do; although I did not want to be all closed in the room, so maybe I will just wipe off my car and maybe even start a polishing job and only until it starts to get dark.

Chapter 20

Second Semester is Over

The second semester for Mira Rose has ended and she will look forward to summer vacation, for her it is the accomplishment of her 3rd year in High School and the first year at this current school. It will be of interest to hear what her opinion is of the school and its program for this past year and what will the next year be like.

I especially wish to hear if she has been happy being in this type of school program, has it been okay for her, because there is a loss of personal freedom when a student has to realize that there is no going, out, no visiting with parents, no eating out or going to the movies on a regular basis.

Early Friday Evening

There have been students who will leave after one year or so because of the school's restrictions and inability to have more freedom to be out nights and weekends with friends.

The message that Rose shared with Michael, in person, mid Friday left such an impression in his mind that he was doing the best he could to deal with it through the course of the day and he was not looking forward to the next day which was graduation day for all senior, and all classes are expected to attend, but this Saturday will not be important.

Michael did not attend the usual dinner at the 6:00 pm time, instead he chose to sit in the car; he just sat there and was dealing with the very real consequences and after effect from Rose's recent disclosure of what her plans are for later.

Comments she had laid on him without any emotion whatsoever; almost in a matter of fact tomorrow's graduation day, he was sitting on the exterior steps of the auditorium, his head hung low he was just staring at the sidewalk, his mind was blank, he had no feelings of any kind. He had tired himself of sitting in the car.

Just beyond on the path from the dining room Delia and Josie were walking toward the driveway that leads to the girl's dorm, as they had been helping in the kitchen and dining room. Delia looks up and in the direction of the auditorium and sees that Michael is there.

Just sitting on the steps, he did not look right and seemed awkward in his sitting there, she wondered what was wrong. She had not seen him at dinner time and she wondered why. She motioned to Josie, let's go see what is wrong with Michael, *Josie is not aware of the feelings she has for Michael.*

They both walked up to Michael as he sat there, she asks, "sorry Michael to interrupt you, but is there something wrong?" Can we help and are you going to dinner?" He muttered back, "I will probably go to eat at Larry's Drive-in a little later, why?'

At that point Josie says to Delia, "look you stay and talk to him I need to go, see you at the dorm." Delia proceeded to sit next to Michael and said, "please tell me what is wrong, I want to help if I can, and I do not mean to interfere, okay?"

"Thank you Delia, but it is personal and I do not know how to explain it to you, but I will if you really want to know." He started out by saying,

"at noon Rose told me that she needed to talk to me and to meet her under the trees by the dorm. We met and she was sort of cool and to the point, and she said, "I know tomorrow is senior graduation, my parents will be here for the day,

Once it is over I will be leaving with them to Taos and will spend the summer there, I do hope to be able to work at the Saavedra's Drug Store for the summer.

"I have decided to go to college the following year, I hope to enroll that fall at a Colorado University. That may come as a shock to you now, but I wish to be more independent starting now, because I have concerns about us and our relationship in the near future."

"You will be graduating next year and then you will receive your commission and then you will have to go off to active duty; Where will you go?"

"What troubles me is that you will leave and who knows where you will end up and that I may or may not be able to go with you; besides we have not made plans about our immediate future or beyond, have we?"

and I am not sure how I would deal with you being gone." "There is no future for me in Taos and I need to know what I can count on for now." "Please forgive me, as I am unsure of the future." That was her last comment as she walked away.

Michael continued to looks at Delia and says, "well that is all I know and what I was told, so in so may words; I was just dumped and left to figure out what the real issue is or was, so you can now see what kind of a blow I felt after receiving that message."

Delia looks at Michael with a sad and passionate expression on her face, she reaches up and touches his face and says, "I am so sorry to hear the bad news you are dealing with, I can't imagine what you are feeling right now." "If you can let me into your heart I wish to comfort you, be with you and show you my feelings that you can rely on, again, and as I have expressed before, it can be **now or never** for us, please remember that."

"As I have told you before that I have cared very much for you, those feelings I have for you have become deeper and I have yearned for you these last 12+ months, I have never forgotten that very special night that first summer and it will be with me forever."

She then says, "I am not trying to take advantage of you and how bad you feel now, but I wish for you to know that I have much love for you, it has consumed me and kept me alive with the memories and I want to be with you no matter what, but that is up to you. I want to be by your side and show you what I really feel." Will it be **now or never** for us?" "Will my love for you always be forbidden, can I ever express it to its fullest?" Please think of me in that manner, okay?"

Michael says to Delia, "you better hurry if you are going to dinner." She says back, "Now that I know how you feel I do not feel like going I am just going to the dorm, shower get in bed worrying about you." He looks at her and says, "I sure could use some company, what do you say If I take us to dinner, can you slip away and maybe no one will miss you?"

She looks at him with a wide smile on her face and says, "you would like to do that,!, what a great idea?" "let me go shower and get pretty for you, I can be back while everyone is at dinner, no one will know." He say, I need to freshen up myself, If you get back before I do, just wait in the car and stay low, I'll be out soon, okay?"

Michael was back to the car in less than 15 minutes and she came up shortly there after, he let her in the car and said, pull on your skirt so it will not wrinkle, because I am taking you to a really nice place, kind of fancy but you deserve it for all that you have had to endure all this time."

She asks, "where are we going?" he turns around and say, "we are going to the Yacht Club restaurant where we can forget our troubles and talk about you and I, after all we are the most important ones to us, you and I, right?" she nods with a big smile as usual.

Michael and Delia were received in a very gracious manner and it helped them feel very good at the club, they were led to a sort of secluded table for two giving them more privacy then in open seating.

A very attractive waitress arrived quickly, greeted them and asked if they wished to order something to drink; they both called out their choice, but Michael asked if they had wine coolers? She said yes and did they have a choice of flavors? Michael asked Delia her choice and asked for his.

He quickly says, "miss could I ask if the manager would come to our table as I have a quick question"; she says yes; she will have him come to see us.

The manager is there in minutes, introduces himself and asks how he can help us. Michael introduces himself and says, "my girl friend is slightly under 21 years of age and I am curious if she is allowed to drink the wine cooler that I placed an order for. I am not sure what the alcohol content is I do not wish to cause any concern or problem?"

He quickly answers, "thank you for asking, that is very noble of you to be certain, it just so happens that the alcohol content is less than 9% and it will be okay for her to have with her dinner, plus you may wish to add a clear 7UP and that will reduce the drink to mostly a flavored cooler, so that is your choice, but you will be okay." "Enjoy your dinner and it is a pleasure to serve you both."

Delia looks at me with a very big smile and says, "You handled that very well; I appreciate you looking out for me, now we will look more grownup to them."

They had just left the restaurant and she says, "It is a real pleasure to be with you and it will always be a pleasure; I know I may be thinking ahead, but I only say what I feel," and she gives me that look that plays with my mind big time ! They got in the car and left the area and drove to the campus. She says, "do we have to go back in so soon?"

He looks back and say, "I believe there is a story in your eyes that I have been trying to read and to fully understand, but I do believe you are very sincere in what you say and your body language is in tune with all the expressions of passion and affection towards me; which gives me a sense of already being a major part of you, and there is a part of you that I keep inside of me and I cherish all of it with the utmost respect as a secret not shared with anyone and it has stayed with us both, right?"

As he looks at Delia he sees that she has tears in her eyes and seems to be anxious to say what is on her mind. He hesitates because he knows she needs to respond quickly in the spare of the moment. "Are you okay, I need to know?"

"Oh ! Michael I am so happy and thrilled that I have affected you in that manner. I am over delighted that you are seriously wishing more from me as you say; by looking deep into my eyes."

"I do have a story that has been going on for the last 1½ years since we had our very special night, I would like to share those days and nights if you are interested." "Delia, sweetie I would like to know what you went through and what you have endured all this time since our special night and if now is not the proper time, then I can wait until later."

We continued to sit very close to each other and I would kiss her lightly as I cupped her face and studied how she was affected by the extended length of my affection and kisses I placed on her lushes lips. When I did delay another kiss or two she herself would kiss me tenderly with much passion. I did notice and feel she was getting more excited and aroused and suddenly she unbuttons her blouse, she is warn and continues to open her blouse wider, "she takes my hand places it on her breast.

She says, "please caress my breast I need it I am so hot for you, but should we stop now and just wait?" He looked at her, "I really hate to stop, but we are too close to the dorms and someone could see what is going on, so we better wait for now, it is already 9:45 and soon I need to get you to the dorm."

She was so relaxed and so beautiful; mostly sitting up, so I helped her button up her blouse and handed her my comb, she smiles and forms the words out to me, "I love you" I reached over, kissed her lips tenderly and let her comb her hair for now, as we needed to get going. What a night this has been so different from me just sitting on the auditorium cold concrete steps feeling sorry for myself.!

Saturday Graduation Day
11:45 am

I greeted Mira Rose's family when they arrived on campus and visited with them for a short while .I had to wait until Mira Rose came out from the dorm, as she had brought her personal suitcases and other bags down so that they could be loaded into the car's trunk.

Rose looked at Michael in a somewhat sad manner that was neither inviting to him for a close embrace or a semi-distant goodbye. He was unsure how to close the space, so he just reached over and gave her a light hug and said, "have a good trip home and be safe." He then let go and looked again at her parents.

After Michael finished his greeting Rose's parents and was backing away from them, he did wished them a safe trip home, he also turned sideways and looked intensely at Rose, he was not sure how to make a break from her and treat her as if nothing was any different than at other times.

They hugged and stayed close while she talked to her mom and dad about their return trip back home. Now that they were here to pick up Mira Rose for their trip home.

They talked like they might stay the night and go home the following day. They worked that out and said to Rose, "well, we better go and see about a room for the night and then head out tomorrow a.m."

They asked, "can you still stay the night here in the dorm or would it be better that we all go eat later and then stay at a motel and head out tomorrow?" Rose was quick to answer, "we better go and then be ready to leave town in the morning, you see all my stuff is in the extra bags, I am all packed and ready."

Rose said to her parents, "give us a few minutes, I need to visit with Michael before we go." We walked over to the steps of the auditorium to talk. She looks at me as if she is ready to tear up. "I have thought over what I expressed to you about going home for the summer."

"I will not be coming back for my senior year here and that I am going to Colo. Springs to visit with my cousin, she is trying to talk to me about planning to go to college there. There is a lot on my mind right now, so I still think we need a little time for both of us to think about summer and then next school year. okay?"

Again she says, "I hope you will not be upset; we can still talk, maybe visit and see how things are."

I said, "Okay whatever you want, I'll also have thoughts and will wait and see what goes." I walked her back to her parent's car, I again wished them goodbye and gave Rose a pat on the shoulder and turned around and walked away towards my dorm.

Rose just stood there, and as he walked off, she looked sideways from where she stood; he walked away, never looked back; all of a sudden thinking to herself; what have I done and how did I really present my response to him yesterday at noon. She also felt a sense of remorse and guilt.

will I ever see him again or will I ever talk to him again !! what have I done to our relationship and will I regret the outcome, am I that self centered or detached from the real truth and what have I grown into that I can just throw it all away without regards for his feelings?

Rose realized it was all over and she may have hurt the one person in her life that had real meaning, and that her love for him had been genuine, until now? and there is no doubt that his love for her had always been sincere, so what went wrong? She may never know, and who's fault is it? Will they ever know, sooner or later?

He had walked away and never looked back!

Those Were My Days?

Are those days long gone forever?

Miranda Rose Ledoux

I had found a love I have never known before and I did
wish to share my love with you and I was just Like you
and lonely too?

I looked into eyes and they sparkled and there were
slight tears starting to show, but her smile gave her
away, seems they were tears of joy

Chapter 21

Part One

Those Were the Days

Epilogue

In some circles it has been considered that there may be two significant episodes that initiate a phase in life and at some point during the extension of that first phase in life, that there will be a second and final episode in life that has evolved from the first.

It is known or suspected that the final episode in life has more meaning more rewards and carries a more than satisfying peace of mind, of which the result is that what was learned and experienced in the first, now contributes to the wellness and satisfaction in the second episode of life.

This story transcends into a second and final episode in the life of Michael who still holds on to the same values and beliefs of a young man with his own set of dreams and desires for a life of many accomplishments. The satisfaction in love holds primary and foremost value because it contributes the most peace of mind, wellness and endurance to the life of two persons totally engaged in its existence

In the final episode the readers will have first hand knowledge of how this love story transcends to the second level in a similar but different manner with a new loving, giving and passionate young woman, which was hardly expected. On behalf of the young school girl who for at least 1½ years; with her caring, devotion and desires that she said were well managed and directed to only one person who meant to whole world to her and how she craved to be a real partner in that persons' life, forever if possible and how she managed to endured the unknown of how her feelings would survive in the future for the one person for whom her love seemed that, little by little, it became more intense and open.

The readers shall be aware that the content and context of the initial experiences of both parties to the episode may be very explicit and very sexual in a manner that opens up the whole relationship. It does go back in time to a period approximately 18½ months, with the consequences that she initiates and then she evolves into a mature young woman who is bound and determined she has discovered who her soul mate will be in her future.

The initiation and aspirations of Delia, the girl in the center of the episode, has no further opportunity to be a part of a relationship, but has to accept the fact that Michael is not available for a relationship as he is already in a commitment and she has to live with the consequences of their initial highly intimate affair.

She understood clearly, as he explained, that her initiation of her feelings and her wishing to be his girl friend were not possible at the time. She was willing to accept the fact that they could be close friends with little or no contact in the realm of the close knit school campus.

Delia was disappointed but not broken hearted and delegated herself to what had been agreed upon. She still kept her hopes alive, never giving up the possibility if there was a change in the future. *She feels it was now or never, did not wish to be unsure about the future and be destined to go on with a broken heart!!*

She was not going to give up, if luck or fate should have a hand in the end result, she was not going to cross the line from being a friend to being a girl friend for the love of her current love object. Michael does not know what he is missing and what would be in store for him, God help them both if it does come to be a relationship, neither one can hardly imagine.

PART TWO

It's Now or Never? *

A Story of Forbidden Love

The on-going love triangle story that has suddenly taken a negative turn, was only known as a friendship between Michael and Delia, and Rose was not even aware that there was someone else accidentally on the sidelines of her and Michael's relationship

The readers shall determine the unknown unpredictable consequences as the story unfolds in another dimension with the unpredictable coming together of Michael and a lover who had been on the sidelines during the ongoing relationship with Mira Rose, that lover was undeniably a breath of fresh air,

Delia is her name, a beauty that knows what she wants and wastes no time in exploring and placing herself where Michael could not run from himself as there was no place to hide; did he really want to run and hide; as a reader, that is a question to ponder, the undeniable truth is he is about to face not what he has totally imagined or would be expecting in the unpredictable days and many months ahead.

- This was the expression that Delia has shared with me in our previous conversations that has been deep in my mind, what does ***never*** mean?

Be prepared for an emotional coaster ride
through the lives of each and everyone in
this three-way love story !!

It is time to look back 18+ months, may you not be shocked but enlightened as to the clarity and explicitness of the past and very intimate sexual experience between the two persons who are not even involved romantically or were they?

She is so wrapped up emotionally in Michael that taking it beyond just a date is just what came naturally for both, and for her it was a beautiful and everlasting personal intimate experience.

Be fair to the author as it came naturally for him to explore beyond the limits what this couple dared to exceed in simple but honest expressions of love on her part and the intimacy that he dared to exceed in order to satisfy her needs.

If it offends you the reader, please feel you have the right to overlook and go on with the story as the persons continue to explore their potential future relationship.

****

The evening was no different than other days after having the meal of the day. Neither one had the expectations that this evening's outcome would be such a departure from other evenings.

Michael had just walked out of the dinning room when Delia walked up to him and said, "walk me to the dorm, I want to ask you something." he said "okay" and they proceeded to walk and chat and she shared something he did not expect. Michael does not say anything for the moment, but listens closely to what she has to say.

She says, "I like your car do you not go places after dinner or later on before it gets dark?" He looks at her and responds, "very rarely only if I need to go buy some items I need, why?"

She gives him that sly sexy look and boldly says, "take me for a ride tonight?" I dare you to do that, are you brave?" He says, "How can we manage that?" she says, "the house mother is out for the evening and we are on our own with no supervision and no one is keeping track of what we do."

I say to that, "we could go for a ride, but lets wait till it is almost dark. My car is parked beyond the Admin Bldg. You know where. Do you want to walk there and meet me say at after 7:30?"

She had a big smile on her face and she quickly said, "yes yes I will come meet you there, be waiting." I let her go and she went into the porch and I left for my dorm. I brushed my teeth, put on some aftershave and change my shirt; I do not know why.

I was sitting in the dark with the car facing the direction I would drive out, I had the car window open, I heard her say softly, *"I am here"* "I said, come around to the other side, and I reach over and opened the door for her.

She let herself in, "I am ready, but wait," she reaches over to me puts her right hand around my face and gives me a very passionate kiss, one I could not resist and was not expecting, Wow !

I started the car and pulled out slow without the car lights on, I waited until I got to the front gate and then turned them on to go onto the main street. Meanwhile she is clinging to me holding me tight and says, "I am so thrilled we could go out together like this, where can we go?"

I said, "sweetie there is a road on the other side of the property beyond the boys dorm we can go and park there and visit if you wish." She says, "good I do not wish to go anywhere in particular, I just want to be with you, now !"

I drove beyond the north property limits of the campus and parked near some trees, turned off the engine and locked our doors except for rolling down the windows for fresh air.

I turned to her and said, "is this okay? she says, "if it is okay with you." I had my arm around her on the back rest and, so she just leaned into me and was ready to be kissed. I had just enough time to kiss her and we kept on kissing.

She moved in closer and was running her hands around my body and I could not help but do the same. I had my right hand around her shoulder and it slipped down and it ended over her right breast and I could not help but massage her breast and she started to sigh and get more excited.

She reached up from her arm position around me and started unbuttoning her blouse and moved her bra away from over her breast, she took my hand and placed it directly over her breast.

I continued to caress and then I bent down and cupped her breast and put my mouth over her nipple and sucked it tenderly but steady. At that one point she was very excited, moaning and her body was vigorously gyrating against me.

I reached down and started to caress her just above her crotch and she liked that, so I unzipped her shorts and move my hand inside her panties and started to stroke her, she was soft and bushy and then I moved two of my fingers down and entered her vagina and I was so excited to feel that she was so wet and I started to finger her colitis and she became totally aroused and said,

"let me take my shorts off, She took them off and turned to me, then she said, I am so hot for you I want you and I want you bad and I want you inside me, now,! should I take my panties off?" " If you wish, I said, yes."

She said "I have never done this before, but I think I know what to do." I reach over and unzipped my pants and pulled out my penis; believe me, I was totally erect, she saw it and put her hand on my penis and started to stroke it . She said," I want to lie down," so I mover her body so her head would be in the driver side and she slipped off her panties and put them on the back seat.

I spread her legs and asked her, "sweetie are you ready for me, she said, "yes yes very much so, I said "but first I want to give you the best treat you have ever had, I am going to taste and lick and suck you first and get you totally excited. and further aroused."

She pulled my head down to her bushy labia and I proceeded to nudge her pubic hairs around and then spread her vagina lips and touched her colitis with my tongue and then with my lips,

She was so excited she move up and down and sideways and made noises as she was experiencing ultimate excitement. That went on for many minutes and then she relaxed and her movements subsided and she says, "that was out of this world, I felt an eruption inside of me."

I had already reached in my back pocket and pulled out a condom package so that when I was ready I slipped on the condom and knelt down over her I asked her," sweetie are you ready for me to go inside of you?" "I will go slow , be tender let you enjoy what you are going to experience, okay?"

She says back, "I am ready, I want to experience you and what you are about to do. I placed my penis just on the outside of her vagina and moved it up and down and in and out slowly, each time going in a bit further, because I wanted to see how she was going to react; she started to react in a very excited way and then moaning and moving her hips up and down; I told her to move towards me when I went in further, so that she could get a better feeling inside.

With those movements and with her excitement and my pushing in and pulling out, that added more to the inner feelings she must be having, because she showed it by moving in and out with me. I was very worked up with the vigorous thrusts of my penis, I was getting to the point that I would let loose all that I had, for her.

I point blank asked her, Can you feel another "out of this world" feeling inside?" She said, "yes I will be ready very very soon, help me reach that great feeling inside of me.

Within a few more strokes as I talked and persuaded her, she all of a sudden lets out the most sensual outcry that I have ever heard.

I comforted her, kissed gently on her lips and kept on kissing her until she calmed down, she looked at me and said, "that was beautiful Michael I seemed to be in 7th heaven as some say" I never knew the first time could be so beautiful and satisfying and I love you for it. We hugged and kissed and she was all smiles. I could not see her eyes clearly in the dimness of the car's interior, but I know they sparkled with joy and delight for this experience of a life time.

At this point she had removed her blouse and bra and that was quite a sight, her breasts were very round, full and firm and I gathered them both to the middle of her chest; what a beautiful sight I kissed them, played with the nipples and just caressed them gently and she seemed to be enjoying that.

I caressed her, hugged her, spoke softly to her and I made sure she was okay and satisfied, I asked her, "how do you feel now was it good for you?" her response was exuberant with happiness. "I have never ever experience such pleasure and I am happy it happened with you, you were wonderful.

I helped her get dressed, but first I took 2- napkins and cleaned and wiped her vagina very carefully so that she could be dry and clean, then I asked how did that feel?

She said, "you can keep doing that all night, it feels really good." we slipped on her panties, her bra and blouse and then she sat up and we put on her shorts.

She had to look in the mirror to see the condition of her hair and face; she looks lovely and radiant like never before. She combed her hair and put on a thin layer of lipstick, which she had in her shorts pocket; she was prepared for it. I massaged her over her shorts and she just could not sit still.

At that point she still was not ready to go, she reached over to my semi-erect penis and stroked it and soon enough I was erect again. She looks at me and says, Wow, I want it, can I have it?" "I do not know, you tell me." I said, " you kiss it and then put it in your mouth a little at a time and all of it, then you go suck it up and down and feel it in your mouth."

She went thru the motions and it felt good for the first time for me and first time for her, so we decide to quit for the time being, we needed to get going.

I asked, "are we ready to go, where else do we want to go", she looks at me and says, "you got to be kidding me, "I suppose we need to get me back to the campus and hope I can slip in quietly and since I do not have a roommate it should be easy for me, hopefully." She reaches over and kisses me lightly and gives me that look she is very good at.

I drive off, make a U-turn beyond and head back to the main street; we are only a few blocks away, so it is not far; we reach my parking spot, quietly without talking we leave the car and I walk with her in the shadows of the building and the trees towards the girls dorm, she kisses me goodnight and walks away quietly and I wait till I see her enter the porch and into the dorm.

That 2nd showing of affection and then intimate sexual experience was the highlight for us, 18½ months ago but never forgotten by either one of us.

Will there be another time for us to show our affection in the form of real devoted love for each other? That will come with time as how a new relationship may by chance develop and if it is serious.

Only time will really tell, can this out of the ordinary love interest survive the near and far future?

Only Time Will Tell

Chapter 22

Saturday mid-Afternoon

2:30 p.m.

Michael is in his dorm room, he was just trying to deal with the emotional setback that he had just experienced late this morning before lunch time. He is here sitting on his bed having decided to skip lunch in the dining room.

He is dealing with the turmoil in his mind of having to say goodbye to Mira Rose after she had given him her own decisions about the summer away from school and how she implied that he would not be part of her summer.

The phone rings, he wonders who that could be, certainly not Rose, but he answers and hears a voice he knows; Delia is calling. He says hello, what is going on?" "Michael can you talk?"   "Yes I can."

"The reason I am calling, I am at the phone booth, and that my parents have arrived from home and are here to take me back with them. I am having a real problem with that, but first, are you in a mood to meet them, as we are parked close to your car where it is less public from the girl's dorm?"

I answer, "I guess so I have nothing else to do, just sitting here as I skipped lunch for now. "you know I will always talk to you, you are very precious to me."

"I will walk out to the cars in a couple of minutes." As I was near my car both the dad and mom got out of their car when I approached them. Delia rushes over to me and throws her arms around my neck and kisses me on the cheek, she seemed very glad to see me.

Her parents were smiling and were ready to be greeted by me; her mom says "Hi Michael we really wanted to meet you since we have heard so much about you from Delia." We greeted, I said, "I am very pleased to meet you both as I as well have heard much about you both. You have a very beautiful daughter whom I admire and cherish her friendship."

Delia could not stand still, she hugs me around the waist with a broad smile; says "thank you for that." Her mom says, "thank you for your compliment and her dad and I think she is special, but lately she has, you could say, been acting different and very concerned about you." "We appreciate how you look out for her and talk to her and advise her."

Her dad speaks up and says, "we are here to pick her up for the trip home and her summer vacation from school": he looks to the mom and then Delia, as if looking for some help in what else to say to carry on the conversation.

Delia looks at her mom and says, "do you need to go visit the bathroom and gives her that look that they need to talk, now ! . they go into the Admin. Building, Her dad and I just look at each other he starts a conversation, wants to know about my university courses and when I am done for the year.

In about 10+ minutes Delia and her mom come out and approach us, it is obvious they did some serious talking, so we waited to see what they have to say. Her mom starts out and directs herself to her husband, "Delia has two issues she expressed to me, one, she feels that she needs to spend some time here with Michael; they have much to talk about, but then our trip to pick her up is wasted." "If she were to stay how or when would she go home?"

"Her second point is, if we leave, she will not be able to see him for how long? we do not know that." "Michael still has one more week of school and then he is done for the school year."

Delia interrupts us all and says, "mom I have cared and adored Michael for the last 18+ months; in fact I do love him; she looks at her parents who seem somewhat surprised at her sudden announcement; right now he needs me to stand by him after what he has been through lately."

Neither one of her parents were able to speak to what they had just heard from Delia, they were, I believe, caught totally by surprise and were even bewildered.

In a few moments they gained their composure, smiled and her mom said, "well now that we know for sure what Delia means, Michael can we hear what your feelings are about her, I hope I am not out of turn to ask that of you?"

Michael speaks up, as he holds Delia close to him, "I appreciate what her one concern is, you should not be disappointed in going home without her and I do appreciate that she wants to stay to visit with me. I suggest this; Delia should go home with you and that I promise to come to Las Vegas to visit her next Friday for a few days. That allows me to give my full attention to my last week at the university and by next Friday noon I should be completely done."

Both her parents look at each other in agreement and her mom says, "That is a wonderful idea, but for sure Delia may not fully agree; what do you think Delia?"

Meanwhile Delia is fully embracing me and looks a little sad and tearing. She says to me, "I understand that you do need next week to finish off the year, I will miss you for a few days. I am happy that you will come up for a few days and it gives me time to get used to my home and the town again."

Deli directs her attention to her parents and says, "Can you stay here in town and not leave until tomorrow? Let me suggest; you should go out to dinner, go to the movies get a motel for the night and call it a date night for you two."

"Michael and I can have dinner here at school, visit the rest of the evening before bedtime. I still have my room at the dorm and he has his. We'll have breakfast together and you can come by when you are ready, I will be ready since I am mostly packed."

Her parents look at each other with a smile in agreement probably thinking we can be alone tonight! They both said in unison, "we will do that, but do you not wish to join us for dinner?" Delia say, "no you enjoy your time alone, Michael and I will be okay here for the rest of the day and evening."

Michael thinks, by now, we are getting tired of standing around, so Delia tells them, "go get a room freshen up and enjoy a good dinner, okay?" She looks at me with that wicked little smile she is so good at, she always does get my attention.

Michael and Delia walk off towards the girl's dorm, hand in hand and acting normal, after all there is no concern as to who sees them. They are about to enter a new episode and a new adventure in their own lives and it appears that it was meant to be.

Delia turns to Michael and says, "I am so delighted and thrilled that each of our lives has come around to just what I have been dreaming about and thinking about every single day for so long."

There is no one in sight or in the area, so they stop in the shade of a large tree and stand at the tree on the opposite side of view from the dorm doors. Michael holds her around her waist and she puts both arms around his neck and they embrace tightly and they enjoy the best kiss possible, better than last night after their dinner date away from the campus.

Delia seemed content for now, but was she all that satisfied? I was willing to wait too; the rest of the evening will bring on more intimate expressions from us both; I guess we have been waiting for this time to come. It is 4:30 dinner will be, I guess, at 6:00 pm.

Delia says, "I would like to have time to rest for a while and then shower and dress for dinner and for you. I want to be especially pretty for you and am looking towards a second night together, how great is that."

Michael says, "It is a good idea, today has been different then most Saturdays and with some stress, probably just for me, because of the turn and change of events that was totally out of my control, but it is now over and you and I can start a new chapter." She cupped my face and gave me a nice wet kiss.

I walked over to the girl's dorm about 5:55 to wait for Delia to come out the porch doorway; in just a minute or so she comes out; Wow she was nicely dressed, looked radiant and was smiling for me as she would normally. She reached her hand out to me and I squeezed it gently and we walked off. When we walked into the dining room there were some people there waiting; I guess we raised some eyebrows as we walked in as a couple, unexpected?"

We both greeted different persons or students as we sought a place at any table that had vacancies. We decided to sit at the university table, they were my fellow students at the university. I introduced Delia to them in case she was not familiar to them; it went well no questions were asked and we were free to sit and wait for dinner to be served.

After dinner we all left for our intended events? since it was Saturday I am sure most of them had no real purpose or intensions for the evening ahead.

Delia quickly reaches for my hand, gives me a very warm smile; it is her form of affection without touching, and asked, "my dear Michael what have you planned for our evening?"

I gave her my best smile and squeezed her hand and said, "Honey we can stay here or we can go to a movie; you know we have never been to a movie on our own to be alone?" She quickly says, "that is great and we do not have to ask permission from any one and stay out late if we wish." I am so thrilled and happy I just can not believe how it is now so different for the two of us today, of all days."

I said to her, "honey you are so beautiful and you look gorgeous tonight I truly adore you and want you with me; always by my side as possible." While under a tree she reaches up and kisses me and then hugs me with all her might, then gently, at least for now.

She said she needed to go up stairs for a few minutes and would return soon. I said I would go to my dorm for a few minutes too and would drive the car up close by and wait there.

We all of a sudden realized that her parents may be out there at the movies, is it wise for us to be out there too?" I suggested we just go out and have an ice cream sundae and then return here and find a place to park and visit tonight.

From the A&W Drive-In, I drove us to the campus and parked where I normally park beyond the Admin. Building, very secluded and quiet at that time of night. After arriving we both took a stretch and got comfortable, I took my arm and placed it on the seat and around her shoulder. She moved over close and looked up at me with those bright brown eyes.

I then reached up to her face, took her face in my hands, kissed her eyes, her nose and then laid a very gentle kiss on her slightly wet lips, we held that kiss for many seconds, she pulled back and said, "I am so delighted to be with you and you take my breath away, especially when I kiss you."

"Delia, sweetie the time has come for us to tell each other what we want from a relationship from now and into the future. There is much that I wish to ask of you and I in turn would also like to share more than I have shared until now, considering that I did not know where I stood with someone else, but as we both know that is going to be from the past."

I know that you have expressed your most personal feelings for me and I have been very impressed that you would do so being that we were not together. Can you say for certain that what you feel is truly from the heart or; this is tough to ask, have you been or just "infatuated" with me as a person or have what is known as a "crush" for me, to feel you can say you love me?"

"One more thought is; were you having those feelings because I was not available to you as you had asked if we could be boy/girl friends?" "forgive me for asking.

"I have become so impressed with you over the last 18+ months and today, that I am becoming more and more sure of my wanting to be with you, I can see how I need to be affectionate, caring and treating you as you deserve to be treated; since I have known you, I have grown more and more interested in you as a person, frankly I love the attention you've given me, I wish to give you that same attention."

She reaches up to me, places her finger over my lips and says, "Michael, I think I can understand why you are asking those questions of me, is it because you really wish to know what I am really feeling deep inside me?" "I know that a relationship you had was not what it may have seemed, and you are concerned about being in another one so soon after what you learned in the last few days."

"I feel I have really grown up in the last year and half, I've made sure that I did not depend on anything that could never happen, I was willing to accept and be disappointed if there was never to be a closeness and a relationship between us."

I stepped in and said, "Delia sweetie it is my own understanding that there are reasons why one can love someone. It can be you like, you trust, that person treats you with respect and does not mistreat or abuse you. You also need to have things in common which there are many to consider at this point in time." "It is best when you are loved back and in that manner two persons can share a bond."

Chapter 23

"Delia, may I ask? How do you want me to love you and care for you In return for all you have shared with me; all those wonderful deep feelings?" Will you base how you wish to be loved on how you have come to love me? you have been very clear of why and how."

I also said, "believe me I am searching for a simple interpretation, what you as my girlfriend wishes to receive back in return for how you shared with me your affection, feelings, and devotion during the time since we first met."

She says back to me, "I am anxious to experience, in return, now that we both seem to be free to be together, how you will respond to my affection and closeness . I know you can be tender and affectionate, express yourself by how you hold me, caress me and look at me with such warmth and it seems that you are saying a lot in a very quiet way."

"From the way we have shared ourselves lately, I know I can trust you and I believe all that you share with me; I do feel there are issues or feelings that you may hold back for now and I do hope it is only for now and that some day soon you will share them so we can have a happy understanding."

I looked into her eyes for a moment and cuddled her face in my hands kissed her eyes and then her tender lips and held that kiss for what seemed like a minute or so. I pulled back and said to her, "Delia, now that I have found you, let me love you in the best way that I can, so be my partner."

"I want us to be together from now on and no one will be able to tear us apart, no one.! I know that I have just come out of a situation, but I am prepared to be completely separated from it and I hope you can trust me to be done; it is in the past, okay?"

She comes back at me; "Oh ! I am delighted you have shared with me and want me to be with you from now on; I love you dearly, I am truly yours now."

"I know that we still have the rest of the summer and then the full school year; not only you but me in order to complete my 4-years of courses and the ROTC program and then an unknown future ahead."

"You are still looking forward to your senior year at the school in order to graduate, at that time in the future you will be mostly free to decide your near and far future." "What have you seriously thought of so far at this point?" "As for me, I will have my next 4 years after graduation planned for me and I will have no choice in the matter."

"If we stay together after our own graduations, I sincerely know we could have a very bright, exciting and fulfilling future together, but we would have to work on it and think about it, starting now."

"I would not want to think that we would invest our time, energy and passion and then, you for example could decide otherwise and kiss me goodbye and want to have other experiences beyond that time."

Delia's eyes lit up and there was an expression of shock on her face that I had never seen or even imagined that I would see. She quickly recovers and her face takes on a different look and her eyes begin to tear and she sobbed a few emotional cries before she was able to respond to my serious comments.

"Oh ! Michael, I feel really sad that you would be unsure of my feelings and devotion for you and that I might possibly throw away all this and future great times and days and do like someone else did to you." I know I seem young to you and that I could change my mind any time I would wish to. I assume that all young persons who are nearing adulthood would and could change their moods, ideas and objectives and mind about their future after they have graduated."

I pulled her to me, hugged her lightly and kissed her on the lips and said, "sweetie I did not mean to upset you but to share thoughts that I have been tossing around in my own mind as to what the future brings from now on, I am beginning to love you and care for you more and more as we have become closer and more accustomed to each other."

"I do not want to take away future opportunities to be with friends and parents and miss out on having good times by going out to movies, dances and other ways of having a crazy time all us young persons wish for. You certainly deserve those experiences."

"What you need to realize that once I graduate and have to go into the Air Force active duty, it will be more of an adult situation, but we can have our own separate life and go dancing, go to movies and have our own crazy times, because we will make friends with other persons, after all we will still be young for as long as we wish."

Delia answers back, "I am so glad and happy that you have shared those feelings and questions, so what does our future look like?" I have, as you say, tossed around many ideas and personal wishes for my own dreams and expectations for a real relationship, with you my dreams can come true, because I am ready and have an open heart and I am fully prepared to be with you from now on."

"Please give me the opportunity to further prove myself to you during the next 18-20 months as we continue our schooling requirements and we can then face our future as a couple. I am fully devoted to be with you during that period of time and I will be so happy and thrilled to know that we can see, talk and show our affection from day to day."

She shares further thoughts, "I am so sure about my love, devotion and passion for you that I will work on keeping us both happy. I know that you have been through several days of some form of stress and maybe you are not too sure if any form of a new relationship is what you really are prepared for."

"Michael, let us take our time and I promise I will help you through any rough days ahead, as I plan on being here for you from now on. It will be somewhat difficult since you will be in the city and I will be here, but we will find a way, okay?"

I looked at her beautiful brown eyes, reached over and kissed her gently and held her tight as she had already wrapped her arms around my neck. I moved back just enough to be able to see that she had tiny tears in her eyes. I asked, "are you okay, why are you tearing?" She smiles broadly and says, "my dear Michael they are tears of joy.

I cupped her face again and said, "are you ready to be my sweetheart at this point in time, I do need you at this time and do accept your understanding and patience for us to see better times."

She quickly says, "Oh I am so pleased you wish me to be your sweetheart. I am so delighted and thrilled to hear you ask me, yes, yes I am ready."

"I wish to say that I can visualize a bright, positive and successful future for us, especially after we are both graduated. There is a whole new world out there that we can experience and we can create our own destiny." "I am preparing myself for at least four years of active duty as an Air Force officer and you with me will make it even more rewarding."

She quickly responds to me, "You asked how I wish for you to love me; again, I wish for your continued tender attention, your affection and mostly I really care for how you treat me like your equal and that you are so considerate of my feelings."

"For the last 18 months you have treated me like you really believe in me, did not reject any of my attentions and when I expressed how I cared for you, it appeared that you really believed me and were very kind in your responses to me, personally, I guess that is why I kept up my hopes and continued to care for you and tell you how I still feel."

"I think that we were destined to be together and someone up high let it happen only because I had the faith and patience, I endured the wait and when you were dealt consequences that you did not expect there was some hope."

"Our relationship should grow and we should thrive on what we both will bring to it over periods of time as we look to each other for support, affection and personal help in our daily issues." "Our daily contact will be limited to evening visits after dinner and then on the weekends based on entertainment and church functions." "We should keep our spirits as high as possible and stress minimum."

"I believe sweetie that I should get you over to the dorm, because it is already 9:45 and I do not know how long they keep the doors unlocked up front, so let me drive over there to make sure you can get in."

"We were successful and she was able to walk into the front doorway, as it was still unlocked. Delia mentioned the following morning that the house mother was up and met her in the hallway and she said nothing but goodnight and see you tomorrow.

Next day Michael was up early, showered, shaved and dressed In clean clothes and it was time to walk over to the dining room for breakfast; he glanced towards the girl's dorm but did not immediately see Delia, so he kept going.

He had just been sitting for a few minutes when she did walk in the entrance doorway and was looking for him as well. He stood up and waved at her and she smiled and was headed towards the table where he was.

Michael says to her, "good morning are you ready for some breakfast this early?" She says, I sure am, for some reason I am hungrier than normal then very shyly she says, "I wonder why?? and gave me one of her sly looks and licked her lips, I hope no one was looking at that moment. Michael then helped her with her chair, she sat down and he took a seat at the head of the table, then he says, " you see I am the "big shot here" or so I think, anyway we greeted the few others that were at this same table.

One of her friends did ask her, "You are still here, are you going home for the summer?" She quickly answers, "In fact I am, my parents are picking me up later this morning, they were delayed yesterday and were not able to be here."

I noticed that we both ate with much vigor, as I too was hungry after last night's heavy duty discussions about our future. It was very productive and we accomplished a lot, which I did not expect to happen so soon.

After breakfast we both walked out in close but separate distance, as we proceeded to the girl's dorm where Delia needed to finish up her packing and to wait for her parents to arrive.

I left her at the front door and turned around and headed for my dorm room; make my bed refresh myself and wait, because her parents were to arrive around 10:00 am or so.

Personally and quietly I was tossing thoughts through my mind about the fact that very soon this morning within an hour plus Delia would get into the back seat of her parents car, wish me goodbye and they would ride off to their home and I would be left here to deal with the loneliness of being alone, the separation and missing her after the last few days of being together; how am I going to handle it ??

Delia has been my saving angel; Her closeness, her affection, declared devotion and expressions of commitment has given me the strength to put aside the results of the bad news and sadness that I had been shared with me and not expected at all. I just need to get over it, as I know there will be better days ahead. With help of a most wonderful loving and caring Delia, in fact I feel rather blessed to have her.

Her parent's car was just pulling up near the girl's dorm, parked in the shade of one of the large trees. I quickened my pace to meet them again and see if I could be of help with Delia's luggage as she would be leaving the dorm porch.

Her dad saw me as he turned around to open the car's trunk; he looked up, smiled and waved hello. I said hello and approached him and greeted him with a hand shake. We turned to look as Delia called out to us that she had her luggage ready inside the porch. I rushed towards her, she hugged me and said, thanks for coming, I love you for it. We carried all her luggage to the car and I put them in the trunk.

Her mom left the car on the right side and came around to greet me and Delia, but I reached her, gave her a kiss on the cheek and hugged her close.

We all looked at each other not knowing who was to speak first, so I quickly said, "did you enjoy your evening and rest?; you sure deserved it after your trip here yesterday." "Well it looks like the time is here for Delia and yourselves to head home and I do wish you have a safe trip."

"Oh ! Delia will you call me later after you have arrived home to tell me you arrived safely; I will be waiting and then we can talk for a few minutes?"

Her mom said, "thank you for taking care of her since yesterday hope you two had a good visit and we sure hate to take her home. Will you still plan on coming up to see us this next Friday?" :Listen we will give you two a few minutes to visit and say goodbye."

Delia looked at me and she already had tears in her eyes and her expression was; "I do not want to go, she says to me, "I need to stay and be with you, I know you need me now; how else can I say it as she threw her arms around my neck and kissed me hard and then started to cry openly and then said, "I feel like I am deserting you and I feel very sad."

I could not help but feel rather concerned that she was leaving and I was to be left behind. So I said, "Do not worry I will be okay you will call later and we will reconnect and share further feelings, as there is no time at this moment. Be safe and do not distract your dad while he is driving okay?"

I kissed her again, open the car door for her, wished them all a safe trip again; she looked at me and there were still tears in her eyes and she squeezed my hand and it seemed she could not let go.

As they drove away she appeared at the car's rear window and was waving vigorously and I waved back as the car disappeared towards the main gate. Moments later I felt a sadness like no other sadness, I had never felt this way that I can remember, not since someone left town without notice.

it was consuming me with despair and some disconnect within myself and I was now very lonely. I look towards the girl's dorm and then to my dorm I was unable to move.

I suddenly felt all alone and detached from my normal surroundings and could not let go of the anxiety I was feeling; like where do I go from here? Do I just go to my dorm room and sit there in a chair in the corner of my room? I did turn towards my dorm and walked slowly, passed my car and stepped up on to the entrance porch and went to my room.

So much has happened since last Friday thru early today; much more than I had even imagined would take place in my past relationship to the new and current personal and intimate sharing with Delia and my meeting of her parents.

I just laid there on my bed, flat on my back my arms and hands folded in my lap and just staring at the ceiling running all the facts through my mind and digesting everything over and over as I could best recall all the important and less important issues.

Chapter 24

I looked over at the clock and saw that it was about 5 minutes till lunch; on Sunday they usually have a very good meal and dessert, because it is the meal of the day, there is no evening meal, just a brown bag with a lunch type of goodies. So I wondered over to the dinning room and took a seat at my normal table with my fellow university mates.

Two of Delia's girl friends caught sight of me and after the meal approached me and asked about Delia, I told them, "her parents came for her and they left for Las Vegas around 11:00 this morning,

I told them you and your parents would be home soon. They looked at me with a look that was wondering what was going on with the two of us, but I did not care to share any of our very personal relationship secrets.

I went back to the dorm, to my room, and sat there sort of waiting in case Delia would call after they arrived. I am sure she would be anxious to call as soon as possible. I had not been there more than 5 minutes when the phone did ring; I answered it quickly and sure enough it was Delia.

She says quickly, "Hi my darling we arrived 10 minutes ago, unloaded my stuff and here I am so anxious to talk to you. How are you, please tell me you are okay, I guess." "Me, I am a wreck, I will tell you what my parents had to put up with on the way home."

I managed, "Sweetheart, I am a mixed up soul now that you ask; as you left and were waving at me and the car disappeared towards the gate, I all of a sudden experienced a sadness I had never felt before and felt so alone and lonely. I want to say to you that I then was convincing myself that I do love you and the effect I felt was because now I know why I felt that way when you rode away; was I going to see you again?" I am so glad you got home safe."

She could not wait to say to me, "Honey I too felt a strange sense of sadness and felt that I had deserted you by leaving and I was crying real tears in that back seat. My mom was looking at me and asking me; are you okay, I know how you must be feeling and I understand why. You have developed an extreme emotional connection with Michael."

Mom says, "what can I do or say to help you feel better until we get home so that you can call him to fill that void.?" "I finally settled down and I believe I may have dozed off for a while, when shortly Dad left the interstate and onto the ramp leading into town."

"We managed to get home okay finally !, I just could not wait any longer to talk to you." "Michael I really did try not to distract my dad who needed to keep his eyes on the road and I am sure he appreciated that, so my mom wanted to know if she should get in the back seat with me, I said no."

All the way home, off and on, I cried and told mom that I did not expect I would be so emotional. My concern was that now you would be all alone."

"I am really missing you It is really strange to believe that we have only been together for nearly 3 days and here I am so thrilled and delighted but oh so anxious to see you again. I can hardly believe that after all of the 18 months and the yearning, waiting and dreaming to see how time would tell us what would be our destiny, good or not, good I had hoped."

"I think I will have not only a restless night but also a sleepless one just trying to get used to my bed again and only wishing that you were here with me." "I am here talking to you about how I would give myself to you with all my heart and just like before. Oh ! I have something happening, I felt a surge of wetness down below and I do not know what to say."

"Please forgive me for being and feeling this way, I just can not help it, please understand." "Delia I do understand and I am equally pleased that we are now together and I can hardly wait until Friday when I will come to see you and be with you and family."

"Honey I am so sad to hear the feelings you had this morning as we left and were out of sight. I was very upset and sad that I had to leave and leave you behind. I had not expected to feel so bad, otherwise I might have told my parents I wanted to stay but I am sure they would not have wished to hear that.

I gathered my thoughts and quickly needed to tell her that I will leave here about 3:00 pm and should be there at approx. 5:15 to 5:30. When we talk again tomorrow will you give me your address and now I need your home phone number so I can call you tomorrow night. Can I call you; after dinner?"

I said to her, "I hate to let you go, but I was thinking earlier that it is so quiet and dead here and the mood that I am in is not helping matters.

"I think I will go into town and see one or two movies just so that I do not have to be here in the dorm all alone, I do not know if I can handle it today."

"Honey that is a good idea, at least the movies will distract you from how you are feeling today. Please try to be feeling better by this evening, okay? I miss you terribly and care for how you are doing."

I did see two movies one right after another and when I left the theater I decided I needed to find a place to have dinner before I head back to the dorm, maybe just maybe I can go watch T.V. at the girl's dorm, as it is allowed until the usual bedtime hour.

I managed to get back to being somewhat normal after watching T.V. with some of the students who were there for the summer and so I marched myself back to my dorm. It was approx. 9:15 and the phone rings ! I wonder, who could be calling now? I answered, said hello and it is was Delia, "honey are you okay?

"I called about 15 minutes ago and there was no answer. Did you go to see a movie?" I answered back, "yes I did see two movies back to back and then stopped at a restaurant for my dinner, came back to my dorm room before 7:00 o'clock. I still did not want to be alone in my room so I walked over to the girl's dorm to see if anyone was watching television and a channel that might be interesting.

Sunday evening shows. There were several warm bodies there so I sat down and watched T.V."

"I had just walked in when you called now. What a surprise that you did, never expected it at all, it now makes my night so much more pleasant, how beautiful of you, my day is now more complete hearing your voice."

She says to me, "I was trying to kill time after our dinner so I too had sat down to watch T.V. but it was not helping much, so I asked mom if I could make a quick call to you, she smiled and said, " of course".

"Mom thinks it is rather neat that you have your own telephone, from now on that will surely help us stay in touch with each other and us not feel so separated." "I just wanted you to hear my voice before you went to bed; too bad I am not there to tuck you in; not sure how that would go?"

"Thank you sweetheart for the pleasure of hearing your voice so soon. I meant every word I said in our conversation earlier this afternoon; about how I am getting to love you more each day for what and how you are to me and your affection and passion are now very important and that I want you to be a part of each and every one of my days and nights."

"Honey it is my pleasure too, as you are a part of each and every day and night and I will thrive on being there for you and it will be better for us both, this late call has made my evening too, I am so thrilled."

"Sweetie, I had a bright idea yesterday, do you think that your mom can find a photography studio in town that would take a couple of pictures of you, all prettied up so that I could have one, or two, for here in my room, "so I can look at you when I get lonely so I can see you as I see you in my mind.?" She quickly says, "What a great idea, I would love for you to have pictures of me in your room, will I be able have some of you also?"

 I said, "sure I know a studio over on Lomas NE where I can have some pictures taken for you. I painted that studio on the inside when I was working with Horton Const last year ; I will do it too and soon, I'll say goodnight for now okay?."

I called on Monday night and Tuesday night and we had some very interesting talks and somewhat emotional connections. Delia's mom asked her to work and assist her at the city library so that she would not be sitting at home with nothing to do. I guess it really helped her to deal with the day time hours until we had a chance to talk.

Tuesday after 9:30 pm the phone rang, this was after Delia and I had spent at least 45 minutes on our call. I answered it, said hello? a response came back as, "Michael this is Rose, can you talk? I did hesitate for a few moments, so I said yes, what is going on?"

She says, "I just wanted to talk to you about what was said on Saturday before my parents and I left for home. I just do not know how I left the situation at the last minute, it was cut short, as my parents were anxious to get going, they also had a stop to make in Santa Fe.

"I know that I may have left you very confused as what was to follow after I talked to you on Friday and what I was thinking and what my possible intentions were for this summer and the next school year and possible intentions for going to college." What did you gather from all of that?"

"If you really must know, I gathered that, as you have planned, you were saying that we were done and that you had chosen to be more independent and that you would not be back this next school session.

"It was rather shocking to me, but just keep in mind that it was you who left me and not the other way around, right?" Look do not be sad, I know it is over just be glad that we had some time to spend together.

"Oh! that is not what I was trying to get across to you, it was that we could still see each other from now on, especially when you would come to Taos for a weekend as you have done before. Is that still a possibility?, I will be here of course, as I am already working at the drugstore for the summer."

"I do not know how you can expect that of me being that you were very clear before you left and how you left the situation; there was no discussion, no conditions expressed. My impression was that you wanted to be free, independent to do as you would choose."

"Will you consider coming to see me when you are in town on your next visit with family?" I said back, "I will have to think about it, but I can not make any promises, maybe on those weekends you may be out with someone; a boyfriend from the past, or other friends, so do not plan on me being there."

She did not say anything for a few moments, I could sense that she was a bit emotional and maybe sobbing slightly to my response. I asked, "are you okay? What sort of an answer would you like from me?

She says, "well I did not think I am throwing away all that we had been through for the last 20 months or so. I only wanted to change how I finish school and then going to college."

"The concerns that you mentioned about my having to go into active duty after receiving my officer commission and where I would end up, very much sums it up, it appears that you would be reluctant to go with me or to be away from home, especially if we ended up on the other side of the world."

"I would also like to say that we did have a very good 20 months in our relationship and I have no regrets at all. What is the old saying:

It is best to have loved and lost, then not to have loved at all" so do not beat yourself up!, we are really done and that we are parting ways.

"I do wish you the best and happiness in what ever you accomplish. You will look back and think of our relationship as a positive step towards a future with a more rewarding relationship with a soul mate of your chose."

Between sobs and sniffles she says, "Michael I am so sorry of how I left our relationship, I have loved you all along and appreciate what I learned about being with someone, I had no experience at this and I hope for your forgiveness, maybe I have just been too young to appreciate what I could have had with you in a future time."

"Again I say to her, "do not be sad, it is over and life will go on for us both." "Well Rose, we will both get over it, just look to having the future you can wish for and work for and be happy, positive and do not worry about what has come about, we both need to think positive, okay?"

She said goodbye and wished me a good night as she sobbed and sniffled and we spoke for the last time, I do not think I will hear from her in the future. I do not think I was too matter of fact with our talk.

Chapter 25

This is Wednesday, I am at the office trying to keep my brain functioning and concentrating on my project at hand. It has been a rather strange day for me considering the two totally opposite type of calls I engaged in last night, I hope it does not happens again.

I decided after work and after dinner to call Delia and have a sincere conversation with her about the unexpected phone call of last night. She needs to know; for her peace of mind as to what direction she and I are headed.

I was somewhat nervous and not quite sure how to go about telling her that I had heard from Rose, I did feel like she will be okay with me being honest and up front with her.

she was going to be pleased to hear about the ending of that cloud that was hanging over my head and was not going away, so I decide to call her and not wait around anymore.

Thursday after dinner I called it rang three times before she answered and I said, " guess who? She says, "Michael you silly guy of course I know it is you, but Delia is not here, is out for the night, then bursts out laughing and says, see two can play this game."

"anyhow honey I am surprised to hear from you, are you okay?" I jumped in and said, I have some news for you; good and bad, which do you want to hear?" she hesitates for a few moments and then says, the good news, I guess?

"Well sweetheart there are no bad news just some super good news I know you will like. Are you sitting down? If not please sit now." Rose called me last night after I had talked to you, I was not sure who would be calling at nearly 10:00, anyhow she started the conversation, asked how I was, was I working full time and how had I been lately?" "I was not giving out to much information and just played along and then I asked her why she called."

She said she was trying to clear up anything I may have misunderstood from last Friday and Saturday. She said she was upset at the way she left the situation and did not handle it well. She wanted to know if we could still see each other even though we are in different places.

She was asking when I would be going to Taos to visit my family and could I come by and see her, on those weekends. I told her I did not think so, after all she had made it quite clear that she wanted some space of her own for the summer and next school year. I told her that she had expressed too many doubts about any future between us.

"I told her she had been rather clear that it was over between us regardless of what she now thinks and besides what kind of a relationship can we have if either one of us has doubts of what is ahead."

I wished her good luck in her future and that she should go out there and experience other things and have friends and make the best of it. I told her I was going to make the best of the breakup, because I have a future planned for me."

"So Delia sweetheart that is about it, it is over and there is no more concern, my mind is clear and I am totally available for you so as to get whatever we want out of our own personal relationship. I have much love for you and I want to make it all good for us. So, are you ready?

She bursts out, "Oh ! honey I am so delighted to hear that it is all behind you, I can now express how happy I am, bursting with happiness; wait until I see you next Friday when you come up, you will know !!, so I wished her good night and promised to call again tomorrow night after dinner.

Believe me it was strange to say good night knowing she was far away in another town and I will not be seeing her at breakfast in the morning as we did before classes ended. Now I have to deal with the separation for the next till few days, although we will be able to exchange telephone calls in the evenings, so better then not at all, until Friday evening.

Starting tomorrow we will be separated in this manner for three months, but able to visit when I can go up there on a weekend ever so often to visit with her and catch up.

Here it is Friday morning, I feel somewhat blah and not as energetic as usual and just looking forward to working every day; each day will be just like the one before it. I will need to be creative about my evenings; find something different to avoid boredom and even loneliness now that there is someone else in my world.

We had much to talk about on Saturday evening's call, she sounded so sad and restless and had been anxiously waiting for my call; she said her spirits were down and did not really enjoy dinner with family

She says to me a few minutes into our talking back and forth about how good the last weekend had been for the both of us, "honey it has only been three days since I left and to me it seems like more than a week."

"Help me figure out how to deal with us being apart, especially when it seems like it will be almost one week till we can possibly see each other. Promise me you will come this coming week on Friday?"

"I promise I will be there, I too can hardly wait until 3:00 pm that day so I can take off to see you."

"Sweetie, I am also having the same concerns about being apart, last night after our talk I too felt a similar sadness and restlessness and being alone here is really of no help to passing the time." I need to also find ways to fill my alone time." Let us do this; we need to think positive, you can visit with family.

"Maybe you can start a friendship with your brother's girlfriend, enjoy conversations with your mom, ask her about relationship issues, say positive things about how you feel and what is going on in your mind. It might be helpful to ask her advise. Since she runs the town library where you can check out books and novels, buy some new magazines that can give you ideas about girl or women fashion stuff."

"Maybe take in a movie in the middle of the week." "You can tell me what movie you saw and what you thought of it; is that like something to do? although I hate to see you go alone, maybe invite your brother's girlfriend; that would be interesting."

"Mostly be happy with what we now have, dream some things for the future you wish to have and experience and gather information of about just everything that you have interest in that is good for you and possibly for us." "Also feel positive with the fact that I have expressed my love and devotion for you, that should be very satisfying, okay?"

I say, "I too need to find positive tasks and challenges to work with every evening after dinner and on the weekends that I am here, I do read my mystery books and do odd tasks in my room and clean and occasionally wax the car."

"I would like, again, to ask about taking two couples from school to a movie or two, so that they too can experience a change of scenery during the week; gives me a break from the campus as well." Does that sound okay?"

"I can also go to my church on Sunday mornings and then plan on some shopping in town, as you know Sunday afternoons and evening are boring. I know now that I think about you constantly and wish you were here. ! hey ! that would make a good song."

"Oh ! I have something interesting to share with you, I had a dream last that totally blew my mind, the dream took place at some sort of outdoor function in your neighborhood.

I was there and for some reason so was your dad. I came around the corner from somewhere and ran into him, we were both surprised. He said that you were supposed to be there but had not yet shown up. He mentioned your mom was around; he was looking for her, but was concerned that you had not shown up."

"We both started to look around for your mom but also keeping an eye out for you. I walked away In a different direction and then someone caught my eye; I did recognize that it was your mom. She had on a flowing black dress and she was just going in a different direction in a very loose stride, almost as if she was floating away... then I woke up, looked around and realized it was just a dream.

"I was totally surprised that I would dream about your parents, but where were you?? The mystery girl was no where to be seen or found, so think about that, are you going to be that elusive to see or to find? "Am I always going to be looking for you in my dreams, hope they do not turn into nightmares, but not with you in my dreams, what a treat."

She could hardly wait to say "I do not think that I am, as you say, elusive, in the real world, in all this time that we have known each other was I ever difficult to see and to find? and I hope to God not in your dreams, because I would always be with you, holding on to you by touching, kissing and caressing you."

"I am sorry sweetheart I do not mean that in our real life that you would be elusive or that I may not be able to find you when I needed you. On the other hand I really would like to see you in my dreams and I would cherish the fact that you would be in my dreams over and over again; here I am now dreaming, wide awake, and hoping I dream of you."

"Honey I too want to see you in my dreams, but so far you have been "elusive" in my dreams, so I guess we are even. I would love to hold you, kiss you and hug you very tight and would hope the dream would not end."

She quickly says, "I really prefer you in real life, because as you know, our kisses, hugs and affection for each other are so much more real, right?"

"I guess I better go and let you get your beauty sleep; stay beautiful for me and smile and think great thoughts for us both." "I want you to know that I adore you, love you and you are on my mind all my waking hours, so I wish you a night full of pleasant dreams and I look forward to hearing your soft and sexy voice tomorrow night?"

"Honey let me call you tomorrow night instead of you, so wait for my call, okay?" Good night to you, get your rest for tomorrow since you are working."

Monday evening at 7:30 the phone rang and I right away knew it would be Delia, so I answered calmly, but it was not her, it was Rose, darn it what now !

She responds to my hello by saying, "Hi this is Rose can you talk?" So I answer, "not for long, I need to go off campus."   She starts out, "I wanted to know if you had given thought to your coming to Taos this coming weekend?" "Did think you would come to see me?"

I quickly responded, "What gave you the impression that I would do that?" I thought I had made myself clear, that you had made it clear that we were done and there would no longer be any type of visiting."

"Well I would still like to see you and maybe I can explain myself better as to what I had said when I left school for home, can you at least give me a chance to explain it?"

I had no choice but to say, "I do not need further explanations from you, you said your piece and I did understand completely, lets not kid ourselves." "I am so sorry" she says and then starts to cry and sob loudly; I had to just hold back for a few moments and give her time to regain her composure.

She was still sobbing while she tried to contain her emotions and finally says, "I am so sorry it had to end this way, I am not sure what I did and I feel I owe you more explanations, I know I hurt you, but I do not know how badly it must be for you."

"Look Rose the last time we talked I shared ideas and opinions about how you could go about making the best of your summer and your near future, so let us leave it at that and I wish you the best, again okay?" "I do have to go, so long." I hung up as she was still sobbing lightly, and says, "Okay the best to you too."

No sooner had I hung up and went for a drink of water, the phone rings again. I stop to think for a quick moment: I hope it is Delia this time. I answer it and it is Delia.

She comes on and says, "Honey are you okay, I tried a little while ago and your line was busy, so I thought maybe you were talking to your mom."

I responded, "no, I was listening to someone else and I hate to tell you who." "If I had known it was Rose I would not have answered, but I was stuck listening to her run her mouth." She wanted to know if I was coming to see my mom this coming weekend and of course she asked if I would go see her.

I made myself very clear that I was not going to see her, the last time she called, but she did not care to listen before. I told her again, we are done, as she had implied before, so I was a little rough with her and I told her I could not talk anymore, I hung up."

"Sweetheart I want you to know about that call because I want to be totally honest with you and there is nothing for you to worry about. I have no intentions of seeing her for the reasons that we are done and you and I have our own relationship, I am very happy and comfortable with you."

"I hope you are not concerned that she called and that I did manage to sever that situation for good and I hope she has understood there will not be any more back and forth. I hope I do not have to change my phone number."

"So sweetheart talk to me, what have you done since last night? We did talk a lot and I feel much better about what I need to do to stay busy and keep happy thoughts about us."

"Honey can I say something real quick?" I said, "yes go ahead, I did not mean to dominate our conversation." "Honey I want you to know that I do completely trust you and believe how you feel, I am so proud of how you are handling all the issues you are faced with, does it appears that it is over?"

"Sweetheart I already miss your kisses and your passion that you share with me, I feel so lucky and I wish to tell you that a kiss is not a kiss without your love, because I know you mean it so completely that there is no doubt how your feelings are so real."

"I guess I need to go, it is getting late and another day of work is coming up before the end of the week; can we wait till Saturday night to talk again?" I need to call my mom to see how she is doing and also to call and talk to my dad, as it has been awhile since." I miss you very much,

It was very satisfying to be able to visit and have a personal and honest talk with Delia about our on going experiences. I was really ready for bed after that long talk, but it helps keep me tuned into her.

Tuesday came and went and here I am faced with an other evening without her, but just a memory of her from our visit last night. I called and talked to my mom and then my dad. At least that helped me get through the first of the week.

I managed to find tasks and things to take care both in my room and with my car on Saturday I had made the best of my time to stay busy so that I would not be lonely.

Chapter 26

Delia and I talked again on Wednesday night after dinner. She was ready to talk and share her thoughts from the past two days. I told her I was planning to go to a movie where I could be around more people and also to be part of the overall gathering; it is rather comfortable and gives one a feeling about being part of a group who is there for one purpose and one purpose only.

Half way into this week I decided to go do some shopping for at least three different items. For the most part I want to buy Delia a nice blouse and maybe a bottle of wine for her dad and a large box of fancy chocolates for her mom. I did accomplish my goal and I was getting ready for my drive on Friday to see Delia and her family.

I was so looking forward to seeing them, especially Delia; I need to touch her, to caress her. and those wonderful sweet kisses are the icing on the cake, for me that is not enough; she will be waiting with open arms when I arrive there.

I sailed through the rest of the week Friday I quit work early and rushed back to my dorm room and within a half hour I was climbing into my car and off I went, not quite driving off into the sunset but close enough.

I drove into Las Vegas about 5:10 pm, worked my way to Delia's street and home. Like magic, there she was sitting on the porch lounge and straining her neck looking up the street for me. The moment she saw my car, she rushed off the porch out to the driveway to meet me as I drove in.

There seemed to be no other family cars further in on the driveway; so I was the first one there? I had barely parked on the side when she is at my car door just smiling and anxious for me to get out.

As soon as I did, she threw her arms around my neck and kissed me with those hot wet lips of hers' I in turn wrapped my arms around her and returned her kisses, but to start, she was much more passionate than I was, guess I needed to catch up.

I said, when I was able to catch my breath, "sweetheart it is so great to see you, I guess you have missed me as much as I have missed you." Please slow down, I am here.!

She responded, "Honey I sure have missed you so much it hurts and the two weeks have been so long and I have been practicing what you and I talked about last week, but my mom thinks differently some times she says I am climbing the walls." She said the other day, "I do not know what I am going to do with you like that for the rest of the summer."

We pulled apart and I walked back to the trunk of the car for my luggage, but I did not reach for the packages in the back seat, I was going to wait until after dinner then bring them in.

She led me to the room I slept in last time here, she hung up my clothes and I placed my bag next to the closet; I would empty my stuff later. We walked out to the living room together.

we sat on the couch and her arms were around me again, I did not resist the passion that was boiling inside of me, and boy neither did she, what a way to make up for lost time.

We finally came up for air as I did not want her to faint on me, but oh ! what a joy and what a pleasure. She still held on around my neck and whispered in my ear, "honey I surely missed you and the phone calls really help, otherwise I just know I would have felt rather lost; I looked into her eyes as she had a few tears running down her cheeks.

"Sweetie please do not cry I am here and you are here and that is what is important. I have had to make the best of the days we are separated, so I just go in the closet and do my crying in there." I chuckle and she laughs and says, "I do not believe you cry like me"; she looks at me with her head tipped to one side like I do not believe that. We both had a good laugh about my joke.

We had just finished laughing when her mom walked in the kitchen door and saw us laughing. She says hello to me and then asks, what is going on and what is all the laughing about?" Delia says, Michael said something that was funny and we started laughing."

I got up and walked over to her mom to greet her and gave her a nice hug, she is getting used to my greeting her that way. She says, "have you been here long?" I responded, "not more that 15 minutes."

Make yourself at home. "Delia did you offer him some form of drink? With that question I could see it in her eyes "were you too busy hugging and kissing? "Delia jumps up heads for the refrigerator brings a drink and says, sorry mom and gives her a wicked little look and smiles at me, her mom asked her to help with a few things so that they could have dinner ready when her dad arrives.

We all gathered around the table for dinner and I said, "I Thank you both for having me here for dinner, I feel like I am imposing, how can I make it up to you both?"

They both speak up and say, "we like and want you to feel at home and enjoy meals with us, after all you drive from the city and came to visit, so you are our guest and even more; she looks at Delia with a smile on her face knowing full well that it would be understood by Delia.

Saturday morning I was able to convince Delia's dad that I could help him with chores or other serious tasks if he wanted to tackle them for the day, so we worked a good 6 ½ hours at various tasks and when we were done; he paused for a few minutes, took a swig from his cold water bottle;

He looks at me and says, "you sure are a hard worker and we really accomplished a lot compared to what I would have done by myself, you do not know how much I appreciated your help."

"I believe it is time for us to quit for the day, so what you say?, lets go in and relax, I do know I need a good shower, sure you feel the same. We walked in to the kitchen thru the rear door and Delia and her mom looked at us as if we were unrecognizable and there we were, all sweaty, tired and ready to shower.

Delia's mom says, "well I know two guys that need to shower, cleanup and relax and you can tell us all about what you accomplished today."

Dinner was ready when we were back in the living room, they called us to sit and they would serve us; at the point Delia comes up to me, puts her arms around my neck and kisses my check; then says, "well! ! you smell okay, in fact very good, chuckles and leads me to the dining room.

After dinner we sat back and relaxed in the living room, her dad and I looked at each and he says, "you feel okay, not too tired I hope.?" I answered I was okay and would feel better soon. I said out loud, "that is the hardest I have worked since I quit working in const., but it felt good to do some heavy stuff."

Delia sits next to me and says, "remember I said we were going to a movie tonight, my treat." Are you okay, but I hope you do not fall asleep in the theater?" and then laughs I answered, "of course I will be okay." We sat for several minutes and then Delia says, "I will go ahead and get ready; are you ready as you are?" I said, "sure I am ready to go."

In about 15 minutes or so she comes out from her bedroom. I was so amazed at how beautiful she looked, she was wearing the blouse I had just brought her with a colorful skirt and low heels and her hair was combed just right to suit how she looked. She says, with a little shy look, "I am ready if you are." I was stunned could not say much.

Her parents said, "you two go enjoy your evening, you have not had an evening together for two weeks." "Delia is It a double feature tonight?" "Yes mom it is, but we will have to see what it is about and how long it is, but we shall see, so see you later."

On our way out to the car, I stopped her for a moment and said, "sweetheart you are so beautiful and I love the way you look; guess you liked your new blouse?" She says quickly, "I love it and it fits just right. You have very good taste.

"Good taste also shows how I feel about you and why I am loving you more each day and miss you when we are apart." The days and weeks seem so long in between the times we are together."

I helped her fix her skirt so it would not crease or wrinkle when she got in the car, but she does know that it makes a difference to do so and does it.

She knew we were early but she just wanted to be able to be in the darkened theater and just talk and take time to be affectionate. It felt so good to have her next to me and so close with her warmth and passion, it is just so relaxing.

The first movie was the featured one and the last one is considered the lesser of the two, so we enjoyed the feature show and decided we would go, so that we could spend some time alone, in the car before we would go to her home.

I said to her, "sweetheart we need to sort of behave even though I would rather not, we need to be presentable when we walk in the door as I do not want your parents to think otherwise, right?"

She looks at me with a sad face, head looking down and to one side and says, "Oh! honey that is not fair to us, because I want to spend the night kissing and hugging you.... stops for a moment and then burst out laughing, I am kidding, I know what you mean. Mom and Dad really trust you, are very comfortable with us; sure they must figure we want to be intimate, but to what extent, so I guess we do have our limits as to how far we go being intimate."

We did have our share of closeness and wild kissing, but we quit soon enough so we could go home and be presentable. We arrived, walked into the living room and they were both sitting on the couch and her dad was half asleep. They both perked up and said, your home early?"

Delia said, "we only stayed for the feature show because it was long enough and the second show did not seem too interesting."

She guided me to the other small couch and we sat down and we all just looked at each other. Her mom rises quickly and says, I think the two of us need to get to bed, as you see your Dad is almost asleep and I am halfway there too.

"You can stay up if you wish, okay; oh! there is some dessert on the kitchen counter, enjoy and see you in the morning." We had dessert and continued talking,

she kissed me and I did the same, we kept it cool and just talked about the weeks to come. She says to me, "I have a secret that I have kept from you for several days and I just can not hold it any longer. Because of the manner in which I have been since I came home and how in the evenings mom notices how quiet or reserved I am, so let me explain how the discussion went, "mom came right out and asked me."

"Are you that sad or lonely because you and Michael are separated and only see each other every other weekend?" "It is going to be a long summer for you until school starts in the fall and I can imagine how you must feel, do you think you would like to go back to the school campus and work and be there for the rest of the summer?"

"I did ask her if she and dad would be okay if I did not spend the summer here. I mentioned to her that I had spent last summer there...I said, "quickly, mom that is when I met Michael and had a different attitude about being away from home for the first time during the summer."

"It was a summer I will never forget and it would mean a lot to be there again this summer. "You really do not mind me being gone again for the rest of the summer?" she says, "I will have to talk to your Dad first."

"Mom looked at me in sort of sad manner and I did see some tears in her eyes, so she says, "I want you to be happy from now on; you have such a great relationship with Michael and I can see that you need to be together as much as possible. We will miss you but lets wait to see what may happen.

Next week we will call to talk to whom makes the decision, okay?, they held each other for a few more moments as they cried, each one emotional for different reasons; her mom was crying because her daughter would leave for the summer and "I no longer have a young girl growing up and attached to family, but that she is now changing and growing, attached to someone, and there is not much I can do."

Delia is being emotional and crying because she does not want to disappoint her parents and for them to be sad when all of a sudden she is no longer that young high school girl trying to grow up.

"My dad walked into the kitchen where we happen to be and finds us standing there sort of crying and wiping our tears. He looks at us both and asks what is going on? Mom speaks up first and says, "Delia and I have been talking about her wanting to go back to school and work for the summer, but the main reason is she wants to be where Michael is, so we were saying that we would call early this coming week and see if they will accept her now for the rest of the summer for credit."

She asks, "what do you think about her going back to the school for the rest of the summer before she starts her senior year there?" my dad speaks up, "Right now, since you've caught me by surprise, I do not have a real objection and like you say, she wants to be closer to Michael.

"I can understand that they are very close and maybe they both need to be closer to each other. I suspect that it is good for them as they seem to know what they feel and want."

Mom also says, "I will miss her not being here with us at least for the summer and we are aware that she would be returning in Sept. for her senior year and will then graduate. I think you and I need to realize that it is going to happen and we can not deprive her of what she must feel and want.... remember it is her future?"

They both look at each other shrug their shoulders and seem to agree without saying it. At that moment, Delia spoke up and said, "I have an idea, but do not know for sure. I think and feel that Michael would agree to bring me up every other weekend to visit, that way we can still see you, visit and then go back."

"I know how he thinks. He is very kind, flexible and he wishes me to be happy. After we call the school and they agree then I can share the final decision we have come up with, so lets wait and see."

Both my parents seemed satisfied with that thought and said, "Okay, we can still talk more later?" So I left it at that point and we have not talked about it since then." "What do think about what I suggested to them?" Mom will call."

"I have thought about it quickly and I see that it can work, but the only thing that comes to mind is will the house mother or Ms. Brown be acceptable if you are leaving the campus every other weekend. I guess you and I will have to wait for that decision to be accepted or declined; as they may say that the school is responsible while you are there and may not want you leaving, even if it is with me."

We kissed and decided it was late and needed to get to bed; tomorrow is Sunday and I will need to leave mid afternoon. Do not look forward to leaving her again but it can not be helped, but on the other hand it was a good weekend.

We all had a very good breakfast and just relaxed, her parents went to church, so Delia and I went for a walk in the neighborhood.

We shared the Idea of her possible spending the rest of her summer working on campus till school would start, so she finally said, "I am so excited that I can go back, just think how great the rest of the summer will be and how we can see each other on a daily basis. I feel bad about leaving my parents and only seeing them every few weeks, but I think they understand."

She stayed very close to me, squeezing my hand and reaching up and caressing my cheek as we stopped for her to just look at me straight in the eyes, and says, " I love you so much and I really look forward to the near and far future with you."

I could just hold her tight, play with her hair and kiss her cheek; had to reserve more contact until we were in the privacy of her home. We returned about half hour plus and sat out there in the porch and then we kissed passionately and she hung on to me as if I was trying to get away, but I sure was not, as I knew that we would not be doing this for a awhile, when??

After a light lunch and when I was finally packed up and to ready to leave, I talked to her parents and we thanked each other for a great weekend and I then turned to look at Delia. I could tell she had some tears starting to show, so I said goodbye to the parents.

Delia says, "I will walk out to the car with you, she did and she was holding my hand tight, like I do not want you to leave. Since the car was not visible from inside the home, we were able to kiss long. She says, "I will be waiting for your call after you are settled in. By now she was really tearing, I hugged her very tight and said, "sweetheart this is, "see you later and not a goodbye, so be strong and happy."

I had a good trip back and stopped to get an early dinner just so that I would not have to go out again after I had settled in for the evening. It was good to be back in my own space, I am alone again but have great feelings about us.

When I unlocked the door to my dorm room there was an envelope on the floor which had been slid under the door while I was gone; I guess Saturday's mail. When I picked it up I saw that it was from Taos, not from my family but from, guess who? It was from Rose, I was puzzled she wrote.

I flipped the letter on my desk, put my clothes and small luggage case away and threw myself on the bed, just to relax after that long drive and a good dinner to tide me over till tomorrow; the letter could wait as I need to call Delia and say I arrived here safe and a bit worn out. I did not want to do anything for now.

I Called Delia, got a response, Delia did not waste any time in answering, she says, "Hi honey I am here are you okay, get there safely?" She was almost out of breath, when she did catch her breathe, says, "I had to run from the kitchen to the living room; mom and I are cleaning up after dinner."

"I had a good trip, no problems, had my dinner and got back to my room, I am okay feel a bit worn out but I will live." How are you doing, so you already had dinner?"

"Honey, I guess, I am okay as mom has been talking to me and keeping me busy, since she did not like how I looked after you left and she saw tears on my cheeks, so she has been comforting me and just talking. She did not want me to end up in my room, I am very glad to hear your voice, that helps me a lot." We said good bye for now, talk tomorrow.

Once I had sort of settled down for the evening, I glanced over at the envelope toying with the idea as to what to do; open it read it or just put it in drawer 13.

I stared at the front of the envelope for several moments and then turned it around and sliced the envelope at the top, pulled the letter out and unfolded it and noticed it was dated this past Thursday and arrived here on Saturday. I proceeded to read it. The letter is from Mira Rose.

I thought to myself, I was not expecting any form of communication from her, but I guess a letter is better than her calling, because then I have to talk to her and try to get around what ever her purpose is for calling again, so I sat down to read to see what was on her mind.

Wednesday night   8:30 pm

Hi Michael

I am writing you even though you may not be expecting anything from me, especially now. I know we had a conversation two weeks ago and it ended rather emotionally and abrupt

I am trying one more time to talk about what I said or did on that last day of school and the Impressions that I left with you

I have thought about everything that I said without thinking what those messages were telling you. I know it was bad timing and I should have discussed them further much earlier.

I am really upset and ashamed of myself for having left it in such a hurtful manner. You did not deserve it and again I wish to apologize for my behavior. Do you think you can forgive me for it?, because it was cruel. Of me

                                   Page 2

to have been so insensitive about our relationship. My parents, especially my mom, questioned my attitude towards you and said I was cruel to have left things as I did and it *would be on me if you never got together with me or spoke to me again*

I am not asking you to take me back, but I just wanted to clear the air about me, not you and hoping that maybe some day you would reconsider us starting over again

Meanwhile I will have to deal with myself and plug along. I guess I will be going back to the high school here and after graduating I will still consider my cousin's suggestion to move to Colo. Springs for college

I wish you the best on your last year at UNM and your career in the Air Force, if when you are up here to visit your mom, if you would call maybe just maybe we can at least talk and share thoughts; you are not obligated to do so forgive me for asking, It is late and I need to get to bed, goodbye??

Rose

Well that was the end of that letter and I will not be reading it again; I already know in what direction my days, nights and months are headed and it is with the comfort, passion and caring from Delia that I now hang my hat on, so to speak,

I walk over to my easy chair, sat down and gave a sigh but I do not know if was a sigh of relief after having read the latest letter or a sigh of frustration. I was not expecting any more communication, because I wish to put the immediate past out of my mind; as I now think of that time period as "*Those Were the Days?*", for better or for worse.

I needed to clear my head about the issue at hand and think positive about what I now have on-going in my life. I do not know exactly what went wrong in that relationship; it seemed to be going well and the future seemed secure and well planned or so it seemed.

I think in the back of my mind that Rose was and is still young and has had a somewhat sheltered life and does not have much experience in dating.

She also does not have any experience in relationships; she might have thought it was great to have a boyfriend and think of it as on-going but not necessarily a permanent one. She did have the right to change her mind and alter her thinking about our relationship; I do not fault her for that.

Next day, I wanted to start off with a steady undisturbed attitude towards my day, my duties and to look forward to my daily thoughts about Delia and our relationship. We lean on each other for affection, attention and moral support; I have come to really love every move and expression radiating from her bodily moves and facial expressions. I look forward for all of that like I look forward to seeing the sunrise each day.

The following evening I called Delia and she answered as quickly as always and greeted me with such a happy mood that I had to wait a few moments to let it all soak in.

She starts our conversation with the fact that her parents had each talked about her returning to the school campus for the rest of the summer and had reluctantly agreed but Delia could tell they were somewhat saddened to let her go, but waited until earlier this evening before dinner to confirm that they did agree for her to go back to the school campus.

Her mom was the first to tell her and she said, "we agree that you may return to the school and we understand what you are feeling and what your real reason is for returning."

Delia says, "Michael you can not imagine how surprised I was when she made that comment to me, my heart just skipped a beat and I was off the couch, I threw my arms around her and asked, "do you really mean I can go back for the summer?, are you sure, because we need to call there and see if they will agree."

I waited until she finished sharing with me the extent of their discussion about her and the fact that she would be going back to the school; she was just all excited and she probably was jumping up and down.

I finally had a chance to get a few words in by saying, "sweetheart I am delighted for you and for the both of us."

Delia responds to me quickly, "Honey I may be able to go as early as this next weekend if not the following Saturday, since my parents both work they will not be free until that day, so this coming Saturday may be too early."

"Sweetheart would it be possible if I came for you this coming weekend and bring you back; of course it would depend on how your parents feel about that. I do not wish to interfere with that task, but see how they feel about getting you here and then maybe suggest it, but do not make it sound like I am pushing to do so. We need to keep them happy about getting you here, okay?"

"Mom has promised me she will call tomorrow morning and talk to Miss Brown about my being interested to work there the rest of the summer and make the arrangements for me. I really look forward, it makes me happy that they agreed for me to go."

"You said that you suggested that I might be interested in us going up home every other weekend for visits with your parents. I have no problem with that, in fact I very much like the idea, because that will easy the separation of you from your parents through the summer, so make sure your mom inquires if that will be acceptable, okay?

"sweetheart I too am excited that you and your parents are working together to allow you to come back to the school campus. I certainly look forward to you being here full time for the rest of the year. Can you let me know which weekend it will be so that I can be prepared to visit with your parents and then see you, my beautiful girlfriend and partner."

"Honey I can hardly wait to see you soon, until then mom will really be seeing me climb the walls." I need to start putting my clothes in order and gathering all the items that I will have to take for the summer and for working." "I also need to bring my pretty clothes for us going out if it is possible during the rest of the summer."

I quickly said to Delia, "I guess I need to let you go, it is getting late have to work tomorrow, you need your sleep?"

"Honey I probably will not get much sleep tonight, I am all jittery and super anxious for time to fly till the weekend, so I wish you goodnight and wish I could just hold you tight and kiss you, but it will wait until the weekend."

With this coming week I will do my best to keep my mind on my work at the office and also wish for time to fly, especially if it will be this next Saturday when she will arrive, although I will be disappointed if it is scheduled for the next Saturday, O! well either way I look forward to her return.

Monday and Tuesday days went by rather quickly and that evening I was just wandering around after dinner, so I ventured over to the girl's dorm to kill some time with the group there and spent some time till 8:45 and then decided it was time for me to go rest up for tomorrow.

I waited until Thursday night to call Delia and see how the planned return to the campus was working out for her; I assume her parents were bringing her and not her brother.

She answers the phone and blurts out, "Honey I missed hearing from you last night, but I guess you were busy?" I do understand that you can not call every night, but it sure is great to hear from you when you can call."

"I know that after this coming weekend you will not need to call, because I will be with you not just on campus but with you and that means a lot to me." "Just think now we will be able to see each other every evening and visit and share and be close; I am so looking forward to that and I am very excited to go back now that I am so sure about you and I.

"Several weeks ago I was very unsure at what the future would be, not only for you but for me, I was preparing myself for further disappointment and possibly walking away with a broken heart, but my love for you would still be there."

At that point she started to cry and was sobbing hard and I was feeling bad for her, but then she slips in and says, "Honey I am not sad, these are tears of joy not sadness, for I am so happy and delighted for us both. I love you so much that I get this emotional, please understand me, okay?"

"Sweetheart I totally understand and I am so fortunate to have you and cherish every possible moment with you and I too am looking forward to you being here on campus. I will walk around on a cloud knowing you are here. We will be in our own little world and nothing else matters.

"Let me know that Saturday morning when you are about to leave home so I can estimate when you will be here so I can be around to meet you and see and talk to your parents." I'll let you go for now but I will call tomorrow night and visit with you.

Saturday morning at 9:45 am Delia called and said, Hi honey we are just getting ready to leave and Dad says we are driving straight thru. How long do you think it will take us to get there?" I answer quickly, "about 2 and ½ hours or so"

She says, in a very cheerful and excited voice, "Honey I am so anxious to see you I am so excited, can you tell?" I will tell you all about our trip in when we get there, okay?"

I say to her in closing, "sweetheart I too am anxious to see you and waiting with open arms for you. Will your parents be going right back or are they staying overnight?"

Saturday morning I decided to take a shower, wear clean clothes and be prepared for meeting her and the family again; it will surely be different after today and for how long; I hope for a long time in our future.

I waited near the girl's dorm, sitting on the bench under the big shade tree hoping it would not be too long till they arrived. It had been no more than about 15 minutes when I see Delia's parent's car come around the curved row of trees and shrubs and proceed towards the girl's dorm.

I am in full view of the car and they seem to see me sitting there, they pull over closer to me and stop, I got up from the bench I was on and walk over to the passenger side.

I greeted Delia's mom and wave at her dad, they greeted me back and the mom said, "Hi have you been waiting long?" I answered back, "just a while, anxious to see you."

Delia steps out of the back seat rushes to me and gives me a very tight hug and kisses me on the lips real quick so that it is not noticed for the time being. We are just talking to each other and finally her dad says, "need to unload luggage?"

I quickly respond to what he said, and offered to help him carry the luggage to the dorm porch while they talked briefly. Delia did have various suitcases and a couple of boxes plus two bags packed full of personal items.

Once we took in all of Delia's luggage, we all went back out to their car; we gathered around, the parents were in the front seats and Delia and I sat in the back seat with the two doors open for fresh air and so as not to look like we were being too close and visible to others to get any ideas.

Her parents decided they needed to leave soon, but were reluctant to leave their daughter; her mom looked at Delia in a slightly sad way and then me and they both said, "okay let us go and we will call after we get home, okay?" Her Dad was trying not to show any emotions at this time. Delia showed a bit of sadness when they pulled away, but turned her attention to me and reached out for my hand.

As they pulled away up the driveway, I could hear the music on the radio and it sure was a strange coincidence, but it sure fit the occasion:

The song was, **Sealed with a Kiss,** *I have heard it before, but it never occurred to me it would have such a profound impression as it does now, too weird to be real.*

I will ask Delia this evening and ask her what she thought of the song, hearing it as her parents happen to leave the campus, and then I will express my opinion as it hit me when I did hear it; I want to hear what sense it made to her.

Chapter 27

Our Summer Chapter Begins

I am trying to get it into my head that Delia is now here for the rest of the summer, it is almost like we have turned the page and that our relationship will now transform itself into a more easy going day to day seeing each other, touching each other and sharing private moments and expressions that before were short but sweet.

It is surprisingly difficult to realize that her parents finally did come to the conclusion that Delia was not going to be happy being away from here and me. They did admit that she is more adult in her manners and expressions of what she wants for her future from this time on.

I personally am very pleased to see that she will be here within the campus environment and very near to me, so that we can develop a deeper understanding of each other and fulfill our personal needs for companionship and build on that for our near future and the future beyond.

I asked her, "sweetheart are you going to be okay now that your parents have left?" "I know that you must feel some form of separation from the family you love and wish to please." "I am here for you and it will not be long until you [we] see them in 2-3 weeks."

She moves into my arms and holds me tight and says, "I will be okay, it is sad to see them go and hope they do not think I have abandoned them so I could be here with you. It is different then when I first came here 2- years ago just to go to school and for no other reason, but this is quite different, and I always went home for the summer." "For now this is my home and I am here with you, which means a lot to me."

So I say to Delia, "shall we walk you back to the dormitory, because we need to get ready to go to lunch, I am getting hungry by now." she places her arm thru my arm and smiles with a big smile and says, "I am ready if you are, as I too am in the mood for lunch; we had an early breakfast and I did not eat that much because I was ready to come back."

As we are walking away I turned and looked at Delia to see her facial expression and to see if I could see any form of sadness, so I asked, "sweetie are you okay now?" "I know it is probably sad, you'll be away from the family again."

She says back, "honey you know that I want to be here, with you, I am looking forward to share myself with you, to care for you, and I am so delighted for the closeness that we will be able to experience on a daily basis."

"I know that sooner or later, if it weren't for you, again I would be here for my last school year and then I would not know where or how I would direct myself for the future." "Even though I had not, to this point in time, given any thought to what I would do after graduation."

"Now my darling Michael I know exactly what I feel and how I expect my future and of course our future together from this day on, as we have discussed our relationship and how we have sort of planned what a future for you and I will be." "As for being away from mom and dad and my home, I know that there will be many times when we will see each other, here or at home.

"I said to her, you need to talk to your mom and find out if she can call the main office and the housemother about them agreeing that you can be allowed to go see your parents every 2-3 weekends between now and the start of the school year. I would drive us to Las Vegas spend 2-full days there, giving you the time to visit with your folks."

"Oh Michael that is a great idea, I would really like that and I am sure mom and dad would like seeing us both."

"Okay that is one problem solved today and I look forward to solving many more as time goes on for us both. Do you want me to come back or just wait for you when you are ready for lunch?"

She quickly says, I can be down in about 10 minutes or so, if you want to wait, is that okay?"   I nod yes, so I found a spot on a bench in the shade and waited.

Delia had freshened up, changed her clothes and wore that fragrance that I adore, she really is amazing and she's always full of surprises. "sweetie, that was quick and look at you a sight for my sore eyes and how I have missed seeing you just as you are, beautiful, I am sure glad you are here."

We walked hand in hand to the dining room, walked in close to each other and students and staff who decided to show up for lunch, especially because it is a Saturday, looked at us, some were surprised to see Delia since they had no knowledge that she would be back. Some of her classmates who had not seen her arrive and move back into her regular dorm room were also surprised; given the expressions on their faces.

After we all said our hellos and selected where we would sit down, everyone went about talking and visiting, also waiting for lunch to be brought to the tables so we all could serve ourselves as we wished.

After lunch Delia and I bid our goodbyes and left; we were in no hurry to be anywhere or to do anything, as it was now Saturday afternoon and the day was ours to do as we wished."I asked Delia, "do you feel better now that we are beginning a new chapter for ourselves?"

She looks at me with that sort of wicked sexy smile, the smile or smiles I have become so accustomed to, because I know that she shows her happiness and it is always a part of her way of expressing passion and affection, which she did automatically by wrapping her arm around me, tightly.

I asked her, "do you think it would be wise to ask the house mother if I could take you to see a movie this afternoon?" we both stopped In our tracks, looked at each other; there was a surprised look on her face and she quickly says,

"Do you really think that she might say yes, since I just got here, what would she think?"That we want to go off and make out and to be alone; I do not know what to say. Let us not do that because I do not want her to be suspect of that."

I wait and then answer, "I guess that is not a good idea, at least not today, maybe later this coming week we can get permission for several of us to go to a movie, how does that sound for now?"

She agrees, "I would be the first to suggest what you said, as I want to get you alone because I need your kisses, hugs and all the affection I can get, so I guess we wait, right?"

"I suggest this, lets just take long walks around the campus, over to the football field and around just so we can be alone but visible so no one gets any ideas, okay?"

"Michael, I love you for your thoughtfulness and good thinking to protect us, especially me since I have more responsibility to behave and not cause any concern. I truly want to be here for the time we have left; its just you and I"

As we are just walking around with no purpose at all, I just remembered that the Den [a place where the students can vent their frustrations and buy treats and best of all listen to music on any of the local stations], has been rather idle lately because there was no one to chaperon and keep an eye on the students.

I stopped in my tracks, looked at Delia and said, "Hey why don't we go get permission to open the Den tonight and let all the guys and girls know so they can come there this evening and have a good time. I can be the chaperon and enjoy it as well, what do you think?" "Michael that is a great idea, I would like that myself and we can be together."

We walked over to the girl's dorm, found the housemother in her office, we knocked on the door and called out to her. She invited us in, we said hello and we presented our idea about the Den; she looked at us for a few moments and then said, "I think that would be fine and you Michael will be the chaperon?"

I said, "yes I will take on the responsibility, but first we will go and see how much of the treats there are and check the cooler for drinks. Can we be there for at least 2 hours; 7:00 to at least 9:00 p.m.?"

She says, "that seems okay, but let me call Miss Brown and arrange the time and I will ask her if she can also lend you the key, so wait a few minutes while I call her."

We stepped out side into the hall and waited while she made the arrangements. Soon she comes to her door, invites us in and said, "Miss Brown says that it is okay and you can come over for the key at her apartment in the Teacher's Building, so good luck and be safe, but I'm sure Michael that you will take care of everyone, so good luck."

Delia tells me, "you can alert everyone at dinner time so they will know if they wish to be there for a good time. Oh! Michael that was a neat idea I am sure that my friends and the other girls will be delighted to do something else with their time besides watching TV and or staying in their rooms; it does get very boring when there is nothing to do."

"I am sure they will appreciate you for what you planned and they will be good; they will just want to visit, tell jokes and dance and have a good time, they can even play ping pong, and listen to records, I have forgotten what else is there for entertainment."

While she was talking, I was thinking; "Delia I tell you what I am going to do, I will buy everyone their first soft drink and a candy bar or chips of some kind, how does that sound to you?"

"Michael that is super, they will love you for that, how great is that, but I am the only one that can love you, catch my drift?"

"I said, "you know I can bring my small collection of records and we can also listen to those; do you or your friend have some records you or they can bring over?"

We secured the key to the Den quarters when staff and students gathered for this Saturday dinner, we were able to meet Miss Brown just before we all gathered and I promised to return it on the following day along with cash earned for sales.

Those that were interested and ready for an evening that would be much different than most weekend evenings began to show up minutes after I had opened the Den. Delia and I went about familiarizing ourselves with all the different goodies and checked the soft drink cooler.

The cooler was a bit low on drinks, so we found a couple of cases of cans and put them in the cooler; behind those that were already cold. We dusted off the record player, laid out the records I brought and those by her friends who set them on the counter as they arrived. One of the boys asked if he could go to the dining room kitchen a get a big pan of ice.

It did not take long before we had music going, they were enjoying the drinks, different chip selections and just visiting with their buddies or best friends; it was going well, they were all well behaved and just having a great time.

We also had fresh ice from the kitchen for our cups to cool off drinks as needed. They started dancing and singing to some of the music they knew the words to.

I had promised them that we could stay and enjoy the evening until about 9:30 or so, they all agree to that. A few, at a time started to leave close to that time; they were very nice about helping to clean up and put away items in their places.

Delia and I checked the Den, took out the trash and had already counted and placed the money from the sales of all the goodies in an envelope. I decided to itemize the drinks separate from all other items so that the money matched the amount of sales and made sure everything was in order.

There was no one left but us and no one around to check up on us, so we took advantage of being alone in the Den and we hugged, kissed and caressed each other for at least a half hour; wow what a treat for us both, since she had just arrived here today, we had not seen or touched each other for over a week.

What a beautiful ending to the day, it really meant a lot to us both. Delia was happy, radiant and just so passionate and she needed it all to satisfy her longing for me and the outwardly passion that we had for each other.

We locked up, walked back to her dorm arm in arm, when we arrived at the porch she turned around and cuddled into my chest and arms and says, "I am delighted I am here, this is where I belong, with you and this is great place to be and live for a good while longer. "I love you so much and care so much and do not want to be separated again.

I kissed her goodnight and wave as I walked away; What a delightful evening we had and with all those crazy persons having a good time; something they do very rarely. I am glad I was able to make it possible for those that chose to be there and make the best of it. It was good clean fun without problems. I will assure them that we will do the same during the balance of the summer time left before school starts.

I arrived at my dorm room feeling quite satisfied and happy as to how my relationship with Delia is progressing, the rest of the summer will be the best summer I will have had.

Sunday morning came early and I showered, shaved and put on a clean set of clothes and readied myself for a good breakfast and looking forward to seeing Delia again.

As I was approaching the dinning room I noticed that Delia and some of her friends were just a short distance away, so I decided to wait before approaching the front entrance so that I could greet her before we entered the dining room.

As soon Delia saw me she quickly started to walk faster and met me and rushed up to me and hugged me and was in my arms; smiling, gave me a kiss on the cheek. She looked so refreshed, her aroma and the fragrance she was wearing was just so delightful, such a beautiful sight this early in the day.

We had an easy going breakfast with all the others, after all it was Sunday, no hurry to go anywhere, no schedules and no work. I looked at Delia, I lean over and whisper in her ear, asked her, " do you think you and I can volunteer to stay and help with the cleanup?

She quickly answers, "Honey I really would like that just so we can still be together for a while longer." I will go ask the cook or dietitian. She quickly returns and says, "the dietitian was surprised but happy that we were volunteering to help."

We finished our breakfast and walked over to the kitchen and greeted those there and told them we were ready to help and how could we help. We were asked to start bringing in all dished and silverware from the tables and then clean the tables so that they would be ready for Monday's meal.

Since it was Sunday there would be no evening meal today and not till Monday. Delia and I spent about 1½ hours helping out fixing the dinner bags with an acceptable assortment of sandwiches and other goodies, she was in rare form,

Every time she caught me busy bending over a table she would poke me in the ribs and say, "How is it going poky you need to pick up speed."

She is such a delight and always with a big sexy smile and always walks away teasing me to go after her, which I did twice and caught her in a corner and she puts her arms around me and kisses me with such passion. I sure hope we weren't setting a bad example if someone were watching us.

It may seem rather goofy but it is really important to have a bright and flirty relationship, but at the same time a sincere loyal one that is as serious as any relationship. We are so tuned into each other and we do not skip a beat.

When we are in a semi-private location together, we hold each other close and those tender moments really count. Those moments generally are in the evenings when dusk is on its way and we can stroll around the campus and can experience some privacy together.

Now that school is not in session, the evenings and the weekends are very loose and there is no real control of any of those students that are working for the summer.

Delia and I really enjoy the closeness and semi-intimacy when we are together; we cherish those periods of time each and every day, as the summer is really very precious, we have no concerns or worries about anything in particular.

We both are currently living a sort of sheltered life here on campus; I work all day at the office and she participated in the tasks and chorus they are assigned on a daily basis.

Our day to day passage of time is sort of a routine, but it is satisfying and we both seem to have the peace of mind that is very comforting and allows us to communicate our thoughts and wishes and I encourage Delia to think of our future and I wish for her to have her own dreams of what she needs and expects from the months and years ahead.

On this particular evening after dinner I suggest to her that we just take walks around the various open spaces where we will be visible by anyone and think nothing of us being out there in a very casual manner.

We finally find a place to sit on some benches that are slightly sheltered from view but not hidden. We make ourselves comfortable and she gets very close and looks at me and says, "Honey I am dying for a kiss, I have thought about that all day long, come hold me tight and do not let go." I am so delighted and happy that I am here with you."

She moves her face close to mine and gives me that look that I love so much and I move my hand to the side of her face and I kiss her gently and look at her; her eyes are closed and then I kiss her with the kind of passion she cares for and she just melts into me and holds on tight.

After we have kissed several times she relaxes her hold on me, looks up and gives me that look of satisfaction and then just lays her my head on my shoulder. The fragerance that she wears just cranks up my desires; so heavenly and on her it is just so unbelievably satisfying.

She says to me, "Honey I love you with all my heart that some days I just can not stand myself with those feelings and emotions that I have deep inside."

"Sweetheart I love you too and have my own feelings and built-in passion for you."

We finally decide we need to take a walk and cool off before we get into trouble, which we do not need at this time.

We take our time walking to her dorm, there are other girls and some of the fellows just having a good time by teasing one another and making jokes. We walk up to their spot and one of the girls looks up at us and says, "What are you two up to?"

I quickly respond to her, "You know that is a good question and I have no real answer for you." They all look at her like saying, its none of your business; she gets the hint and says back, "I am sorry I do not mean to ask like that."

I answer back, "that's okay, we do not mind and no apology required." We both took a seat on the nearest bench and I asked, out loud, "Would any of you want to go to the movies sometime this next weekend?"

They all spoke at once, "we would like that!, can you get permission to take us?" I say, "I will try and see if I can get the small bus and have more room to take more of you, okay?"

I had a resounding response from all of them, so I said, "let me get permission first before we announce the day, if they give me the okay." Well that was taken care of, for now.

Delia and I visited for at least another half hour and then it was time for her to call it a night. We moved around the corner in the porch where it was semi-dark and exchange a very deep and passionate kiss; it will have to last until later.

I took my time getting back to my dorm and my very quiet space, the space where I do my best thinking and putting many ideas together, but I do have a favorite pastime when alone; I am currently reading one of "Mickey Spillane's "Mike Hammer", detective mysteries. It occupies my mind and I also seem to calm down and relax before bedtime.

Tomorrow is another day in this new and interesting chapter in Delia and mine's relationship. It is very pleasing that now and for the rest of the summer it is very low keyed here on campus and there are no unreasonable demands on those that stay here for the summer and of course the same applies to me since I am only working during the day 5- days a week and there has not been any demand on overtime at the office, at least up until now.

Chapter   28

 discovered the following day when I approached the Dean of Students about my request to first of all to take some students to the movies and secondly to be able to use the bus for transporting the University students, like me, to and from UNM. I was told that the bus probably needed fuel and I should check it before we use it, so I guess that was okay with the dean.

I was able to fuel up the bus, check the oil and water and make sure it was all in order. In fact I am the one person who drives the bus with us UNM students on a daily basis as the previous driver graduated and is now gone.

I had Delia or one of the other girl students arrange for those who wished to go to the movies to clear it with their house mother for the drive into town for a double feature showing. We all had a good evening off campus and every one behaved well and they all were very thankful to me for making the evening happen.

For several days, we, Delia and I, were involved in what is our daily routine that can be somewhat boring and time does drags on and there is nothing we can do except do what we have to do and enjoy the time each that we spend together.

That time element that is cherished by us both, is our visits during evenings after dinner time, but there are days when I actually have to use more of my evenings studying, planning and executing my own next day projects for my classes at the university; that is coming up soon, in September for one more year, sure looking forward to getting thru the school year and finally, if all goes well, graduating.

Delia fully understands that it is of most importance and she will encourage me to keep up with those projects as she understands the value of the education that I place on the objective of me graduating as scheduled.

It has been 2½ weeks since Delia did come back for the summer to work and prepare for her senior year. I asked one day, "Sweetheart would you like to go visit your mom and dad this coming weekend or the following weekend?"

She looks at me sort of surprised and lowers her head and says, "Honey honestly I had not thought to do that. I feel sort of bad that it has not been on my mind, that is terrible to be so absent minded about that."

"I know that mom said she would talk to the dean and get permission to do so. Can we call mom tonight to find out if she has even done that, and yes I would like for us to go to see them soon." "Are you willing to take me, I would hate to take the bus there?" I quickly responded, "Of course I would like for us to go and besides I enjoy seeing your folks, they are very important to me."

"Also it is a short period of time when we can be together away from the campus and not be restricted on time."

Arrangements were set up for Delia to go home for a long weekend and it was agreed that I would be driving us both there. I am very pleased that there is trust in me on both sides; the school and her parents.

We did go the following Friday afternoon shortly after my week ended at the office and Delia was done with her chores and assigned work for the day. She was ready, excited and rushing around waiting for me to get my act together. It was about 5:30 when we were able to drive off for the weekend.

I asked Delia, "sweetheart what do your friends and any of the other girls think of the fact that you can go home for a weekend and especially when I am taking you there and us spending the weekend with your family?" "Do they say any thing or express any comments to you or indirectly to others?"

"My two friends say, "How lucky and fortunate you are to be able to go and then it must be great to have a boyfriend to take you there; we are jealous but we still care for you and we hope you two will be safe going and coming.

Through the course of the month of late June and then July and August, Delia was allowed to leave the campus a few times and that really had a positive effect on both Delia and her parents, especially her mom whom she closer to.

The enrollment days for all students returning to school and any new potential students would be happening in about two weeks. Of course to Delia that would mean that our very casual summer time for us both would soon come to an end; In her mind, as she spoke out loud recently, it was okay for her, which meant the sooner the better because in her mind she was thinking, planning and wishing for next summer.

She understands that next summer a whole different world of occurrences will take place for us both. To her it means finally becoming more of an adult and looking forward for a permanent relationship for us.

It just so happens that one evening last week we were being very close and being very close as we walked around the campus, held hands, shared an occasional deep satisfying kiss. She looked at me very intently, I was not sure what she was searching for and I was waiting to see what she would express to me. Her expressions were not serious and I hoped not earth shattering.

We sat down in a comfortable location on the field bleachers and she cuddled up very tight, kissed me on the neck and said very quietly, "Honey I am so happy we are both here and that I love you very much and I am so content."

She says, "I hope you are thinking and looking forward to next summer like I am and as I wonder how we will finally graduate, me here and you at UNM." I looked at her very seriously and said, "Sweetheart I've had the same thoughts over and over again."

Chapter 29

Our Summer Chapter Ends

September 4th, the campus is crawling with students, parents in their cars and trucks, it is as if they opened up the streets and directed all vehicles to one location; this school campus, it is so wildly different from the tranquility of the good old summer days when we hardly experienced any form of vehicles on campus.

Delia's parents again were here as well to formally enroll and sign her up for her last year of education and overseeing her so that she completes her 12th year of courses and does receive her diploma next late May.

September 12th, Monday morning, my day for rushing around and getting our group of UNM students on board the bus and off to our own campus, for a few of us, this is our last year as well and we need to make sure that we have all of our credits and credential in line so we can also graduate next June.

Everyone one of us UNM students, both on and off campus, begin to get into the routine of classes, sports and unrelated activities that makeup the yearly composite of activities required for that graduation,

I myself have one activity that is ultimately very important and required under the program of the USAF ROTC. Last year we began to receive a financial stipend from the Air Force so that we could meet some of our fiscal and educational requirements in preparation for graduation and then receiving our commissions at graduation time.

We had been in classes one whole week and two daily sessions of ROTC instructional classes, when they informed us that next week we would be getting the squadrons together for on-the-field practices and marching and we were told that we all better be there, no excuses accepted.

We were advised to get our uniforms and dress shoes in order and if some needed replacement, to let the person in charge of issuing those items. They implied that if we had gained weight or damaged our shoes or boots, to get them replaced sooner.

I shared those demands with Delia just so she would know what we have to live with and how we join in the ranks. She smiled at me and then said, "Honey I feel for you, but you are very strong and will be able to take care of your assign- ments, I hope some day to be able to go watch you and your squadron practice and march around the field as you have mentioned before."

I agreed, sweetheart, I will know soon enough once we are in our routine of classes for two weeks and then gathering of the squadrons to begin our first practice march.

"Here is what is going to happen, they will call us to form ranks of one's squadron, then the lecture and thanking us for being in classes again for the new school session.   Then they will start giving us commands, about face, salute, eyes right, eyes left and then forward march."

"At that time many of us will start stumbling and messing up, then starts the comments, "what is the matter, you people act like you have never marched before, get your shit together or you will be out here until it gets dark. It is really embarrassing to hear."

At this point Delia can not hold back and starts really laughing and giggling at what I have expressed to her as if she could not believe what I have just said.

When she finally calms down she says, "honey does that happen every year when the program starts? How long does it take to get back... into shape ?"

We both had a good laugh over that ridiculous expression of how our first day at forming ranks and getting our stuff together. I said that it is rather comical, especially when some of us are going the opposite direction from the commands, not funny to bear the frustrations.

This exchange of information and laughing our selves into a frenzy: someone who do not often carry on like that, it did surprise us both, so I said, " lets take a walk and talk about more serious issues about this coming school year and what we hope to accomplish."

I began to get tuned into the routine that I need to establish off campus and on campus with my responsibilities to pay for my board and room. I also need to make time for visiting with Delia, especially on weekends when we are both free of any school studies.

School had only been in session 2 1/2 weeks and on this particular Saturday I was busy most of the day with personal tasks; laundry, cleaning my room and then outside washing my car after neglect for 3 weeks. When it got to be time to get ready for dinner and the early part of the evening I clean-ed my self up so as to look halfway decent.

At dinner I met up with Delia just before entering the dining room. She was mostly her usual happy self, but I noticed it was not really her usual. I did ask, "are you okay and did you have a good day?" She answers back, "I did but there is something I need to share with you later, okay?"

I nodded yes and I followed her into the dinning room, we both sat at our own tables for dinner. Occasionally I would glance towards her and she seemed to be preoccupied, with what I have no idea, so I became concerned, what did happen since we were very close last night and happy.

I waited outside on a bench under the one tree close by and as she came out with one of her friends I walked over to meet her. I extended my hand to her and she closed her hand into mine and she was shaking a bit, so I held her tight to show her I was there for her.

I looked at her and she looked back with a slight sadness and she seemed upset about something, so I asked, "sweet- heart what is wrong, how can I help?" She said back, "Lets walk around the area to take a little longer to get to our favorite bench, okay?" I agreed and held her closer.

When we reached a spot on the auditorium steps we sat down quickly and she got really close and put her arm around my waist; at this time I kissed her lightly on the neck and she was immediately responsive with a kiss on my lips.

"Michael, last night after our visit and I was in my room with my roommate, she said she had something to tell me that she found out from Lupe, our classmate next door. Josie claims that Lupe told her that she had received a letter from Rose, I guess they write each other once in a while. Rose wanted to know how school was and they gossiped about some classmates."

"Evidently Lupe had informed her during the summer that you and I were very close and seemed more than just friends and were a couple, a very serious couple. I guess that Rose was not too happy. She wrote Lupe a letter and said that she was upset about us and she thinks that I stole you away from her. I guess she had a few choice words to say about me and was upset that I had taken up with you, I was her classmate last year." She did not know why.

"Honey it really bothers me that she should speak that way about me, after all I do not know what she thinks happened and she was the one that broke it up with you. We both know what it really was and I never let it known that you and I were quietly visiting on occasions, right ?"

I agreed with her and at that time she started to tear up and was sobbing lightly, I drew her closer and kissed her lightly on her cheek and was comforting her and I said, " we know what the real truth and how this came about, let her and her goofy friend or friends think what they think. Do you think that more of your classmates know, are they talking about us?"

"Honey I have not heard much about it except what Josie has told me since Lupe only received that letter yesterday."

"Tell you what, sweetheart, talk to Josie and ask her to go to Lupe; that she should keep the letter issue to herself and not talk to others, after all they do not know what the real truth is and that it is unfair to gossip about it."

"No matter what they say or do, you and I have a solid relationship and we share a love like no other, sure there are some that are jealous of you because of what you have with me as your partner and they can not take that I away from us. It will blow over soon. Do not let it get to you, I wish you to be happy as before and I love you as never before."

She reached up and drew me in closer to her and she kissed me with so much passion, I am glad no one could really see that happen, for our sake. She quit being emotional and I dried her tears, I held her very close and she looked into my eyes and said,

"Honey I love you so much no one could ever tear us apart and I am so proud of us and how we have the best love as you say and I will not let it upset me anymore. If someone says something I will just smile and walk away, happy and content with what you and I have."

Our evening visit ended better than I expected, especially after the sad or unwanted news she shared with me, but the way we talked it over helped her quite a bid and it also was satisfying to me, because now she has a way of dealing with any comments directly or from the gossiping group.

It is day after the emotional and frustrated sharing of the subject that neither one of us would have cared to deal with at the time, but it was unfortunate that it occurred. The subject did involve me and my past relationship with Rose. I did need to deal with it in a personal way with Delia, she did not deserve what she had been informed of and how she was accused without any proof.

I did the best to perform my duties in the office, but I could not help but occasionally toss the situation in my own mind; I thought how could I further, in a very personal manner, guide Delia to deal and ease the emotional aftereffect without any consequence, again so she did not deserve what she was accused about.

That evening after dinner she and I met and she came to me looking the best that she could for now, I opened up my arms and motioned her close and held her tightly as she also held me very tight. She said, "honey I feel much better today and it is only because of your help in dealing with the accusations."

I kissed her on the cheek, since we were out there in the openness where other students are going in different directions. She took my hand and held on with her other arm as we walked away and shared that closeness she really needed.

We managed to find a semi-secluded place to sit and direct our attentions to each other. She said to me, "honey I do not know how I would have handled what I was confronted with on my own, you really saved me from dealing with the situation and hearing your advise was such a support, that is why I love you so much and I do not care what anyone thinks and says, because I will do what you suggested to me last night."

We had a very close visit tonight and I assured her that I am always here for her, she smiled and said, "honey I am yours from now and ever, with all my heart."

We wished each other goodnight and sealed it with one of our passionate kisses, I know it is what we both look forward to each night, because it is both a very satisfactory way of ending our day as well an exchange of affection that will keep us until the next day.

The next few days of classes, work and most of all the fact that we both look forward to those precious minutes of the time element that we are able to visit and exchange our very most intimate thoughts and ideas; it is as if we are our own island, very much apart from others; it is our time capsule that is very special since there is no other way.

It is Friday, 5:10 pm , I just left the office and was glad to see that the weekend was upon us. I plan on refreshing my body and my mind to see and visit with Delia in a more relaxing frame of mind, since there are no classes tomorrow and I can manage to go to into town, do some shopping.

Friday evening dinner is usually a bit more boisterous, even my fellow university classmates demonstrate that relaxed attitude, their persona is just I how feel.

I meet Delia outside after dinner, she walks briskly to me and throws her arm around my waste and says, "Hi honey I missed you today, but here we are looking forward to another weekend, I want to get you into a quiet place so I can kiss you with one of my wet kisses, do you think you can handle that?"

I said to her, "sweetheart, I can handle anything you dish out, how does that sound?" She gives me that shy sexy look and bumps me with her hip and says, The way I feel tonight, I do not think so, ha ha, but since I have to behave I will keep it mild."

THREE DAYS LATER

Today, this Tuesday, of all days that so and so squadron commander decided yesterday that we would practice our marching at 3:30 after classes. I was not able to work at the office. We were told yesterday to wear our uniforms and be prepared.

Well it turned out to be a somewhat cloudy and then to boot windy as heck, but we had no choice in the matter and so we had to "man up" as he tells us.

After it was all over and done, we all departed for home with a lot of dust in our eyes and mouths and not very happy with our day, we will hope the next time will be better.

I went back to my dorm room at the campus, sat around a little and moped and then laid down for a little rest, which was a mistake, Woke up jumped up and went for my shower. I dressed quickly after showering and the clock said 5 minutes after 6:00, so I rushed to the dining room, and was late.

I walked in the dining room and everyone looks up and sees it is just me, but only one set of eyes was studying me and of course that was Delia; she seemed puzzled to see that I was late today.

I was glad when dinner was over, I sure needed to move on as I was not in the best of moods. Delia waited outside for me, looked at me with her head cocked and with a sympathetic look, walked up to me and wrapped her arm around my waist and said, "Hi honey are you okay, do you feel alright?

I kissed her forehead and said, "I'll be okay now that you are by my side". She very intently looked into my eyes I then said, "honey it is just leftover burden of the very trying and nasty march practice we experienced today, but we have to take and deal with what we get or get into, so I will be okay and I am looking forward to our evening together."

"Honey" she says, I have thought about you all day long and I even had sort of a feeling that was very strange to me because I am normally okay all day long and usually just thinking about us and how I want to share my feelings and my latest thoughts with you; at the end of the day. I do want to tell you, I love you and can not help sharing that with you to say that I am here for you."

"I feel that we are really tuned into each other and the fact that I had those strange feelings; I guess it meant that I was there with you as you and your classmates were dealing with the conditions of the day, I guess I was just feeling what you may have been experiencing out there at the same time."

"Honey in fact the afternoon here was very unsettled, the wind was blowing and moving the dusts around as we left classes for the day on the way to the dorm."

We had a very quiet time for the rest of our visit she talked about her day, asked me about mine aside from what she already knew. She sat very close and cuddled into my shoulder and occasionally kissed me.

The next few days before the weekend were still rather hectic in the classes I attended as they gave out assign- ments that we are expecting to turn in during our Monday classes.

Friday evening after dinner Delia and I found a quiet place to visit and I said to her, "sweetheart the ROTC Ball is in three weeks, we need for you to get a formal dress and what ever you may need to go with it." Lets do this, let us go to see your housemother so I can ask for permission to take you into town to look for and try on gowns so as to pick one.

She quickly says, "Yes let us do it now, but one problem, I do not have the money to buy such a dress, is it going to be expensive? I will need to call my parents so they can send me what I will need."

I quickly said, "You do not need to worry, we will go and buy what you need, I can take care of that, no problem."

We went in to see the housemother, found her working on some papers, she looks up at us and says, " hello". I am here to seek permission to take Delia in to town for her to look for a gown , she said, " yes please sit down," so we did.

I started the conversation by asking, "I believe we had mentioned to you that our ROTC Ball would be held some time in October, well that time is nearly here and there are some preparations to be made by us, the critical one is that Delia will need to acquire a formal gown and accessories in plenty of time so as to be ready."

"We are here to ask your permission for me to drive her into town to go to a few stores and for her to see what is available, if not she may need to order one, I am asking, may I take her in for that purpose?"

"I hope I am trustworthy to do so, her parents are in Las Vegas and it is a little too late for them to travel here for her and to help her find what she needs."

She looks at us both, smiles and says, "Of course you are very trustworthy and I know that you are and will be looking out for her, so I do approve of you taking her shopping. When do you wish to do that?"

"I would like to do so tomorrow, Saturday, because as we both know it can not be done during the week, I do not wish to wait till next weekend, so will tomorrow be okay?" "Do you need permission from her parents, like tonight?"

She answers, "no I do not think so If you will only be there for a few hours or so. We may need permission from her parents for the night of the ball and you can have them call me, in the next week or so."

I said, "thank you very much, we shall go after lunch and be back way before dinner time, we will not let you down, so we appreciate your acceptance and we shall leave you for now, have a good night and we shall see you tomorrow."

After we left her office, we found a place to finish our visit and I said to Delia, "sweetheart, we have to make the best of the opportunity to attend the ball, as it will be our last time to do so, but there will always be many, many special treats for us to be together, catch my drift?"

She gave me that look of surprise but also one of delight for what I just quickly pronounced as a matter of fact. I looked back at her, tried not to make it seem like I had spoken something that was in my mind, but had blurted it without thinking first.

This seemed to be the first real comment or expression, on my part, of what the future could or would be once we were both done with our education. We have been just enjoying our relationship and dealing only with our lives in present terms without thinking beyond this time frame.

Delia just smiled broadly, reached for my hand and gave it a gentle squeeze and did not attempt to question or add any comments, which I can very much guarantee were in her own frame of mind. I adore her for how she accepted my statement but did not respond and left it stand for now.

We both walked to my car, got in and left for town as we had planned as we were given the go-ahead to go shopping. We spend 2 hours plus visiting several department stores in the girls-women's sections looking for her gown.

She was trying so hard to pick a gown that would please me instead of concentrating on how it would fit her and if she indeed would feel good wearing it.

I finally looked at her and said, "sweetheart regardless of what style you select, the only suggestion, pick a blend of colors that goes with the Air Force blues and how it fits you is very important, because I know you will look beautiful and also gorgeous in it."

She relaxed about her choice and selected a very well fitting gown that enhanced her body and was more than just a gown, it was such a pleasure to see her wearing it, I can now imagine how much more beautiful she will look when she also wears the matching shoes she later chose and then we stopped and found her a great necklace that complemented her gown, shoes and her personality.

We took all those great items she choice, and I took care of the purchase. She was in heaven, it seemed, she was very much alive, bouncing around as we left the store and was thanking me to no end. She seemed a little concerned, so I asked, is there something wrong?"

She says back, "honey I can not let you purchase all those wonderful things, my folks will want to pay you back."

I quickly responded, "no they are not, it is with great pleasure that I wanted to do that for you and I will not hear about paying me back, okay?" "I just want you to be the most beautifully dressed and happy girl, in my eyes and that will be the highlight of our attending the ball, since it will be our last; until other functions??

We arrived back at the campus, both of us smiling and I personally was very content at how successful we were at finding exactly what she deserved and liked for herself.

She quickly asks, honey would it be okay if you kept the gown and shoes with you at the dorm until the morning of the ball; I do not want to see the looks I will receive if I were to walk in with the big box and shoe box, I do not think that is needed, at least now?"

"That is a great idea, I will just put them away safely behind my clothes in the closet; no one needs to know and of course I will not tell. Let them all wait till that Saturday when you will walk out of the dorm, dressed like a young princess on her way to the ball !! Let them feast their eyes then and wish it was them and not you, it will be something for you to remember and cherish for as long as ever."

The next two weeks, in anticipation of the day, passed quickly as we were both involved in our daily tasks and the normal routines that could not be avoided.

One evening after dinner, we joined hands, walked as one towards the girl's dorm but in a round about way to kill time and have our own bit of privacy. She turns to me,

"Honey I get these really short vibrations almost like chills, they only last a few moments, but it is because they come when I think about how I will feel on the night of the ROTC Ball, it just makes me so happy and I am so delighted that we will be there as a couple; just as I have began to think of us as…. a real couple for always."

"Sweetheart I also am thinking ahead as how it will be the very first time that we will be somewhere as a couple to enjoy, live it to the most and cherish it for a long time."

TWO WEEKS LATER

It is Saturday noon, that special Saturday, the day that Delia will experience a night of wonder and pleasure that she will cherish for a very long time. It is after lunch, I am now carrying the "big box'; her precious gown, and the box with her matching dress shoes. I know she can hardly wait to be dressed, all prettied up and looking like her own version of a princess, a princess for the night, this is her night.

She knew she would be meeting me in the porch so that she could take her gown and shoes upstairs. She meets me there and she is all smiles, very lively and bouncing around. She comes to me and throws her arms around my neck and gives me a very wet sweet kiss. Luckily I had put the big box down for the moment, I expected that to happen.

There was no one around to see the action between the two of us; something to be grateful for, .to avoid unwanted chatter or gossip.

We quickly disengaged from that hug and kiss and I looked at her and I said, "sweetheart, we just need to wait until tonight, because we will have plenty of time for many hugs and many kisses, okay?"

"I will come by for you at 6:30, I will meet you in the front entry hallway so I can help you with your gown as we walk out to the car and help you get into the car."

She looks at me and says, "Okay...." puts on that little act of being sad, but I have learned to see through that smoke screen she is very good at putting out there, so I tickled her and squeezed her arms and said, "I need to go and most important is that you need to go also because you have much to do to be beautiful for the ball."

I left for my dorm room to likewise to get myself ready, put on that uniform and a white shirt. I have already polished my black low boots and I will be ready for tonight.

We arrived at the large event building where the ball was to take place, good thing there was ample parking near the main entrance, but I still walked her to the front lobby, held up the back of the gown so it wouldn't get soiled going in.

I rushed back to the main entrance and I had Delia place her right arm inside my left arm so that I could leave my arm to be able to salute any and all commanding officers who are to be attending the ball. We went through that routine and then were able to find a table to get comfortable for the evening. We found one with a couple of my fellow friend cadets and their dates and just took seats and relaxed.

I looked at Delia and I could tell she was impressed with the fact that she was there, she had a broad smile on her face, she leaned sideways and momentarily placed her head on my shoulder and then kissed me on the cheek.

We danced, we joked, we ate, we drank refreshments and just had a great time. Delia was the happiest I have seen her and she was enjoying every minute of it. She was all bubbly and excited. Those slow dances are a great way to be close, for her to cuddle and she whispered all those ....I love you and said she was so thrilled to be there and having such a great time and especially the two of us together.

We had planned to have the best time possible, because this was my last year and opportunity to do so, especially having Delia with me really was what made it the very best.

I was committed to bring her back to campus, on time and safe and sound, so I did so and Delia advised the house mother after she entered into the hallway near the office, so we would be in the good graces of her, us having proved that we had made a commitment and had kept it.

I'm sure that Delia was faced with all kinds of questions the following morning, which was Sunday. She informed me that her roommate and other friends asked many questions about the previous evening; I guess they wanted to know everything about the ball.

She shared as much as she could recall, one question after another; as she related them to me, she did so with a sense of pride, and I could see that she was very pleased to have been there and be looked up to as so fortunate to have been there and had that experience that none of her classmates would probably ever enjoy, in that manner.

Little by little she and I talked about what great memories we will have about that very very special night out consider- ing a school with very limited social opportunities to be out as we were that night. She is so thrilled and it was only because of me being what I am, she tells me.

Two Weeks Later

We both were back to our so called normal routines, but with very positive thoughts about us as a couple and after that experience with the ball, the mystery of our future and how we would go on after we left the limits of school and the campus.

One evening after dinner as we visited and kept to ourselves, she brought up the subject of where would we be at this same period of time after we both had graduated and left here. She says, "honey may I ask, where will we be, where will you be? and what about me?" She looks at me with a bit of concern and some sadness and in a sense questioning, what is to happen to us as a couple.

"I am asking because I love you so much and do not ever want to be separated from you, in my heart you are here, I want to be in your heart as well," as she gently puts her open hand on my chest and says,   "honey am I there in yours?"

"Sweetheart how can you possibly think that you are not there." you are sharing a very large part of me and I could never leave, go away without you, you are a very permanent part of me."

I pulled her gently closer to me, caressed her face gently and then kissed her lips and looked into her eyes and said, "sweetheart please be assured when we leave here next year we are going away together and no one will be able to stop us or tear us apart, never." "I will want you to be the happiest person at that moment in time."

"I am so looking forward to that moment in time when we have both completed our education and then we will decide exactly what we will be doing and where we are going."

It was now time for us to move on to our dorms for the night and be ready for classes the next day, I walked her to her dorm and found a spot where I could kiss her good night and tell her, "please be happy, tonight, tomorrow and always from now on, okay?"

The next day after I got back from work and checked my mail and rested for a few minutes, I decided to make a call, now that I was thinking about certain issues.

I picked up the phone, I dialed Delia's parents home, in 3 short rings her mom picks up says hello and I said, " hello, this is Michael can you talk for a few minutes?"

She says, "Sure, but is there something wrong?"

I quickly say, no! nothing is wrong I am only calling for two reasons, one is that next weekend [Saturday] is school homecoming with all kinds of activities and I want to know if the two of you are interested in coming, I am inviting you, so the four of us can visit and you can enjoy it, for the last time.

Secondly, is your husband home? If so can he also come to another telephone because I have a question for the both of you at the same time."

She says, "sure let me call him and he will pick up the other extension." She calls out and he goes to the other phone and says, "Hi Michael what's up?"

I speak up and say, "I have a very important question for you both and I hope I do not shock you for now." I am calling to ask this…. I wish to ask for your daughter's hand in marriage, but wait, here is what I wish to say, I want to propose to Delia soon, but this is only, how can I put it."

"She and I have been discussing our near future and our far distant future and she has been a bit concerned about us and is a bit sad because she wants to know how we feel about each other and where we will go from this time period into another period of time."

"As of now I wish for her to be happy, to have no doubts about us now and later. I do love her dearly and I will never leave without her by my side."

I sincerely believe that if I propose to her here soon and assure her that we will keep the "engagement" secret from everyone because the more outward and official proposal would be next summer after our graduations. You will know from now on and I hope you will be comfortable with the on-going relationship until that time comes."

There's silence from them for just a few moments and finally they both spoke, one at a time, her mom says, "What a surprise I would not have been expecting that you would be asking for permission to marry our Delia yet, but I am very pleased at this time and I know that the two of you are really together in a relationship and because I know how she feels about you, I have no concerns in that respect."

Delia's dad comes on and says, "Michael what a surprise and I am sure Noreen too appreciates the fact that you have decided to call us and ask our permission before you take the next step to propose to Delia. I give my sincere yes to your request, "Noreen what are you thinking?"

"I very much also say yes to you Michael. You are so thoughtful and I know deep inside that you are very sincere and you have shown your love for Delia and you are so good to her and thoughtful for her happiness and safety and I will wish you both the best of everything in the future."

"Delia has really grown up in the last 18 or more months, since she met you, that I know that she knows exactly what she wants and expresses what she has never felt before."

I slipped in and said, "you have raised such a beautiful and joyful daughter that I feel like the lucky one to have such a relationship with her and she has been very honest and has been very bold in expressing her feelings all these months."

I will never let her feel anything less than happy, loved and protected as well very much needed all the time."

Her mom spoke up and says, "Michael we really do appreciate what you have said and what you wish to do in sharing with us and your honesty and I can just see Delia jump up and down, so be prepared for her reaction, best of luck."

Delia's dad closes the conversation by saying, "again you have our yes without any doubt and also we will be here for you both in the future and will wish you the best, so thank you for coming to us first, good luck."

The mom quickly says, "for the both of us we accept your invitation to go to homecoming, let us know later when to be there, okay?" "goodbye for now and say hello to Delia."

The Following Evening

Yesterday was Thursday, I planned it that way, so that I could give full attention with my surprise to Delia today; Friday evening and looking forward to a good weekend with her. We met while entering the dining room for dinner. She squeezed my arm as we entered and expressed quiet kisses.

I said hello and squeezed her waist and said I would see her after dinner.

I caught up with her and her friends outside and beyond the exit way; she turns around and comes up against me and she says, "honey I have missed you since yesterday, did you work hard today?" I said, "sweetheart for a Friday, it was a tough day both at school and then at the office, but I am very happy to be here with you."

"besides I have some interesting thoughts to share with you here shortly when we are more alone." She turns sideways stops and says " what kind of thoughts?" "What are you up to, you better tell me soon or I may need to hurt you, laughs."

"Why, are you going to hurt me?" "Yes I will hurt you and it will not be fun." She starts laughing more and is poking me.

I said, "Okay I give up, lets walk a little further and I will tell you what I am up too, you may not be too happy." "I spoke to your mom and dad last evening before dinner, we had a nice talk, boy are you in trouble."

She quickly interrupts me and says, "Why are you calling my parents, I have not done anything wrong and besides you should have told me last night, not waited."

"I can not tell you why I talked to them, but I did invite them to come next weekend to homecoming and to see you be an attendant to the homecoming queen. I think you should get on the phone now and call and also invite them to come down and visit, okay?" "Come I have change for your call."

She looks at me and sticks her tongue out and says, "you are telling me what to do?" I say to her, "here are some quarters, lets go to the phone booth, there is no one there now." she took the quarters I handed her and stepped into the booth and called.

"Mom this is Delia, can you talk for a few minutes?" she evidently says yes, so Delia is asked how she is doing and is everything okay. She says back to her mom, "there is this pushy person who told me I had to call you; can you come next weekend for homecoming?

"I have forgotten to tell you and dad that I am one of the attendants to the homecoming queen". She gets back a yes answer and she turns around and sticks her tongue out at me. That girl is full of surprises and full of it.

She puts her hand over the receiver and says to me, "mom wants to talk to you, hands me the phone to talk. I say, Hi how are you two doing?"

Her mom, says to me, "how is it going with our friend there have you done anything yet?" I say not yet, Delia could not see what I had said into to the receiver , but I did say louder, "are you coming next weekend?" I got an answer of yes.

We said our goodbyes and walked off to find somewhere to sit and enjoy the nice pleasant evening, but it is now the fights will start until I pop the question.

"You still have not told me why you called my parents last evening, what are you hiding from me? You better tell me or I am going to hurt you."

I said, "Just be patient, I'll come around to the bad news."

The look on her face was an expression I did not expect, so she says to me, "why do you have bad news what is going on with all that secrecy between you and my parents?"

We found a quiet more reserved spot to sit and be away from most all couples just sitting around talking. I motioned her to sit and I sat next to her, I reached over and cupped her face with both hands and said softly, "sweetheart I love you very much, can you understand that and how I feel?" Next I kissed her softly and long and then looked longingly into her eyes.

Chapter 30

"I have a question for you…… I hesitated for a moment until I got the nerve and then reached for her left hand, I kissed it and then said softly, "sweetheart will you marry me?" Her eyes went wide open, the expression of complete surprise radiated from her face, her mouth was wide open and for several moments she could not say a word. Finally she says, "oh my god, you, you… just asked if I would marry you !!?

"Am I hearing you right?" you want me to marry you, how when oh my god what is happening here?" She let out a squeal, raised up from her seat and threw her arms around me, looked at me and said yes ! yes ! I will, but how when and what are you saying?"

"I said to her, "sit down and let me explain okay?" she did and I said, "okay I called your parents to ask them for their permission to marry their daughter, you, and they said yes and were very surprised that I called to ask them."

"Honey I am too surprised and I am delighted, happy and everything you can imagine and I just can not imagine that we are talking about getting married, " again, how, when?"

"Well, the other evening we were talking about our future and what we expected from each other and where would I be and where would you be, I noticed that you were concerned and maybe had some doubts about us."

"You were in a mood that I did not want you to be experiencing and that there was no need for you to be in that mood. I do not want you to feel that way, there should be no doubts in your mind. By asking you to marry me, there should not be any more doubts in your mind from now on."

"From this day forward we will be together without any doubts and I want you to be happy, content and thinking about our future together."

"This is what we need to do, our engagement is to be a complete secret to all here on campus. I do not want to know about the gossip, it shall just be us and your parents only that will know this secret. I am not even going to mention it to my own parents for now."

"I am thinking to keep it a secret until after we graduate and are at that point in time when I can officially ask you again and surprise everyone." What do you think, tell me your thoughts, I do not want to just be the one who agrees."

"Oh honey I like that idea, I can walk around knowing that something very special has happened between you and I and no one needs to know for now, something that no one here has and may not experience for years to come."

"I am just concerned that because it is such an unusual personal special occurrence and there will be much gossip going around, something we do not need to deal with."

"Honey I agree with you completely, it is best to keep it a secret; it will still be very special to me when it happens again, now my heart is completely open and there will be no more doubts as we plan for those precious days to come."

She reached over and kissed me with such tenderness that I had not yet experienced from her, I now know that she is truly in touch with her innermost emotions and is probably in a peaceful accepting mood, because she now feels that I have opened up myself to her and verbally expressed all my emotions and feelings towards her by proposing, for what will be the ultimate goal for the two of us.

I held her very close and caressed her face; I asked her, "sweetheart, are you okay now?" She answers, "Oh honey I have never been better or more happy then I am now, you have expressed those four words that makes me feel like I have gone to heaven."

We held each other for a few minutes not saying much but absorbing the intimacy and passion we had exchanged. It seemed she was just in a state of bliss and very peaceful.

She pulls away slightly, looks up at me and says to me, "I now know that we are really meant for each other and that no one can come between us." "For me this is the second most beautiful experience that I have ever had."

When visiting hours were over, I needed to walk her back to the dorm and call it a night; a very enlightening evening with all the passion that spilled out from Delia as she poured her heart to me and I offering very much the same to her.

Saturday Homecoming Day

Delia's parents arrived around 10:33 a.m. I had been keeping an eye out for their arrival, since I knew the car and color. I managed to walk over quickly so they would know that we were expecting them. Delia also was waiting and she walked over to them and they exchanged hugs and kisses.

I stepped up to them and greeted them and mentioned to them that it was great to see them and had missed seeing them since school started, meanwhile Delia is moving around and all excited, humming ..... I can not imagine why.

Her mom looks at her in an inquisitive way and says to her, "you really are glad to see us, I guess you missed us or something else is going on;" she had a smile on her face that was really saying that she suspected.

Delia is all action, could not stand still and blurts out, "I have great news for you both."

She quickly tells them, "Mom and Dad, Michael proposed to me last night I had no idea that was going to happen and I was completely surprised and he told me, after I had settled down, that he had called you and asked for permission. I just could not believe what was happening."

Her mom interrupted her and said, "we are fully aware, except we did not know that would be soon, so that was really quick;" she looks around at me, smiles and says, " also it is a surprise to us, meaning your dad and me, that it happened so quickly."

"Michael has asked me that we not tell anyone here or anywhere, that we should keep it a secret, because he is concerned about all the gossip and discussion that gets started if they know." He wants just the four of us to keep it to ourselves until later and that includes our relatives, okay?"

Delia, stops, then cuts in, says, "I need to go start getting ready for my part as an attendee with the queen, so you will be seeing me in the procession around campus and the football field at different times during the game."

I invited her parents to follow me to the dining room so that we could get some cold drinks and sit around and visit. We spent at least 45 minutes there and then I walked them over to the gym field and sat in the bleacher waiting for the game.

The homecoming and the game went well, in fact the school won the game and everyone was having a great joyful time with the events, later in the evening there were some celebrations and awarding of awards to players.

The parents decided that all four of us would go out and enjoy a nice meal, we acquired permission for Delia to go with her parents, we had a great visit; they were all very pleased to have been able to see each other and they went off to stay at a motel for the evening and then head back home the next day. Delia was okay seeing her parents again, but she did realize that her place was here now, and that she and I had taken that next step in our relationship. She says to me, "honey I now accept the fact that I belong here with you and I just feel that much more mature, pleased that I now have that peace of mind that I guess comes with having crossed from one frame of mind into another and the future."

We told ourselves that homecoming had come and gone and some day we will look back, think of it as a stepping stone to our future and would not experience that again.

The next three weeks were hectic with classes at UNM and then working part-time added to additional scheduling and compromising with other personal issues. I found myself not being able to visit certain evenings with Delia; it bothered me and I know it bothered her as well, but we are both strong and have the peace of mind that we are there for each other.

In three weeks it will be the Thanksgiving break for all of us at school and here for the students, who will be ready for a break and a chance to go home and kick loose and enjoy their freedom away from this campus.

I would be away from classes for at least 5 days and I asked my supervisor at the office if I could have Friday before the weekend and the following Monday. I wanted to go up north to see my folks and also spend some days with Delia at her home; a relief from being cooped up here on campus. That period of time would be very good for the two of us and I am sure there would be discussions about the new surprise I dropped on everyone concerned.

Her parents made the point to ask what my plans were and how Delia would be part of those plans. Did I even know where I might be stationed for active duty; as I had at one time informed them how the process works after one receives a commission in the Air Force. I assured them I had no idea where but maybe just maybe I could suggest the type of functions I would prefer based on my education and past and current experience in planning and design.

The days off for Thanksgiving were what we both needed desperately, it just allowed our minds and bodies to relax and cool down from the rushing and frustrations of the every day, meeting the demands of our own educational tasks.

Delia acted so peaceful, she was very helpful to her mom and she was very talkative with both parents she seemed so much more mature. She and her mom were on occasions very secretive about what they talked about and I could see that Delia was very attentive to her mom's instructions or advise. She is definitely more grownup and confident in herself.

She has a great attitude around her parents but she is still the flirty, sexy, teasing Delia that I have gotten so used to because that is her personality and I hope she never changes, not for me or for other reasons.

Once back at the campus, schedules and tasks were back to haunt us and demand that we get back to fulfill each and each and every one. Looks like lots of work till the next holiday which will be the Christmas holiday.

Within the week since we returned, I took some time off during the noon hour and stopped at a jewelry store to view some casual rings of some type or another, but of course it would not be an engagement ring. I just wanted Delia to have and wear what is usually called a "friendship ring" I figured it could give her the feeling of an intimate connection and really not give out any other form of interpretation.

That evening after dinner we strolled along in a different direction towards the gym and the football field, I wanted for us to be a ways from others so as to have some privacy.

We sat on a bench under a tree beneath one of those good shade trees. I had the ring in my right trouser pocket, easy to pull out the small box with the ring I had bought today. I pulled over so as to have more room between us, had the ring in my hand and I said to her, "let me see your left hand."

She looks at me with an inquisitive look, but moves her left hand towards me and looks up at me like saying what is going on.

Well, I did not give her more time to think, I took the ring in my hand an reached for her left hand finger, and again said, " I again ask that if you will marry me, as I have this ring for you so that my asking you is a bit more official for now."

"Oh, honey what a surprise I just can not believe it." She looks at the ring, is admiring it, reaches for me, kisses me as she normally does but with much passion and again she can not contain her joy and she is totally off-the-wall happy.

I said to her, "sweetheart you should not wear it on your left hand finger where an engagement ring is suppose to be worn, so wear it on your right hand and from now on it will be your "friendship ring', does that make sense to you?"

"Honey I do know what we agreed upon but I was not aware that you would give me a ring at this time. Can I wear it all the time or just occasionally?" I will be careful with it, it is a beautiful ring and I love it and for what it means."

I squeezed her hand and kissed the ring and then her, I made my kiss last a long time and caressed her face; she seemed so happy, a nice smile and her eyes just sparkled, mainly because she had tears in her eyes.

"It is up to you when you wear the ring, do what you think best and the times will matter to you if you are exposed to more closeness to others. I hope I am making sense."

I guess it did not take long for her friends and some of the inquisitive ones to notice her ring and ask questions, Delia says she was very casual with her responses and said it was a "friendship ring", some had never heard that term, but did accept it.

The time was slipping by fast; the days and weeks were just disappearing rapidly between Thanksgiving and the up and coming Christmas vacation. I know that the both of us were looking forward to it with anticipation.

Delia would have an opportunity to go home and visit with her family. I was looking forward to the time off.

Recently she asks me, "You will be off for the holiday with no classes, but what about your work at the architect's offices? Do they take off for the holidays?"

I looked at her and said, "honey business goes on no matter what, but they usually close the office for a few days for Christmas and also for the coming of the New Year, so I think I will be working if they need me."

"It will be good because I will need more funds for 2nd and last semester. It helps feel more secure if I have the money to pay for tuition, journals, and materials for design classes." "I am very fortunate to be able to stay here and work for my board and room, so I am very grateful."

She squeezes my hand and kisses me and says, "honey you deserve it and we know you are very loyal to this place and I am so proud of you for what you have by now accomplished and you will reach your goal with next years' graduation."

We realized it was time to return back to the dorms, so we walked there and hung around for a little while longer and then I said, "sweetheart I guess it is time to go."

She hugged me and said softly , "I love you and thank you for my ring, it means the world to me and I will wear it with pride and will keep the secret here;" and she pats herself near her heart, we kissed good night till tomorrow.

year closing in on the both of us

The senior class was told that they were to get together and come up with a theme for a Christmas play to be presented at least a week before the holidays start. They had choice in the matter, Delia falls into the middle of all of this because her extra circular club deals with the drama club and with literature studies in their English curriculum.

I asked her, how she felt after they were given their instructions about the play.

She says, "honey I wondered if we had enough time which is 3½ weeks till we put on the play, so all seniors are to get together tomorrow after dinner and go over 2-3 ideas about a play and start selecting a cast. I suspect we have a lot to do beginning soon …. practice practice. You may not see much of me during our weekly evenings."

There was not much I could say regarding her describing how the next 3 and half weeks will come about.

I say to her, "If we just have a few minutes here and there, I think we will survive and our relationship will be the stronger for that matter, because we will miss each other more and more. I will miss seeing you for periods of time like we normally see each other."

This was one night visit that we made sure to make the best of it, because it will be short, I will walk her to the dorm, our personal touch and closeness will last for just minutes.

We made up for lost time on Saturday evenings, and most of Sunday; if we went to church and visited in the afternoons. We made sure that we could go to church so we could be together and close to each other before Sunday noon dinners.

I made the separation work for me by studying and being more detailed in my technical courses and studying the nature of our assigned design projects. I spent more time trying to be more creative with my presentations for review by our class professors.

I think each of us could hardly wait for breakfast and especially dinners so that we could catch a glimpse of each other and being together for less than 15 minutes at most.

We were so hungry for each others attention, touching and trying to get off a kiss or two. I was starting to unravel and crave those lush lips I was so hungry for. I told myself, how desperate can one get, my patience was almost gone.

I might have to declare war on the school staff for what they did to the senior class; I was feeling like a deprived male that had no direction. Time came when there was one more week till the weekend when the play was to be performed on the last Saturday before the holiday.

The senior play went on as scheduled, I was amazed on how well they performed their parts in the play and they had a good finish and the audience was pleased for it.

I caught up with Delia after the change of play dress up and getting back to normal; I was pleased and happy, because I got my sweetheart back, oh how I missed her for the last 2 ½ week of play practice.

I praised her for her part in the play and her ability to perform the part she was assigned; she took it in stride.

We met quietly where we could exchange hugs, kisses and the opportunity to hold each other, we needed it very much.

Our routine caught up with us again after all the personal intimate exchange of me presenting her with her ring, it was the high light of those days before the senior play had taken place.

Our break for the Christmas holiday was interesting to say the least; even though we were on vacation from our studies, I chose to work during the week days but would visit with family on weekends and also Delia at her home.

I arrived at Delia's home on late Friday evening to spend the next 3-4 days with her and family, New Years was on Sunday this year, so New Years Eve was Saturday. Her family planned a special dinner and gathering with their own family.

That evening turned out to be very special indeed; her mom and dad decided to dedicate that evening's function to us both. Her Dad spoke up first before the midnight hour by saying, "To us as a family and for the sake of Delia and Michael, I herein bless and dedicate the up and coming new year to our new couple as they have united themselves through Michael's asking our Delia for her hand in marriage."

"We are very proud of you both, you're such a perfect couple and are so grown up at your young age and her mom and I wish you the best future in the new year and years to come."

Delia's Mom spoke up next; you could tell she was some what emotional as she had tears in her eyes, but she went on to speak well of Michael and Delia's relationship; saying "I have never seen such well suited, to each other, personalities as the two of you."
"Michael is so good and generous and takes such good care of our Delia and then she gives back so much to him and I see nothing but goodness coming of this relationship, I too give them all our blessing as I feel that they will be a very unique couple on their own."

This was the best New Years Eve I have ever had; all this time Delia was just hanging on to me, so happy she could hardly stand still, so we had some champagne just to fit in with her parents and older brother and bring in the new year; the beginning of a year that will be full of memories and blessings never to be forgotten.

After the holidays we were back at the campus to face the beginning of this new year and any and all occurrences. Delia was very much looking forward to beginning the last semester of her last year. She has just been so bubbly and happy in the last few weeks, I just wonder.....why?

The why is that; she is so looking forward to the ending of the year and she is anxious for us both to take the next step and our trip into our future and beyond.

My classes for the last semester did not start until January 7th, first had to register for the last of my classes and then had to report to the ROTC main office to reestablish the forms to continue to receive our monthly stipend and to order any items of our uniform that we may have outgrown or even damaged with wear and tear.

It was a Tuesday after classes and working at the office, I do not know why but I had a strange feeling that I could not understand, so I kept it in the back of my mind and I went ahead and cleaned up and was ready for dinner by 5:45.

I left a few minutes early to be at the main entrance to see if I could catch a glance of Delia as she may also be coming for dinner. In the next few minutes her two friends that she hangs out with approached the entrance but Delia was not with them. I could not believe that, not here for dinner !!

I stopped the girls at the doorway, asked, "where is Delia? One quickly answered me, "she is not feeling well, in fact she left classes in the middle of the afternoon, went to the infirmary to see the nurse and now she is curled up in bed and they are not sure what is wrong, except it is also that time of the month for her. She did say to say hello to you for now."

I had a sort of nervous dinner, guess I looked distracted because it was noticeable to my fellow university students, so Robert asked me; "hey dude what is wrong, did the girl friend dump you?", seriously what is wrong, I or we have not seen you this distracted and JUST looking out and beyond."

I looked up from what may appear to be a bad case of the blues and guess I looked rather pathetic. I quickly answered, "I am just concerned about the fact that Delia, whom you all know, is seriously ill today and in bed under the nurse's care.

I looked at Robert and said, "and no she did not dump me as I am just concerned because she is very healthy as a rule."

They all almost spoke at the same time offering their concern as well and were wishing her a quick recovering, so I thanked them and they said, "She will be okay do not worry too much and stay in touch with the nurse and follow up on how she is doing. I thanked them and we continued with our dinner and I was able to cheer up enough to make the best of the last of my dinner.

I found her friend Josie and asked her to tell Delia that I am very sorry and sad that she was not feeling well today and that I would check with Lucy about her condition later.

I had a rather restless evening and night, did not sleep very well thinking about her hoping she would be well and be her usual, which I care for so much, love her outward personality when ever we are together and around others.

The following noonday after my morning classes, I headed for the nearest drugstore to find an appropriate "get well" card that would express my feeling admiration for her so I can send or maybe give to her at the evening dinner.

I managed to keep my head on straight and concentrate on my tasks at hand, must always be very precise and clear on all those architectural drawings I work on.

I could hardly wait till 5:00 or so to complete my hours for the day and leave with high hopes of seeing my sweet Delia.

I was very surprised to see, coming down the path, Delia with her friends Josie and Lucy ! She looked okay from where I was, but as she approached me standing outside, I noticed that her face coloring was different than the bright, smiling radiant look that she usually presents, so I walked up to her and extended my arms to her and she pressed herself against me and seemed delighted to see me.

We walked together, into the dinning room and went to our respective tables to sit and have dinner. I know that after dinner we will be able to visit privately and hope she can visit for a short while.

Our evening together was quiet, intimate with some passion just to reconnect after several days; we also made it known, we missed each other. I held her tight and was gentle and spoke quietly to her. She says to me, "honey I am glad to be almost myself after my getting sick, I missed you much and I love you for being concerned about me, but I will be okay according to the nurse that treated me, so in a couple more days I hope to be back to normal."

The next few days were days in which Delia little by little went back to being herself, it was very satisfying to me that she was now her normal self, the side of her that just goes on and on and I never wish anything but that side of her.

In another week the month of January will be over and we will step into February the start of colder sometimes more bitter than January. It will be much cooler, colder than before and mostly impossible to visit outdoors after dinner, which is rather sad, because we both need to see and touch each other in order to fill the gap of time during the days when we are both in class, she here on campus and me at the university.

I inquired with the housemother if there were times when they do allow couples to visit and watch TV in their large living room.

She did say it is permitted and it is only 4- evenings during the week; said to inquire with her later. And there has to be a mixture of other girls since it is a girl's dormitory.

I met Delia at the dining room the following day, she was all bundled up in a winter coat with her hands in the pockets, it was obvious she was cold and was trying to keep warm. I squeezed her arm said hello and she responded with a lip/mouth I love you and I winked at her. I was able to walk with her back to the dorm, hand in hand but in my pocket this time, my coat has large pockets…..very convenient for that sort of holding hands.

The days, the nights and weeks go by and mentally I always look forward to those final days of classes, but it is not the time to be concerned as of now. I tell myself that Delia and I need to just invest in our time that is left and make the best of it. Our destiny will come soon enough; worth waiting for.

I asked her one of the following days after she was well and herself again, " have you thought much about where we are now time wise and look forward till the end of the semester?"

Wow ! that turned out to be a very wide open question, I had just opened the door to fast talking fast ideas and more than I expected at this time and place.

"Oh ! honey you just do not know all the great ideas and things that I dream about, hope for and wish to happen when I graduate and you graduate. I am keeping it all to myself and keeping all that a secret, even from you, so do not even think that I will give away what I wish for, …… so there."

I looked at her in amazement, shrugged my shoulders, looked at her and said, "well I guess that tells me I should not have asked, but so be it. You are such a sweetheart and I know that response was just a tease job, trying to tell me that you have it all under control and I will just have to wait and see; you are so sneaky you take the No 1 title."

"Oh ! honey I am not trying to be sneaky and mean, but I should have the right to keep my wonderful ideas and what I expect when those great days come around, you know I love you and would never hold back later, but now !!!! ......

Two Weeks later

It is now 2 days till Valentine's Day, I reminded myself that I needed to make a path to the drugstore to find a very suitable card for Delia, it has to be just right, hopefully.

That evening at the dinner gathering . the staff member in charge of the school store and "The Cave" announced that she had a new fresh major selection of goods and cards for all to see and purchase, so the store would be open two evenings in a row before Valentine's Day starting tonight. She says, "So do not break the doors down getting there," she smiles and walks off, everyone is just looking at each in amazement.

Delia says to me, "Honey will you join me at the store to see what they have?" I looked at her, said, "sweetheart, I do not need to be there when you select what ever pleases you, besides I have already made my selection by sneaking around to the drugstore, so I am all set, it will be a surprise for you."

She gives me that sly inquisitive look, like what are you up to, no good this time, then she cuddles up to me and kisses me like I am accustomed to; "that is why I love you so much."

This is our second Valentine's Day together in the sense that we were able to be here and not separated. We exchanged our cards with our personal messages; her card to me was very passionate with much to say about our finally being together as she has been secretly wishing for, included were her personal declaration of her feelings, her openness as to what our future can be and hopes for.

Well, February is on its last leg luckily it only has 28 days and then we can look forward to a new month and one month less towards our final episode of our education and then starting our destination.

Our destiny is in the hands of our creator who will guide us. At that point it is my hope that we are adult enough to carry on and carry through and begin all the dreams we possess and surely hope we can.

Our weather, some days cold some days warmer, last week our ROTC commander decided, sight unknown, that this coming Thursday we would meet out at the football field and do perform more marching maneuvers, and he has some new marching techniques planned for us.

He was very adamant about those new marching techniques because he wants us to be at 100% as he is scheduling us for the day of graduation, so he says, "buck up and get it right." For his sake I hope the weather is much more pleasant then it has been usually or for our last march.

I shared that bit of information with Delia. I said to her, "well our illustrious commander says he will drive us to the ground until we are at a 100% with his new marching techiques."

She looks at me and says, "honey how do you and your fellow cadets;, she knows the term/ title we go by, feel about the new schedule for this week?"

"Well several of us stood around after class and griped and complained. "One of us did say, "hey ! guys we are almost there to complete our tour here and we need to understand that we need to take what they dish out and accept the assignment, we owe it to the ROTC program, as he has commanded, 'buck up' live and deal with it.

Delia was so sweet about it, smiled at me a said, "honey as long as you do not break a leg in the march..... smiles from ear to ear and then chuckles, but stops and says, I know you guys can do it after all you have been at it for four years."

She steps up close, touches my face and says, "honey I am only teasing you and from what I have seen you guys on the field before, you can do it, I bet even with flying colors. I so wish to be there on that graduation day and I will be very proud, specially of you." She follows it with a great kiss.

I thought to myself, "time marches on", and that is what we will be doing this coming Thursday.....march, march will be the theme, will need to wear our marching boots and our blues !

Thursday came and went and we did our best, took instructions well, got yelled at, cussed out but at the end he looks at us and smiles, "you guys did well, I thank you much."

We are still practicing our marching and coordination at least once every two weeks, believe it or not and our commander is not on our case anymore than is needed.

For once he did compliment us and we all look at each other like saying, Wow !!, but we all seem to be content that he feels that way and we do not want to disappoint him, as our graduation, commission is very important to us cadets.

Spring break at UNM is coming up and I understand that the school here will also take a break and allow students to go home for a few days; lucky for them. Turns out their break coincides with my break, so maybe I can take Delia up to her home so she can visit with family and I too can visit with them

The up and coming retreat will be an escape into the real world away from all tasks that keep us tied down to what may be considered as an artificial form of living just so we can be better prepared and educated to function in our ever changing society.

Delia and I did escape from the campus that we have been tied to and obligated to do our duties and perform our educational tasks as, each are soon approaching graduation.

We left on Friday late afternoon, no need to stay longer, as they were not serving dinner for the entire student body, just to those remaining staff and a few student stragglers.

Delia had called ahead at noon to advise her mom that we would be up after school classes were let out for the day. Her mom asked about dinner and Delia said we were not getting dinner here, so she said they would wait with dinner.

We did arrive shortly after 6:00 p.m. and sure enough her mom had dinner ready and hot, we both looked at each other and said, "Oh ! it will be great to have a home cooked meal for a change, much different from school cafeteria meals.

After a very fulfilling meal we and her family members were content and everyone looked like, I am ready to relax and not do anything, but Delia offered to help her mom clear the table, gather up all dishes and to do pots and pans.

What a great feeling it was to just sit back and relax without having classes, books and tasks to look forward to. We must learn how to appreciate these very simple but important times in our lives as we grow and explore other horizons.

We enjoyed those 3 full days and nights visiting and going out to movies, eating ice cream sundaes at the drugstore and a bit of shopping there in their town. It was so satisfying for us both to go out as a couple, hold hands, hug each other without the feeling that we're being watched and had to behave.

Delia looked so beautiful, she was so relaxed, content to our being together she was radiant and I could tell she was about as happy as she could be. I for one was very relaxed and felt comfortable with her parents and I could tell that they too were very comfortable with us being there.

Delia and her mom were very close, they hugged and her mom had that gleam in her eyes that said she was happy and proud of her daughter and now it seemed that they were comfortable with the fact that we were engaged.

They both wanted to see Delia's engagement ring as it was now proof of what had happened a few weeks ago. She went to each parent and hugged them and showed off her ring and there were those tears of joy as her parents admired her ring.

When there was a break in the display of her ring, mom and dad looked over at me smiled and both said, "thank you for the joy and happiness you have bestowed on Delia, it is an honorable gesture and she is so happy and so lucky that you have each other, we know that you both are and will be very happy together from now on."

"We both welcome you, prematurely, into our family, we are extremely pleased and happy that you found each other and we have never seen Delia so happy and content. We both sort of felt that she was too young to be in such a relationship even before she finished high school, of course you are a few years older, more mature and have a great future ahead, but now we do not have anymore concerns about you both."

Her mom continued saying, "We feel that you are both very smart and feel that Delia will want to continue her education at the higher levels and that you will work with her and guide her as she has complete trust and confidence that you are there for her."

Meanwhile Delia and I sat there and listened to the most interesting expressions of feelings from her parents that was unexpected at this time. I must say, it was a very interesting acknowledgement of their approval directed at us both and there is no doubt that we have their blessing, 100%.

I personally thanked them for their faith in us and how they offered to be there for us in the future if we were to ever need their advise, help and support. I told them, I and as a couple, would not ever disappoint them.

The weekend plus extra days went by rather quickly, but what a treat to be able to have those precious days together, it just restored our desire to be closer than it is possible while limited and restricted to the school campus.

I know that I personally am able to come and go as I see the need to attend classes and work in the architect's office, but Delia is limited to the campus, and for good reasons.

Here it is the end of the first week in March, in two and half weeks it will be the start of spring, look forward to warmer and longer days and nicer pleasant evenings to visit together. I just realized that in about 2½ months those long awaited days for graduations will be upon us.

I can speak for the both of us; we are so looking forward to the time for our graduations, but we must have completed all of our requirements for graduation; I must fulfill my credit hours plus all the ROTC requirements in order to receive that long awaited commission, I have felt anxious but some what nervous, just hope nothing goes wrong, as it means so much.

This coming Saturday night will be a special night here on the campus, they will be showing a film in of all things; Technicolor, beats those black and white ones we see here.

This is Tuesday of the week after that great movie they showed in the auditorium on Saturday. They announced in ROTC class that we were to have a swimming competition on Thursday evening at 7:00 at the indoor swimming pool with the naval ROTC team. This evening I will go to the pool and do some practice runs and diving just to build up my confidence and my own techniques; I know what they will be expecting.

After dinner that evening, as I walked with Delia, I mentioned to her about the up and coming competition on Thursday. I looked at her into her beautiful dark brown eyes and said, "sweetheart, I will not be able to visit you now as I want to go to the pool on campus and do some practice routines and build up my confidence for the meet."

She looks at me and responds, "Honey I understand and I know how important it is to be ready. Kind of short notice is it not?" "I guess you have no choice, so I will be okay, I'll just go read the novel I have been reading and or look at those great magazines you have bought me, so it is okay, we will make it up tomorrow night."

I said, "thank you for being so understanding, have no choice, after all it is all part of what we are looking forward to." ,The swimming meet later this week was competitive, very competitive. At first we were ahead several categories then they caught up and then we picked up a few more points but at the end they beat us by two lousy points; well that is the last time they will ever beat us… it was the last one …forever.

As always, Delia was full of questions about our ranking in the meet itself and of course I had told her about our past swim meets, so I explained to her that overall we finished the year, the entire 4 years behind the other team by two losses.

She looks at me with a slight smile and I knew it here it comes whatever she just dreamed up to say. She says, "well it appears you guys got your butts beat" and then chuckles, so I reached over and poked her in the ribs.

She comes back to me, "honey you are always my No.1,and starts to run off saying " no matter who beats your butts."

I ran after her, reached over and pulled her to me from her waist, she turns around still smirking, laughing and then reaches up and kisses me nice and wet, says, "I am sorry honey I was only teasing you, but we should do this more often I like it because it is exciting and personal and fun."

"And no matter how may times you lose, I will always love you and care for you, I will even clean and dress your wounds." Still smiling and says " honey kiss me its your turn.

I changed the subject; I did not want anymore of that foolishness she was dishing out at my expense.

I guess I need to be a good sport and put up with her teasing, but that is what she does to me, quite often.

I kissed her many times and we walked off headed for her dorm.... visiting hours will be over in 15 minutes.

As I walk away to my quarters, I think back to the teasing and exchange of comments about what I went thru during the swim meet and I said to myself, how lucking I am that I have such a spirited and beautiful partner in this love affair of ours and I love the fact that there is never a dull moment when she is with me. I hope it last a lifetime for us.

Two Days Later

As a surprise during this current week I found out that the administration had declared this coming weekend [Saturday and Sunday afternoon] as open for anyone of students who would wish to go down town, do some shopping and even to attend a movie or two movies in a row.

Students could take the city buses but should return before 6:00 p.m. because of dinner on Saturday evening and for the sack lunch that is normal for Sundays.

I checked with the girl's housemother and asked if I could take at least 3-4 students with me in my car and bring them back as required. I did mention one of the students would be Delia and maybe her friends and that I would be responsible for their safety and they abide with the requirements for us to be back at the campus by at least 5:45 p.m., she agreed and it was settled. We left shortly after 12:30 noon.

The weekend trip down town worked out well, five of us did some quick shopping and then managed to see 2-short movies in a row and kept our agreement with the housemother by returning around 10 minutes early.

"Time Marches On", because of me, who uses that phrase quite often, Delia and I have made it our declaration when ever we are keeping track of the weeks and the few months left until both of our long awaited graduations.

One Week Later

It is Friday 5:00 p.m. I have been ready for the end of the day and the start of the weekend, I am hoping that there will be an opportunity to go into town with a group of students who wish to see a movie or two, again, hope we are permitted to do so.

I rushed back to the campus, got ready for a shower, it was about 5:20 or so, but my phone rings; I say to myself who in calling me now? I answer and I hear this soft sexy voice say to me, *"you are in for a surprise this evening so you better be alert and you better not panic; be a big boy"*   and hung up.

Strange but I was not sure who called, was it Delia?, she must have disguised her voice or had someone else act for her, so what the heck am I supposed to do with that threat, if it is a threat...... and the worse part of it was she did not identify herself. I know not, to think now, bummer !, but I will be prepared for the worst and I better not let my guard down.

I went on to dinner and looked around to see Delia but I did not see her at that moment, I went on into the dining room, took my favorite seat. I still looked around and there she was, at her own favorite place; think she does that so she can keep an eye on me.

She looked my way and I waved at her, she waved back and threw me a silent kiss. Dinner was served, but I was a bit distracted, but managed to work on my dinner and dessert. As most persons are moving out of the dining room, I waited until Delia did approach near me and then I walked up to her and gently took her left arm as we walked towards the doorway.

When we were outside and away from others, I leaned in and kissed her on the neck and said, "sweetheart I was running a bit late and missed you when you arrived.

"I want you to know that I have a date with a sexy gal that called me earlier and said I had some surprises to deal with."

She pretended not to know what I was talking about, so I let it go and changed the conversation to her.

"Are you okay, did you take a little nap before dinner, you look so refreshed and radiant.?" Something must really agree with you that you look so good , good enough to lick and munch on, lightly of course."

"I missed you today and thought about you all afternoon at work, but I was still able to perform my tasks Some days are like that."

She says, "Honey I too miss you during the days and so look forward to dinner and the early evenings to spend with you, now tonight will be special. I need to go up to my room for a few minutes, I hope you do not mind, okay?"

I looked at her with a mild sensation and said back, "It is okay, I will just wait right here at this bench, our favorite."

I sat there and it finally occurred to me that there was some thing different about her, the way she was acting and she was dressed somewhat different then usual; I will check her.

I look up and there she comes she was sort of cupping her left hand within her right hand as she approaches me. I say, "is there something wrong with your hand?"

She smiles broadly pulls her hand away and gets real close she shows me her hand and is real happy and ..... she is wearing her engagement ring.

"I wanted to wear my ring, because it feels so me and that big part of you is there on my hand and it represents our bonding and the meaning that we are one together. I just wanted to wear it for you and so I can admire it as we visit for the rest of the evening."

That is only part of my surprise for you, the other one is; she moves in closer and says, "I am wearing some very special pieces of clothing you never get to see or to feel and admire; I am wearing a see-thru bra and panties with very delicate lacing and I know you will love them, very special just for you, my sweetheart."

She also says, "honey can we walk somewhere else where it is more private, just for a few minutes, you will not regret it, okay??

I looked at her for a moment and asked, " why do you want to go where it is more private?, she puts her fingers on my lips and says, "I want to show you more of this and she points to her chest and down to below her waist"

"Are you looking for us to get you and me in trouble? So we walked over towards the gym and around the corner of the auto mechanics wing, no one could see that location.

She opened her blouse and took my hand and placed it on her left breast and sort of rotated so I could feel then she did the unexpected; she raised her skirt up to just below her waist and took my hand and placed it on her lower tummy.

She tells me, "please rub me, stroke me up and down and see how it feels; see how you can see right thru my panties?" do you like what you see?' "Of course I love it all, but we must quit before we get into trouble, straighten your skirt and button up."I really hated to say that, but had no choice."

We walked around to the other side, and I motioned to her, "let us look in the shop windows and see what is in there, just so as to look innocent, even though we are not."

We circled around towards the one other building in line with the girl's dorm and crossed the grassy area towards areas around the dorm; there was no one in that area, so we were safe at least for now.

As we crossed the grass areas under the trees I say to her, "sweetheart that was a treat and surprise I never expected and you took my breath away, I am just barely recovering, you just do not know what you have done to me."

"Well honey I really felt like you needed that treat to lift your spirits up on a Friday of an all day busy schedule, tell me what do you think?" "Now you know what you have to look forward to after we are on our own and gone from here."

"Sweetheart I was over whelmed and truly surprised, I hope you do that again under different circumstances, okay?"

That was certainly an interesting evening visit with Delia, as much as I was surprised and then treated to such beauty, it is too risky to take any more chances.

She says, "honey I am glad you enjoyed yourself tonight."

Chapter 32

One week later and here I am still saying to myself and chuckling about the big surprise that Delia pulled on me, sure glad we did not get into trouble.

When we are together and either one of us brings up the subject, we break out laughing close for several moments, and then Delia finally says, "honey when I am in my dorm room I start sort of laughing and my roommate will ask "what is so funny with you.?"   "I will tell her it is an inside personal joke that you and I share, no way am I going to tell her anything."

I asked the following day after she wore her engagement ring if she had taken it off and stored it. She responded that she had, in fact when she went into the dorm she had turned the ring around so only the band showed and she was cupping the stone in her hand.

Again the days and the weeks were starting to go by very slow, I guess it is because we are looking forward to the beginning of the end.

The following evening after dinner when we got together outside of the dinning room. I extended my arms and she walked right into them with the usual very sweet smile.

She took my hands and spun herself into my arms and said, "honey I love you more and more each day. Will you be mine tonight even after I was a naughty last week?"

I just stopped momentarily and then we continued walking away, I was not sure what I was going to say, so I too said, "sweetheart I too love you more. Your surprise was absolutely unbelievable but great. I do agree that you were a very naughty girl, but under different circumstances,

It would have turned into a second night to remember, even though we will remember it from now on and we will laugh about it." We walked around various areas near and close to the dorm, because it is required that we visit within limits.

Delia asked if we could sit at a particular semiprivate bench. She seemed to have a quiet look on her face she took my hand moved over and kissed me gently and said, "I just want to say again that I am so happy, content and sort of bewildered as to how far we have come since we did bond together.

"I am so much a part of you and there are times, especially when in my dorm room that I want to dance around the room, and want to stick my head out the window, and call to you and let everyone hear me shout; Michael you are the love of my life, but then I come to my senses and just say it to myself quietly, and then those tears come down my cheeks. They are always tears of joy and my love for you."

"I can hardly wait until that very special time when we will graduate, and cross the threshold into our own special world. Forgive me honey but that is how I now feel; it is so close and yet somewhat so far away, right?"

"I too am overly anxious for time to fly, I, like you can hardly wait, I too count the days, the weeks and I have, in my mind, many vivid images of you, of me and of the both of us. I have not expressed to you how I am dealing with the waiting, but we are the same, waiting, thinking and all that planning we need to start putting all the pieces in the order in which we will probably wish for them to happen."

She places her head on my shoulder, kisses my neck and just sits there; we are both enjoying the closeness. I know she needs more, wants more intimacy from me but she also knows we are limited in what we can feel and express in the environment we currently live in.

"Honey I want to say that I feel strongly about our future and I so look forward to the beginning of being together and being a part of our own destiny."

We were both quiet for quite a few moments, or two minutes or more, I was the one that spoke up first, I said to her, "sweetheart I love and cherish your attention, your passion, and your love of life, our life together here, for now."

"Not a day goes by, in which I recollect in my mind all the wonderful feelings, memories of the many and I mean many special bits and pieces of affection, passion and your wonderful sexy kisses you shower me with, all of that means so much to me and I feel so blessed."

"I feel so lucky, so fortunate that we met like we did and I am absolutely ecstatic about how you were so persistent with demonstration of affection and showering me with all those "I care for you, then later "I love you" no matter what, and how you were so willing to wait to see if my situation would change, just maybe." I looked into her eyes as they returned my gaze and I could see tears forming in those beautiful eyes.

In one split second she reacted by quickly throwing her arms around my neck, sobbing lightly and saying out loud, "I now know why I really cared for you and then why I chose to love you no matter what."

"Honey my love for you was a distant love, one that I could not just ignore and I did not know where it was taking me, but I was willing, and I prayed, believe it or not, that in some distant space of time I could be there for you and you would be there for me and so now here we are, honey I guess my prayers really were answered."

I reached over and wiped her tears from her eyes and she quickly says, "sorry honey that I get emotional that way just as you had shared all those wonderful feelings."

It was time to call it a day or a night as far as our very own private visit; we both seemed to dig further into ourselves and share more of our innermost delicate feelings.

We walked over to the dorm, we stood close in somewhat of a shadow momentarily while we exchanged a couple of kisses; and I wished her pleasant dreams, Its never enough.

It is now one week later since our emotional and fulfilling sharing of feeling, but time marches on again!, but it is closing the gap to those long awaited days when we will be crossing from one time dimension into a somewhat unknown dimension when our individual world will take on an entirely exciting and sort of a scary time wit many variable diverse scenes and scenarios.

It is now Mid May, two and one half weeks until I begin taking my final exams in five different courses and then our final participation in the ROTC and a dry run at how us cadets   will engage in our own graduation.

Delia has informed me that they got their class graduation pictures with cap and gown, they have been included in the class album. They too will be rehearsing their own graduation process. Slowly but surely it will be coming to the conclusion that she and I have been wanting, waiting for the last two months for sure.

I have advised the office manager and the architects too, that I have two weeks till finals and ROTC functions and that my days, for now, are limited until total graduation. I advised them there are various personal arrangements to be taken care of and some very personal ceremonies to attend.

I will leave my schedule open after all functions are over, because I will not know when I have to report to active duty after graduation, after achieving officer status from the ROTC program. Potentially I may be able to continue work here at the office, but will have to wait and see.

Chapter 33

Delia and I met for dinner, we managed to take a long walk around the campus and then chose to sit on a semi-private bench and talk about the next two and half weeks.

We had very intimate discussions of the many issues that we both needed to fully understand, how to prepare for them and how to include our families, some friends. She wants to invite some of her school friends to our wedding, I agreed.

One Week Later

Here we are, two weekends before the final day of graduation here on campus and my graduation is seven days

Myself and the other cadets scheduled to graduate in June were advised how to prepare for the presentation of any medals or rewards and our gold bars. There is supposed to be a reception after all the presentations for all including any family members invited and wish to attend.

I shared all the requirements with Delia and I said I needed to arrange for invitations to my receiving my degree and then an invitation to the ROTC presentation of the commissioning of all graduating cadets to the Second Lieutenant status.

That evening when we met and visited, it was Friday after dinner, we sat very close together on a bench in the cool shade of our favorite tree. It was very apparent that Delia just needed to be close, she seemed a little upset, and she was fidgety, so I turned her face towards me, I kissed her and asked her, "sweetheart is there something bothering you, can you share with me?"

She hesitates a few seconds and then she responds, "Oh I have had a funny and strange feeling all day today and I can not quite figure it out." I have this sense of impatience and I am anxious for the days to go by fast. "Forgive me for being like this today. Can you help me clear my mind of my anxiousness?"

I looked deeply into her beautiful brown eyes, took a few moments to compose a reaction and organize ways of assuring her by trying to interpret what she was feeling and how we can clear up that feeling or even anxiety.

I continued to look at her and I said, "I think I know what you are feeling and maybe why you are having those feelings." I too have been having feelings of anticipation and wishing that all those expectations become the reality of our destiny."

We continued to share how we were feeling and little by little she loosened up; I noticed that even her body was sort of stiff and not as loose and naturally flexible to the touch, so I massaged her neck and upper shoulders and kissed her cheek and even nibbled on her ear.

That did it, she could hardly stand still and I guess it caused a tickling sensation, she was moving all over and finally was laughing and had that twinkle in her eyes that I am so accustomed to and then I tickled her waist and she was squirming in delight. I said," that was what you needed."

She continued to giggle lightly and then stepped up closer against my chest tilted her head and said, "honey that is what I needed from you and I want you to kiss me, kiss me."

After all that change from an anxious and tensed Delia to a giggling and smiling person, and then the demand for my kisses that she is always ready for; hopefully we are back to our normal selves given the fact that we both expressed the desire for a faster pace of the days and weeks left for the long awaited graduation days for us both.

Friday evening Delia and I approached the house mother and asked If it would be allowed for me to take Delia into town to look for and buy some items of clothing she needs for the graduation ceremony. She thought about it for a few minutes and stated that yes she could allow her to go but to be back on campus Saturday by no later than 5:00 p.m.

Delia suggested to her if it would be possible if two of her friends could also go and motioned to me that I would lookout for their safety as well as herself; she quickly agree and asked who would her friends be, and we thanked her.

Saturday: we left for town at 12:30+ and those girls were absolutely happy to be able to leave campus and go shopping, they were also very grateful that Delia invited them to go along with us. Delia said to them, "That is what friends are for, right? As she looks at me for assurance."

I indicated to Delia if either of her friends found themselves a little short on cash for something they really wanted, to offer them some help, so I slipped her $15 to use as she would need just in case. I wondered around nearby, kept an eye on all of them and assured them that I was nearby.

We were back on campus slightly before 5:00 p.m. and the girls had their bags of purchases, were smiling and carrying on about what a good time they had shopping. Even the housemother was smiling, pleased to see them happy.

We were reminded that dinner was at 6:00 p.m. and also that there would a showing of two movies in the auditorium at 7:30, so be ready, and not late!

All in all it was a great Saturday, especially for the 3 girls; and I too enjoyed it; was satisfied that they had a great time. Delia gave me a hug and said she would see me at dinner.

Saturday; a great dinner and very good movies and the greatest part was Delia and I being together for a longer period of time and to be closer, Delia loved the entire evening.

She says to me later after dinner, "honey I really enjoyed our afternoon out without the feeling that we are always being seen wherever we are on campus. Thank the Lord that soon very soon that will be over and our lives will really change, and of course for the best, right sweetie?"

"I always love every minute of the time we spend together and always feel a little sad when we have to part and you go to your dorm and I go upstairs." I am always happy we spend more time together, but it is not enough for me."

"Hold me honey so I can tell you I love you so much and I am always thinking about you when not with you. I know you tell me to try to be happy as much as possible and to just look forward to the next day when we are …together."

"I occasionally feel sad, lonely and detached from you. I have no one to spend time with at the dorm; I have no room mate or friends, because all the fellows there are students and we do not really relate to one another."

"I too am very anxious for that time to arrive so that we can take our finals, prepare for graduation and most of all I am really anxious about receiving the 2nd Lt. commission, so that you and I can go off on our new journey and our destiny."

She tightened her hug on me, began to speak, but then her voice changed and I lifted her face by the chin and she had tears in her eyes and said, "sorry honey I am very emotional today." I had a very strange dream last night, it seemed that I was still here on campus and you were gone, and you had not told me you had to go and how long you would be gone."

"It almost seemed as if you were not coming back to me and it seemed you had avoided telling me. I was very upset and I was tossing and turning half the night after that dream was over."

"Hold me tight honey, kiss me, tell me you are not leaving me, my whole world would fall apart and I am so anxious to leave this campus and to be your sweetheart as we go off as a couple."

"I know that some time back I told you that I needed to know if you loved me and asked to tell me because we were at a point in time that my love could not wait and maybe tomorrow it might not wait and we might not meet like this ever again and I would have to walk away with a broken heart."

"In my heart I was very anxious to know how you really felt and how serious or sincere you were about me, knowing that you had been dropped from the previous relationship. I did not know at that time where you were emotionally and if you might still be attached there."

"Sweetheart, I have come a long way emotionally since you were asking what I was feeling, I hope I did not give you an impression of that kind. I was very thankful that you were so attentive to me in those moments and days following the breakup.

"You saved me from a possible period of trying to find myself and how to carry on from there, I was surprised."

I do not know how I would have carried on. You rescued me from who knows how long I would have just moped around and lost interest in school and my social life. I am most grateful that I had you to lean on and to distract me from a more serious setback ,

"You were and have been such a fantastic distraction and at times it has been sort of overwhelming, but I have found it to be so soothing; with your passion, emotion and attention."

"Honey you do not have to thank me, because I was right in there with you and besides I just wanted to show you how much I really cared and care for you, and as I have said before, I have loved you for quite a while and I would not have been able to stand by and see you suffer, even though it was not really obvious that you were, to others, but to me, I could sense it right away after it all took place."

We hugged each other, I kissed her lips tenderly and I now could whisper to her "I also love you very very much." We now had to part for the evening; this time I wished her happy dreams. Thankful that tomorrow is Friday, time is closing in on the final last days.

Next week I will be completing my finals on all courses, I need to bone up on all and need to turn in our last design project for grading; I feel confident that my design meets the assessment our professor will give me, hoping for the best.

I am now three-days into finals, thanks to my being prepared, they are now in the past. One more day of finals and the design submission and I am done. Now comes the waiting for final results; hope I passed !

I have not been working at the office for almost a week, had to take time off for finals, need at least 2-3 more days in order to be completely done, they understood I needed the time to get through it all. Next week will be the last finals and to report to the ROTC commander of our class.

On this 3rd. day, I left the University campus, went home feeling like I had been hit by a two-ton truck, worn out, very hungry and needed a shower badly and maybe a little nap.

I was up; showered, dresses and tried to look normal, but not really I just needed to put up a good front.

I walked into the dining room just as everyone was getting seated, they were listening to the dietitian explaining the meal for the evening, so I quietly found my sitting spot and sat down. Two of my college classmates motioned a hello and smiled, good, had not seen a smile all day long.

I glanced casually toward Delia's table, saw here intently looking towards me, catches my attention and smiles at me broadly. That is the smile that makes my day and brightens my outlook and I now know it is going to be a great evening with her by my side for a few hours.

Some how I managed to eat faster than normal, looked forward for the dessert that was brought to our table, downed it in record time and boy was I ready to leave to be with my Delia and have some quiet time again.

I waited for her under the shade of the closest tree, she sees me and makes a beeline for me, rushes up to me and throws her arms around me and kisses my cheek, sure there were others watching but she could care less. I was aware that we had not seen each other the last three evenings, and that is why we both were so anxious to embrace as best we could under the circumstances.

She quickly says, "Honey I have missed you so much it seems like a week and not just three days." How do you feel, you do look a bit worn out and are you okay?"

I answered very quickly, "sweetheart I am worn out but I am thankful those three days are over and next Monday I will have two more days of the same, but will finish up."

We ducked into a recessed doorway and we kissed long and hard, our mouths were just so hungry for each other.

After that initial share of affection, I saw a few tears in her eyes, but I know they were tears of joy and her being very happy that once again we could share our affections and also be emotional.

We walked away towards an area under the trees for a little more protection from the harsh sun setting along the mesa. Lucky us, soon it will be more private in the dark.

She asks me, "Honey how did your finals go? Hope you did well; they are more important now then at other times." "I want to tell you about the finals I was also taking these last three days and I too feel somewhat worn out after taking them, but surely they are not as technically involved or heavy as your courses."

"Sweetheart your courses can also be very involve and some what heavy for the fact they are basically testing you with material that you had been processing throughout the the entire course, right?"

She says back. "you know that is very true, and you should know, you have been through that process in the past. That shows me how smart you are, but do not get big headed okay?".... "I am just kidding you." "Love you."

I poked her gently in the ribs, put my arm around her waist and held her close and kissed her on the nose and Her eyes, she loves that form of attention. She is such a beauty when she is happy; I feel so lucky.

Being that it was now Friday, we could just relax for the Week end and look forward to some more time together for the time being; It Is a matter of only days now until it is all over for the both of us. Thanks to the Lord.

Delia says to me, "Honey we are so close just a few days, so I want to take this special moment; now look into my eyes and listen carefully, I am here again pledging my love to you and my continued devotion and to love you as never before, or just in a more complete manner."

"I am more in love with you then I have been in the last several months and it is just because you proposed to me, you have been so devoted to me and to our relationship it is as if we are one and as you have said before "no one can or will tear us apart."
"Kiss me hold me tight and I will always be by your side."

I reached out brought her close to me and kissed her very gently and said, "I am so much in love with you too and plan to always be devoted to you and to our one and only intimate relationship", so I squeezed her tight and she began to tear up she seemed overjoyed with so much happiness she was barely able to contain herself, as she was shaking lightly and needed me to hold her tight until she was steady.

She finally steadies herself, looks up to me and said, "honey I apologize for being such a baby, it is that I just have this overwhelming emotion when we are together in such a sharing manner of ourselves, I just can not help myself."

"I understand how you feel I too have very similar feelings but somehow I am able to hold back and it is because I am spending my moments devoting my attentions to you as you are so important to me and your feelings are most important too and then my own."

"Thank you honey I am okay now and lets just visit and talk about the next couple of weeks and plan on when my own graduation comes up, I need to plan on what I am wearing."

That day and of course the night before, my mom wants to buy my dress and we would need to go to shop in Santa Fe because the stores in Las Vegas do not carry a nicer type of clothing, especially for girls or older women."

"She might come here this coming weekend and take me shopping downtown, there are much better selections here, I think I will encourage her to have dad bring her here."

I finally had a chance to speak up and offer my ideas of what shopping will be for me for my graduation the week after her graduation. "I will just go into town, buy me a pair of dress slack, a neat shirt and maybe a nice tie. It is no big deal for me, as our gowns cover up our whole bodies."

"That is quite simple as no one looks at us guys to see if we are in fashion or if we have coordinated our colors and if our shoes work color wise with our trousers, am I right?"

Delia gives me that look and nods her head and says, "Honey you are better than that and smarter, I hope, and she laughs and continues to make fun of me and says, "I may just have to go shopping with you to make sure you make good selections. You guys do not know how to shop; guess I will have to teach you."

She just can not stop laughing and giving me that look like she is saying she may have to buy my clothes from now on, so she finally quit picking on me and hugs me and kisses me and says, "Honey no matter what, I am here for you even to buy your clothes. She walks away from me. I had to catch up with her and gave her a smack on the butt.

It is now Friday Evening

Delia rushes up to me as we were entering the dining room for dinner and is somewhat excited and takes my hand says,

"Mom and Dad will be here tomorrow mid morning to take me shopping and I get to shop for a new dress, have not had a new dress in over a year."

I say to her, "I sure can see you are quite excited, but I have not had a new dress in a year also and then I start laughing and she quickly shrugs her shoulder and says "that is not funny, besides you would look quite weird and ridiculous In a dress, so there and go laugh somewhere else and she turns around and sticks her tongue out at me and then she motions me with her finger, like saying, "come to me."

That method of conversations and exchange of smart answers is what makes it all so much fun and lightens up and adds interest to a relationship. It gives different ways or manners in which to enjoy each other, and have respect and to appreciate one another.

I walked slowly to her, she extends her hand to me and we hug each other then she looks at me and seriously says,

"Honey you really do not want to get caught wearing a dress it will not do anything for your reputation."

I stand there, shake my head and wonder to myself how will I live this night down, I guess I need to be careful and not leave myself wide open, she is unbelievable.

We stood in the shadow of the nearest tree, we held each other close and she kisses me touches my face and says, "Honey I am sorry I picked on you tonight please forgive me.

As she walks up the steps into the porch she turns around and says quietly, "Wait till mom hears about your dress joke, waves goodbye and throws me a kiss.

I just can not win tonight, so I'll go to my dorm and stick my head under the pillow, but I will not cry or even whimper.

Delia and her parents ventured to downtown to shop for Delia's dress, etc... Who knows how her dad is doing just following the two women around or is he over in the men's side of the store doing his own thing, I hope so.

I met them after the shopping trip near the girl's dorm; I do understand they were planning to spend the night in town, so they left to spend the night and Delia and I made the best of the time left before the evening ended.

It is Monday ! this is the last week of torture that I have to bear and wait for graduation exercises the following Friday afternoon. This coming Saturday is graduation for Delia and classmates and they will be done.

There is a full week till my graduation and then the following week is ROTC graduation and our swearing in as new 2nd Lieutenants and our celebration, we'll finally make it.

Tonight I need to talk to Delia about whether she will leave for home for the one week till my graduation; I know she wants to be here. Then what about the ROTC gathering?

It is late Friday afternoon, I am around the Admin. Building and I see a car I recognize as Delia's parents, they are here for tomorrow afternoon class graduation. They visit for a few minutes as it is almost our dinner time at 6:00 p.m.

In just a few minutes I see someone rushing towards me and I see that it is Delia, I could tell that Delia is all excited as we approached the dinning room, she rushes up and says,

"Come on honey my parents are treating us to dinner , but not here, hurry !!   they are waiting."

We walked up to their car at the dorm area, I greeted them and hugged her mom and shook her dad's hand, as I said, "I appreciate you including me for dinner."

Delia was all smiles and fidgeting, I did not understand why, but then she holds up her left hand and there she was wearing her engagement ring, she shows her mom and dad and we all smile with her. She takes my right hand and we start to get into the cars' back seat.

We all had a great time at dinner, visiting exchanging questions and answers to both our up and coming class graduations. It was good to see them.

Delia's mom ask me about my final days and graduation and when was the ROTC function taking place.

She says, "your graduation is a week later than Delia's?
I said yes, "and then our swearing into the Air Force is not till the following week." She looks at Delia and asks,   "what are you going to do in the time in between?"

Delia did not know what to say, she was a little sad, says, "I do not know if I should go home with you, but I need to come for his graduation and then also the next week; that one function is very important to the both of us. He has worked hard towards that day when he is commissioned an officer in the USAF, so please mom and dad help me figure it out okay?"

Her parents look at each other not knowing what to say and mom started to talk, when Michael steps in and says to them, "wait why not do what we did last summer when she was in a dilemma about going home."

"Remember we checked with the staff and the house mother to see if she could stay a few days longer?" "If she can stay until next weekend, she can probably help at various tasks and chores and if need be, I can pay for her weeks' stay and meet their requests."

They all look at each other, smile and mom says, "you always come up with the best ideas, dad what do you think, would that be okay? I know she does not want to miss his graduation."

Her dad nods his head and says, "I could not have put it together any better than that, sure is a good plan." "You do not have to pay, we will do that ourselves."

Michael steps in and says," let us not worry about that now, on Monday I can make the arrangements for her and we will let you know right of way."

Delia is waving her hands and says, "wait, mom and dad, Michael does wish to invite you to his graduation next Saturday we had just forgotten until now." I guess we could go home providing we do come next Saturday morning?"

"we can not mess up because I would be very upset." Her mom speaks up, "we are delighted to accept the Invitation and can see no reason not to come, but if you would be more comfortable staying and then we can still come next weekend and attend the function with you both."

Delia speaks up first, but pauses for a few seconds and looks at Michael, "would you be upset if I do go home for the week and we all come back on Saturday morning for your big day and night of celebration?"

Everyone stays quiet, all looking at me, so I finally speak up, "I will not be upset but will miss you, I promise to survive."

Delia again says, "then I will not stay but we will come back for week's function and celebration for your graduation, okay?"

I agree and say, "that seems like a good idea and all of you can visit and then we will see you all next weekend."

Delia says, "so please stay overnight so I can gather up and pack what I will need for this coming week?"

Everybody seems pleased with the final decision and her parents decide to stay and pick up Delia next morning after 10:00 a.m.

It is now 8:35 and the evening is drawing near, her dad looks at his watch and says to the mom, "Honey we need to go find a place to stay for tonight."

He directs his attention to Delia, "young lady we will see you tomorrow morning and you too Michael if you happen to be nearby, okay?" They left and we are standing there arm in arm waving away to them.

Delia and I looked at each other as we walked away towards the dorm, she speaks first, "Honey that worked out well I will go home tomorrow and we all will come back next Saturday morning to see you graduate."

"I am already starting to have that feeling that I am going to miss you terribly and it will seem like a long…long week. Hold me honey talk to me give me enough love so that I can manage to be okay." "I know I will not be okay."

"This will be a test of time, time we will be separated may I call you every evening after dinner?"

"Of course you may if not I will be calling you Just to hear your voice and for me to complain about being lonely."

"Sweetie, I too will miss you immensely, but I will have tasks and studies and turning in test results for review and credited to my portfolio ; I still need to be concerned that I do have all the credits I need to graduate next Saturday.

I reluctantly wished Delia good night as we kissed for now and I will head back to my own dorm room, and call it a day.

Delia's graduation Day

Saturday morning, there are cars and people everywhere and it Is amazing how quickly the campus is overrun with them both. I had to take my own car and move it to the north end area of the dorm to make room where I normally park.

It is 2:30 p.m. the ceremonies start at 3:00 p.m. and I did find a suitable seat to be sort of close to the stage and place where they award the diplomas,

Luckily I bought a camera that takes color photos. I never told Delia I had it, want it to be a surprise to take pictures for her photo album.

Ceremonies were 45 minutes long and then a procession of all graduates into the main hallway, a place to receive their congratulations and personal wishes from attendees.

Delia was such a beauty, she looked taller and more adult then ever before, as it seems she has matured and filled out into a more sensual young woman ready for her destiny. I do wonder what she is thinking at this very moment as she stands and receives salutations and best wishes from us.

It came my turn to walk up to her and quickly she threw her arms around my neck and here come the tears, she did seem a bit vulnerable and excited, after all this is a first time, one only graduates once at this educational level.

I comforted her and said I would be waiting for her with her parents outside in the shade of the trees.

Very soon she pulled herself away from the line of graduates and came looking for us, found us and she threw her arms around both of her parents. She appeared relieved and her face radiated and reflected a very calm attitude.

She then directed her attentions to me and hugged and kissed me openly no matter that her parents were there. She very shyly raised her left hand, showed her engagement ring on her finger, we all just were surprised that she had been brave enough to take that step, wonder how many of the crowd might have noticed that, well now who cares.

Her parents accepted the entire scene as they too were very happy to see her as a new persona, she had just reached a whole new position in her life and pleased to see that she now was a young adult woman.

I must have had an expression of admiration and pleasure on my face as I viewed this beautiful creature that stood before us as if she had just evolved out of her own shell.

Her parents were studying my expressions and I caught that look of pleasure and contentment on their own faces. They said to me, "Michael are you ready for the next chapter as you are going to have your hands full with this new Delia."

All I could do was nod my head and say, "I am ready for her, but she will also need to be ready for me as well."

As the crowds were moving away, we looked at each other and it was obvious that we all had to move along, they needed to travel to Las Vegas as I knew what was coming up. Delia and her parents would leave soon so as to get home at a decent hour before dark.

Her dad moved their car close to the dorm entrance so that Delia's luggage could be loaded and they could say their goodbyes and I would be left behind to lick my wounds.

Delia started to tear up and hugged me ever so tight and kissed me again and said, "honey I am going to miss you for this coming week, but will call tonight after our arrival, okay?" I said goodbye to her parents, wished a safe trip. I said back, "I will wait for your call and I too will miss you for the week, we will talk every day."

She stepped into the back seat, she was really tearing and very emotional, it is hard to part like that even if it is for only a week. As they drove away she was waving goodbye until they disappeared from the campus entrance.

I resolved myself to be alone in my dorm room, it was going to be a very lonely night and every night for a week.

There is a song called, "*Saturday night Is the loneliest night of the week*" I sure will know that tonight !

Sunday morning I decided to go to church, it had been at least 2- 3 weekends since I had been there because of all the weekly effort into school and work.

Monday Morning

How I hate Mondays it just seems like there is never enough weekend, but I am at the threshold of a new beginning and a new future just two weeks away, I have to be as strong as possible and ready to " march on" After next weekend as I will have with me the most wonderful person in my life as I see it now and we will both be more than ready.....

This week I will be dealing with the last of all issues related to graduating and looking forward to moving on and .... the week went by quickly, the days yes but the evenings dragged on, I sure missed Delia on those evenings after dinner.

There were very few students left, only those that will stay and work all summer long. Week went by quickly for me.

It is my Good Friday

It is now noon on this long awaited Friday the day before I am done with the UNM scenarios and tomorrow is the end of the journey through the never ending halls of the university.

I do expect Delia and parents tomorrow at least by 10:30 am tomorrow so that we can all prepare ourselves mentally and especially me, as I am starting to feel the pressure building up both in my mind and body.

Delia had called early this Saturday morning to say, "Good morning honey we are just about to leave and will be there in about two hours plus, I am so anxious to see you again I can hardly stand myself, so see you soon."

The school campus here is practically deserted since this is a week since their graduation, so I went and sat in a bench under a tree close by so I could wait for them, and sure enough at approximately 10:30 they arrived.

Delia did not even allow the car to come to a stop then she was out the car door and dashing towards me as I quickly, left the bench and met her. She was besides herself , she hugged me and kissed me ever or so hard and hung on.

"Oh honey I kept telling my dad, "can you drive any faster?" He just looked at me and smiled, "driving at speed limit."

Her parents were glad to be able to get out and stretch their legs, we greeted each other and her dad says "Are you ready, this is your big day?" I answered, "oh yes I really am, quite a bit nervous but ready."

"I hope you had a good trip, I know you had a back seat driver asking you to drive faster, I can certainly understand how funny that must have been.

"Oh I took it in stride I know she was very anxious to get here, she just wanted to fly in and it was a long week if you can only imagine." We both had a chuckle over that as I approached Delia's mom and said to her, "how was your trip, with a nod of my head and a smile."

She quickly says, "you can just imagine she was overly vocal and anxious to get here, like her dad said ..she wanted to fly in, so maybe now she will calm down and we can enjoy the rest of the weekend."

We gathered in a huddle and hugged and greeted each other again. I said to Delia, "maybe your mom and dad can relax in the shade of that tree on our favorite bench?"

"We need to unload your luggage and take it up to your room?" she looks at me with that little wicked smile, "Oh you want to go up to my room?" "You will need to be careful"

Saturday Afternoon Graduation 2:30

We had arrived at the UNM Gymnasium where large gathering and performances are held, I had my cap and gown, was in the hallway. I said to them, "Try to find good seats as close to the front as you can, the ceremony will start at 3:00 pm... I kissed Delia and excused myself to the reserved sitting area at the front.

The ceremonies started on time and we, sat through all of the calling graduates and presentation of degrees and finally it came to my name as I am almost at the end of the list and there were cheers for me from friends, family and Delia and her parents.

It did not take long, the awards were over and everyone threw their caps in the air and the audience was covering their heads so as not to get hurt and they started leaving and going out to the open receiving areas to wait for their own graduates to meet them.

Delia was the first to throw her arms around me and kiss me generously and then her parents offered their own congratulations. They now could see the sight of relief on my face as it was all over too.

That evening. Delia's parents decided we were going to celebrate both Delia's and mine graduations. They had planned to stay over night. They took us all to the hotel at Second and Central Streets they have a great dining area.

We had a great time, Delia for one was having the best of time, she just hung onto me and was just bubbling with so much energy and laughter. Her parents just watched her with admiration until her mom could not hold back.

She says to Delia, "honey we are so amazed at how you have matured and become such a unique person in the last two years but especially in the last year….

"We know why and we see that your relationship with Michael has done wonders for your growing up, you are such a lovely daughter and you are so happy and we are so proud of you and we are now wishing the two of you the very best as you will soon look forward to your careers."

"Now we wish to formally congratulate you on your engagement and we will wait to see what your plans are." Her dad also added his blessings and was delighted to do so: he asked, "can we help with anything or shall we just wait until you make your arrangements?"

They both hesitated and it seemed that they were both done for now. We toasted with a glass of wine and enjoyed the after-dinner dessert and just visited until it was time leave.

They drove back to the campus to drop us both off and then they were headed to their motel for the night and would leave tomorrow morning. We bid them good night and a safe trip tomorrow. Delia had to hug and kiss them, she sure was in a delightful mood; she knew she belonged here with me.

The parents were now aware that Delia would be staying for this coming week so she could attend the swearing in of the future officers and I was the main reasons for it all.

Delia reminded them that I would receive my officer's commission next Saturday afternoon. I stepped in and said, "you are invited to attend, it should be unique and very different from the ceremonies you've attended so far, but if you folks may be busy and can not come, I accept that."

Delia's dad came right back at me and said, "we will not miss it no matter what as it will be our pleasure to be here to support and experience such a personal accomplishment."   "We will be here Saturday mid morning, so plan on us."

Her mom said, "Michael we would not miss the occasion as it will be the one and only one in our life time that we are sure it will be very unique and one of a kind, so be well prepared and we will be here for you."

Chapter 34

We all stood there on the driveway, I think we were all somewhat worn out after such a fast paced day of activities. She looks at me with her arms around my waist and very clearly says,

"Honey now you too are a graduate and one of great accomplishments in your field, I am totally proud and super happy for you and you have one more to receive your bars as you say.."

Delia says again, "Honey I am so glad to be back I surely missed you even though we talked every evening, it is still not the same."

She became somewhat emotional hung on tight and said, "I had some very emotional personal talks with mom and she was so understanding and helpful. I am so blessed to have such a great mom for her guidance . She is so proud of me and boy you ought to hear how she adores how you are and how you treat and care for me."

"When will we travel to see and visit with your mom and dad?" I hope it will be soon after this next week?"

"Sweetheart we will go very soon so they can see you again since the last rushed trip up there; we will now have much more time to do so."

We stayed outside together for at least an hour and half, as of now there are no restrictions to our being together as we are both adults in the eyes of those in charge around here.

The following morning we joined the few staff and leftover students that work here for the summer at breakfast. There was much talk about what the summer was to be and where either one of us was to be. they were surprised that there would be a wedding very soon and there were many cheers.

Week of Commissioning Ceremonies

The reception we received at breakfast was more then we expected as we were not aware that there was information out there that alerted the few people there, we were on campus and engaged. We took the response with great surprise and we enjoyed the attention.

I asked Delia, "sweetheart do you want to go to church later?" She said, "sure what a great idea, we haven't been to church together in quite a while, I look forward to going."

The weekend was short, I guess because of all the fast paced activities and our Sunday together. I have a few errands to run, get my Air Force blue pressed, and I need to shine my shoes, wash and press my white dress shirt.

Delia says, "honey how can I help with your uniform?" If you want I can get your white shirt ready and press your tie."

"sweetheart that would be good and I will take care of the rest, during the next few days.

I need to run over to the architect's office and visit with the staff, I told them I would come by after graduation and before the ceremonies.

My visit with the architect's staff went well, they were very glad to see that all had gone well, if fact, they all want to go to the ceremonies; they said, " we may never have an opportunity like that in the future, so they are all going.

Delia and I were just having a great time in the evenings, she had offered to help others in their assigned tasks during most of the days so as to pay for the opportunity to stay in her old room and have access to meals along with me.

Tuesday evening I asked her, "sweetheart what do you wish to wear to the ceremonies on Saturday?"

She looks at me in a great surprise and bewilderment and says, "Oh my God I had not even thought about it yet. I will call mom, she had said they would buy me a new dress if I wish to have one; darn, are we going to have enough time?"

She was all excited and moving around like crazy, so I stepped in and calmed her down by holding her by the shoulders, and said, "lets do this, tomorrow afternoon we will take you into town and buy what ever it is you need, okay?"

She looks at me wide eyed and bewildered again and says, "You will do that for me !, oh my gosh, but mom said she would take care of it."

"There is not enough time, besides it will be my pleasure to buy you a beautiful dress, shoes maybe even a necklace to go with your new dress, okay?"

"Tell whom ever is in charge of the tasks you have been helping with that you need to go shopping tomorrow and we will take care of it and then you can even have your hair done Friday afternoon?

"You think I should also have my hair done? Oh my gosh, it is your ceremony not mine.!

"Sweetheart you are just as important as I am and tomorrow we are going to show everyone how beautiful and important you are in my life and our relationship, besides we want to surprise your parents even more."

She was besides herself, she was covering me with kisses like crazy, "oh honey how good you are to me , I can hardly believe what you said, I really really love you dearly."

Next day after lunch time she said, "honey I need to go shower and wash my hair and wear something decent to go shopping. How much time do I have?"

"Take whatever time you need, and if you need some help in the shower I am available." She looks at me wide eyed and said, "we can wish right, and she laughs.

"I am afraid they will not let me in the dorm much less your room, so we can forget about that neat idea.... some day."

We ventured into town, hit all the women stores and the big department stores. We finally found exactly what she liked, she tried on and finally selected a beautiful blue dress, a pair of open toe silver dress shoes, nylons, a white half slip [it is the style nowadays] and a nice necklace with matching earrings. Those had her birthstone; I am not sure what that month was, but I did not ask.

We left the stores with many bags, she was so happy she could not stand herself, but we managed to get to the car and back to campus. It so happens she is the sole person in her room, so she does not have to share anything with anyone for the time being.

After dinner she was antsy to call her mom and share with her what she had selected. I took her to my dorm room so we could use my phone instead that uncomfortable phone booth.

There was no one around to hear us. I had the door open to the hallway and I stood out there while she made the direct call. I heard her say, "Mom I am calling to tell you that Michael took me downtown and had me select my dress for the Saturday ceremony."

"What do you mean " what did I use for money? Michael bought it all for me; a beautiful blue dress, open toes silver mid height heeled shoes, he even asked me to choose a necklace and earrings and some other things."

"Oh mom you do not need to worry about that, he wanted to do that, he was very generous and wants me to look, as he said, "beautiful and important as him that day."

"Mom do not concern yourself about it, he wanted to do that for me and I am so happy and delighted, mom it is going to be a great day for us all, Say hello to dad and see you on Friday evening or Saturday morning?" let me know."

Chapter 35

Saturday morning, I wake up I get up make a few circles in the middle of my room and I say to myself "what am I doing here? What am I supposed to be doing now?

It is 7:15 am, breakfast is served soon, I need to eat to keep up my strength and distract myself from doing this.

I finally focus, I look around and it dawns on me it is my day, my day to strut around after all I have fully earned what ever it is I want to strut about.

Today it will be all about me, not to be self centered, but I have worked for this moment for the last four intense years.

I look at the clock on my side table and realize, Delia's parents will be here mid-morning and I must be at least a little bit presentable until I dress for the final hour, the hour when along with all my fellow officers to be will stand at attention and each of us will receive our gold bars; oh how great that will feel.

I quickly dress, rush to the dining room eat a hurried breakfast and see Delia because I am sure is already there and sure enough she's waiting patiently at the nearest table.

She greets me, "honey I have been waiting for you, did you oversleep?" "I, not really its just that I did stay in bed more than I thought, but here I am just for you."

She looked great as she usually does, so we both ate quickly because she had to be ready for her parents arrival..

I did get back to my room to shape up for the arrival of my beautiful girl's parents and I strolled back to be with her to wait their arrival. It was now 9:50, so we sat in the shade of the tree on our favorite bench.

I told her, "sweetheart you are looking so alert and clear eyed, how do you do it with all the things we are doing and expecting to go through today and even after today?"

"Honey it is my way of dealing with this time period, it is so precious to me and am so excited for you and for me, because today will fulfill your dream of being an officer in the US Air Force and for me to be alongside of you from now on."

"You may not be aware but It has, as of lately, been my purpose and my goal to see you fulfill and accomplish the requirements so that this afternoon you can stand proud and receive those 2nd. Lieutenant gold bars you deserve and have worked so hard for."

"Thank you sweetheart, I do know you have been on my side and cheering me on so that I could get through it all and you have stood by my side all along, I love you for it and will always cherish your loyalty."

It was 10:20 and all of a sudden her parent's car comes around the corner from the administration building and does approach where we are seated.

Delia rushes to them as they leave the car, they hug each other and her dad looks over to me and says,

"Hello young man how are you holding up?"

I answer him as I shake his hand, "I am some what nervous but I have Delia for support and I think I just might make it through the day. I think that four years of part- time military training and brain-washing should have prepared me for an interesting swearing in later on today and the very important resulting reward for hard work and determination."

We exchanged greetings and Delia's mom looks at me and says,   well Michael this is your day, are we ready?"

We all sat down and enjoyed the shade and quietness of the campus, in fact mom and dad voiced out loud the beauty of the campus and green areas and how quiet it was there.

Dad says quickly, "will we all be ready for a lunch, we were up early and I am getting ready for a nice quiet lunch nearby?"

Delia and I look at each other; we both knew it had been at least three and one half hour since we had a hurried break- fast.

I said it first, "I think Delia and I would be ready soon and at your wish we can go anytime soon."

Delia blurts out when I paused and says, "mom ,want to go up to my room and see my dress?"

Mom says, "of course honey let us go see, I am very anxious to see what you described to me yesterday."

I get close to her mom and say, " ask Delia to loan you her 'friendship ring' I want to use it at the end of the ceremonies to propose to her again while everyone is there, she has the regular engagement ring which she'll wear later."

Dad and I just sat there and I said, "do you need to go visit the boys room before we head out, we can walk over to my dorm building if you wish. It may be a while till they are ready."

In the next 20 minutes plus we were all ready to go eat some lunch. Her mom hands me a ring box which I assume has the ring I requested for later.

We drove over to the local family restaurant that we had frequented at other times when they had been here.

Delia was her usual bubbly, happy full of energy and passion and just hung onto my arm while we waited to be served. We had a great visit. Her parents are in such a good mood, so much has been happening which was needed for all.

Chapter 36

Time has marched on: The hour of reckoning is now here as it is 2:00 pm, Delia and I are driving into the university campus and her parents are with us so as to save parking there.

We are all dressed up and me in my Air Force blues, but no one stands out more than Delia in her entire attire all in blue and silver and so much in harmony with my uniform.

Her mom was so delighted with her attire and she just marveled as how beautiful she was and so mature looking.

I said to them all, "she will out shine me and maybe other young women accompanying their boyfriends or even husbands for that matter, we are so proud of her."

Delia says to me, "honey that is not fair that you think I will out shine you, this is your day and you shine in that uniform of yours, I will never forget how you look and who you are, is it not true mom?

Her mom says back, "You are so right and Michael she is right, but I must say you two are an outstanding couple and deserve all the credit for what you stand for and what you are , such a blessing to each other."

Delia and her parents found good seating considering the gym [acting as an auditorium] for such ceremonies as this one is nearly at capacity today.

Myself and the graduating classes are seated in the first five or so rows and all the top brass is on stage ready to start the ceremonies. They have photographers on hand to take photos in general at random for the year book.

Our Air Force commanding officer had the privilege to begin the service and enlighten the audience as what the procedure was to be, and called out all the steps taken to proceed thru the program.

He called for all cadets [officers to be] to stand up, at attention and salute the American flag and the 2-star general who is the honorary speaker and our commanding officer would do the honors of pinning on the gold bars on everyone as they are being sworn in.

It was very obvious that it was going to be reasonable lengthy ceremony, there were 50 plus cadets receiving their bars. There are also certain awards for various categories such as swimming, marching abilities , scholastic rankings..etc....

All recipients to officer categories are awarded in alphabetical order, so of course I was to be near the end of the awards and pinning of bars. A complete surprise to me was that I had not ever missed a single class attendance and was second in-grade level in my class in final ranking, I was given a framed award for each category and was issued both as they pinned my gold bars, one on each side of the uniform collar.

When the general stood, he congratulated all the new officers, a prayer was perform by a military chaplain and the audience was asked to stand and give a loud sounding ovation as cadets left their seats.

As I was surrounded by Delia and her parents, two members of my family [brother Ted and his wife Mary] her mom gave me a hug and the ring box, I then turned around and faced Delia, I knelt down on one knee took her left hand and I said, "my dearest Delia will you marry me? She was totally astonished and surprised that it was happening right here amongst so many people it sort of embarrassed her but she quickly got over it.

She quickly responds, Oh my gosh, " yes, yes I will, I quickly slipped the ring on and stood and she fell right into my arms and kissed me passionately, it was the passion I expected; just as before,

Everyone who caught sight of what was going on started clapping, whistling, making vocal sounds; we drew plenty of attention, it was the hour for us both to remember for as long as possible.   My parents were very happy, surprised and started clapping along with the others.

Family and brother with his wife continued to offer their congratulations on my officer accomplishment and the surprise in my asking Delia to marry me.

My brother is a former now retire naval officer who also went through the ROTC program many years ago here at the university, so he knows what it is all about. I have always looked up to him as a professional scientist and he set the example for me to follow, in also becoming an officer.

We said our goodbyes to him and his wife Mary Jane and my mom and, then we, all four of us, started to walk out to the car. Delia was hanging on to me, she had tears down her cheeks, but they were tears of joy and happiness.

I drove us back to the campus and we decided to just go in and make ourselves comfortable in the main living room of the dorm while we decided what we would do this evening.

By now Delia had exchanged her 'friendship ring' with the real engagement ring on her finger because now it was real and official to her, to us and for anyone else known to us.

Her dad again decided we should go out to dinner, it is beginning to be a standard occurrence when they are here. I wanted to help money wise for dinner but he would not hear of it. We had a great celebratory dinner for us both.

Chapter 37

We finished off a great satisfying dinner, considering Delia and I had been surviving on quick meager meals the last two days and now we were having what could be the best dinner for a long period of time in the near future.

I spoke up and said, "now comes the fun, what do we do after today, where will we go from here?? " Can we still have a home here for the time being, who knows?"

We returned to the girl's dorm where Delia is camping out for now and she decided we should all go relax in the living room, but we should advise the housemother we wish to do so if it is okay for now, we did and she said yes.

We sat there, made small talk and her parents [mom and dad] from now on, as I will soon be part of the family for good. They were asking if I knew when or how soon I would be called into active duty.

I did not have an answer so, I said, "It will be a matter of time for the Air Force to absorb all new officers and attempt to assign them where they could be needed,

"I believe that the type of degrees, experience, training and other personal attributes will have some bearing on where each one will be assigned for duty.

I turn my head towards Delia to see what form of expression she might have on her face; she seems to be puzzled and maybe even concerned about how I am explaining how active duty might be.

She cuts in and asks me directly, "honey will you be sent somewhere where I can not join you at first, because I will be very concerned or unhappy here without you."

I reached out for her an cuddled her and said to her, "let us not worry about that; I should be able to have some input and can request for some form of assignment for us both."

I do not know if that was of any comfort to her and her parents look at her with some concern and then look at me to see if I have any other words of comfort.

"My personal interest is in the field of design, planning and management of facilities on any given base and I do hope it will be here in the US. I am not yet, this soon, interested to be located at a foreign base in a country of different languages and cultures."

"I feel it should be that I [we] should become used to being in the service first and then look forward to new environments and different languages."

"Delia I certain will make good choices for our benefit but generally I believe that in the services one does not have many choices for assignments."

I studied her facial expressions for a few seconds and looked her in a manner in which she lightened up and then she reached over to me and hugged me lightly, and then said, "honey I do realize from what you have mentioned that there are no real choices, but wherever you go I go too, right?"

I quickly said, "of course never will you be left behind; I plan for us to always be together."

Her mom pops in with, "I believe your dad and I need to get going to the motel, it sure has been a very interesting day and evening for us all. thanks Michael for inviting us and having us be a part of this special occasion it will always be imbedded in our memories."

"My question right now is what are your plans for the next few days or week and how can we be of help in how you will transition from your former way of being here to actually not having a home?" Can you still stay here?"

Delia jumps up and says to her mom, " we need to get together very soon and talk, but not today, Michael and I need to make some plans; I am sure you know what."

We exchange goodbyes and walked them out to the car so that they may be on their way to the motel, too bad we can not go too, have our own room?   Not a chance, not yet.

As they drove off Delia turns around and hugs me and says, "It is a bit sad to see them drive away and me not being with them, but I now belong with you and it is us now !. but we will see them in a few days?"

I sat us down on the swing in the porch under the light so that no one could say we were off doing the unthinkable.

> "Sweetheart now that we have some time to our selves, can we talk about plans for our wedding, and real soon too." I believe you are as anxious as I am and besides, I would like for us to be married before the time comes to be assigned to a base, don't you think so?"

> "Oh honey I agree and we need to get started on our plans, that's what I meant for mom to be ready and you and I need to agree at what church we wish the ceremony to be held."

> "Do you have a preference, here in town or maybe if it suits you, how about up north in my Las Vegas?" It would be closer to your folks in Taos an our friends and relatives up north."

I looked at her in a bit of astonishment, smiled and said, "That's two good places, but the only connection we have here is the church I, and you with me, have attended."

My concern is that we do not have many friends or even relatives here in town, so maybe we can have it in Las Vegas, as you say closer to all and if any of my sisters or even my brother come, then can drive up for the day."

"Oh honey you are so agreeable and helpful, I love you, so I do agree about having the wedding in Las Vegas."

"Did you say you have made arrangements for us to sort of camp out for a few days until we decide to what our priority will be for the time being?"

"Yes I talked to the office and paid them for at least a full week and we can still be in our rooms and just have the meals as we wish."

She says, "too bad we can not be together, but I can dream can't I?"

"Your first night and days and nights after are yet to come and I too know it can not come any sooner, but I want your first night to be that of happiness, bliss and fulfillment like you have never had before."

"Oh honey I so look forward to our first night and it will be a night of pure pleasure and passion."

I looked at my watch it was getting close to 10:00 pm, I know it is time to call it a day, but how can I call it a day or a night when I have this precious person here with me, it is just not fair to us, but I have to bite the bullet for now.

"Sweetheart tomorrow we will call your mom and you and her can start talking, making plans and ask her about the church and arrangements."

We kissed goodnight and I told her, "Pleasant dreams and I wish to say that you were so beautiful and gorgeous in your lovely blue dress and boy did those silver shoes set you off as a marvel to look at, I bet there were a lot of envious girls or women at the ceremonies, many eyes were on you."

I felt a bit of a let down after that rush rush day and busy with her parents and the marvelous dinner, and now at the end of the day it is so quiet, so dark and here I am in my dorm room and all that joy and fun is done with, for now?

I was ready for bed and am alone with my own thoughts, ideas and going over in my mind the precious and delightful partner that I am blessed with from now on.

I was wide awake at 6:45 the following morning, I just lay there hoping someone special would just walk in the door and greet me with a kiss and a few caresses, but no such luck today, some day soon.

I got up showered and got dressed for breakfast and to go see my Delia, she will be wide eyed, fresh looking and I know she will be dressed well since it is now Sunday.

As other times I asked Delia, "Sweetheart do you want to volunteer to help out in the kitchen and dinning room after breakfast, I feel like doing something worthwhile and then you will be there too."

> "I see you are wearing that special ring, it just makes you a different, special mature person way beyond what you were prior to graduation, now you are someone to look up to."

> "Yes I would like to stay and be helpful, I will go check with the dietitian and see if it is okay, be right back. thank you from the bottom of my heart for how you feel I looked yesterday, I love you for how you see me as that special person in your life and I can see how my parents were also looking at me too."

We helped out for a couple of hours. The dietitian came to us as we finished helping and thanked us and said she appreciated us a lot. Then she looks at Delia's hand sees the ring and says, "Heard that the two of you were engaged and were planning a wedding soon, how great is that, I wish you two the best of everything. Are you both done with all your schooling?"

> I said, "Yes we are in fact, yesterday I was fully commissioned as a second Lieutenant in the Air Force and will soon go into active duty, but first there will be a wedding."

We excused ourselves and walked to the dorm area, I said to Delia, "Do you wish to go to church, it might be the last time here." She says, "of course I would love to go.",

We both spent most days of our last week here on campus thinking and planning and she would talk to her mom every evening after dinner to find out what she was able to figure out for church schedules, catering, invitations, and of course later it would be flower arrangements.

The most and desperate arrangement that was needed; who was to be the maid of honor and the bridesmaids also I was told to decide who for the best man as well, the brides groomsmen, I needed to make some contacts to see who would accept, and be available to meet our schedule.

I had conversations with at least three of my friends and also the one that he and I agreed would be best man. I will try to reach each and everyone to confirm if they will be available and interested.

Delia was also dealing with the same issues, and she talked to her best friend who also graduated with her. They had been having conversations with at least three classmates, because it happens that Delia only had friends there on campus and not there in her home town.

We left on the weekend to her home so that she and her mom could start making plans, and arranging for all the points of importance that make up a wedding and reception.

Delia and her mom were having initial success with local arrangements, but they did need to travel to Santa Fe to search, view, and try on wedding dresses for Delia to find what she would be the happiest with.

I asked her how the search for her dress was and she gives me that look then says to me, "that is a secret and I can not share that with you, you'll just have to wait until that day" so just walk away from me; her usual manner of teasing me just to prolong the mystery of the subject.

Her dad and I have been left out of the process, but in a way it is a blessing. Just watching them going back and forth, talking, laughing and being emotional is enough for the both of us.

After several days of intensive calls, visits and another trip to Santa Fe by Delia and her mom, they had achieved all of the main issues in preparation for that special day.

Her dad and I were now faced with the fact that he and I needed to travel to the nearest rental outlets to see and select either a suit or tuxedo. Color was important to both and then we needed to convey that selection to the best man and bridegrooms in Albuquerque.

The women heard our conversation about looking for suits and immediately Delia rushes over to us and says,

       "Michael, mom and I do not want you to wear a suit or a tuxedo, we want you to wear your blue uniform with your new gold bars. Please honey that will be   so   much   more original for us both and I would be so proud of you."

Her mom steps in and directs her attention to her husband and says, "Honey you have a practically new suit that you could wear, do you not think so?"

Her husband changes his mannerism and looks up to her and says, "I did not want Delia or Michael to think I would want to wear a suit I already have, what do you think?"

I just stood there and kept quiet while the discussion was on going. Then Delia's dad directs his attention, first to Delia and then to me and says, "What do you think? I do not want to offend or have you think less of me."

       I looked at dad and said "I do not mind at all, please do wear your suit that you really like and I agree to wear my blue uniform; I agree with Delia and mom."
       I further said, "It will be a special day for us all and

I am positive that we will all shine, especially when you walk your beautiful daughter down the isle to meet me, I think all eyes will be on Delia not either one of us, maybe me but not much."

The discussions about our suits or otherwise was over and mom and Delia were satisfied that we were to dress as was agreed and dad and I eyed each other in a manner which silently said, hey ! …. there is no need to go shopping.

The following day we set out to take care of many areas around the house needing, straightening and cleaning up. The front yard was in need of clearing. Their concern was there would be some persons invited to visit indoors after the reception. That task we delegated to Delia and her mom.

This was the early part of this first week of us being completely free from school and work and we were looking forward to the wedding taking place one week from the coming Saturday, basically nearly two weeks from today.

Our wedding attendants have been in touch by telephone and my best man said he would be here one day early. I called three of the local motels and set up reservations for all five of them for at least two nights and arranged for me to be there on the first evening and to take care of the payment.

I wished to do that because I thought it only fair to have a place for them to relax, get ready for the wedding and then the reception which usually carries on into the middle of the night. I did not want any one of them traveling in the night.

Here it is just before dinner time on Tuesday, I have been visiting with Delia on the front porch, she is so lively and just moving around, she hugs and kisses me and asks if I will be ready for dinner soon.

I said, "No sweetie I need to go shower and shave and change my clothes." She looks at me with that wicked little smile and says, "honey can I join you in the shower?"

I look at her and say, "You are kidding right, what would your parents say about that?"

"You and I know that will happen soon, very soon and I am sure you are not going to say no, right?

We hear a call from the kitchen, "Delia, honey I need your help to finish up the food for dinner, can you come and help me.?"

Delia calls out, "I'll be right there mom, she smiles at me and says, you really got lucky this time   trying to talk your way out of a response to my suggestion, right?"

Delia's dad drove up, honked and waved at me as I was moving around on the porch, I walked down to the driveway and asked, "do you need some help with something?"

He says, "as a matter of fact I do, I have some heavy packages in the trunk that I need to get into the house for now, so please help me get them inside."   We greeted each other and went to work.

He went on to freshen up for dinner and at that same moment mom informed us that dinner was ready and for us to fix our own drinks; there was at least 3- different selections.

Dad asked us to join hands and he said a short prayer prior to us sitting down for dinner and the usual conversations about the day. We all shared our tasks of the day and hope- fully our accomplishments. Everything was related to the needs for the day of the wedding.

After dinner Delia looks at me and says to me "Michael can we go to a movie tonight? I drove by the theater and I would like to see that particular movie. "I have heard about it on the radio."

I responded as she finished and said, "sure if mom and dad do not need some help with some chores." I looked at them as if to ask, and they both

answered, "no not tonight, so go ahead and enjoy
a movie, you both deserve it."

Delia looks at me and says, "the first showing is at
7:15 we can make it if I take a quick shower
and change clothes."

As we waited for Delia to be ready, her parents and I sat on
the benches in the porch, and her mom spoke up first to me,
"the both of you are taking this time before the wedding very
well, you are not nervous or running around, like, I would be,
confused and flustered."

I smiled back at her and said, "well the both of you have been
a very good example, you have been very calm and helpful and
besides you both are making progress with the self assigned
tasks in preparation for the wedding."

As soon as Delia came out from inside and said she was
ready, I was too. I said to her parents, "tomorrow night she and
I get to do the kitchen chores, okay?"

I helped her into the front seat and said, "smooth out your
skirt so it will not wrinkle and she smiles and says, you all- ways
look out for me in so many ways ....I love you my dearest and
tonight I want to show you how much."

I looked at her in amazement and was not sure how to take
that comment or should I even comment on it, so I let it slide
and just went around to my side of the car.

As I got into the driver's seat, she looks up at   me
and says, "with a straight face, you ignored me
so what is up, do you think I was kidding or what?"

Again I did not know what to even respond to   that
additional declaration, she knows how to put me
on the spot and test me and tonight is one of those
nights and I hope I can survive her tests for now.

I looked at her and said, "sweetheart I know what
you are up to, you tease me, rag on me and then

you sit back and laugh, enjoying my inability to give
you the response that hopefully you are searching
for,   am I right? If I gave you the response you wish
for and I act on it, you might be very surprised and
even reluctant. Well you just wait till the end of the
movie and let's see what you are implying."

She smiles with that wicked sexy smile and
says, "oh honey I do not want you to be all confused
with what I had said, I am serious about showing
you how much I love and adore you and not in the
way which you might be imaging, although I know
you have quite an imagination, so just wait and see
and you will be okay with my passion and affection."

She kissed me passionately and hugged me tight and said,
"let us go see the movie and wait for the rest of the night.

We went into the theater hand in hand, many of the patrons
looked with curious expressions on their faces, because they
really did not know who we were.

After the movie we did spend some time in the car in a sort of
secluded area and talked and she was so passionate and she
did show me how much she loved me, but we have our limits,
but it is so difficult to be passionate but with our own limitations
because we are at her home with her parents.

It is a waiting game and we both so look forward when we can
be free to take our love making to the maximum and feel no guilt
or concern about our relationship. Our love for each other will
take us there.

When we arrived at her home we saw that her parents were
still up watching a movie on the TV, we walked in very casual
and sat down on a separate couch and gave them an account
of what the movie was about.

Her mom asks, "would you like some dessert, since we did
not have any before you left for the movies?" We all gathered
for dessert, talked and discussed further plans for

the dinner the night before the wedding and then the reception after the wedding.

After all that discuss and comparisons we did agree on quite a few of ideas, mainly that her mom said that she had picked up the invitations and she would need our help tomorrow to address and mail them all out.

Next day shortly after 9:00 am Delia and I sat at the dining room table and took on the task of addressing all those invitations, all 75 of them, most were instate, but several were for out of state persons like members of my family.

We looked at each other when we finished with the envelopes and then we had to insert the invitation inside, we did quite well and soon had them all ready, licking that wicked glue was another matter.

As I studied Delia while she was licking those flaps, I could not help but laugh, but in turn I was also making faces, so I asked her, "you like that taste huh?"

> She counters back, "no I do not, and my mouth
> seems to be coated with that stuff. I am going to
> keep some of that glue and then I am coming over
> and give you a one wet kiss, a French kiss to be
> sure and lets see how you handle that, smarty."

We told her mom we were ready to take them to the post office. She said, "wait I need to give you some money."I quickly said, " no you do not, I can take care of this expense this time is mine and it is not a problem."

I poked Delia lightly and we went for the door so we could take the bundle of invitations and buy stamps for them.

> "Delia sweetheart, I wish you to know and be
> aware that I do have funds for me to help out with
> many of the costs that we are facing. I managed to
> save my US Air Force stipend that I received for my
> last year in the ROTC plus from my working for the
> architects, so we are going to be okay.

Delia looks at her mom and says, "mom it is okay, Michael does want to help because it is for the both of us and he wants to help in any way he can."

She answers back, "thank you Michael we will not try to upset you if you do want to help, as you may know it is always the responsibility of the bride's parents."

Delia says to me, "I can hardly believe we are sending out the invitations to our wedding, in my mind it was only a very far and distant and unknown special happening that I only dreamed of since I met you, but our lives were so disconnected and the future certainly totally unknown."

"Yes sweetheart we have come a long ways in the last year and a half, I know that neither one of us had any concept of our own future and much less a future together."

"This will be a future I would not have missed for the world, I am so thrilled and super happy that we have what we created together, a relationship that will take us into our own destiny."

Delia could not help herself, she threw her arms around my neck and kissed me as if it would be her last, finally I was able to come up for air, and she was so happy, full of joy and was just moving around and could not stand still.

We managed to get to the post office without any incidents, we behaved until we got back into the car, then Delia could not keep her hands still as she was all over me.

I told her, "sweetheart we need to behave we are on our way back home and do not want your mom to look at us and think we are up to something."

She says, "not for long do we need to behave, I know it is frustrating for both of us. It is just that I need you, want you and I am sure you feel the same for me, I can see it your eyes and feel it in the way you hold me and caress me, honey it is just normal, We kissed and she caressed my face and said out loud, "honey I can wait two and a half weeks."

The next few days were busy, entertaining for us all, I guess we all were just going through the motions for the special day. I explained to her dad that I was capable in helping with costs related to the reception, the church donations; I had to work hard at convincing him, so he finally agreed with me.

Six Days Later

We have survived those past six days and seems like an eternity and here we still have another nine days to go until that special Saturday afternoon. We all are starting to look a bit raged around the edges, but not the bride to be.

Delia does not seem to be looking like the rest of us and she walks around, wait ! she flows through the house spaces very happy, smiling, and humming a song.

I asked her, "what are you humming I do not recognize the tune?" She gives me that chin up and a slight smirk and says, "wouldn't you like to know" and then off she goes.

One particular evening she was really going to it, I and her parents just looked at each other in amazement and could not believe what we were seeing, but could not do anything.

Her mom calls out to Delia as she flows from the kitchen thru the living room, 'honey please slow down your making us all dizzy and what are you up to?"

   Also mom says, "I have never seen her like this it is totally unreal, but I guess she has reasons to be happy and she is not nervous but anxious."

Her dad and I just smile and nod our heads and accept   her actions and hope for the best.

   Her mom then says before she thinks, "Michael see what you have done, you have created some one who does not resemble our daughter, then she puts her hand to her mouth and says, I am sorry I did not mean how it came out.

I smiled and looked at her, "I agree with what you said, she is not the same daughter you knew and happy with, when she was more normal, until lately, right?"

All three of us had a good laugh with those comments and when we were laughing Delia comes in the living room and says, "What is so funny in here?"

"Are you talking about me, she says, what did I miss and what is so secret and important that I am not being told?"

She looks at me first, tilts her head like she normally does, and gives me an inquisitive look, like I want to know, now!

I quickly say, "no, there is nothing to worry about, your mom was just saying how much you have changed and how much more mature you have become, right? As I look at both her parents for agreement. They nod their heads and leave it at that. *Will she be satisfied with that answer, God I hope so!*

I motion to her to come sit down next to me, she does and leans down and places a kiss on my cheek and surprises the heck out of me by saying,

"now tell me the truth, what did I miss while I was gone to the bedroom?" "I said that was it and nothing else, so that is it okay?"

Saturday Afternoon

It was 3:30 pm, Delia had been busy helping her mom with what was to be dinner and also other chores in the house. All of that was happening after our encounter with her in the living room after lunch.

Her dad and I had still been tiding up the side yards of the house and putting many tools away from view, This is the third weekend we have tackled the yards, but we have made great progress and are just about done, *good thing, finally.*

When done for the day we called it quits, went indoors and helped ourselves to some cold drinks and sat at the eating bar and nursed our drinks. We are just minding our own business when guess who comes storming, or should I just say flowing in….none other than Delia.

She puts her arms around my neck, turns to her dad and says, "oh do not mind me checking up on both of you, hum! do not smell too good, you two need to hit the showers.

As I am about to get up she pulls my arm and says, "honey do you want to go to the movies?"

I look at her and say, "sure why not, we have nothing else to do, and besides we need to get you out of the house so you can get some fresh …then I start laughing, air, your mom would appreciate that" Her mom or dad did not say a thing, they smiled like saying that they agreed and approved.

I guess I do not value my life and body too much when I leave myself open for who knows what kind of punishment, so I say, ☺" I am sorry sweetheart it came out wrong, I will enjoy us taking in a movie and enjoying the evening"

Sunday came and went and we were on the last few days until our special day. On Monday Delia and her mom went to get her wedding dress and I took the afternoon to get the last few articles of clothing I needed and picked up my uniform blues that I had taken in to be cleaned and pressed.

Tuesday afternoon we went on our appointment with the minister at the church to rehearse out portion of the ceremony and to have a very personal discussion with him about our future.

Wednesday afternoon the entire wedding party was to go in to practice with the minister and he was to clue all of us on the different steps from the time the bride walks up the isle to the podium and who stands where and then the little girl who is the rings bearer comes up to the podium.

Delia and her mom were busy going from place to place taking care of last minute issues such as the catering, drinks, arranging for the church seating for the amount of persons to be attending.

Delia and her moms also made arrangements for flowers, I told them that I would pick up and pay for the flowers and all the corsages for all attendants and bride's bouquet of flowers.

I would do that on Saturday morning around 10:00 am and deliver them to the church to place in their refrigerators.

I made arrangements to also pick up dad's suit and white shirt at the cleaners. He had gone and purchased a new pair of dress shoes for the wedding, I had my dress shoes issued to me with my uniform so I only needed to polish them, and boy did I put a shine on them,

I am sure most persons there will not be looking at my shoes and ignoring me in my slick blues uniform, but I am okay with that, because the bride is the most important one and is the center of attraction, the bridegroom is there for the ride.

In two days, by Thursday afternoon early, all the bride-groomsmen and the bridesmaids are planning on being in town, whether by car or having been brought in by a family member.

I know that my Best Man will be flying into Albuquerque and then one of the other friends will pick him up and they will both be here; hope it goes as planned, as we need them here no later than Friday noon?

Delia and her mom are just so busy here at the house and coming and going for the final arrangement of services for the reception.

It is Friday 1:15 afternoon, we had just finished lunch and were discussing the last few issues related to tonight's practice with the entire wedding attendants when we heard several cars drive in on the driveway they did honk good and loud, so I went out to where the noise is coming from and meet everyone there.

The entire group and friends join the rest of us inside the living room, we all exchange hellos and I introduce the bride's parents and the bride since some of the attendants do not know her personally.

We had a good visit and they were all thankful they were here as expected, but I gathered that they were a little antsy and needed to go to their motel rooms I had arranged for. I asked them to follow me and I would take them there now.

Delia did not waste any time, she rushes to the door, is motioning to me to get with it, as she had not been out of the house all morning. She just needed to go out for a while.

Delia's dad and I had made arrangement for the entire wedding party, so I advised them to be at the restaurant no later than 5;30 for our dinner because at 7:30+ pm we are scheduled for the practice, they were all very agreeable.

Incidently, I forgot to mention that the maid of honor and the bridesmaids arrived about an hour later since we were back from the motel. Delia introduced them all, had them sit and relax for a while and instructed them about their motel accommodations. Some parents had driven them up here and the rest were local friends of Delia; her friend Josie was to be the maid of honor.

We all gathered at the church, met the minister, he sat us all down and went over the process for tomorrow's wedding. The mom of the flower girl with the young girl also came in a few minutes after us; as we receiving our instructions from the minister.

Our pre-wedding guidance and instructions went very well with the minister, he seemed comfortable with the entire party and wished us all well for tomorrow. The flower girl was full of joy and happy and she told her mom that she was ready and tomorrow she would be walking down the isle like the bride; she thought that was a really big deal.

As we all were walking to the exit doors, the minister caught my eye and motioned us to wait a bit as he wished to have a final talk with us.

We stopped and waited until all party members left and then he said, "please sit down and lets visit a bit and talk about the both of you and the wonderful union that you are about to form tomorrow. I see you as a very serious couple and determined to be together and from what you have told me, you will have a wonderful future together."

"Do either one of you have any concerns or doubts about The union and marriage you are about to enter into, remember it is supposed to be a union for a lifetime and are you prepared for such a journey.? If you have any serious questions please do not hesitate to ask, for now it is the best time to speak up."

Delia and I both looked at each other and she said that I could speak first and she would follow if need be.

I looked at the minister and said, "We are totally devoted to each other, we both feel we are making the right decision and have been talking about it and planning it for nearly a year, but were waiting to finish our education which we did just 1½ months ago."

"In the next few weeks, plus or minus, I will be assigned to an Air Force base, and I hope it will be in this country and not over seas and we will go together no matter where, right Delia?"

He looks at Delia and asks her, "how she feels about the wedding and the fact that you, with your new husband, may be moving out of state and being away from family and any close friends?"

She smiles and says, "I have thought of the very same circumstances and what it would mean to me not being close by to visit family or friends, but I am so devoted to Michael and our future that I will go anywhere he has to go, besides that is exactly what I wish for and want and for us to be a couple."

He looks at both of us, smiles and says, "I am very satisfied with your responses on the issues and you both are very adult in your thinking, planning and I know you will both succeed and thrive as a couple no matter what, so I now give you my blessings and I will be honored to bring you into a union that you both deserve, see you tomorrow."

We left our visit with the minister and left the church to go home and see what everyone else was doing, but first we did need to stop at the motel and check on all those single guys to make sure they were behaving themselves.

I turn to Delia in the car and said, "sweetheart I think you better stay in the car for a few minutes until I can see how those guys are doing. I'll be back quick."

As I returned to the car I asked Delia, "do you wish to check on the girls and specially the maid of honor to see how they are doing, remind them they need to be up early to have plenty of time to make themselves presentable?"

"Honey I can do that, so lets me drive to the other end of the motel where they are staying and I will go in and see what they are up to and I will tell them that you want them to be alert for tomorrow."

"Just tell them I said they have to be bright eyed and certainly beautiful for tomorrow, okay?"

We placed the girls in rooms away from the guys for very obvious reasons; to avoid concerns about their behavior and them not getting enough sleep and be ready for the big day.

Delia came back out from the two rooms that she went into and came out just shaking her head sideways and smiling as if she had just seen some wild actions going on in there.

When she got in the car I said, "I really hate to
ask but what are they up to, Are they decent?"

She answers, " honey you would not believe
what the are up to, they are having a good time, but

I warned them, to keep the noise down and turn off the
lights off early, or someone may call the cops on them." They
stuck their tongues out at me and said   "we will see you
tomorrow am for breakfast, okay?""I am happy for them, they
should have a good time for now", so we drove home
because I knew Delia needed her beauty sleep too.

Once we arrived home, we found that Delia's mom was
taking care of a few leftover items that needed to be ready by
early tomorrow. I stepped in and ask if I could be of help, as
Delia was saying she needed to take care of personal items for
tonight.

Delia came to me gave me a hug and kissed my cheek and
said to me, "honey, which came out of no where; this is your
last day and night of freedom, are you still hanging in there?"
and then just walks away, and waves at me, see you later."

Even her parents were rather astonished at that sudden
comment she threw at me. Her dad says, "where does she
come up with some of those comments she throws out at
different times, Michael you are in for a roller-coaster ride, so
hang on tight."

I looked at both of them and said, "I know she does that on
occasions, she has done it in the past and it impresses me that
she does those out of the blue, but that is one of the special
things that I love about her; she can keep me on my toes and
I am going to really enjoy it, but I will have to beware cause it
can come without a moments notice."

Her mom says, "I better go see what she's up to and I know
her dress is ready for tomorrow, but I need to check on a few
other things to make sure she is ready, so wish me luck."

Half an hour later I decided to call it a day, was saying good night, and her dad says to me, I hope you sleep well that was quite a threat or impression and hope you do not have any nightmares, do have pleasant dreams about the two of you."

The Wedding

The entire family was up and rushing around to get our breakfast prepared and out of the way, because there were various tasks to accomplish before noon and no later.

It occurred to me that Delia and I needed to go check on the best man, bridegrooms men and the bridesmaids, so I got her attention and said we needed to go.

We stopped at the room where the guys were, I went to the doors of both rooms and got their attention. stressing the fact that they needed to be at the church no later than 1:30 and ready for the ceremony, especially the best man.

We next went to the rooms where the girls were, Delia went to two rooms to remind them as well, she spent some time going over the final details with the maid of honor and the bride's maids and the time to be there at the church.

Delia says to me, in the car, "honey to refresh your memory, me, the maid of honor and the bridesmaids will be getting dressed and prettied up at the two dressing rooms the minister's assistant told us to use to get ready, okay?"

I said, "I really was not aware or just forgot that it makes sense that you girls get beautiful and dressed there at the church, would not want you all to have to get into a car at the house and struggle keeping the gowns or dresses clean."

She kisses me and says with a smiling face, "it is alright I forgive you for being absent minded", sticks her fingers in my ribs and just laughs as she usually does when she decides to pick on me. I may have left myself wide open for that one.

We arrived at her home, her parents look at us with a surprised look, and asked, "are all the guys and gals doing okay and are they on schedule?"

Delia quickly says to her parents, "Yes, I went to both rooms where the girls have been staying and they are ready to proceed to the church, in fact mom you need to take me and my dress and stuff to the church now because it is getting late; so she rushes to her room to get her dress which is wrapped so that no one can see it.

She looks at me with her head lowered and says, "that means that you can not see what I will be carrying out. Don't you have to get ready too?", I see dad must be getting ready."

I said, "you are right and I am on my way", I head for my room and I see them rushing to the door and out to the car.

It did not take me more than 15 minutes to shave, I had already showered earlier, and I proceeded to put on my blue uniform and polished dress shoes, I combed my hair and went out to the living room; dad was there waiting and we both looked at each other; I compliment him and he did likewise.

He says to me, "wow I have never seen you or anyone in military uniform before, and you look great son you make us all proud and your family too. We are ready to go and get into our places at the church and we do not want to be late."

It is 1:25 pm dad and I arrive there, park our cars, the bride and I will need my car so that we can later leave the reception and come go back to the house.

We entered the church from the front, but that was not too smart wow could not believe the number of persons who were already seated and just waiting for the ceremony to start; we were just 15 minutes before the 2:00.

We went out, turned around and went to the back of the church and entered a side door into a hallway that led to a waiting room where the best man and brides groomsmen were gathered and having low key conversations so as not to attract attention.

I greeted the fellows, asked if they were nervous and the response was rather loud as they all spoke at one time, so I put up my hand, motioned to lower their voices and said to them, "guys if you are nervous do not feel bad, just imagine how I must feel as of right now I am shaking in my boots and dad here has been trying to calm me down."

"You all must realize that all those wonderful people sitting out there in the Sanctuary, they do not bite and they are here to see you be part of a ceremony that we are to participate in, me more than yourselves, so I want all of you to go out there smile do not be nervous, because if all of you are calm, that will surely help me contain my own nervousness, okay?"

Dad looks at them smiles and greets them and says, "I am very pleased with all of you as Michael and I and the family really appreciate that you have come to be part of the wonderful union that is to take place with Michael and my own precious daughter Delia,"

I too am sort of nervous as you can see I have never done this before; I have to walk my daughter to the podium and I too have to contain myself, walk straight at an even tempo, as I will be under more eyes watching us come forward, so just remember that, watch us come forward and that will take the attention away from yourselves and the bridesmaids."

I stepped in and said, "all eyes will be mostly on the bride and then of course me, so just relax enjoy the ceremony and I am sure that you all will forget that you might be nervous."

Dad stepped in and said, "I need to get back to the front foyer and wait for the bride and no sooner had he said that then there was a knock on the door, "is the father of the bride in there?" "You are needed at the front foyer."

When dad left, one bridegroom asks me, "How does the bride get to the front there without going through the hallway and the Sanctuary?" I said back, "I have no idea, I do not know if she already is there or is taken separately, great question, I will have to ask after it is all over."

The Ceremony

The front foyer to the sanctuary double doors opened wide, by two of the fellows assigned to usher guests who stepped aside quickly, why? because! the bride and her father appeared and are walking slowly with eyes focused to the podium with the intentions to reach there where the groom and the minister anxiously wait for the bride to ascend the two steps to the stage.

In front of the bride and her dad, as they proceed forward, all eyes look down to a small girl ..the flower girl..who has in hand a basket full of flower petals and is spreading them in front of the bride; bright red rose petals.

Someone else who is walking behind the bride catches the eyes of the guests, it is the ring bearer boy as he follows the procession, in his two hands he is holding a very colorful pillow and in the center are the groom and bride's rings.

The bride reaches the podium, stops and her father raises her veil, kisses her on the cheek and she turns and is helped take the two steps up and stands to the left in front of all the bridesmaids in their red rose colored gowns.

She is now projecting that aura of joy, smiling from ear to ear and looks at the groom with those dark brown eyes, and the minister calls the ceremony to begin.

The minister starts, as usual, to address the guests "we are here today to bring this bride and groom together in matrimony: he reads from his book and then he turns to the father and asks, " and who gives this bride in marriage? Delia's dad speaks up and answers, "I her father do give her hand in marriage."

The minister looks at the groom and asks him. "Michael do you take this woman to be your lawful wedded wife until death do you part? Michael says, "yes" then do you wish to declare your devotions to her?

He reaches out to the bride and says, "Delia my beloved I love and cherish you with an intensity that bears no match to other feelings of joy and I wish you to be my beloved wife."

The minister then turns to Delia and says, Do you Delia here now take Michael as your lawful wedded husband for as long as you shall live?

She directs her attention to Michael takes his hand and says, "My dearest beloved Michael I offer you my soul, my body and mind and I will love and cherish you for as long as I live.

The minister then says, "you shall now take the rings; Michael place the wedding ring on her left finger and say, with this ring I thee wed. Delia also took his ring in hand and his left hand and says, "It is with great love and devotion that I, with this ring do wed you.

Minister says, as he directs his attention to Michael, "you may now kiss the bride and I now pronounce you man and wife and wish you the best and the most happiness.

Michael assists Delia down the two steps to the isle and they proceed; the congregation has stood up, they are clapping and smiling as the couple walk forward to the foyer where there will be a viewing and congratulation time period.

After all the wishes, kisses and hugs are over, the visitors and families have left the church, the bridegroom man brings a car up to the front of the church for the newly weds to be driven to the Reception Hall where the balance of the festivities will then complete the overall celebration of the wedding between Delia and Michael.

After the reception is over, and all those happy joyful participants have enjoyed themselves, have visited and eaten to their hearts content; they little by little wish the newly weds the best of their future and leave happy.

The final step is for the couple to pose for pictures by themselves and then with members of each other's families.

The newly weds are driven to the bride's home where they will momentarily be with family until they depart to the local hotel where they will spend their first night as a couple.

Delia's mom and dad are there to receive them and welcome them with open arms, again as they had not had the opportunity since they were also part of the receiving line

Delia's mom is the first to speak and says,
"That was a beautiful wedding ceremony and it all went so well, even the reception was outstanding and all the wedding party looked so well, it was a lovely group.

Delia's dad steps in and says, "we now welcome you both as a couple and it was a pleasure to be part of the wedding. My most pleasure came when I walked my beautiful Delia down the isle to be with you Michael, It will be the only opportunity I will have in my life time."

We all sat in the living room for a while to relax and catch some relief from the ceremony and the reception and all the excitement in the entire process. Dad was removing his tie and shoes, and mom was removing her flower arrangement on her dress.

Delia was sitting there just looking like a princess, but she did look somewhat uncomfortable and was fidgeting, so I say to her, "sweetheart you need to change your wedding dress for a comfortable one, as we will be leaving soon?"

She answers, "of course but I am so relaxed and still all excited, after all this is the greatest day of my life, right?"   I could not compete with that response.

I asked mom and dad, "Do you wish for the four of us to go out and enjoy a light dinner so mom does not have to do any cooking?" There is no hurry now, right."

Delia decided to go change her dress and be back, she asks her mom, "would you help me change briefly, I do not want to tear any one part of it.?, what did you think of the wedding?,

 "I was so nervous that I could not concentrate on anything but being there with Michael and sharing that most beautiful connection and experience."

Her mom answers her, " oh honey I was so impressed how well you managed to get to the podium, stand there so in control and handling your vows with Michael, I can certainly understand how that must have been the greatest experience that you have had or will have for a long time."

"It will take you a few hours, a few days and even a few more weeks to come to the realization of that glorious most personal connection with now the most important person In your life, so for however long it will last; hopefully for years."

Delia came out of her bedroom, so radiant, her hair in the most beautiful way and dressed like no other time, in fact, she was wearing an amazing dress and shoes I had not seen before, what a great surprise, here she was so much the beautiful person; my wife, and smiling like never before.

> She looks at me with the look like never before, and says, "honey are you ready?, meaning we need to go to dinner and then to our hotel, it is our night."

Her parents look at us, her mom says, "You have reservetions at the Plaza Hotel restaurant, enjoy your dinner and your special night together… we knew what she meant."

Our dinner was indeed very special, a glass of wine to wish each other happiness together and the start of a new episode like no other we had ever experienced. We did enjoy our dinner and proceeded to leave for our arranged room suite for the night in the same hotel.

Without going into a detailed coupling of two persons with the greatest desire to be one in body, in soul and in mind, the rest can be left to the imagination.

What a peaceful and intimate way of coming together as two persons with love, devotion and the most of passion.

Waking up to a sexy creature such as Delia, just lying there half asleep, I did not realize she had so many curves within those curves from the tip of her toes to the top of her tousled hair is just beyond my imagination.

I leaned over and kissed her softly on the tip of her nose and then ever so gently on her slightly puckered lips; goodness she stirs and reaches up and puts her arms around my neck and kisses me back.

I asked her, "sweetheart did I wake you? She looks back at me and says, "no I was just pretending to be sort of asleep just to see how you would react seeing me in what you would say, "in all my glory," see how you have influenced me: I am beginning to act, talk and think like you, and I love that very much."

"Good morning sweetheart how does it feel to be here all by ourselves as a married couple and not have a worry about who we are now and being together in what ever manner we wish to be."

"Oh, my honey this is what I dreamed about all those past

months, days and hours. I would let my imagination go wild at times and I could not contain myself and keep it together."
"I am here with you where I want to be and I am so delighted and happy beyond my wildest dreams of the past."

So I say to her, "how do you feel about us and how we got here after all those months of waiting and talking about how it would be."

"I am super delighted too and I am here with you as only I imagined it would be, but I am overwhelmed knowing that I know that we are here for each other."

We quit talking, we showered and headed down stairs for the dining room; we were both starved and needed some good nourishment that our bodies were craving.

After breakfast we drove to her parents home, it is Sunday morning, we wanted to catch them soon incase they might be heading off to church.

Her parents were still home, greeted us with a reserved hello and good morning, her mom wished to know if we wanted some breakfast, but we informed them that we had breakfast at the hotel and were fine.

They asked us to sit, relax after all it was Sunday and all the excitement and pleasures of the wedding and after the wedding are over and it is time to take it one day at a time.

Her dad asks, "so what are the newly wedded couple up to now, are you going to stay here in town or are you going back to Albuquerque?"

Delia and I looked at each other to see who would have the answer he was looking for, so I jumped in and said to dad,

"Delia and I have to put our heads together now today, and think about what our priorities are, since I am still waiting for orders from the Air Force, I can no longer work in Albuquerque, we have no place to live even for a short period of time."

Mom steps in and says, "you are welcome to stay and spend time here as much as you wish, now you only need one bedroom.   *I liked how she did emphasis that particular suggestion, but Delia and I did not comment immediately, we let that one slide for now.*

Delia quickly says to her, "Michael and I talked last night and we are considering taking a few days and sort of go on a honeymoon, right honey?"

Delia asks her dad, "We would like to go visit Las Vegas, Nevada and see what that city is like what do you think?" "Just for a few days and then come back here."

Her dad responds, "That is a good idea, a lot of couples honeymoon there and enjoy the difference."

We both looked at mom and dad and acknowledged their acceptance of our thoughts for the time being, it will be nice.

That one decision is now decided upon and other decisions will have to wait until that period of time when they need our attention, so we relaxed and spent time sharing our thoughts about the wedding and the reception.

Her parents were very pleased as to the outcome and how everyone participated to what was expected of them.

Her dad looks at both of us and says very mildly, "I gave my very own and only precious   daughter away, I will never have that opportunity again." Then looks me in the eye and says, "so do take good care of her."

Monday we were both up a bit early, joined her parents at breakfast and just sat around and relaxed, in no hurry to do anything for the time being. After the parents went off to each of their jobs, Delia decided she needed to sit on my lap, she was quick to do so….could not stop her,. She settled in facing me with her dress hanging down around me, what a delight that was.

She says to me, "Honey this is how we will end breakfast every day from now on, so be prepared for and be ready for what is to come, get my drift??

to travel there on our own, a new experience for us both.

>I curiously looked at her and said, "How are you going to manage that if we are in a restaurant in a Las Vegas casino?"

>"I guess we will just go back to our room and misbehave there instead, so you are not going to get away too easily, I will not let you."

We both had a laugh over that and she sat there on my lap and just took advantage of me, as I just let her have her way with me, but generally it is the other way.

We took time to relax after that very intimate sharing and she was very pleased and content, gives me that sexy side look and says, "sweetie I love you so much and I am totally yours now and forever."

I looked at her and said, "let us get serious now and talk about our trip to Las Vegas, we need to pack, I need to go get the car ready for the trip and need to go cash a check at the bank where I deposited the funds transferred from the bank in Albuquerque.

>"Are we ready to leave tomorrow afternoon and no later than 4:00 p.m. and I will tell you later why then and the time."

She raises her body and looks at me in somewhat of a surprise not sure what she is hearing from me. She knows we are ready to go, just when?

>"Sweetheart we need to both agree that is what we have been planning all along, to do, right?

I look at her and try to read her expression, her eyes and what she is thinking right at this moment. I extend my hand to her face, touch her tenderly and reach over and kiss her, then I say,

"Sweetheart I know how you must feel that all of a sudden we are leaving your parents and my parents and all our friends and it might be more of a shock or sadness"

Think of it as only a short temporary period of time and that we will be back before you know it and of course we have to wait and see where we will be going; that farewell will leave more of an impression on both of us, but we will work through it, okay??

She looks at me rather sadly, but then cheers up, wipes her tears, smiles at me and throws her arms around my neck and kisses me gently but deeply and says,

"Honey I know and understand exactly what you have said and I am in full agreement with you,   but it just hit me that we are leaving the comforts of my parent's home our friends and it took me by surprise but will be okay; I'll be with you and your loving care and me to be there for you, just like I   have been dreaming and wanting all this time."

Tuesday morning 9:00 am breakfast is over and her parents are ready to leave for work as usual, and said they would see us at lunch time.

Her mom looks at her and then me, smiles but with a certain sadness that I had not seen before, her dad is just smiling with his head lowered as she says,

"Okay you two we will see you at noon and talk about your trip; you are leaving today right?"

I step in and said, " yes later, but we will be here at lunch time, in fact we will have lunch ready."

Lunch time came and went, they liked and enjoyed the good lunch we prepared; not too shabby, we talked, laughed and the women were very teary eyed but we made it through lunch.

We said our goodbyes, exchanged hugs and kisses on the cheek and they wished us well and a safe trip west to L.V. but we had to call them when we arrived and to tell them where we were staying and for how long.

Delia and her mom and her dad exchanged the last hugs, dad and I shook hands and he said, " drive safely my son."

Our Trip West

I placed all our luggage in the trunk, placed a cooler with drinks and assorted snacks for the drive and hung our clothes on the hooks at both sides of the back seat; we were slightly packed, but we would be gone for 5-7 days for sure.

Delia had tears in her eyes and looked back at her home as we drove out of the driveway, I felt sad too but had to take care as we drove away towards the main highway that would take us south to Albuquerque and then west on I-40 to Las Vegas, Nevada, of all places to go to, but this will be our own short honeymoon. It was 4:00 p.m., we were out the door.!!

Michael and Delia literally drove off
into the sunset to find
their destiny

Earlier in their relationship,
Delia to Michael, "honey
Is This love of mine forbidden?
hold me, love me tonight it is now
or never as I may not wait, I do
not want to walk away with a
broken heart"

About the Authors

Those Were the Days

A.Miguel Trujillo is an Architect in practice, in a passion by which he has created many projects functional and user friendly projects. He decided to seriously involve himself in a new passion; writing and creating stories and expanding meaningful past experiences and writing stories that can inspirer readers of all ages.

Miguel has in his portfolio various other creations: wrote an introduction Handbook to the Field of Architecture and the Profession He will also complete two other novels well on their way to being completed, ready to publish after years' end or later, the other one in early spring or later.

Amy Russell, an aspiring writer, and deeply involved in the publishing industry and with the beginnings of a new serious, passionate and insightful novel of her own, was very much delighted to participate with the author in this novel by reviewing the story and offering insight to the compassion, dialogues and the sort of exchanges that take place in a romantic relationship within a young couple that embarks on a one to one partnership.

Amy is meanwhile, on her own, deeply involved in promoting, creating and the production of major world wide Book Fairs, internationally & in the USA.

Those Were the Days

Michael knows there is someone out there, a young girl in his
home town that he has not seen for nearly a year. He wishes
to locate her, why does he want to find her?
What has happened that he needs to find her
how should he go about it? He does not know
where she lives, if she does she still attend the
local high school or is she out, working; he expects he will
have to exhaust every possibility, roam the halls,
drive all over town, and visit the local theater,

Appears that he has a real task ahead and
will she even want to see or talk to him, only time
Will tell when he does find her

Its Now or Never

Without notice, in a very casual way a dark
haired beauty suddenly presents herself to
Michael in a sutle, without personal pressure, she
Becomes an attraction that presents confusion in his
daily routine and distracts him from his open relationship with Mia Rose, how can he deal with the smart,
sassy, fresh, assertive distraction and keep his senses, his
emotions are shifting from one persona to another, then
one day he will be confronted with, "love me now,
"it is now or never" what does never mean?

Read the novel and be surprised with the ending

Stratos Writer's Studio

www.ingramcontent.com/pod-product-compliance
Lightning Source LLC
Chambersburg PA
CBHW061422150726
47987CB00001B/56